I0806674

# ASSAULT ON ABSALOM STATION

STARFINDER®

# ASSAULT ON ABSALOM STATION

Tim Pratt

paizo®

This is a work of fiction. All of the characters, organizations, and events portrayed in this novel are either products of the author's imagination or are used fictitiously.

ASSAULT ON ABSALOM STATION – A STARFINDER NOVEL



Written by Tim Pratt.

Cover illustration by Mirco Paganessi.

Published by Paizo Inc.
15902 Woodinville-Redmond Rd NE, Suite B
Woodinville, WA 98072-4572
www.paizo.com

ISBN 978-1-64078-814-5 (print edition)
ISBN 978-1-64078-815-2 (e-book edition)
ISBN 978-1-64078-816-9 (audiobook edition)

The Library of Congress Cataloging-in-Publication Data is available upon request.

For information about special discounts available for bulk purchases, sales promotions, fund-raising, and educational needs, contact Paizo Sales at sales@paizo.com.

First Edition: August 2026

This book about nonbinary weirdos in space

is dedicated to the founders and organizers of WisCon,

the feminist science fiction convention

that always made me feel welcome

as a nonbinary weirdo on Earth.

# 1

## INCITING INCIDENTS

(Tyrcell / 7 AG)

I'm scribbling this note a long time later because, it turns out, the funny thing about living through major historical events is you don't always realize that's what you're living through at the time. Initially, they just seem like... events. But after reading back through my journals, I'd say this next part is when the war started, at least for me and my friends.

The Magefire Assault, the trap in the Thousand Moons, all that death and undeath and devastation... it began here, for us, with a walk through the park.

I was ambling through Jatembe Park, beneath the great gleaming dome of the Eye, on my way to a meeting (about having another meeting), when I ran into Mikiel, head of the combined orders of the Hellknights on Absalom Station. He was a broad, tall human in shining armor, now with an elaborate mustache instead of his usual white-streaked beard, and he'd personally ordered my death on at least four separate occasions.

We happened to arrive simultaneously at a spot where two cobbled paths crossed, right next to the Dread Memorial Gazebo, and we both stopped and stared at each other. You run into people you know all the time on Absalom Station. Sure, there are tens of thousands of people living there, and more arriving every day, but in certain fundamental ways, it's like a small town. Sometimes it's *too* small.

I was outnumbered, since Mikiel was flanked by two other knights, a human and a devil. They also stared at me, clearly recognizing me from, I assumed, an unflattering Most Wanted poster. I had a pistol on each hip. Mikiel had a fangblade at his side, and his armor was probably full of embedded weaponry, not to mention the brutal armaments his bodyguards were carrying, both openly and doubtless concealed. One of them wore gauntlets with spikes all over the knuckles, which seemed a bit excessive for a day in the park.

Mikiel stroked his stupid mustache for a moment, then dipped his head in a brief nod. "Greetings, Citizen Tyrcell."

I dipped my head too, in a precise mirror of his motion. "Greetings, Lictor Mikiel." I paused. "How's our... mutual friend?"

"Lictor Astrachios?" Mikiel made a face. Neither of us were huge fans of the head of the Order of the Eclipse, a rare point of commonality between us. "Last I heard, he was chasing Zo! around the galaxy, trying to stop the old monster's broadcasts. The chasing happens much faster now, with Drift engines, and yet, somehow, Astrachios never seems to get any closer to catching his quarry."

"I've met Zo!," I said. "Astrachios might not enjoy the experience if he actually caught him." Picking fights with millennia-old talking corpses with eyes made of fire is generally a bad policy. They don't live that long by being cuddly and forgiving, as a rule.

"Quite," Mikiel said. "Will we see you at the meeting later?"

I resisted the urge to duck my head and look sheepish. "Ah, well, probably not. Valentine is the head of the Society these days. I try to let her get on with things without my meddling. I'm just a... consultant."

"I'm sure you undersell yourself," Mikiel said. "May the law bind and protect you, Citizen Tyrcell."

"And also with you," I muttered as he tromped on by, his guards giving me murder eyes as they went. It was hard to believe that it had been just seven years since my Society and his Hellknights had started shooting at each other on a regular basis... and only four years since I'd been forced to hide out inside a hollow moon for months because Mikiel and his goons had taken over fully a quarter of Absalom Station and declared me, specifically, one of their public enemies.

But since then, the station had unified—become "civilized"—and the days of criminal gangs, armed fiefdoms, violent religious sects, and active warfare in the corridors were long gone. We were all living in peace and harmony, governed by a ruling council composed of the leaders of those former criminal gangs and armed fiefdoms and violent religious sects, but hey, that's progress for you.

I continued strolling along the path, and the bushes rustled off to my right, in the direction of the cathedral. There is some wildlife in the parkland under the Eye, if you can call generations of squoxes fattened by hand-feeding "wild," but this creature was considerably bigger, and it emerged to block my way.

"Hey, Carn," I said. Carn is my co–best friend (semi–best friend? Half best friend? What I'm trying to say is, I have two coequal best friends, and he is one of them). I don't know if you, dear reader, encountered the first volume of my memoirs, *The Chronicles of Tyrcell: A True and Accurate Account of Events on Absalom Station and in Other Regions of the Galaxy in the Immediate and Medium-Term Aftermath of the Disabling Mass Amnesia Event Known as the Gap* (sometimes called *Era of the Eclipse* by the impatient), or if you're some random person who found a few loose pages stuck in a wall during a renovation, but in case you're the latter, let me catch you up. Carn is an ysoki, the species sometimes and somewhat rudely known as ratfolk; on the short and stocky side, even for the short species; usually dressed in dark overalls; and almost always trailed by a fist-sized mote of black energy. He's a solarian, which means he can do terrible things to you with gravity. He can also fix just about anything, he can break *absolutely* anything, he has a disconcerting habit of sticking a finger in his ear and wiggling it around when he's thinking hard, he's blunt but good-natured, and I would die for him. Though admittedly, I'd rather not.

"Ty." Carn fell into step beside me. "I thought I was gonna have to hit the head of the Hellknights on his actual head with a hammer for a minute there. And then it would've been a whole—What do you call it?—a thing."

I nodded. "A civil war, which we're trying to avoid these days, yes. I appreciate your restraint. You don't have to lurk around looking for opportunities to do violence every time I go for a walk, you know."

He sniffed. "Sure I do. I'm your bodyguard."

I stopped in the middle of the path and swiveled to face him. "You absolutely are *not*. You're head of security for the whole of the Society!" (The Society is our mutual-aid collective, currently constituting a few thousand citizens concentrated around the Lorespire Complex. I technically founded the Society, pretty much by accident, in the days immediately following the Gap. But we all realized quickly that I wasn't the best administrator, and I like being sneaky too much to be a figurehead, so I shifted to just lurking around the edges of the upper echelons with my cofounders, having opinions.)

"Pah," Carn said, in one of his myriad syllables of dismissal. He combines the worst attributes of an immovable object and an unstoppable force, which is great if he's aimed where you want him to be and incredibly frustrating otherwise. "My team can handle the Society. But you're the one everyone wants dead."

He had a point. I resumed walking, and Carn stumped along with me as I continued objecting. "We don't murder each other in the corridors around here anymore, Carn. No more than the people in any settlement do, anyway. We've all been pulling in the same direction for years. Last time I saw Astrachios, even he just made a rude gesture at me, and his devil buddy Rakhiel actually waved."

Carn gave another dismissive snort. "You act like things are stable forever now. I could personally disrupt food distribution and tear up the electrical grid and make the whole station descend into a lawless, barbarous, chaotic murder-fest within maybe... a day and a half."

"Sure, but that's only because you're a trusted member of the engineering and logistics subcommittees, with access to the levers of power, and that means you *wouldn't* do something like that."

"I'm just saying, when you expect the worst, you're never disappointed," Carn said. "I only experience happy surprises."

We passed by a couple of sauntering worlanisi, delicate four-armed blue people with cone-like horns sticking out of their heads, and they nodded at us amiably. They're an interesting species—stellar nomads who've *vastly* expanded their range since we were all gifted with Drift technology—and I wanted to recruit a few of them into the Society; they have psychic powers that do interesting things to luck, and we could always use more of that.

Looking around, I saw a few more denizens of the Vast who'd taken to visiting or even living on Absalom Station in the intervening years. There were four mostly naked moyishuu having a picnic on an expanse of grass, their skin in shades of sky blue and leaf green, with hair like shining crystal. They're some kind of fey, and they project their emotions the way unstable nuclei emit radiation. Even though I'm resistant to psychic things (being an android), we passed close enough for me to catch the edge of their radiant joy. That put some pep in my step, and Carn started grinning.

An osharu in elaborate ceremonial robes oozed past us on the path, very slowly, nodding his moist head in greeting. They're... well, look, they're four-foot-tall slugs, basically, and professionally they tend toward being either monks or scientists or a combination of the two. This one was clearly heading toward the Arcanamirium, the leading magical university in the system and one of the immense, impressive landmarks within the Eye, the central dome of Absalom Station. The main building in the university complex is a confection of towering, elegant spires, even more impressive than Swordlight Cathedral, in my opinion. You'd never know that seven years ago a bunch of Hellknights literally blew the front doors off the place in an attempt to murder me and my friends... and successfully managed to murder one of the best of us, a contemplative named Soubrette's Last Elegant Algorithm, known as Sue to their friends. The current peace of Absalom Station was built on a bloody foundation, but isn't that always the way?

"It's kinda nice seeing so many new kinds of people on the station," Carn said, and I nodded. "Especially since they aren't automatically forming into criminal gangs and claiming territory and shooting anybody who trespasses on their turf."

"I do not miss the old days," I said in agreement.

Carn turned uncharacteristically philosophical. "We're like if somebody got a big pot and put in a whole bunch of different ingredients... I'm saying, like the station is the pot, and the people are the ingredients, you know, and you'd think it wouldn't all work together, but it does, and it's really delicious, it's like a soup. Or a stew. Absalom Station is like a... big stewpot."

"Good metaphor," I said. "We should put that on mugs and shirts in the visitors' center. 'Absalom Station: The Big Stewpot.' With a picture of a cauldron. That can be our new symbol. We can put it on our flag too. You're a marketing genius, Carn."

"I've got a lotta talents. People don't even know."

I was teasing him, because that's what we did, but Carn was right. Ever since Triune had gifted us with Drift technology, and it turned out the station's mysterious power source, the *Starstone*, was a rare natural Drift beacon, Absalom Station had become a nexus of galactic travel, and we were prospering as a hub of tourism and trade. No matter what distant quadrants of the galaxy you explored, Absalom Station was just a short jaunt away through the mind-bending realm of the Drift. We welcomed everyone (and their money), and we cherished our neutrality about their problems, so as a consequence, we were everybody's favorite port of call. The Society was reaping the benefits of that new prosperity too: We were an unusually multicultural group, even by the standards of Absalom Station, so it was easy for us to make connections with the people of other settlements. We'd also... acquired... several ships over the years, entirely legally of course, at least if no one examined the paperwork too closely. Lots of our members had wanderlust and curious minds, so we'd developed a reputation as liaisons and negotiators and explorers and traders. And smugglers. I admit that one's true. It funds the exploration missions.

"There's Mel and Val." Carn pointed, and I smiled, this time the rush of joy coming not from proximity to fey emotion and friendly aliens, but from within. Two other founding members of the Society were lounging on a horseshoe-shaped array of benches next to an ornamental fishpond encapsulated in a floating orb of water, deep in conversation.

On the left was Melezheun: my *other* best friend, a lashunta mystic. Mel was tall, slim, and pale green, with short antennae on her forehead and colorful swirling ridges contouring her face. She wore flowing, shimmering garments that covered the protective mindmail she invariably donned before going out in the world. It had been a few years since anyone had tried to kill her, but I knew she felt better knowing she was protected. Mel is radiantly beautiful, like many lashuntas, but she's also beautiful *inside*, even if she doesn't always believe it; she's the kind of person who always tries to do the right thing, and even though she's one of the best people I know, she can't forgive herself for some of the mistakes she made in the past. Carn and I are pretty good at keeping her focused on the future, though.

On the right was Valentine, a tall blond human dressed in strappy pants, a low-cut top, and big stompy boots, laughing her head off at something Mel had said. I met Valentine on day one, year one, when everyone in the galaxy woke up with their memories erased. She was out in the hallway at the time, menacing a terrified stranger with a knife. That stranger was her wife, Starla. There was evidence they were probably married before the Gap stole their knowledge of one another, but they'd fallen in love all over again, after I helped talk them through the knife incident, and I'd officiated their new wedding a few years back. Val was reliable, no-nonsense, unsentimental, and could shout very loudly, which made her well suited to serve as the actual official leader of the Society, instead of me. (Plus, Val was physically on the station a lot more than I was. That wanderlust I mentioned? I've got it too. In fact, I'd just returned from an extended sojourn on my beloved personal ship, the *Venture*.)

The two rose from their seats when we approached, and I wrapped Mel up in a hug. I hadn't seen her in weeks, and her company always made me feel like the machinery of the galaxy was humming along properly.

Val yanked me into a hug once I let Mel go. Her hair was different, one side buzzed to the skin while the other hung long, and there was some kind of holo-projector in her hair clip, giving her an aura of rainbow sparkles; flashy, but it looked good. A shimmering, nearly invisible drone bobbed in the air above her, recording her every move to an encrypted data crystal that only she could access. Val was determined not to lose her memories again. She couldn't do much about another probably-divinely-caused event like the Gap, which had even corrupted data storage to steal our pasts from us, but she could defend herself against head injuries or magic psychic mental meddling by creating a comprehensive record of her life. A little odd, but we all react to trauma in different ways.

"Did you have fun gallivanting across the galaxy?" Val asked, releasing me from her crushing embrace. "Leaving me behind, burdened by the burdens of leadership?"

"I had the *best* time," I said.

"More importantly, did you bring me a treat?" She mock scowled at me. Our arrangement was that she'd take on the aforementioned burdens of leadership, and I'd bring the treasures of the wider universe back to her after every journey.

"I brought you caffeinated chocolate from that one planet you like," I said. "The one where the beans are... biologically processed."

"Eaten, digested, and pooped out by the indigenous cute furry fauna, you mean." Val rubbed her hands together and grinned. "That stuff is so *smooth*. It's because of the enzymes. Gimme, gimme."

"Repulsive." I reached into a pouch at my belt, pulled out a foil-wrapped rectangle, and handed it over.

"It's not like they don't wash the beans *off* first," Val said, tearing into the package immediately. "You all talk amongst yourselves, my mouth is going to be full."

We all sat down on the benches, comfortable in each other's company. It occurred to me that if, say, an asteroid crashed through the dome of the Eye, that would pretty much wipe out the senior leadership of the Society, apart from Dr. Bindi, who was terminally cranky, and Starla, who was too kindhearted to keep the inevitable malcontents in line. The Society was a robust and not-very-hierarchical group, though, so the organization would probably survive even if it lost all of us.

Back in the bad old days, when Absalom Station was in a state of near-constant multidirectional civil war, we made a point of not clumping up the senior leadership in public like this, but it was peacetime, right? Once upon a time, there'd been sixty or seventy armed and competing groups on the station, mostly organized along species or religious lines, with a few multicultural oddities like the Society, the Arcanamirium, and the Conductors (who controlled the transit systems). The Hellknights had done the best job of actually uniting and imposing order during those chaotic years, loath as I was to admit it (because I hate them, and they suck), but nobody enjoyed living under their brutal regime. Fortunately, the Hellknights never managed to take over the *whole* station, despite a lot of plausible forged documents claiming they had the authority to do so.

Our current peaceful regime was the result of everybody almost *dying*. Some years back, a runaway system malfunction nearly vented our entire atmosphere into space. There was still debate over whether the crisis was an act of sabotage or simple lack of maintenance, but fixing the problem required station-wide cooperation. It turned out the prospect of imminent death was enough to make everyone work together, and in the aftermath, there was a big summit to sort out a sensible future for the government of the station. That led to the heads of the various gangs forming the first Syndicsguild (basically our governing representative body) and electing our Prime Executive, Loqua Tem. (She's fine! A compromise candidate, sure, but a sensible one, tough enough to stand up to pressure and personable enough to charm her way out of most sticky situations.)

You'd think that whole everyone-almost-dying-and-civilization-emerging-from-the-horrors thing would be a big part of *The Chronicles of Tyrcell: A True and...* etc., but me and Mel and Carn were away on a starship when it all happened, meeting with an avaricious arms dealer who sold us a set of so-smart-they're-almost-people autocannons to protect our settlement from persistent Hellknight incursions. By the time we got back, we didn't need the big guns anymore, so we curried favor with the Syndicsguild by donating the cannons to Absalom Station's galaxy-class defensive batteries.

"So this next gathering of the Syndicsguild," Val said, dragging our catching-up chitchat back around to the point of this meeting, which was to talk about another, more important meeting. "I'm going to talk to them about Bindi's emergency medical first responder pilot program, and expanding it beyond the Society to the station as a whole. The public medical drones are all well and good, but with all the new people on the station, the automated systems have made some mistakes, giving out meds that are toxic to different physiologies, things like that. The drones don't have a robust enough dataset with species-specific information, but Bindi has been building a database of cross-references for years to treat her patients, since we have such a diverse population in the Society."

"Sounds good. Go forth and heal the people." I waved my hand grandly.

Val rolled her eyes. "Is there anything else we need to bring up at the meeting?"

"Carn and I are open to doing more work on behalf of the Syndicsguild," Mel replied.

"Good," Val said. "It's not an explicit quid pro quo situation, but we all know the Primex is more open to helping out groups who step up to help *her*, and there's always some disaster that needs mitigation from senior people."

"That's me," Carn said. "So senior my bones ache. And mitigating? Forget about it. Nobody mitigates like I do."

"You're selfless," I said. "As for me, I'm selfish, and I waited nearly an hour to dock the *Venture* this morning. We could use some better traffic-control systems."

"What we *need* is more capacity in general," Val said. "Some of the people down in Botscrap are working on building these orbital hubs—basically mini stations where people will be able to refuel and resupply and get something to eat, and maybe get drunk, without having to enter the station itself. In the meantime, there are a couple of big ships out there that basically never go anywhere—there's the casino, of course, but there's also that big freighter that's basically an overflow hotel."

"There are thousands of people on ships out there who've never set foot or pseudopod on the station proper at all," Mel said.

"Didja know people are saying there are actually *five* sectors on Absalom Station now?" Carn asked.

I frowned. "There's the Eye"—where we were sitting—"and the Ring and the Arms and the Spike. I'm not the most mathematical android, but even I can count to four."

"The fifth sector is the Armada," Carn said. "That's what people are calling the swarm of a zillion or so ships that semipermanently hang out in a big buzzy cloud around the station."

I grunted. "'Armada' is a little... militaristic. We have a navy now?"

"It's one of those—What's it called?—ironies," Carn said.

Val nodded. "They're pretty much all civilian ships, and a lot of them hang out there because that way they can be close to Absalom Station and our resources without having to follow all of our laws. Like the casino, which doesn't want to pay taxes, and even bans worlanisi patrons on sight because they can manipulate luck."

"The Prime Executive is squeezing the casino owners, though," Melezheun said. "She doesn't like all that money flowing off the station with none of it coming back to us, and a species-specific ban angers her too."

Val wrinkled her nose. "Yeah. If we're going to ban a whole people, maybe we can ban *those* instead." She gestured.

I turned my head, surprised. Val wasn't usually one to paint people with such a broad brush, and I couldn't imagine a species she'd dislike that much; Hellknight isn't a species, after all. Then I saw who she meant, and I understood. I coughed. "Well, that's not... as I understand it... that's not so much a *people* as a... condition? Like, that one's an elf."

"That used to be an elf," Val said. "Now it's a borai. An undead... monster." The borai in question hurried along a nearby path and was tall, extremely pale, dressed in black robes, but he was hunched and twisted, like he was waiting for a blow to fall. He would have looked like an ordinary elf, except for the veins of negative energy that pulsed all over his face and hands like black worms.

Carn wiggled his finger in his ear. "Borais aren't monsters. Their soul is stuck in their dead body, right? Botched resurrection, cut-rate necromancy, that sorta thing. So they're like a ghost haunting a house, but the house is their body. They still eat and breathe, even. They aren't so creepy."

"They creep *me* out," Val said. "I mean, honestly, I want nothing to do with undead in general, and there are more and more of them around lately. I know they don't *all* come from Eox, but some of them do, and there are... *tensions* with the bone sages. That's going to be the really big subject at the next Syndicsguild meeting, I suspect."

"What kind of tensions?" I asked.

"You *do* spend a lot of time gallivanting," Val said. "The bone sages of Eox, their undead rulers, offered to 'welcome' Absalom into their sphere of protection. We said, 'No, thanks, we like our independence, and we don't want to be farm animals for a bunch of bone-faced liches,' only in a more politically courteous way, of course. The Eoxians reply was not pleasant. Their ambassador left the station last week. They've made some threats and—"

Val didn't get to finish her sentence, because she was interrupted by a huge explosion.

# 2

# CHK CHK AND DAE FIND THE WAY

## (326 AG)

"Of *course* we're going to look!" Dae snatched up the first crystal and turned it over in their hands. The usually glamorous and vivacious pahtra was looking a bit frazzled—descending through a series of challenges in a god's dungeon on a desolate moon will do that to a person—but the imminence of discovery had them revitalized and sparkling again. They'd come to this ancient temple, and finally to the charred cavern sanctum deep belowground, in search of the truth, and that truth was at hand.

Then Dae looked at their best friend, Chk Chk. "Right?"

*"A chance to find the answer to the most profound mystery in the galaxy?"* the shirren mystic sent telepathically. *"Yes. I think we should look."*

The ancient android, Tyrcell, face hidden in the hood of their green cloak, made no comment, seemingly content to let the youths choose whether or not to explore a secret hidden for centuries: What, exactly, had happened to the lost world of Golarion? Dae crouched, looked over the projector, and then carefully slotted the crystal, hidden centuries earlier by the rebellious goddess of wisdom Yaraesa, into place. The data crystal nestled neatly in the aperture.

"Just flip the switch there on the side. The projector should be charged," Tyrcell said. "I tested it before I left Absalom Station. I wasn't about to come all this way and be stymied by equipment failure—I've actually got a spare projector on my ship, just in case."

The pahtra put their hand on the switch, looked at Chk Chk, looked at Tyrcell, took a breath, and turned on the projector.

A bright light shone from a lens, illuminating a large square on one fire-blackened wall.

Words of white fire shimmered into existence, and Tyrcell, Chk Chk, and Dae all released long, awed exhalations of surprise.

The message began:

SO YOU'D LIKE TO VISIT LOST GOLARION

Tyrcell snorted a laugh. "Yaraesa sounds like a cultural ambassador trying to drum up tourism."

*"I think the tourists would be lining up to visit Golarion without much encouragement needed,"* Chk Chk said, but Dae just sat and stared, rapt, as the words shimmered and changed.

THE WAY IS LONG AND WINDING AND PERILOUS

"Just once," Tyrcell said, "I'd like it if the way was short and straightforward and really quite pleasant, actually."

"Shh!" Dae leaned forward.

"It's not like there's a soundtrack I'm talking over," Tyrcell muttered, but they subsided.

YOUR JOURNEY CONTINUES
AMID THE BLACK MOONS OF EOX
SEEK MY FAVOR THERE
FOLLOW THE GUIDANCE PROVIDED
TO UNLOCK THE WAY

The words flickered, replaced by a complex string of two dozen numbers and letters, which glowed for one second, two seconds, three seconds, and then faded.

There was a pop, and sparks burst from the projector, followed by a spurt of flame. Dae jumped up and out of the way, and Tyrcell strode forward, kicking the projector across the cave. "I think the data crystal Yaraesa left for us just exploded."

"We're supposed to go to Eox?" Dae said. "They don't really like... alive people going there, do they?"

*"Not famously, no,"* Chk Chk said. *"But it is one of the Pact Worlds,*

*so it... should be safe? -Ish? I don't think anyone will eat us."*

"Oh, some of them might try." Tyrcell sat cross-legged on the floor and put their head in their hands. "Ugh. Eox. I hate that place. Though, the black moons... that probably means the asteroid field around the planet, called the Thousand Moons." They paused. "I hate *that* place too. I got into some serious trouble around there once, and the bone sages aren't too fond of me..." They shook their head. "Anyway, I recorded those numbers, and they look like another one of Yaraesa's math puzzles. You can probably decipher them to get coordinates."

Dae had never been to Eox, but they knew it was a dead world, the planet destroyed by some cataclysm or war (or both) long before the Gap, leaving behind a dry, irradiated husk pocked with craters and chasms. Just because the place was dead didn't mean it was uninhabited, though; indeed, it was teeming with the undead. From the infamous bone sages, the necrovite spellcasters who ruled the planet, down to the common citizenry of corpsefolk, ghouls, vampires, ghosts, borais, varculaks, and who knew what else. Only the undead could easily survive on such a desiccated husk of a world.

There were a few enclaves of the living, mostly in domed or underground areas, where life-support systems could sustain them, but Eox wasn't a very *nice* place for the living to inhabit. Such people were often forced to participate in... entertainments... for the undead aristocracy. Some of which were so gruesome and cruel that not even Zo! would have been willing to broadcast them.

"You're coming with us, aren't you, Tyrcell?" Dae asked. "You've waited so long, you must be especially excited!" They bounced up and down, unable to hide their excitement and, honestly, not bothering to try.

The android considered. Their face was impassive and unreadable, but Dae knew that didn't necessarily mean much; androids didn't tend to show strong emotion, but that didn't mean they didn't feel things. Dae had read Tyrcell's firsthand account of the days and weeks following the Gap and knew Tyrcell felt plenty of things—and felt them deeply.

"My sense of self-preservation says, 'No, stay far away from Eox.' Those people live forever, and even though I don't *think* the ones in charge know my name, underestimating necrovites is a bad mistake. But..." They sighed. "This is a mystery I've been waiting literally hundreds of years to unravel. Figuring out what caused the Gap, what happened to Golarion—that's what the Starfinder Society first set out to discover, until those... unpleasant setbacks... made them stop investigating. I'm a lot older than you two, and I remember the nightmare of the years and decades following the Gap, and... I'm mad about it. I want to know why we had to go through all that. So, yes." They took a deep breath, then let it out. "I'm in. Let's figure this thing out."

Making their way out of the dungeon was much simpler than making their way in: Yaraesa had provided an easy egress through smooth lava tubes leading from the crystal cavern to the surface, and Tyrcell knew the way, having been there centuries earlier. They sealed their environment suits before clambering out of a hatch concealed in a heap of boulders, onto the desolate surface of Elindrae, the grim industrial moon of Castrovel, barely inhabited apart from those few people responsible for running the automated factories. Castrovel itself remained beautiful, in part, by outsourcing pollution-spewing heavy industry to places like this. They trudged through the dust silently—even Dae, who was seldom silent—back toward their ships, which were parked close together. Dae's runabout, the *Light Fantastic*, was a sleek little two-person racer, while Tyrcell's craft was a dented, battered explorer vessel, anonymous, old, and inelegant.

"Uh-oh," Dae said, as their ship's comms system pinged them once they were in range. "We missed some calls. A... uh... lot of calls."

*"Ah,"* Chk Chk said. *"I thought we might."*

A shimmering square appeared in Dae's heads-up display, containing the face of Seraphina: a very annoyed-looking human with her hair in a messy bun, wearing ornate glasses with purple lenses. "Junior Probationary Agents Chk Chk and Dae," she scolded. "*Where* have you gone? You were given a very simple assignment, to read a trove of old documents and provide a brief report on their contents, and now I find out you've left Absalom Station?" She took a deep breath, clearly trying to control her temper. "This is *not* the way to make a good impression as junior agents. Venture Captain Chronis only has a couple of spots left on the crew of his next long-range exploration mission, which I thought you were eager to join, but this latest stunt is not helping your cause. Get in touch with me immediately and give me a *good* reason for your dereliction of duty." She flickered off.

"There are three more messages," Dae said miserably. "They look like more of the same, but increasingly impatient, based on the automated summaries."

They had arrived at their ships, and Tyrcell leaned against their explorer and crossed their arms. "Call Seraphina back and loop me in on the call."

"Um," Dae said. "Why?"

"Oh, I don't know. I might be able to help, is all."

*"Tyrcell founded the Starfinder Society,"* Chk Chk said.

"We didn't call it that back then. But, yeah, my Society became yours, eventually. Live as long as me and you get used to change, even if you don't like it much. Go on, call."

Dae shrugged and placed the call, sent across the system to the Lorespire via the powerful transmitter on the *Light Fantastic*. Seraphina picked up instantly. She had clearly not become any less annoyed since her first message. "Where in the *layers of Hell* are you two?"

"Uh, we're, uh—" Dae began, but Tyrcell smoothly interrupted.

"I think I can help clear things up," Tyrcell said. "I've requisitioned the assistance of your junior probationary agents for a matter of some delicacy and urgency."

"And who are you, exactly?" Seraphina glared, and even in miniature, her glare was intimidating.

"Look up the call sign Secret Society," Tyrcell said.

Seraphina glanced away, and then her eyes widened. "That's... these authorization codes are *ancient*."

"But still active," Tyrcell said. "There's even still a budget and a discretionary fund, isn't there? With one agent on the payroll, who has the power to requisition equipment and personnel on a case-by-case basis."

"But *why*—"

"Ah, ah, ah," Tyrcell chided. "What does the authorization say?"

"'Render any and all assistance,'" Seraphina said flatly. "'No questions asked, and no explanations required.'"

"Well, there you go." The android spread their hands. "I'm not sure I'll have your junior agents, as you call them, back in time to join this venture captain's expedition, but they've already done enough to earn a couple of commendations. They are, unfortunately, the *secret* sort of commendations, so no one can know about them, but still, it's satisfying to be appreciated. I should know; I have *lots* of secret commendations."

"I know I am not supposed to ask who you are or what you're doing—"

"You can ask," Tyrcell said. "I'm just not obliged to answer."

"—but please tell me. Will Chk Chk and Dae be safe? They're *new*, and they haven't been on a single mission yet, do you understand? We had them working in the Archives!"

"I do understand," Tyrcell said. "But trust me when I say the collective experience of this team rivals that of any Starfinder expedition you've ever heard of."

"Do you two want to go with this... person?" Seraphina asked. "Chk Chk? Dae? I can send a shuttle for you if you say the word."

"*We are exactly where we want to be, Archivist,*" Chk Chk said formally. "*We thank you for your concern. Truly.*"

"Yeah!" Dae agreed.

"Fine," Seraphina said. "I look forward to... not hearing all about it, probably, when you get back. Good luck." She sighed and cut off the connection.

"There," Tyrcell said. "That's all sorted. I hereby authorize you as junior probationary covert operatives of the Secret Society."

"That was amazing," Dae gushed. "She just listened to you! It's like you have the cheat codes to life!"

"*What exactly is this Secret Society?*" Chk Chk said.

"It's the somewhat silly nickname for the officially nameless covert operations branch of the organization I cofounded," Tyrcell said. "A branch that is still on the books of the Starfinder Society, and has been for centuries, mostly because it's very cheap, and very quiet, and at this point, there's only one member: me. Of course, if Seraphina ignores all the please-don't-talk-about-this stuff in the file and runs to tell the

Forum or the First Seeker about what we're doing, someone might do an audit, and that could be the end of my lovely line of credit. But it's a risk I'm willing to take to keep the two of you from getting in trouble. So. Shall we go to... ugh, I can't believe I'm saying this... Eox?"

Dae jumped up and down and clapped their hands, and Chk Chk nodded solemnly.

Tyrcell said, "We should all go together in my ship. It's faster, and it has more amenities. You can send your ship on autopilot back to Absalom Station."

"*This* is faster?" Dae looked the battered explorer up and down. "No offense, but it looks like it was built centuries ago."

"It *was* built centuries ago." Tyrcell slapped the side of the ship, and, somehow, an avalanche of rust didn't come showering down. "This is the *Venture*, my personal vessel, acquired through almost entirely legal means back about, oh, five years after the Gap. Though honestly, I've replaced so many parts of it over the years that I'm not sure anything of the original vessel remains." They cocked their head. "Hmm, isn't that a philosophical puzzle? If you start with the ship of Tyrcell, and gradually replace every bolt and panel and bit of wire until, after many years, nothing of the original ship remains, is it still the same ship? If not, when does it *stop* being the same ship? When over half the original parts are gone? Or—"

"*Please stop,*" Chk Chk said. "*We just navigated a dungeon where we had to answer questions like that or die. I would dearly like a break from philosophy and mind games.*"

"Fine by me," Tyrcell said. "But trust me, the additions I've made to the ship are fantastic. These engines *go*. You two haven't met any real resistance yet on your quest for the truth, but past experience tells me that where there's a secret, there are people who want to protect that secret. My old Hellknight pal Astrachios may be long dead, but the Order of the Eclipse he founded still remembers me—institutions have long memories."

"*And you said the bone sages also dislike you,*" Chk Chk returned. "*What sort of trouble did you get into on Eox, anyway?*"

"It wasn't *on* Eox, it was *near* Eox," Tyrcell said. "It's a long story, but if you really want to know, I can tell you on the way."

"An enemy of the Hellknights *and* the necrovites," Dae said. "That's kind of impressive."

"I've always said you can judge a person by the quality of their enemies," Tyrcell said. "And by that metric alone, I'm *amazing*. But don't worry. There's no reason for us to run afoul of either group. We'll be sneaky, we'll be subtle, and we'll be fast. Though I will have to turn my transponder back on. You do *not* want to be mistaken for a pirate anywhere in the vicinity of the bone sages. Most places, the worst thing that will happen is they execute you. On Eox, the worst thing that will happen is they execute you and then bring you back for more."

"*We don't know exactly where we're going, though,*" Chk Chk said. "*We'll need to decipher that code the crystal displayed.*"

"Yes, but I'm sure we're headed for the Thousand Moons," Tyrcell said. "Because it's one of the last places in the galaxy I want to go, so where else would Yaraesa send us? Once we're on board, I'll set a course for a Drift beacon near the debris field and see if we can decipher more precise coordinates on the way. Though centuries-old location data might not be super accurate. The moons shift around."

"If worse comes to worst, we only have to check a thousand moons!" Dae said. "If we split it up, that's only three hundred and thirty-three each!"

"*The name Thousand Moons is an approximation,*" Chk Chk began to explain, but Tyrcell interrupted and said, "That's the spirit. Let's go, Junior Probationary Covert Operatives. The mysteries of the universe await."

"We just got a ping from one of the sensor arrays we compromised around Eox," the ghost named Alcyone said. "A ship on a watchlist emerged from the Drift near one of their remote monitoring stations, at the very edge of the network. The vessel fled and almost immediately went back into the Drift again, though. Hmm. This is a very old flag—it's from 7 AG! Gods, I was *alive* back then."

"Huh," Groth, her ghoul copilot, said. "Is it a rogue necrovite?" The ghoul and the ghost crewed a small fighter ship together, trailing along at the back of a detachment of the Corpse Fleet. "Come back from a sojourn in the deep black Vast for trouble and shenanigans?"

The ghost manipulated the computer with spectral hands. "No, it's an android. They can live for centuries too. The dossier is... look at this, Groth."

The ghoul didn't immediately rise from his seat at the console. His exocortex—a computer implanted in his brain and bulging out of his skull—connected with the ship's system and streamed the data directly into his heads-up display, but there wasn't much data to be seen. There was a file creation date, and several subsections bearing later dates, but the contents were all redacted, classified above their authorization levels.

Groth rose and stomped over to the station where Alcyone hovered, shivering when he brushed against the edge of her immaterial presence. The physical screen didn't show anything different. "7 AG," the ghoul said. "Wasn't that the year of the Magefire Assault?"

Alcyone fluttered in what might have been a nod. "Yes, but I think you mean the War of Absalom Aggression. Those vile meatbags almost destroyed all the unlife on Eox!"

"The ship's registered home port is Absalom Station. I wonder if this android is a war criminal from way back then," Groth mused. "Who's the administrator controlling access to this file?"

Alcyone's phantasmal form interacted with the systems, and the screen flickered before displaying an image of a face they knew well: an elebrian woman with pale skin and stained-black lips, just a hint of cheekbone protruding through the flesh to reveal her undead nature, and a smile full of pointed teeth. "Lady Mnephalon," they murmured at the same time.

Groth stiffened as cold fingers caressed his mind, and Mnephalon stepped out of the shadows, dressed in sinuous flowing black, face as bone-white as sunlight reflected off a dead moon. She hopped up to sit on the console and perched on the edge, crossing her legs and kicking one foot back and forth idly. She wasn't *really* there—this was a mental projection—but she was a necrovite, with near-godlike magical powers, and the illusion was so realistic Groth could smell her sweet mix of perfume and decay. The real Mnephalon was aboard her flagship nearby, being very busy and important, commanding this detachment of the fleet.

Alcyone whimpered, but that was her usual response to proximity to her lady, even false proximity like this. Ghosts only really stuck around the mortal plane because of unfinished business, and Mnephalon herself was Alcyone's tether to this reality.

"Hello, darlings," the necrovite said. The leash embedded in Groth's mind tightened. They were Mnephalon's personal lieutenants, and while they were allowed a greater degree of autonomy than many of the necrovite's minions, she didn't ever let them forget that they were puppets on her strings. She could take direct control of them if she wanted, and she would if they displeased her.

Displease her enough, and she might make them pilot this worthless ship right into the heart of the nearest star. Though probably not. That would be too quick and merciful.

"I noticed you digging in some of my files. Do you mind telling me why?" She reached out and put her fingertip under Groth's chin, tipping his head back to make him meet her eyes, and the fact that her finger wasn't really *there* didn't make a bit of difference at all. Her black nail dug into his flesh just the same.

Mnephalon still had eyes, unlike most of the bone sages of Eox or the Corpse Fleet. They were ordinary and blue in her death's mask, but cold flame flickered inside them, a promise of deathless ire.

"A vessel registered to a flagged individual passed by one of the monitoring stations on the outskirts of the Thousand Moons," Alcyone babbled. "We were just looking them up and—well, see, Minnie?"

Groth winced. Mnephalon turned her head slowly, slowly, slowly toward the ghost, who took on greater definition under her gaze. Alcyone had once been a living elebrian warrior. Sections of black spectral armor flickered into existence around her form, as if *that* could protect her.

The necrovite's voice was cold wind and ashes. "We've talked about this. However close we may once have been, in our current relationship, pet names are inappropriate."

"Yes, my lady," the ghost said softly. "You have my most abject apologies. I forgot myself."

"Perhaps we should take steps to help you *remember*. We will revisit the subject later. Now, who's this person of—oh. *Oh*." Mnephalon hopped down off the console and looked at the screens, waving her hands to send data coursing across the displays. Most of the information was in her personal cipher, which Groth wasn't *supposed* to be able to read... but that biomechanical exocortex bulging out of the back of his skull wasn't just for show, and he'd broken her encryption ages before. That was one thing about the bone sages, however powerful they were: Since they were effectively immortal, time was more or less meaningless to them, and they weren't diligent about regularly updating their security protocols.

The data streamed by too quickly for Groth to follow, since even his enhanced mind was far slower than Mnephalon's, but he recorded it all for later perusal.

"I can't believe that miserable synthetic is still alive," Mnephalon said. "I assumed they'd long ago gone to the big scrap heap in the sky."

"Who is it, my lady?" Alcyone asked, and Groth winced again. He would never have spoken unprompted so soon after being chastised by their lady.

But Mnephalon seemed to have forgotten her annoyance. "Their name is Tyrcell. I haven't seen them since the end of the Magefire Assault. They *should* be a wanted criminal on Eox, but the powers that be decided the details of Tyrcell's involvement were too embarrassing to remain a matter of public record, and they couldn't *prove* the android was responsible for the worst of the destruction, anyway. But I always knew they were involved. Hmm." She smiled, the skull hidden beneath her parchment skin suddenly more prominent. "Do you know the best thing about living forever, my darlings?"

"No, my lady," they chorused.

"It means you can hold a grudge for a very, *very* long time. Come to my ship. I have a mission for you, and we need to get you properly outfitted first."

She turned, and in the course of turning, twisted into a column of shadow, which then dissolved into tendrils of black smoke and dispersed. *She's always so dramatic,* Groth thought.

"She's always so beautiful," Alcyone murmured.

"What do you think this mission is?" Groth asked, to shake the ghost out of her stupor of adoration.

"Oh." Alcyone considered. "We're going to go kidnap and torture and kill an android, and then Minn—Mnephalon will turn them into an undead plaything."

"Can you even make an android into a zombie?"

"I'm not sure, but they can do wonderful things with cybernetics nowadays. Lady Mnephalon will find a way."

"Probably." Groth agreed. "I wonder what this Tyrcell person did, exactly?" Maybe the truth was in the data he'd slurped up.

"That much is obvious," Alcyone said. "They bothered our lady. And that's an undeath sentence on its own."

# 3

## SEVERAL SORTS OF ZEAL

(Tyrcell / 7 AG)

Ty here again, once again annotating this manuscript from the future. Let me just pause here to say: If you read my account on the immediate aftermath of the Gap, you'll recall I wrote about things I didn't personally witness, based on a combination of reports, research, hearsay, guesswork, and wishful thinking.

The thing about the conflict that came to be known as the Magefire Assault is that it *was* an assault. It wasn't a long siege, and it was all over surprisingly quickly if we're just talking about calendar time. But it was a battle fought on many fronts, in many places, by many people, and if you added up all the hours of fear, stress, blood, necrosis, and horror that individual people experienced... well, in that sense, the assault went on for *ages*.

Because my friends are such nosy meddlers, I received firsthand accounts of what happened in the Armada, in the Spike, and in the Arms and the Ring, and I saw some of the events in the Eye and elsewhere myself. But I reviewed a lot of other footage (including data from Val's omnipresent camera drone—that was especially helpful) and talked to plenty of people in the aftermath and listened to a lot of stories. My friends were all seasoned fighters at the time of the assault because of the period of civil unrest that followed the Gap, and they did pretty well when it came to tussling with the undead. (I say "pretty well" because one of us didn't make it out alive. I'll talk about that later, but only when it can't be put off any longer; even now, compiling this manuscript years later, that wound in my heart feels fresh.) By interweaving accounts of my friends' experiences with mine, I can provide... well, not the *whole* picture, but a more complete one than you're likely to get from anyone else.

I can tell you the truth about how the Magefire Assault ended, and you'll see that all the official accounts get that part wrong.

But before we get to the all-out assault, I should talk about the foreshocks, starting with that explosion I mentioned earlier. Here's what me and Mel and Val and Carn did after we heard the big boom.

We ran toward it.

The line between heroism and foolishness can be pretty thin, huh? But all four of us were big believers in helping people in need, and Mel especially thought she had something to prove, if only to herself, so she was the first one up and sprinting toward the column of smoke rising from the gates of the Swordlight Cathedral. That struck me as a strange choice for a bombing target—who wants to pick a fight with the worshippers of Iomedae? They aren't exactly one of the more peace-loving sects, and there are always a lot of armed priests and champions hanging around.

Evidence of the explosion was obvious: Even apart from the screams and cries of the wounded, there was a fan-shaped stretch of blackened ground starting about twenty yards from the cathedral's courtyard, with trees and bushes burning merrily on all sides. The wedge of charred ash spread outward in a cone of devastation that ended by the toppled remnants of three of the eleven statues in the parvis. The statues depicted things that the goddess Iomedae had done, probably; thanks again to the Gap, the details were a little fuzzy, even for the most zealous of her followers.

The creepiest of the statues—the one where Iomedae stood over an exquisitely and gruesomely sculpted undead knight impaling himself on a big sword—was pretty much vaporized, except for Iomedae's boots and the hilt of the sword. The explosion hadn't notably damaged the cathedral itself, though the "windows"—they were holograms showing shifting scenes that looked like animated stained glass—were glitching out, the scenes interrupted by jagged lines. The imposing, bladelike towers of the cathedral stood as soaring and proud as ever, and there were priests and worshippers pouring out of the main doors, all apparently unharmed. There had to be wards upon wards upon wards in a holy place like that, so even *this* degree of damage meant there was some heavy power and forethought behind the attack.

Melezheun went straight to helping the wounded, and there were plenty of them in need of attention, from people who'd been strolling by in the park to priests of Iomedae to worshippers at the church who'd been unlucky enough to be in the courtyard. I saw a lot of people with injured bodies, though not many unattached body *parts*, so that was good. The injured can be saved in lots of ways, but with the dead, your options get a lot more limited, and some of those options are pretty unsavory.

Carn rushed over to where an elf was pinned, unconscious, stuck half under a fallen statue—this one depicted Iomedae holding the severed head of a ghoul aloft, and the statue blazed with an aura of blue fire, which was still trying valiantly to flare and flicker but had slowed to strobing at a pace that could induce seizures in the vulnerable. There were a few knights and priests trying to lever the statue up, but Carn is a solarian with a particular affinity for gravity, so he gave a few gestures and grunts, and the statue levitated upward, allowing the devoted to settle it upright on the ground and pull out the person who had been pinned beneath.

I looked around for something *I* could do, but the place was swarming with activity, and suddenly nothing seemed all that pressing: Every fallen person had a couple of people helping them, and the station's fire-suppression bots had already put out the burning bushes, so I just took it all in and wondered who'd done this and why. Some kind of sectarian violence from worshippers of a god who hated Iomedae?

Val stood next to me, strangely still and frowning, and I noticed her drone wasn't hovering around her. "What are you doing?" I asked, because she was clearly doing *something*.

"Trying to find the perpetrators. I've got my drone out scanning for anomalous movement, though the algorithms defining 'anomalous' weren't created with the aftermath of a bombing in mind. There are lots of people getting red-tagged in my HUD because they're running away in a panic, but that's pretty normal in this situation." She sighed. "I don't see anyone carrying a bomb and shouting 'Death to Iomedae,' so—no!" Her eyes widened, and she seized my arm, pointing upward.

There was a black dot above us, up near the zenith of the Eye. The dot got bigger, and my guts clenched up: I knew a decaying arc when I saw one. That was some kind of bomb or missile or other unpleasant object coming straight down at the courtyard—and us.

*Classic terror tactic,* I thought. *An initial attack to draw emergency personnel and security forces, followed by a second, more powerful, attack to wipe out the first responders.* My mind was oddly cold and calm, probably because when you're definitely about to die, what's left to worry about? I considered shooting at the bomb, but even if I could make it detonate early, an airburst wouldn't be much better than a ground one, and was probably more likely to damage the great dome of the Eye itself.

The fact that I'm writing this account removes a degree of your suspense, I suppose: I survived. Thanks to my friends and the hardworking servants of Iomedae.

Val's shout caught Carn's attention, and he instantly recognized the incoming missile for what it was. He reached out with his gravity-altering prowess to arrest the thing's downward plunge. The bomb hung in the air, only about ten feet over our heads, an ugly cluster of explosives and grenades that looked like a bulbous mutant mushroom. Several robed clergy stepped forward and raised their hands, and curved shields of golden light appeared in the air, gliding toward the bomb and surrounding it on all sides. The result was honestly kind of beautiful: a sphere of radiance surrounding destruction.

A muffled boom sounded a moment later, and smoke seeped out of the tiny cracks where the magical shields touched. The priests let their shields drop, letting loose a rain of shrapnel that thudded to the ground like a miniature hailstorm. (I'd been to lots of planets and moons by then and had witnessed weather that *wasn't* controlled by an automated atmosphere-and-climate system. I preferred the orderly nature of Absalom Station to any frozen precipitation I'd ever experienced, honestly.)

Val and I stepped forward cautiously and looked at the shrapnel on the ground, the stuff that bomb had been intended to disperse through the whole crowd. They were marble-sized spheres covered in spikes that shimmered with black grease. "I think those are poisoned," Val said.

"Necrotic magic." An older, hard-faced human woman wearing white robes trimmed with yellow joined us at the edge of the debris field. "I can feel the negative energy from here." A bunch of knights rushed by, swords hanging at their belts—more holy symbols than weapons, probably, but they could still chop a head off. If they found a terrorist, they probably would.

"Necrotic. That stuff only hurts the living, right?" Val said. "But it heals the undead. That's... interesting."

The robed priest frowned. "You think this was an attack by the undead?"

"We don't know anything yet," I said.

Val frowned. "We saw that borai elf lurking around earlier."

"He was strolling, not lurking, Val."

She shrugged. "He came from this direction, though, didn't he?" She began to tick off points on her fingers. "They used weapons with necrotic energy—if you were an undead terrorist, and any of *your* people happened to get caught by a piece of shrapnel, it wouldn't hurt them. The attackers targeted the cathedral of Iomedae, a god who famously vanquished vampires, liches, and ghouls—her priests are experts at fighting undead, and if this second assault had worked, it would have cut down their numbers on the station by a *lot*. Which is also good for undead terrorists. Combine that with all the nastiness coming out of Eox lately? The bone sages have been rattling their swords, and the swords are old and rusty and came from a *tomb*."

"You're jumping to conclusions," I said. "Besides, they wield bone scepters, not swords." Then I sighed. "But the conclusions are probably worth considering." I looked at the priest, who was taking all this in, frowning. "Did anyone get a look at whoever threw the first bomb or cast the first spell or whatever?"

She laughed harshly. "Come and see." We followed her as she walked to the point of the fan-shaped zone of destruction where the damage had originated. Then she nudged something with her foot, and I realized it was a boot. Or, at least, most of a boot. I hadn't noticed it before, because it was a lump of char in a spray of char. "It was a suicide bombing."

"Does it count as a suicide bombing if the bomber was already dead?" Val countered.

"We don't—" I began, but she shook her head angrily and stomped off, leaving without even a glance at Mel or Carn, who appeared to be doing triage to help the priests figure out who they should be healing first.

"She hates undead, doesn't she?" the priest asked. "The Inheritor would have probably liked her."

"The who?"

The priest quirked an eyebrow. "One of Iomedae's many titles." She pointed at the cathedral. "You know, the god this large building behind us was built to honor?"

"Ah. Right. Yes. Sorry. Never been the religious type." The only god I'd ever followed in any capacity was Yaraesa, and doing *that* had nearly gotten me killed. Iomedae stood for honor and justice and goodness and all that, but she hadn't stepped forward to explain why the Gap happened, so I assumed she was part of the same divine conspiracy that had wiped out untold centuries of history for reasons that might remain always unknown. I held that against her, and all the rest of the gods.

I held out my hand. "I'm Tyrcell. From the Society, over by the Lorespire?"

"I've heard of you." She shook my hand in a weird arm-clasping style. "Your lot have done some meaningful charity work, though you have a reputation for being nosy busybodies."

I laughed. "You speak plainly, don't you?"

"Iomedae wasn't fond of circumspection," she said. "I do my best to honor her. I'm Eustitia, one of the senior clergy." She looked around and clucked her tongue. "What a mess. I suppose we'll have to involve the station authorities. My lot is adept at vanquishing evil, but we're not as good at investigating it. I wonder if this really does have something to do with the recent unpleasantness with Eox. The bone sages don't much like my church, and I can believe they'd send agents to strike against us."

"It could be. Or it could be someone who wants us to blame the bone sages for their own political reasons. There are always people eager to stoke conflict."

Eustitia clucked her tongue again. "You've got a devious mind, don't you, Tyrcell? I suppose you might be right... but sometimes a thing is exactly what it appears to be. Thank you for your help today. I'm going to check on my people." She walked away and began barking orders at a group of young priests.

I found some menial chores to do to keep me from worrying about Val.

I should have worried more.

Once station security showed up at the scene, Carn stayed to help coordinate the response. Since he oversaw security for the Lorespire district, he got looped in on station-wide problems like all the local chiefs. The investigators were talking about doing an analysis of the bomb fragments when I got bored and went looking for Mel, but she'd gone off with some of the wounded to the hospital. Her mystic powers allowed her to heal bodily injuries and soothe trauma. The place was swarming with priests, so they could have lived without her, but Mel couldn't help herself from helping.

So there I was with no immediate responsibilities and lots of things on my mind. What else can you do in such a situation but go for a walk?

And while I was walking, I could keep my eyes open for shadowy cabals of terror plotters. Couldn't hurt, right?

I strolled along the paths, eventually reaching parts of the park where people had decided that one little terrorist attack wasn't enough to ruin a day of frolicking and feasting, and seeing people go about the business of pleasure both annoyed me and pleased me. Annoyed because there were would-be murderers running around in the vicinity, and that seemed like something people should at least acknowledge, but also pleased because, well, the people of Absalom Station are nothing if not resilient. So there'd been an explosion and some people were dead—too bad, but a few years earlier such things had been a more or less daily occurrence.

Not everything was joyful noise, though, even on this side of the park. Somebody was shouting off to my right, and even before I got close enough to make out the words, I knew the nature of the shouter. The voice was strident but clear, and the cadence was strong. This was someone preaching to an audience and trying to fire that audience up, which usually meant a trickster or a zealot, and I had issues with both. As far as tricksters go, I don't need the competition, and when it comes to zealots, see my entire history with the Hellknights.

I sidled toward the back of a small crowd surrounding a makeshift raised dais, upon which stood an older human priest. You could tell he was a priest because of the robes, the unlikely looking hat, and the staff topped with a white orb, but mostly from his eyes. There are many people on the station with eyes that literally glow, but even without actual luminosity, this man's gaze *blazed*. He was seized by the spirit, and he wanted everyone around him to know it.

He said, "This latest assault is just the beginning! The undead abominations are crawling out of their tombs to feast on the flesh of the living! They sail forth from their grave world to drink your blood, and oh, brothers and sisters and siblings, they won't stop there, oh, no! Death is only the *beginning* of your suffering at the hands of the bone sages of Eox! Once you die, they'll raise you as a rotting corpse, and you'll join their ranks to murder the very people you used to love—the very ones you died to protect! And for the unlucky ones, a vestige of your mind will remain, consciousness without volition, while you look out of your own rotting eyes and watch the atrocities you'll be forced to commit against your friends and neighbors! That is what's coming! That is what we must stand against! Eox must fall!"

There was another android nearby, one with delicate silver circuitry showing on the blue skin of her face, watching the performance with a faint frown, which is a pretty strong expression among synthetics. I moved a little closer to her. "Who's the preacher?" I murmured.

She murmured back, not taking her eyes off him, "Calls himself Ketavan. Ketavan the Vaticinator."

"The... is that someone who, uh, gives inoculations. Or, no..."

She chuckled. "Don't you have a dictionary loaded? A vaticinator is someone who knows the future—often because they received a divine vision."

"Huh. So what god does he get his intel from?"

"He's a follower of Pharasma, the Lady of the Graves, but there are rumors that he's an apostate. Allegedly his methods are too violent for most of her priests."

"Rumors? Why are there rumors about a preacher yelling in the park?"

"Ha. Those of us standing here, we aren't the real audience. See?" She pointed, and I finally noticed a couple of camera drones hovering discreetly around him, catching him from the most advantageous angles. "He does a vidcast, called *The Mortal's Coil*—which I guess is a reference to Pharasma's holy symbol, some kind of spiral—but his audience goes way beyond the faithful. He's been traveling the inhabited systems, advocating for all the 'living' worlds to join together to launch a preemptive strike against Eox, to cleanse the grave world forever, stuff like that." She shook her head. "Some of the stricter governments have made his broadcasts illegal because his rhetoric is so incendiary, and he's been blamed for attacks on random undead people all over the system. A varculak laborer on Akiton supposedly got ripped into pieces by a bunch of coworkers who'd been radicalized by Ketavan."

I whistled. "You seem extremely well informed."

She shrugged. "I work for the Absalom Advertiser, the news channel? I'm doing a story on the rise in anti-undead sentiment on the station lately. I came here to cover the bombing and then saw that Ketavan had decided to take advantage of the attack for his own reasons. He blames the undead, of course." She held out a hand. "I'm Saphenath."

I reciprocated. "Tyrcell. I'm a trader and explorer, mostly. I'm hardly ever even on the station these days. I guess I picked the wrong day to take a walk in the park."

"Have your travels ever taken you to Eox?" she asked, suddenly more interested.

"I've never had the pleasure. The bone sages do *some* trade, but you have to follow pretty strict procedures to visit their world, and I'm a more... casual sort of person." I was more a smuggler than a trader; it's more fun and the profits are better. But you don't tell someone you just met about your criminal activities, especially if they're a journalist.

"Oh well. I'm always looking for more perspectives. I'm hoping to interview this bone sage diplomat who's visiting. Have you heard about that?"

"No," I said. "One of the elebrian necrovites is coming *here*?"

She shrugged. "There hasn't been an official announcement yet, but the Prime Executive's office leaks like a colander. I've heard rumors of back-channel discussions between our governments for a while, and supposedly a delegation is coming from Eox soon to try to de-escalate all this tension. People say the diplomat is a *young* necrovite, relatively speaking, and more open to compromise than her older counterparts."

"Nobody's memory goes back more than seven years or so," I countered. "Aren't we all just as young as everybody else, mentally speaking?"

"In a sense," Saphenath allowed. "But there are certain... patterns of thought, haven't you noticed? There's more flexibility and impetuousness in those who are physically younger. The body influences the mind, after all."

"I'll take your word for it. My body could be ancient, but I think I'm still young at heart. And brain."

"You do seem rather lively," she said. "Where do you live?"

"In the Lorespire district, when I'm on the station."

"Ah, yes, the Society. One of the only little fiefdoms that wasn't basically a street gang."

"Oh, well, we try," I said.

"You've got a reputation for poking your noses into all sorts of places," Saphenath said. "Maybe *I* should move there."

"Where do you live now?"

"Oh, a luxury apartment in the Eye," she said. "I could see the spot we're standing in from my window. I just woke up there after the Gap, with more credsticks in a safe than I could use in a lifetime. I have no idea what I *used* to do, but I took my own curiosity as a sign to do journalism."

Her name finally rang a distant bell deep in my mind. "When you say you're *with* the Absalom Advertiser—"

She sighed. "Yes, I own it too. I don't like to lead with that information. People always want to yell at me about the things we report on or don't report on or both."

"I like the funny cartoons," I said.

She laughed. "I like *you*, Tyrcell." She glanced over at Ketavan, who was punctuating his rant with longer and longer pauses. "I think he's slowing down a bit, and he didn't really say anything new, anyway, just a remix of his greatest hits. Do you want to go with me to get a bite to eat?"

Well, it never hurts to make new friends, especially with a publishing magnate who runs a channel known for investigative journalism. "I can always eat."

We set off away from the park. "Where will we be dining? The Blue Room?" That was the luxury restaurant at the top of Bluerise Tower, and I'd always wanted to see the inside.

She snorted. "I'm more of a market-food-stall person. You like all that white-tablecloth business?"

"My last meal was eaten directly from a can while standing up in the galley of my ship," I said. "I was just curious how the other one percent lives."

"You don't learn much about the world from a vantage point that high," she said. "You can see a lot of things, sure, but they all look very small. I like being down at this level." She took me away from the Eye, into the Ring, through the bustling booths and tents of the markets, to a little hole-in-the-wall place with a counter and two tables. It served dough balls filled with some kind of algae paste, except that makes it sound disgusting, and it was great; I'm just not good at describing food, since, for the most part, I'm an eat-whatever-is-available-to-sustain-life kind of person.

Conversation with Saphenath was easy, and she was completely open about grilling me about my past, my experiences during the Gap, and my position within the Society. I am adept at deflecting, though, so she didn't learn too much, except that I value my freedom to come and go. She asked me a couple of other questions about my experiences with elebrians and Eox—I confessed that I'd met the famous Zo! in person, though I didn't mention that Hellknights were trying to kill us at the time. "You're really focused on this Eox business, aren't you?" I asked.

"I'm following a lead," she said. "Though it would be more accurate to say I'm chasing after a lead that keeps giving me the slip. A while back I heard some interesting rumors about the Thousand Moons—do you know the place I mean?"

"The asteroid belt around Eox, right?"

"That's right. As best we can tell, at some point well before the Gap, the elebrians destroyed some neighboring planetary bodies—part of the same conflict that turned their world into such a lifeless husk of a place, probably. Anyway, the debris field... that's the Thousand Moons, and some of them really *are* moon-sized. There are a few people living among them, mostly sarcesians, the ones who can fly through the void... they have those wings of light? We don't see them on the station too much, but I met one, and being me, I struck up a conversation, and they told me there's some deeply weird stuff in the Thousand Moons. Including evidence of ancient magic and technology. Some of their friends tried to investigate a ruin on one of the bigger moons, and they didn't all come out again, but they claim they found something remarkable inside—and dangerous. My contact claimed to know the specifics about this genuine treasure trove, but they wanted me to pay for the information, and that's not really what I do. There was no way to be sure it wasn't a scam, anyway. I am really curious about the whole thing, but..." She sighed. "I'm no dungeon delver, and hardly anyone goes near Eox. I love a mystery, but I also *hate* a mystery—what I really love is unraveling one."

"I suppose I could jaunt over that way next time I take my ship out," I allowed. "Do you have a specific location?"

"My source was trying to be cagey, but they were drunk, so I got enough details that I could maybe track it down."

"You could come along," I said. "My ship, the *Venture*, has plenty of room for two."

"Are you asking me on a date to a blasted moon of Eox that might contain some kind of deadly space dungeon?" She raised one silver-circuit-lined eyebrow.

"That depends. If I were, would you say yes?"

"I could be persuaded."

I snapped my fingers. "Actually, before we hop on a ship and sail off into the black, we should head over to my neighborhood. The Society members who go off on trading and exploration missions usually write reports and file them at the Lorespire so we can make maps and give each other tips and warnings and all that. The files are a bit haphazard, but if anyone has been to the Thousand Moons, they'll have left records behind. Maybe somebody else saw something in there."

She grinned and actually clapped her hands. "Tyrcell, you might be my new favorite person."

"I bet you say that to all your sources."

"Only the prettiest ones," she said.

Funny, isn't it, how a chance encounter can change the entire course of galactic history? If I hadn't seen Ketavan and met Saph and she hadn't told me about the mystery in the Thousand Moons...

Well. I'd be dead, along with a whole lot of other people, and you wouldn't be reading this.

# 4

# THE ABDUCTION OF CASPIEN BLIGHTWIND

## (Valentine / 7 AG)

Remember I said I was going to share some accounts from my friends? We're doing that now, with Valentine. Last time we saw her, she was in a foul mood and leaving a crime scene. We pick up with her a little later, still in a foul mood, but this time in the halls of power.

Valentine sat in the Syndicsguild meeting grinding her teeth. The council room was a vast circular space, with tiered seating like an amphitheater—maybe it had been an amphitheater, once upon a time—and the Prime Executive and her team were seated in the center, in the comfiest chairs in the room, all eyes upon them. The curved tiers were crowded, jostling as usual with an array of humans, ysoki, androids, and lashuntas, plus a smattering of other species, all representing various localities and affinity groups on the station, all arguing among themselves. Val was stuck on an uncomfortable bench near the back because she'd gotten there late, on account of stomping around fuming and looking for that suspicious borai she'd seen leaving the park. A dragonkin beside her kept poking her in the shoulder with their spines. "Do you mind?" she finally snapped.

"Apologies," the dragonkin rumbled with apparent sincerity, and shifted over a bit on the long bench. Then they tilted their armored head and said, "I've seen you here before. I was wondering: What's with the little recording drone?"

"I'm pitching a reality show about my life to Zo!," she lied, because the truth—"I'm so afraid of losing my memory again that I want to record everything that happens to me so I can catch myself up if it happens"—made her feel pathetic when articulated aloud.

"Is your life super interesting?" the dragonkin asked.

She snorted. "I witnessed a terrorist attack this morning, so it can be."

The dragonkin grunted. "I heard about that. By the cathedral? Must have been scary. The attacker died on the scene, though, and there weren't too many casualties?"

"Only because a friend of mine stopped the second bomb," Val said. "It must have been launched by an accomplice, so it wasn't just a lone bomber. It was some kind of organized attack."

The dragonkin groaned. "That's just what we need. Do you think it was the undead separatists?"

Val cocked her head, immediately fascinated. "The who?"

"One of my guys at the docks was talking about it," the dragonkin said. "There's some kind of movement to found an undead-only section of the station, I guess, their very own enclave. There are a lot of pro-Eoxian people in the group, apparently, and some of them really hate the living, you know? They're undead supremacists who think we're just a waste of good meat." They shook their head. "Ugly stuff."

"What's your name?" Val asked.

"I'm Azhodehya. People call me Azzi. I'm here representing the dockworker's union. You?"

"Val, representing the Society, over by the Lorespire."

Azzi brightened. "Ooh, there's a great noodle place over there."

Val felt a little jolt of pride. "My partner, Starla, runs that restaurant!"

"Give my compliments to the chef. That one dish, with the garlic? Who needs flaming breath when you can just eat a bowl of that and vanquish your enemies with an ordinary exhalation?"

Val laughed, her mood unexpectedly lightened, and then the Prime Executive's assistant was calling everyone to order.

Loqua Tem rose to her feet, poised but dressed casually in a worker's jumpsuit, always careful to strike a person-of-the-people image. She said, "We have a lot of important matters to discuss today, but first, I want to acknowledge the terrible attack on the Swordlight Cathedral this morning. The damage was minimal, though there are some serious injuries being treated. Things could have been worse, but thanks to the swift intervention of citizens in the park, some of whom will be receiving special commendations, a mass-casualty event was averted. We believe that at least one conspirator is still at large, and our security forces are tracking down every lead. I've heard some of the rumors swirling around, and I want to stress: We do not know who orchestrated this attack, or why. No group has claimed responsibility, and our findings are too preliminary to share. I'll let you know more as soon as we come up with anything solid. For now, let's move on to other business."

The meeting proceeded from there in its usual controlled-chaos way. It was better than the first year of meetings after the Syndicsguild was formed—those were mostly shouting matches that occasionally dissolved into minor melees. The assembled syndics had finally adopted some formal meeting rules, meant to keep things flowing smoothly and to allow people to speak and actually be heard, but there was still a tendency to dissolve into small, squabbling cohorts. Still, it was more than a year since anyone had been stabbed in the council chamber, and even that had been more of a hard poke, really.

The Prime Executive brought up various issues plaguing the station and asked for volunteers to run ad hoc committees to investigate and formulate action plans. Val, true to the meddling-busybody ethos of the Society, volunteered people in her organization to help. Melezheun, with her sense of justice and calm demeanor, would be a good choice for visiting the casino and getting them to behave in a more prosocial way, and Carn might be good to check out the problem with warehouse space at the docks. If nothing else, he could smash down some nonessential walls and make a little more storage space. "Don't go breaking my stuff," Azzi said when she suggested that.

"We've got enough problems down there already. Is your friend good with logistics? Because it's a logistics problem, really."

"He's the most logistical guy I know," Val assured them.

The meeting finally reached the bottom of the agenda, and Val had her chance to speak in support of their emergency medical care initiative. It passed without much in the way of debate or objection, but she didn't yield the floor when she was finished.

Instead, she cleared her throat, and all eyes (and sensors) turned to her. "I know it's not on the agenda, but I think it's important for us to discuss the tensions with Eox. This council unanimously voted to refuse the bone sages' invitation to join their protectorate, but it's clear they're not going to let the matter drop. It's possible that today's terrorist attack was ordered by Eox, or perpetrated by undead supremacists on this very station—"

"You bring up a good point, syndic," Tem said smoothly, rising again from her seat. "And you've nicely set up the announcement I intended to end this meeting with. I have, in fact, been communicating with the bone sages of Eox, through both official diplomatic channels and certain informal means, attempting to smooth things over between our nations. Eox is, after all, a major civilization and military power, and since the advent of Drift travel has made space seem so much smaller, it's more important than ever to get along with our neighbors. The fact is, Absalom Station has great economic power and growing cultural influence, and I believe we're an inspiring model for a functioning multispecies society, but... we are still very small compared to the other worlds in the system."

"The bone sages want to invade and take us over!" a dwarf shouted from one of the lower tiers.

"Some of them do," the Prime Executive agreed, without rising to the bait. "Others realize that if they tried to take the station by force, they would destroy what makes the station *valuable*—our reputation as an open port, and a place where all species are welcome, as long as they behave peacefully. *Including* the undead. Some of the younger bone sages are open to more... peaceful collaboration and cooperation. To that end, I am pleased to announce an upcoming diplomatic mission from a dynamic and brilliant young necrovite named Mnephalon. She is the future of the leadership of Eox, and she is eager to forge a mutually beneficial relationship between her world and our own. She's very curious to find out how our station works, and we'll be setting up meetings with representatives—"

Tem's voice had to get louder and louder as various council members booed and shouted at her, Val among them. "This is *stupid*!" Val called out, though her words were lost in the din. "You're going to show some bone sage everything about how the station works? That will only help them attack us later!"

Finally, Tem raised her hands in the air and cried, *"Order!"* And then she simply stood, arms crossed, waiting.

The rumble subsided. "I am not going to hand our visitor the station schematics and security codes," she said in a low, level voice. "This is a diplomatic mission, as I said. Mnephalon is going to stroll through the park in the Eye and visit some of our manufacturing sectors, discuss import and export dues, and buy cheap souvenirs and pose for photographs. I am trying to normalize relations with a much more powerful and heavily armed planet, and I would *really* appreciate it if you could all refrain from throwing rotten fruit at Mnephalon when she walks down the corridors. She is a *progressive* bone sage, or at least as progressive as they get, and she's our best hope for avoiding an actual conflict with her people. Can we all agree that would be the best possible outcome?"

Val sat down, arms crossed, scowling. Azzi scowled too. "Diplomacy can't fix everything," the dragonkin rumbled.

"No," Val said. "As usual, we're going to have to fix things ourselves."

"How are we going to do that?" Azzi asked.

"Someone knows who's behind that terrorist attack," Val said. "If we can find out, and prove it was Eox, then the Primex will *have* to take this threat seriously."

"Wait, is there a suspect you know about?" Azzi said.

"I think I'm the only one who does," Val said. "Nobody else took me seriously, but there was something *off* about this borai I saw fleeing the scene of the terrorist attack. If I could track him down... Do you think *you* could find a private place for me to ask him a few pointed questions?"

Azzi scratched at the scales on their neck. "I... think most people would call that kidnapping, Valentine."

Val squinched up her face. "I'm a duly selected representative of the Syndicsguild, from the Lorespire district, investigating a threat to my constituents. I bet I could find a lawyer who could justify my actions. But if we get results, we won't even need to justify them. You don't have to help if you—"

"No, no," Azzi replied. "I didn't mean that. If you really have a serious suspect, and the authorities won't listen... then I'm in. I haven't been involved in a quasi-legal conspiracy for *weeks*."

Val didn't even know why she found the undead so abhorrent; she'd barely even ever met any. She wondered if it was a vestige of some pre-Gap experience, a traumatic event she couldn't remember but that had nevertheless left an indelible impression on her psyche. Dr. Bindi thought that was how things worked. She said, for most organic species, trauma left a mark on the body and the brain—negative experiences altered your neural pathways, changed hormonal responses, and scarred you emotionally, even if you couldn't remember the incidents that gave you the scars. "The body keeps a tally of every wrong ever done to you," Bindi said, and maybe inside Val there were deep and ugly marks left by some awful interaction with the undead.

Or maybe Val was just having the sort of sensible and pragmatic reaction any living person should have in the face of creatures who wanted to eat your flesh or drain your blood or feed on your life energy or consume your emotions, and everyone else was being ridiculous by suppressing that natural response and pretending the unliving abominations were just normal people.

Whatever the reason, she didn't have any particular qualms about kidnapping that borai elf. She'd dispatched her life-logging drone to track him down after the explosion and picked him up running away from the park. Granted, plenty of innocent people ran away from the sound of a bomb. But guilty people could fake being innocent. It was an essential skill for them, in fact. And everyone knew the undead were adept at hiding their feelings. Something about those inexpressive corpse faces just made Val distrust everything about them.

She was looking at that face on her heads-up display as her drone hovered just outside the borai's apartment. He didn't live in the Lorespire district, but he did reside pretty close by. She'd done some research on the public infosphere but hadn't discovered much. He was a longtime resident of the station (meaning since the Gap), his name was Caspien Blightwind (that surname struck her as overdramatic undead posturing), and his age was given as 175 years, though most ages were guesswork since the Gap destroyed all the records. He'd "converted" to undeadhood six years ago, dying of unspecified causes during chaos on the station and falling victim to a botched resurrection spell that left his soul attached to a walking corpse, more or less. He worked in accounting for one of the corporations in the Bluerise district. No legal partner. No known criminal associates. That was all the records had to offer. There weren't any mysterious and compelling redacted bits either.

Val felt a tiny tickle of doubt. The only reasons she had to suspect this person of anything were that he was undead and he'd been spotted in the park immediately before the bombing, then had run away afterward. There were at least hundreds of undead on the station, and there'd been scores of people in the park... but still. He might know something. The undead were a minority among minorities there, and even if it turned out Caspien wasn't directly involved, he probably knew someone who was.

And actually, forget all that. This was exactly the kind of record she'd expect to see for a secret sleeper agent placed on the station by Eox to destabilize their society and soften them up for an invasion. Blightwind's apparent innocence *itself* was suspicious in its own way, wasn't it?

Having convinced herself of the rightness of her plan, Val brought Azzi along as she followed Caspien, using her drone to do so at an unnoticeable distance, until he strayed into the Lorespire district, apparently in search of a good meal. Maybe even noodles from Starla's restaurant. Borai have to eat like anyone else, and unlike some of the undead, they eat whatever they did back when they were alive, though a lot of them like things spicier, since dying tends to dull one's taste buds.

Val used her highest-level access codes to shut down the surveillance cameras in that stretch of corridors remotely, and then... they took him.

Ghouls have a wicked, infectious bite. Wights can drain your life force. Vampires vary, but most of them can dominate your will and force you to do their bidding. Silicon mummies can inflict mental anguish. Necrovites command magic so powerful they can turn you into red mist with a gesture.

Borai, mostly, just do whatever they did when they were alive, and with this particular borai, that seemed to be shouting, flailing ineffectually, and then pleading.

Val popped one of the panels on the wall that led to the access tunnels belowdecks. Those were mostly used for maintenance and occasionally transporting cargo, sparsely traveled but not wholly abandoned, so they didn't linger, swiftly dragging the borai along. Azzi did the actual dragging, and the borai didn't even struggle after a while, just said, "What do you want from me?" and "Who are you?" and similar queries that they ignored.

They didn't run afoul of any civilians in the depths, and soon they emerged into Azzi's workshop, where the dragonkin did repairs and some personal tinkering. The space was cramped, windowless, and dim, apart from those areas spotlit by high-intensity work lamps; the walls and tables were covered in menacing-looking tools that made the space resemble a torture chamber, even though they were just tools. Based on the borai's wail when they shoved him into a metal chair and he looked around, he didn't know that, though, and took them for more sinister implements.

Azzi wrapped Caspien up tightly in chains, winding them so his arms were pinned to his sides and his legs were tied together, and *everything* was tied to the chair. As the dragonkin worked, Val leaned on a workbench and scowled. "Caspien Blightwind. We know what you did, abomination."

The borai blinked at her. "Abomination? Oh, gods, do you work with Ketavan?"

The name didn't ring a bell. Was he a coconspirator Blightwind had fallen out with? "Tell me about this Ketavan."

"The mad priest with the vidcast, the one who accosted me in the park today and offered to 'cleanse my soul' and 'purify the abomination,' by which he meant, *kill* me."

"Re-kill you," Val corrected automatically. "You already got killed."

Caspien strained against his chains, more in apparent frustration than aggression. "I am aware! I was murdered by Hellknights when they assaulted Bluerise, and then one of my coworkers tried to resurrect me using magic it turned out they didn't understand very well."

Val blinked. Caspien had fallen victim to marauding Hellknights, just like so many people she knew?

The borai went on bitterly. "And here I still am, clinging to unlife, because nobody's sure if the sliver of soul that people like me cling to migrates on to the afterlife when we die again, or if we just get destroyed forever, like any common zombie. I keep going because this awful life is better than oblivion." He rattled his chains. "Or anyway, it *has* been. Getting kidnapped is making me reconsider!"

Val frowned. "Forget all that. Why do you think I'm working with this Ketavan?"

"Because he said he plans to purge the station of the 'undead blight,' which I did take a little personally, since it's right there in my name—"

A mad priest with a vidcast, devoted to destroying the undead? Maybe Val should track the guy down. "All right, I get it. No, I'm not with Ketavan. I'm a member of the Syndicsguild, and I'm investigating the bombing in the park."

He frowned. "So this is like... an official thing?"

"I'm running an ad hoc independent investigatory unit," Val said, and Azzi, standing back against the wall, grunted. It was probably amusement, but it sounded a bit menacing at least.

Caspien scowled. "This is how you interview witnesses? You could've just invited me for a cup of tea. You didn't need to bundle me into a tunnel and bind me with chains. I'm happy to tell you what I saw!"

"This is how we interrogate *suspects*," Val said.

His eyes widened. "What, me? I don't know anything about bombs! I'm an accountant at—"

"Why were you in the park today?"

"Why is *anyone*?" he countered. "I wanted to take the air, feel the light on my face... I work all day in a windowless—"

"Tell me about your ties to Eox," Val interrupted him. Best to keep suspects off balance.

"Eox? I don't have any ties to Eox. I've never even been there! You can check my travel records."

She already had, but just because he hadn't been to the planet didn't mean he'd never made contact with its leaders. "Eox has an open immigration policy for borai, don't they?"

"I've heard that," Caspien said cautiously. "Wait. So you think Eox was behind the bombing? And wait again—is this *species-based profiling*? Did you just scoop me up because I happen to be undead? There are hundreds of undead people on this station! Do you think we're *all* collaborators?"

"I think it's a lot more likely that an undead person would work to further the goals of the bone sages than it is that a living person would, so when we're looking for leads..." She shrugged.

Caspien groaned. "That is, forgive me, total nonsense. Do you know how the people of Eox treat borai? We're the lowest of the low in their social hierarchy because we still do living things, like eating and sleeping. The bone sages *do* have an open immigration policy, and some borai even take them up on it, because we're objects of fear and mistrust in living society, and the idea of moving someplace we *belong* is tempting. But the rumor is, once you get to Eox, you get stuck with the worst jobs, and I'm talking digging-radioactive-materials-out-of-the-rock-with-a-pickax-a-mile-underground kinds of jobs." He rattled the chains again. "They might even treat us worse than *you* people do."

Val frowned. For her, the undead were one big bucket of bad; sure, some of them drank blood, some ate flesh, and some stole energy from the living, but they were all unnatural predators. The idea that there were hierarchies among them—apart from "necrovites are very powerful and never let you forget it" and "vampires can be snobs"—had never really occurred to her. If Caspien's account was true, the borai were, well, working-class types, downtrodden by the tromping boot of the bosses, and the bone sages were the *ultimate* in bosses, ancient hoarders of wealth who wouldn't even ever have the common courtesy to die.

Ugh. Was she feeling class solidarity with the undead? "I don't believe you," she said, which was only about half true. "And even if I *did*, you could still be useful to me. There aren't a lot of you undead on Absalom Station, and it's natural to congregate with your own kind. I bet you've met some undead supremacists and separatists, haven't you? People who work for Eox?"

Caspien shifted uncomfortably, and Val knew immediately she was right. "Well?" she snapped. "Who?"

"I don't know," he said miserably. "I'm just an accountant. I don't get involved in that stuff. I just want to live my life—"

"Unlife," she interjected automatically, then walked around behind his chair, knowing it would make him nervous to have her out of his line of sight. She drew a knife from her belt, making sure to drag the blade along the inside of the sheath to make the metal ring, so he'd hear it come out. "If you're not useful to me, you're just waste product to be disposed of. How do you kill a borai, anyway? Is there some special thing, like destroying a necrovite's electroencephalon? Nah, you're not fancy like that. Cutting you into pieces and incinerating said pieces will probably do the job."

"Wait!" he shouted. "You can't do this, I'm a citizen, I have rights—"

"You're a terrorist. They don't have rights." Val was privately glad that Blightwind was an accountant and not a lawyer. She put a hand on his shoulder and squeezed, like she was bracing herself for a strike. Azzi was watching her very closely, heavy-browed eyes narrowed, so Val shook her head minutely, and mouthed the word *Bluffing*.

The dragonkin relaxed, enough that Blightwind might have noticed if he hadn't been too scared to pay attention. "I'll tell you what I know!" he shouted. "There's a club, sort of, where a lot of undead go, and sure, I've heard some people talking about Eox there, about how life here would be better for us under the rule of the bone sages. That's all I've got! I can tell you where the club is, all right?"

"No, that's not all right," Val purred into his ear. "You're going to take me there, and you're going to point those people out to me. That is... if you want to go on not-quite-living."

Tyrcell here with another editorial interjection. When I watched Val's recordings and saw what she did to Caspien—a guy I got to know later, as you'll see—I couldn't believe it. I couldn't believe *her*.

Just so we're clear: That stuff Valentine did to the borai wasn't clever or brave or necessary. In fact, the moment she kidnapped Caspien is the moment she permanently disqualified herself for the position of head of the Society, as far as I'm concerned. That was

Hellknight behavior, honestly, and she should have known better. She should have *been* better. Maybe there were reasons in her past, but that's not an excuse; it's just an explanation.

To her credit, Val did come to understand the mistake she'd made, later on.

It's a shame that didn't do anything to help with the consequences.

# 5

## OFFSHOOT OF DESIGN

(Melezheun / 7 AG)

We're going to visit someone else now. If you, my book-reading pal, perused my earlier account about the Gap, you know Mel carried a fair bit of guilt for bringing the Hellknights down on us and blamed herself for the death of our friend, the contemplative Sue. I tend to put the blame on the person who wields the gun, myself, but I can see where Mel was coming from. She wasn't ever a martyr about it, though. She just devoted herself to doing as much good as she could, as a path to redemption. Redemption at any cost. Redemption, it eventually turned out, at *all* costs.

Of all the companions I've lost over my many years of life, Mel might be the one I miss the most. Oh, Melezheun.

Melezheun gazed out the window of the little shuttle transporting her from Absalom Station to the vast casino ship enigmatically named *Offshoot of Design*. She was dressed in pale green formal robes befitting an official representative of the Syndicsguild, but underneath, she wore her mindmail, hidden away but ready to sheathe her in protective mesh at the first sign of danger. She didn't expect to be physically assaulted on board the floating den of vice and pleasure, but lots of unexpected things had happened to her since she woke up, bewildered, on the first day of the Gap seven years earlier.

How things had changed since then! The station had been a place of lawless chaos for years, never more than a few bad choices away from total destruction, but it had become, improbably, a center of culture and commerce. Which, of course, made it a target for those who were jealous or avaricious or both. There were so many ships outside her view port, hanging unmoving in clusters, sometimes connected by gantries and umbilical cords like rafts lashed together on a lake to make a larger dwelling. Smaller, colorful ships darted among plodding behemoths, and she was reminded of fish flitting about in an aquarium.

Melezheun sometimes thought of herself as a kind of fish, and the water she swam in was guilt.

She shook off the bad memories, past choices she'd made in fear and their terrible consequences, and tried to focus on the present and the future instead. Nothing she did would bring Sue back to life, but she could bend her efforts to making sure others survived and thrived. She'd devoted herself to a position of leadership in the Society because she wanted to help her people... and somehow, improbably, that had led to *this* job, something halfway between a diplomatic mission and a shakedown.

The casino ship loomed ahead, dominating her view of this arc of the Armada, a whale to her shuttle's minnow—or maybe plankton. The *Offshoot of Design* was an immense vessel, long and bulbous. One side was covered in docking bays, each outlined in glittering lights of red and blue and purple and gold, welcoming in the punters and the gambling addicts and the people who were sure they'd discovered a system that could beat the house. (Nobody ever beat the house; that was why it was the house.)

Mel's shuttle locked on to the proper beacon and sailed toward a smaller docking bay, one that *wasn't* lit up with flashing come-on-in lights. (Fish again: This time she was thinking of those deep-sea ones that lit up to entice prey into their jaws.) The doors slid open to admit her vessel, and the plankton was swallowed by the whale. Her shuttle settled down in a dark space. She waited as the bay's opening behind her sealed up and the small hangar pressurized. Then she sat in the dark a while longer. That was a bit rude, to keep her waiting, but she supposed it was a power play—

The lights came on in a blinding flash, and two striking figures stood directly in front of the shuttle—they must have been waiting there in the dark. Melezheun rolled her eyes, glad that they couldn't see her. Such *drama*.

One of the two was an azrinaran elf wearing a clinging black dress of some filmy material that shimmered with twinkling starlight. Her people were sometimes called "void elves," and her skin was a deep purple with lighter purple highlights, in startling contrast to her long white hair, worn loose and flowing. Her face was beautiful but severe, as if she'd been carved by a sculptor with a fondness for sharp angles. She was very still and watchful.

Her companion was a robot, but something in the way it moved, shifting its weight and tapping its numerous feet, made Melezheun think it was an SRO—a sentient robotic organism, a construct with a soul. Those came in all shapes and sizes, and though this one was only a bit taller than the stately elf at its side, the resemblance ended there. The robot stood on six multijointed, silvery legs, with a cylindrical torso of gleaming metal dotted irregularly with holes of various sizes, and its teardrop-shaped head bristled with compound lenses and antennae that drooped and twitched like feelers or mustaches.

Mel rose and triggered the shuttle's ramp, walking down it with stately calm. "Greetings," she said. "I am Melezheun, of the Society, appointed by the Syndicsguild to serve as your liaison with the council."

"Welcome," the void elf said, her voice so warm and ingratiating and soothing that Melezheun wondered if she was working some persuasive magic—or trying to; Mel was fairly resistant to such things, thanks to her long years of mystic training. "My name is Phaera. I manage this little pleasure craft. This is my associate, Master Fabricant."

"Delighted to meet you." The robot's voice was as rich and mellifluous as a classical actor's, not at all the grating sound she'd ungenerously expected.

"And what is your role on the ship, Master Fabricant?" she asked.

"I make sure no one cheats," he said. "At least, not more than once, and never successfully. Phaera brought me along to intimidate you."

The elf winced. "It doesn't work as well when you say it out loud," she said.

"Why not? I'm just as intimidating either way. Did you know I can spray a cloud of deadly microbots out of my torso at will, Melezheun of the Society? I can. There. Now I'm even more intimidating."

Phaera sighed. "The leaders of Absalom Station have suggested that if we entered into a more formal relationship, I would benefit from the protection of your security services. I invited Master Fabricant as evidence that I don't need your bots. I'd bet on my associate over them every time. I am happy to remain independent."

"I understand your perspective," Melezheun said. "I'm here to make sure you understand ours."

"Come on, then. We can talk in my office." Phaera turned and led the way, Master Fabricant's spiny legs moving up and down like sewing needles as he kept pace with her. They exited the docking bay into a wide corridor with workers of various species passing by in all directions, disappearing through doors and side passages—there were cooks and cleaners but also people wearing elaborate feather headdresses and very little else. They all nodded or greeted Phaera, who returned their attention with a distant, regal benevolence. The workers tended to ignore or shy away from Master Fabricant, but then, he didn't go out of his way to be friendly.

"Could I see some of the casino?" Melezheun asked.

"Casing the joint so you can rob us later?" Master Fabricant asked, sounding surprisingly serious.

"I'm compensated well enough in my current employment," Melezheun said. "I'm just curious. We're here to discuss the fate of your venture. I'd like a sense of what that venture entails."

"Of course." Phaera paused at a seemingly arbitrary point in the corridor and bumped the wall with her hip. A hidden door swung open, and they stepped out of the white corridor into—

Melezheun could scarcely take it all in, her senses were so dazzled. They were in a vast, open space filled with gaming tables and machines with flashing screens, surrounded by milling crowds, members of every species she'd heard of and some she didn't even recognize. The air was full of happy shouts and beeping and clanging and whistling from the machines and game masters calling out odds or rules or encouragement. Feeling overwhelmed, Mel focused on her immediate surroundings. The floor was covered in a lush, dark carpet; the ceiling was elegantly arched; the walls—she couldn't even see the walls, apart from the one they'd just emerged from, just more gaming floor stretching out seemingly forever. The illumination came from floating spheres of light that bobbed close to the ceiling, most bright white, but with a handful of red, blue, purple, and gold, providing a party atmosphere.

"—tables are there," Phaera was saying, apparently pointing things out, tone professional and almost bored. "Over that way we have the sports betting. Drone racing, ship racing, fighting pits, robot wrestling, low-gravity motorcross, brutaris, that sort of thing. Here, we have the automated machines, for those who prefer solitary gaming."

Melezheun considered the rows and rows of gaming cabinets, each with a person seated in front, pushing buttons as lights flashed and holograms from the cartoonish to the erotic cavorted before them. "So you feed in your credits and pray to the random number generator that it produces a number in your favor?"

"You grasp the essentials," Phaera said. She gently guided Melezheun toward a pathway snaking through the tables and machines. "Here we have some bars, a few restaurants, over there we have sleeping pods—available for rental in fifteen-minute increments so you can grab a restorative nap without leaving the floor. There are, of course, proper hotel rooms above, on the upper decks, ranging from the modest to the palatial, depending on how much our customers are willing to spend. Elsewhere on this level we have theaters for our live shows—feats of magic, acrobatics, music, dance. We tried comedy for a while, but finding talent who can appeal to the broad cultural cross section we attract proved too difficult."

"Not true," Master Fabricant said. "That troupe where the gnomes kept tripping the orc and making him fall on his face while he chased them around the stage was a huge success; it transcended all cultural barriers, and we ran matinees and two shows nightly until their contract ended."

"Why did it end?" Melezheun asked.

"They tried to renegotiate their terms with me, so I banned them forever," Phaera said, and smiled sweetly at Melezheun.

These people *really* weren't subtle, were they? But this hardly seemed like a subtle sort of place.

Melezheun paused by an area set up with a plethora of comfortable chairs, all facing the largest vidscreen she'd ever seen, easily fifty feet high. A vastly bigger-than-life-sized nude lashunta woman, her face and body smeared with mud, crouched behind a tree trunk, clutching a crude spear made from a tree branch. A holographic display of numbers blinked over the top of the screen, and the people watching cheered and clapped and booed. "What's this?"

"Zo!'s new show," Master Fabricant said. "*Naked and Stricken with Unimaginable Terror*. They drop a contestant into the remote jungle on some planet or another and see how long they can survive."

"Oh my," Mel said. "What do they win at the end?"

"Nobody knows," Fabricant said. "We're six seasons in, and nobody's won yet."

Melezheun blinked. "Why would anyone agree to participate in this program?"

"They want to be famous," Phaera said. "I've never seen the appeal of fame, myself, but it takes all kinds. If you'd follow me? I'm assuming you've seen enough of our operation. I do have *other* duties to attend to today, in addition to meeting with your esteemed self."

As they walked away, there was a scream and a crunch from the screen, followed by the cries of outraged gamblers, but Melezheun resolutely didn't look back to see what fate the woman had met.

Phaera led them behind a potted plant so large that, pot aside, it wouldn't have looked out of place in an ancient forest. Behind the plant was a seemingly plain wall which contained another hidden door she bumped open with her hip. Melezheun wondered if the panels would open for anyone who tried them, and doubted it.

*This* corridor was much less utilitarian, the walls papered in an elegant gold-and-black fractal design and hung with mirrors. The way was narrow enough that they went single file, first Phaera and then Melezheun, who was forced to endure the disconcerting experience of having Master Fabricant clattering away behind her.

"This passage leads to my office and private apartments," Phaera said, taking them through a series of doors locked with biometric scanners and codes. Mel felt a stir of misgiving. She'd have a hard time getting out of there on her own if she needed a quick escape. But she wasn't in danger, was she? Relations between the *Offshoot of Design* and Absalom Station were strained, but they'd remained cordial. The station had a *lot* of cannons, after all. Once they'd stopped fighting among themselves, the people of Absalom

Station had started worrying about pirates and other threats from outside and had taken steps to protect the station's inhabitants from everyone else.

Eventually they reached Phaera's office. The opulence of the room was ridiculous: The furnishings appeared to be real wood, and there was a huge marble swimming pool. Phaera draped herself on a chair behind a desk that looked big enough to land a shuttle on and gestured for Mel to take a seat on the other side. Master Fabricant stood off to one side, still twitching and jostling and tapping his limbs, *just* within Mel's peripheral vision, doubtless a position chosen with mathematical precision to be maximally disconcerting.

Melezheun folded her hands in her lap and said, "Since you mentioned being short on time, I will be direct. You owe Absalom Station a considerable sum in outstanding taxes."

"Oh?" Phaera said. "I don't see why. I am not a citizen of Absalom Station. My business is not incorporated there." She gestured. "I've never even set foot on the place. In case you hadn't noticed, we're in space. Space belongs to no one."

"You benefit from your proximity to the station," Melezheun said. "Many of your employees are our citizens. Many of our citizens visit your establishment. The majority of your supplies flow through our docks."

"Your citizens can come and go as they please, as I understand it," Phaera said. "And our supplies come from arrangements with individual companies, not from the government of Absalom Station."

Melezheun shook her head. "There's a reason your casino is *here*, and not in some more remote sector. The *Starstone* beacon brings countless ships here, and a not insignificant percentage of those ships end up patronizing your business."

"Have you considered how much *I* help *your* station?" Phaera countered. "People come to my casino, but they can't all afford to stay here, so they pop over to the hotels *your* people run. When my restaurants are booked up, they hop a shuttle to your station and dine there. Our relationship is symbiotic, and—"

Melezheun raised a hand. "The Prime Executive sent me to negotiate a payment schedule with you. If we can come to agreeable terms, then everyone is happy. If we *can't*, then terms will be imposed—and they will be much less favorable to you in that case, I can assure you."

"You can't *force* me to pay taxes," Phaera said.

"That's sort of the point," Mel said apologetically. "They can. Very few people *want* to pay taxes; they pay them because that's the cost of living in a society. As for force... The station is *bristling* with gun batteries. Swarming with security forces, both bots and people. The current government was formed to bring scores of warring gangs into alignment. They won't find compelling you very difficult at all. We prefer voluntary acquiescence, however."

"If it's done at gunpoint, it's not voluntary," Master Fabricant said. "And you might be surprised to hear about *our* defenses—"

"Enough." Phaera's voice was sharp as a slicing sword. "Do you mean to tell me your station will fire on the *Offshoot of Design* if I don't accede to your terms?"

"I doubt it will come to that," Mel said. "They'll just send someone to arrest you and impound the ship in lieu of taxes owed. The Syndicsguild considers the Armada—and you are *part* of the Armada—part of our station's jurisdiction."

"What makes us part of the Armada?" she demanded. "Is every ship that passes by subject to your control?"

"Your ship hasn't moved in almost a year," Melezheun said. "You're obviously a permanent—"

"We'll take the ship out!" she said. "We'll cruise over to Castrovel for a week, and then come back, and then go away again, and so on! Will *that* free us from your tyranny?"

The void elf seemed genuinely outraged at the idea of being asked to contribute to a system she was obviously a part of. Melezheun wasn't surprised, but she was disappointed. Phaera would not have enjoyed membership in the Society, where working toward the common good was the closest thing they had to a guiding philosophy. "If you leave with your taxes unpaid, and then come back, your ship will also be impounded. If you flee with your taxes unpaid, never to return, you will be pursued. Phaera, why are you fighting this? You've clearly got money to spare—"

"You have no idea how much overhead an operation like mine

involves," she snapped. "I assure you, my margins are as thin as microfilament."

Mel made a great show of looking around the office. "Yes. I can see you're struggling."

The void elf rose. "I have a group of VIPs arriving that I need to greet." She had her voice under control again. "If you'll excuse me. I'll have Master Fabricant throw you—*see* you out."

Melezheun tapped the gauntlet on her wrist, and a tablet sitting on Phaera's desk beeped. "All right. Since we failed to do any actual negotiating, I just sent you the bill our assessors prepared. It includes docking fees, property taxes, a flat gaming tax—oh, and we'll be sending over gaming commissioners to make sure your machines comply with the new regulations the Syndicsguild recently approved. There's been some *shameful* gouging in the casinos on the station, but I'm sure you're less... What was the word you used? *Tyrannical.* Oh, and if the number seems large to you, rest assured, there are details for a payment schedule too, with very reasonable interest rates."

"You're no better than pirates!" Phaera shouted.

"No," Mel said. "We're a government. We collect taxes so we can *provide services.* The wealthiest people in our society help subsidize those who are less fortunate. We don't just collect money for our own enrichment, like pirates do—everything we take in flows back out."

"Gods, I think she's a true believer, Master Fabricant," Phaera said. "I daresay we've reached an impasse." She flicked her hands in a dismissive gesture. "I've got to go meet with the Eoxians—"

"Wait," Melezheun said. "Your VIPS are from Eox?"

"Yes. I gather things are rather static and boring on their home world, and they were very excited to visit my casino. They made a significant deposit to ensure first-class service."

"You *do* know Eox wants to annex Absalom Station?" Melezheun said.

Phaera frowned, then shrugged. "I don't follow politics. Well, except for elections... and battles—you know, things you can lay odds and take bets on. And as I've said, I'm not a resident of Absalom Station, so what do I care? Anyway, these VIPs are part of some high-level diplomatic mission, I gather."

"Oh," Melezheun said. "I heard a bone sage was visiting, but I didn't know they'd be here so soon."

"Apparently they're ahead of schedule. They haven't adjusted to the speed and ease of Drift travel, I suppose, being hundreds of years old and set in their ways."

Mel frowned. "Their memories only go back seven years, just like everyone else—"

"Goodbye." Phaera stalked out.

Melezheun rose and looked at Master Fabricant, who was looking back at her, probably, from at least some of those clustered compound eyes. "I'll take you back to your shuttle," he said.

"I think I'd like to stay and explore the casino a bit," Melezheun said. "I assume I'm as welcome as any other guest?"

Master Fabricant grunted, which was a surprising sound from a robot, though it suited him perfectly. "Not in these restricted areas," he said. "Come along."

Melezheun fell into step beside him as they left the office, and as they traversed the various locked doors, he surprised her again. "Phaera will come around," he said. "She knows things are changing. There were a lot of opportunities in the chaos after the Gap, and she exploited just about every one of them. She's having a hard time letting go of that total freedom. But we've talked, and she knows there are advantages to stability—for one thing, we're a lot less worried about getting attacked by pirates when we're this close to Absalom Station. The reason she's anchored here is because all the other planets and Drift beacons she might have orbited all wanted to impose taxes and fees and laws on her too. She's been trying to outrun all that, but it's a losing proposition. The *Offshoot of Design* needs civilization to function—we can't do what we do out in the Vast somewhere or out in the wilderness on some planet. She'll cool off and set a meeting with you soon. My advice is to approach it like a partnership, maybe offer some grants or infrastructure investments or strategic partnerships. Phaera doesn't like zero-sum games unless she's the one *running* the game."

"That is good advice," Melezheun said. "And, if I may say, not very intimidating. It's nice to see another side of you."

"I contain multitudes," Master Fabricant said. "And not just multitudes of deadly microbots."

"Could I get a look at these VIPs from Eox?" Mel asked, since they seemed to be on friendlier terms. "I'm curious about them."

"Me too," Master Fabricant allowed. "I'm also glad I don't have organic parts to consume, frankly."

He led her through another secret door, across the teeming gaming floor, and finally to a reception area outside one of the docking bays. This one was much more opulent than the place where her shuttle had parked, which she remarked upon.

"Oh, we sent you to a cargo entrance," Fabricant said. "Phaera didn't want you thinking you were an honored guest."

They hung back, Melezheun resting on a small couch in a corner conversation area, and Phaera didn't even notice them when she strode in, followed by a pair of willowy void elf attendants wearing gossamer purple and gold, respectively. Moments after Phaera arrived, a small door to the docking bay opened, and a dozen undead strode out—though a few of them were skeletal minions, probably not guests so much as guards. There were two tall, elegant figures in the lead, once human and elf; presumably vampires, to judge by their toothy grins and flowing black garments. They were flanked by ghouls (the smell made Melezheun's eyes water) and corpsefolk—those were zombies, essentially, but with their minds intact—and a couple of shimmering figures, probably ghosts.

There was no necrovite with them, though. The only one of those Melezheun had ever seen in person was Zo!, and he'd been intimidating enough, even though he was basically benevolent. Or at least, not actively malevolent.

"Greetings, esteemed guests!" Phaera said. "We welcome you to the *Offshoot of Design*, the greatest pleasure vessel in this system or any other!"

"What kinds of blood do you have on tap?" the human vampire said, and Mel winced.

Then Master Fabricant, who'd been doing his jostling, leg-tapping, constantly-in-motion thing, suddenly went still, and that was even more disconcerting than his constant, hectic motion.

"What's wrong?" Melezheun asked.

"I'm getting word of... some kind of attack on the Armada, an explosion on a ship... or a ship that exploded? It... it may be an attack on the delegation from Eox. Details are unclear—"

The human vampire sauntered closer to Phaera. "We come in peace," he said, then cocked his head. "No, wait, that's not right." He opened his mouth wider, showing off more and more teeth. "We come to tear you into *pieces*. Yes, that's what it is. Of course, if you cooperate, and give us control of your ship and all the pretty weapon systems our scanners detected, we might let you live." He touched Phaera under the chin with one black-nailed fingertip. "Maybe I'll even keep you around and just take... little nips here and there." He snapped his teeth together an inch from her nose and laughed.

"I don't understand—" Phaera began, which Melezheun assumed was a lie, but it was as good a way to stall for time as any.

The elf vampire suddenly lunged at the attendant in gold, seizing her arms and biting her throat. The one in purple screamed and fled, pursued by a ghost. Phaera stumbled backward, shouting, "Stop, no!"

"I've never killed a vampire before," Master Fabricant said. His sensors flashed a lurid red, and he spun across the room, pointy legs a blur of motion.

Melezheun didn't let surprise paralyze her. She'd been surprised plenty of times before, and it was better not to dwell on the sensation if you could do otherwise. She summoned her mindmail, the cunning nanotechnological arrangement of chain mail and force fields flowing out to cover her face and hands. *I never have, either,* she thought, and joined the fray.

# 6

## THE DOCK DEFENDERS

### (Carn / 7 AG)

Tyrcell here again. While I was flirting with Saphenath, and Val was stalking an undead elf, and Mel was about to try her hand at slaying a vampire in a floating casino, Carn was busy out in the Arms, at the docks, stuck with doing a lot of the heavy lifting, as usual.

"This isn't supposed to be my problem," Cronch said. "Azzi is the supervisor, and they were supposed to show you around, but they called off sick this afternoon, so you get me instead."

"That's how it goes sometimes," Carn said agreeably, sitting in a tiny office made from a repurposed shipping container tucked away at the edge of one of the station's busiest ports. The not-supervisor sitting at the desk across from him, Cronch, was a minotaur-like nuar, and he was about as tall as two of Carn stacked on top of each other. As a result, he looked uncomfortably wedged in there behind a desk, tucked against a row of cabinets stuffed haphazardly with data crystals. "So, this problem you've got. What's the nature of the problem?"

The nuar's eyes widened, and he snorted through his wide nostrils. "You mean the council didn't even tell you why they sent you?"

Carn shook his head. "Could be they wanted me to come into the situation with an open mind and none of those—What do you call them?—preconceptions."

Cronch leaned back, jostling the cabinets and making the crystals rattle. "It's the crates!"

"Crates," Carn repeated. He stuck a finger in his ear and wiggled it around. "I gotta tell you, Cronch, when I got word from my boss that you all needed my help down here, I sorta figured it was, I dunno. Thieves. Sabotage. Something security-related."

Cronch sighed, lowering his head; even his majestic horns seemed to droop. "They told us you were an expert in logistics. Are you not an expert in logistics?"

"Oh, well, sure," Carn allowed. "I've got all sorts of expertises. I just don't usually get called upon to use most of them so much anymore. OK, so there's a logistics problem. Let's take a look. What's the situation? Too many crates?"

"Too many crates?" Cronch's voice was deep and low and doleful. "No. A month ago we had too many crates. Now we have... *way* too many crates. If crates were credits, I'd be rich enough to retire to a luxury apartment in the Eye."

"*Lotta crates* is what I'm hearing," Carn allowed.

"You don't get it. Come on. I'll show you." The nuar rose, shoving the desk inadvertently toward Carn, but the ysoki hopped to his feet and stepped back in time to avoid getting his knees banged.

Cronch led the way out of the office and out onto the main floor, where bots and organic workers were engaged in moving a whole lot of cargo—or at least, trying to. The situation was challenging, with literal tons of cargo already piled up all over the place, most of it in somebody's way. There was a lot of shouting and pointing and traffic jams and queues, and Carn could see the problem.

"I can see the problem. That is a lotta crates."

"This?" The nuar snorted again. "This is nothing. This is what you'd call the spillover." He led Carn through a maze of stacked boxes that managed to make the cavernous space look cluttered, until they reached a wall-sized cargo bay door, currently closed. "Through here." Cronch punched a button on the wall, and the immense metal panel slid upward, revealing a vast warehouse space beyond.

"Oh," Carn said. "Yeah. Way too many crates." The space on the other side of the wall was absolutely crammed with scuffed white polycarbon crates, the smallest ones about three feet wide by three feet deep by six feet long, the largest three times that size. The crates were stacked in towers that stretched thirty feet high in places, almost to the ceiling, in rows that left aisles just barely big enough for forklifts—or big fellas like Cronch—to get through. It was way more cramped than the main floor of the dock, which suddenly seemed roomy and spacious.

"Look at all this!" Cronch cried. "Most of these crates been here *weeks*, and every day, more come! Pretty soon we're going to have to turn shipments away, and that's money out of our pockets! What do we *do* with it all?"

"Doesn't cargo that comes in usually get picked up?" Carn asked. "Where's all this stuff supposed to go?"

"Nobody knows!" Cronch bellowed. "There's some kind of paperwork problem." He began to gesture, though the gestures seemed more artistic than informative, sort of an interpretive dance of frustration. "These crates were imported by a business that went broke and shut down without warning. Now, normally when that happens, we make arrangements to send any shipments back to their point of origin, but the company that shipped all these crates here went out of business too. Both those companies have outstanding creditors trying to recover the money they're owed, and the lawyers are fighting about who these shipments legally belong to, and what their value even is, since nobody seems to know what's *in* the crates."

"What's the manifest say?" Carn asked. "There is a manifest, right?"

"Manifests on manifests," Cronch said. "Every single crate is listed as containing 'proprietary technologic materials,' and look, they're covered in stickers about all the horrible things that will happen, both legally and physically, if they're opened by anyone without proper authorization." Cronch growled. "But nobody has authorization! So the crates just sit here, taking up space, which means we can't move any other shipments in, and the other docking bays are trying to take up our slack, but we're the biggest one, so they can't keep up. I told Azzi we should just have a little paperwork error of our own and chuck these out the nearest airlock, but nobody listens to me."

"Could be a good thing," Carn said. "If you did that, we'd have a thousand or so crates floating around outside the station, causing accidents."

"Causing somebody *else* accidents," Cronch said. "Somebody who isn't me. I'm not the warehouse supervisor! Something's gotta be done."

Carn nodded. "I can see that. I'm not a lawyer... but I've met some. I bet they'd advise us that these very important disputed assets shouldn't be left sitting around in a warehouse where anybody passing by could crack one open or carry one off. In fact, they should be held in some kind of secure location, right? Maybe one of those vaults under Bluerise Tower, hey? Or if it comes down to it, we've got rooms in the Lorespire Complex that aren't being used for anything too important, so we could sit on them for a while. Whoever stores these things is gonna want to charge for it, but their fee will just get tacked on to all the other fees once the legal situation gets sorted out."

"After our port fees, which also haven't been paid," Cronch said.

Carn shrugged. "However it works out. Lemme make some calls; we'll see what we can do about getting this stuff moved."

"That's gonna take a whole lot of crew to accomplish too." The nuar scowled, unwilling to hear good news.

"No doubt, but I can pitch in. I'm good at moving heavy things."

Cronch grunted. "I noticed your little black hole following you around. You're one of those solarians? I thought they mostly made things all bright and shiny, with little suns bobbing behind them, not splotches."

Carn grinned. "Yeah, I can do all that bright, flashy stuff too, but I've always had more of a liking for the gravity side of things. Lemme see what kind of weight we're looking at here." Attuning was as easy as breathing, and the floating black hole that followed Carn popped into existence, hovering near his shoulder. He lifted his hands, craning his neck to look at the crate on top of the nearest heap, and pointed. Controlling gravity felt sort of like extending a mental hand, and he could almost *feel* the shape of the crate. The box was so far up there, it was right at the edge of his power's range, but he should be able to lower it easily enough. He slid the crate off the pile, surprised it wasn't heavier; it probably wasn't more than a couple hundred pounds. "This won't be so bad," he said as the crate gently bobbed and wobbled slowly through the air. It'll take forever to move them all, but—"

The crate lurched as the contents shifted, and Carn nearly lost his grip. He let the box drop the last few feet, where it landed with a hard thump... and then there were *more* thumps, but these were coming from the inside—it sounded like something banging against the top and sides of the crate from within.

Carn frowned. "*Proprietary materials?* Are there animals in there? Constructs of some kind? It can't be *people*?"

"No way," Cronch said. "These have been piled up here for weeks, any people inside would have to be in some kind of stasis. And why would you smuggle people into Absalom Station this way, anyhow? We're an open port!"

"Maybe they were wanted criminals?" Carn hazarded. "Or people trying to leave no paper trail?"

Cronch grunted. "Sure, reasonable theory, if it was *one* crate, or even ten, but we're looking at over a thousand. You could fit a couple people in the small ones, depending, and in those big ones—"

"Right," Carn said. The thumping hadn't stopped—it had become more violent, and in fact, the crate had started rocking back and forth. "Oof, Cronch, I think we gotta look inside there, lawyers or not."

"As long as you take full responsibility as a representative of the Syndicsguild," Cronch said. "But I gotta ask you: How? A lot of us have been curious about these things and figured it wouldn't hurt to take a peek, but we couldn't crack them. It's not as easy as getting out a crowbar. These things are sealed with some kind of powerful magnetic lock backed up with magic, and there are no controls at all on the outside. Usually with these secure containers, there's a keypad for a code or a place to swipe a card or plug in a fob or get your eyeball scanned or give a drop of your blood or something. But these things are just smooth. We figured whoever shipped them had some kind of special tool to unlock them."

"Maybe," Carn said as the top of the crate cracked open with a hiss, emitting a stench like rotting meat and used socks. "Or maybe the controls to open them are just on the *inside*."

The nuar took a step back, looking around, and then picked up a long metal pry bar that was leaning against another crate. Carn rolled his neck on his shoulders and shook out his arms to limber up, then reached out a hand to his floating black mote. He reached into the darkness and drew out the welcome and familiar heft of his gravity weapon, a hammer so black it seemed to exude darkness the way a lamp cast light.

"You OK in there?" he called out toward the crate. "How'd you get in that box, anyway? Do you need medical attention?" None of those felt like the right questions, but what questions *were*?

There was no answer, anyway, or much of anything else. The lid didn't open any farther, and the thumping had stopped. Carn slid his way forward, hammer held at the ready. "I'm going to open the lid, OK, in case you need medical attention—"

The lid slammed back, and a creature clambered out of the box, movements jerky and spasmodic. *That gnome has got something wrong with them,* Carn thought. Because the creature *was* a gnome, with tufts of bright blue hair sticking up from their scalp, but that scalp was dull gray, with flashes of white—Was that *bone* showing through? The creature was dressed in shredded rags, and there was a great gash across its chest, but it wasn't bleeding or even oozing.

"Zombie!" Cronch shouted, and, huh, yeah, it had to be, didn't it? Definitely undead, and the way it was staring blankly and gnashing its mouth full of broken teeth, it seemed to be firmly on the mindless-minion end of the spectrum. It fell out of the crate onto its face, getting tangled up in its own legs, but then staggered upright with surprising speed, snarled wordlessly, and lurched at Carn.

Carn had never fought a zombie before, as far as he could remember, but most things with a head stopped trying to bite you when you hit them in said head, so he swung his hammer—

The zombie's head caved in like a rotten melon, and it went straight down. Its arms and legs continued to scrabble weakly, but it couldn't seem to get to its feet. He tapped it on the back of the head a couple more times with his hammer until it stopped twitching.

Meanwhile, another gnome zombie climbed out of the same crate and scrambled toward the nuar. Cronch roared in dismay and smashed it overhand with the pry bar, knocking it to the ground, then stomped on it for a while in his heavy work boots, the sound of which made Carn wince and suck his teeth.

Finally the nuar was satisfied that the mess at his feet wasn't getting up again, and then he lifted his horned head and gazed at the crates. "Do you think... I mean... *all* of them?"

"Gotta be our assumption," Carn said.

"Who would ship thousands of zombies to Absalom Station?"

Carn grunted. "You don't follow the news much, do you?"

"Not really," Cronch said. "I like that show Zo! has been doing, where they strip somebody naked and drop them into a remote jungle on Castrovel with just a pointy stick, to see how long they can survive, and if they survive too long, they send in the hunters—"

"Uh-huh," Carn said. "Say, do you think that gnome smeared all over your boots there woke up because I moved the crate? Like I jostled it and activated them or something?"

"I don't see why," Cronch said. "We move those crates all the time, and we haven't been too gentle lately because we're all pretty mad, and nothing like that ever happened before."

Carn leaned on the shaft of his hammer and surveyed the snaking walls of crates. "I was afraid you'd say that."

The sound of the lid on a single crate clicking open wasn't very loud. But when it was ten crates... and then twenty... and then fifty... and then a hundred, it sounded like a swarm of horrible chittering insects buzzing your way all at once.

The towers of crates jostled all around them as the big boxes on the bottom—Carn wondered what kind of zombies were in those—tried to open but couldn't because of the weight of the crates stacked on top. But *those* were trying to open too, some of them violently, and a moment later there came a crash as a crate on the top of a pile fell all the way down to the ground, lid popping open on impact, spilling out a ragged pile of flesh and sticklike limbs. Then came another crash, and another, as more crates followed suit.

Carn knew a little something about physics—and not theoretical physics, either, the practical kind. More crates were going to fall and break open, and that would allow *more* to fall, and more, and more, in a cascade of chaotic release. Killing a single mindless zombie wasn't all that much harder than squashing a bug—easier, in some ways, since zombies were bigger targets and easier to hit with a hammer. But a mob of them, a *horde* of them—that was a different story. If you got surrounded, you were dead.

If you were lucky. If you weren't lucky, you wouldn't stay dead. Whatever was left of you would get up and join the guys who'd killed you and start killing your own friends. "We need to seal this room," Carn said. "And then we need..." What? Fire, acid, a hundred priests to bless the sprinklers and rain down holy water? All of those were in short supply.

Zombies began to crawl out of the nearest pile of fallen crates, and horrifyingly, one of them was an ysoki, his snout so badly broken and twisted that he could have smelled his own black jellied eyeballs if he was capable of smelling anything anymore. Could zombies smell stuff? Maybe they smelled the living. Maybe that's how they hunted. They certainly seemed to know right where their prey was, even if their eyes *were*—

"Come on!" Cronch shouted, running back toward the main floor. He began to bellow warnings to the other workers, and Carn chased after him, wishing he had longer legs. One of the zombies—a human, probably, but it was honestly kind of hard to tell, since it looked like a tall skeleton wrapped in old leather—lunged forward and grabbed Carn's shoulder.

Carn twisted away, shouting, and did a little backward dance step. Half a dozen zombies were charging at him, bumping into each other, funneled down the narrow aisle, getting in each other's way. But they all had the same goal, so it didn't slow them down much. The human was joined by another gnome, an elf, an orc, a goblin, and that poor ysoki, and Carn thought wildly of the Society and the diverse range of species that lived in his neighborhood. But really, these zombies were all the same kind of creature, weren't they? Unified in mindless death.

Carn was horrified and fascinated and repulsed, and he reached out a hand, intending to flatten the zombies against the floor, to press gravity down on them until their heads popped and their abused bodies were put out of their misery... but then he heard the heavy cargo door start to come down.

He spun and saw the door lowering, and he knew he wouldn't make it, even if he sprinted. He knew some tricks, though. Carn tended toward the slow and deliberate (some might even say the plodding), but just because he didn't use other gears often didn't mean he didn't *have* them. He just needed to switch his attunement.

The mote of dark energy floating beside him flickered and then blazed, turning from a tiny black hole into a miniature sun.

Carn drew on the powers of stellar energy that constantly coursed through him, and his body began to flicker with radiant light as an aura enveloped him. The zombies behind him cried out in an approximation of pain—they didn't like bright lights or fire, did they? Good to know.

The release of energy propelled Carn forward much faster than a sprint, a stellar rush that nearly lifted him off his feet. He could have aimed himself at the zombies, smashing into them with a burst of burning light, swinging his hammer, scattering and wounding the undead horrors... but dying in a blaze of glory was still dying. So instead, he launched himself toward the door, flinging himself down face-first and sliding through the narrowing crack at the bottom just before it clanged into grooves on the floor.

Carn stood up to face the assembled dockworkers, mostly dwarves and orcs and dragonkin, most armed with crowbars or other blunt weapons, all staring at him like he was on fire—

Oh. He *was* still wreathed in undulating solar energy. He shook himself all over, releasing the energy into the floor and letting it harmlessly dissipate.

"I'm sorry," Cronch said, staring at Carn, face twisted in dismay. "I started shutting the door, and then you turned around, and I didn't—"

"It's OK," Carn said. "I get it. Did anybody call for help yet?"

"Comms aren't working," a dwarf growled.

Right. This was part of a coordinated strike, then. Carn had figured "stuff zombies into boxes in a warehouse and let them loose to mess things up" wasn't the whole attack plan. The terrorists who'd attacked the cathedral earlier were enacting the next phase of their operation, probably. He thought briefly of his friends—Val was in the Lorespire, within a secure perimeter he'd set up himself, so she'd be OK; and Mel was off station on that casino ship, so she was probably safe; and Tyrcell... well, there was no telling where Tyrcell was, but in Carn's experience, his best friend usually made more trouble for others than for themself. Still, it was hard not to worry. Carn shook that off—he had to focus on the right here and the right now and the maybe thousands of zombies right behind him. "OK, so we do this like we did in the old days, when the comms were unreliable. We use runners. Who wants to go recruit some priests and fetch some flamethrowers?"

Every single worker in the place raised a hand. Carn pointed at a few at random, since if people were willing to listen to him, he was willing to take charge. "Come back with help as quick as you can. The rest of you..." Carn looked around at the piles of crates and thought about how the zombies beyond the cargo door had gotten jammed up in the corridor. "How about you all help me move some things around and see if we can't build a zombie trap?"

Carn crouched behind a barricade with Cronch and some of the other dock defenders, listening to the relentless pounding on the closed cargo door as presumably very large zombies hurled their bodies against it. That couldn't be too good for their bodies, but one thing about such mindless creatures was that pain didn't slow them down. The barrier wasn't flimsy, but it wasn't a hardened blast door either, and Carn didn't expect it to hold much longer against an endless onslaught of tireless undead. The runners hadn't come back with help yet, even though they'd been gone a while, which suggested things weren't going great elsewhere in the station. Oh, well. Right here and right now was all he could do anything about.

He was impressed by how many of the dockworkers had stayed to fight the zombies, and a little troubled by how many of them seemed excited about the prospect. It could be they'd played too many fighting sims and thought it would be fun to fight a horde in real life. Many of them were newcomers to the station, probably—it seemed like they outnumbered the old-timers lately. People who'd lived through the chaos on Absalom Station after the Gap wouldn't be excited about fighting in these corridors again.

The defenders had weapons—a few guns from a nearby security services locker they'd cracked open, as well as a whole lot of improvised implements. You could do remarkable things with a plasma torch if you knew how to disable all the safety protocols.

More importantly, they had familiar terrain on their side. They'd used brute force, forklifts, cargo bots, and Carn's gift of gravity to surround the cargo door with crates, stacking them into barriers and narrowing the exit down to a single corridor that would funnel the zombies in the direction they wanted—right into a dead-end canyon made of stacked crates, where they'd set up some nasty surprises.

The people with the self-proclaimed best aim were up on top of the crate pile, lining the corridor and the kill box so they could shoot down at the zombies as they jostled in the chute.

"It's almost unfair," Cronch said beside Carn. "What's that expression? Like shooting fish in a bucket? We're going to massacre these things."

"Hold on," Carn said. "That would be nice. But I think all this we're doing here is just slowing them down. Reducing the numbers a little before the zombies break through our barricades. Because they're gonna break through, and then things'll get a little ugly. But we'll just have to do our best."

"Do you really think—" Cronch began, and then there was a horrible squeal of abused metal. Carn couldn't see the cargo door from his position, just the wall of crates they'd erected in the way, but the sharpshooters up top had a view, and they called down, "Breach! Breach! They're coming through!"

Carn's plan had been to hold his position with his gravity hammer ready, then wade into the first wave when the zombies broke containment and smash as many heads as he could. But not being able to tell what was happening made his brain itchy. "Be right back," he muttered, climbing over the crate pile and scrambling up the side of the wall of crates; ysoki were good climbers in general, and Carn specifically was good at ignoring Cronch yelling after him.

He made it to the top of the pile above their kill box and looked straight down the long, narrow chute to the cargo door. There was some kind of spike, or maybe a horn, sticking through the door, sheathed in metal, and as Carn watched, the horn ripped a great gash in the door and then withdrew. A moment later, the bottom of the door folded up like a piece of cloth, and zombies began to wriggle through the gap, like water flowing through a crack in a dam. The small ones came first, gnomes and dwarves and ysoki, and then bigger humanoids, forcing the opening wider. Once the zombies emerged, they didn't have much room to maneuver, since the chute was only about three feet wide, and they got jammed up against each other, as expected. The sharpshooters whooped in triumph and began firing down into the clump—

Then the zombies started scrambling up the crates. Carn had wanted to grease the walls against this eventuality, but they hadn't really had time, and the general consensus among the defenders had been that zombies didn't really climb so much as shamble along.

These were very motivated zombies, for some reason, and they clambered over each other as they swarmed, until soon they were climbing over each other as much as they were going up the wall. All that sudden verticality cleared out the jam, and many of the freed zombies on the floor began rushing down the chute toward the squared-off killing room at the end. At least that part was working.

Some of the sharpshooters methodically picked the undead off as they climbed, but others broke and ran at the prospect of sharing the narrow parapets up top with walking corpses. That line wasn't gonna hold. Carn wondered if any of their lines would.

"They're coming over the wall!" Carn called down to the defenders below him. "Get ready—"

The cargo door *exploded* outward, smashing into the zombies ahead of it and smearing several of them to paste. A huge figure lumbered through the open door, and Carn couldn't imagine how it had fit inside even the biggest crate—it must have been folded up in a ball.

Carn had no idea what kind of beast it had once been, but it was at least a dozen feet high, with long, curving horns covered in shiny metal, and its face was so rotted out that the yellowish bone of its skull showed through. Its body was irregularly patched with tufts of fur, and its legs were short and muscular, but its arms were long and multijointed, ending in wicked claws. The abomination leaned forward on its knuckles for a moment, huge head swinging back and forth, as if taking in the scene. Carn couldn't tell if it was a resurrected monster from some savage planet or something created in a necromancer's laboratory, but it was big and ugly and looked more or less unstoppable. The remaining sharpshooters blasted away at it, but the behemoth paid no more attention to bullets than it would have to biting flies.

Then it lowered its head and drove its horns into the left-hand wall, making the crates cascade down and opening a breach that the other zombies began to swarm through.

Carn swore and clambered down the wall to join the fight.

# 7

# FEATURING SPECIAL GUEST STARS ZO! AND THE MISERY KNIGHT

(326 AG)

Tyrcell passed the time on their voyage to the Thousand Moons by telling Chk Chk and Dae about the Magefire Assault, because that was all necessary backstory to explain why the android wasn't thrilled about going near Eox.

"I wrote the whole account down somewhere," they said. "Part of my sprawling series of memoirs, written here and there in lonely stretches of interstellar travel. I even pulled a proper historian trick to cover the stuff I didn't personally witness, drawing from other people's accounts, though I admit I maybe"—they waved their hands around—"added a little extra sparkle in there, just to keep it lively and to keep potential readers interested. Not that anything I've written has ever had any readers, apart from you two. At this point, I can't even remember where I hid all the various manuscripts. Well, I'm sure they'll turn up eventually."

*"How did you found the Starfinder Society when you can't even file your records properly?"* Chk Chk sounded mostly curious and only slightly appalled.

Tyrcell snorted. "The organization I started might have become the Starfinder Society eventually, but as I mentioned before, that's not how we started out. We were just trying to stay alive. And then, once survival was secured, we started sticking our noses into places where they didn't belong, driven by a combination of curiosity and avarice. It's a strategy that hasn't always worked out well for us—see the Scoured Stars incident for an example of things going horribly wrong in relatively recent history. My first go-around with Yaraesa's hidden puzzles taught me that some secrets are better off *staying* secret, and I guess I never fell out of the habit."

"Why write things down at all, then?" Dae asked, cocking their tufted head adorably.

The old android sighed. "Because writing things down became a habit. A way to pass the time on those long solo voyages of exploration. The part where you explore ancient ruins and flee from hostile indigenes is a tiny percentage of that life; it's mostly boring trips in space. Journaling is thrilling by comparison."

*"You could have played vidgames, done a VR sim, or binged all two centuries of Zo!'s masterpiece* The Necromancer*,"* Chk Chk pointed out. *"There must be a deeper reason than just boredom for you to write these things, and to hide them."*

"Ugh, the curiosity, the insistence on asking the next question—you two really *are* Starfinder agents." Tyrcell swiveled back and forth in the pilot's chair, gazing thoughtfully at a spot of empty air between Chk Chk and Dae for a long moment. "I write them because, deep down, I *do* want these questions to be answered and these mysteries to be explored. The reason I hide the things I write is a little more complicated, but something I learned in the course of delving into more wrecks and ruins than you can imagine is that people value things that are hard to find. If I published my complete works on every infosphere node, like a million other wannabe writers, nobody would pay any attention to my stories. But if you hide a pile of century-old pages, or ancient data crystals, in a secret cache somewhere, when people find it later, they get *excited*. I've gotten a lot of joy from discovering forgotten lore in hidden places. I guess I just wanted to get in on the fun." They paused. "I also write them because it's a way of honoring the dead and their sacrifices."

*"Plausible,"* Chk Chk said after a moment. *"Perhaps I should hide some of my sculptures where they won't be found for a thousand years, to increase their eventual market value."*

"You've both lost your minds." Dae leaped up from their chair and did a pirouette. "Art is to be *experienced*, and the way you write your histories, Tyrcell, they're definitely art. Besides, am I supposed to hide away my new dance routine in a space tomb for somebody to find in a thousand years? I want my applause *now*."

"I'm more of a stick-to-the-shadows type, Dae, but I celebrate your irrepressible... you-ness," Tyrcell said. An instrument on the control panel beeped, and Ty swiveled around to take a look. "We're getting close to a Drift beacon on the outskirts of the Thousand Moons, on the far side, away from Eox. It wouldn't be a good idea to pop out into normal space too close to the debris field—those rocks aren't in a totally stable configuration, and I'd hate to crash into one." They sighed. "I can't believe I have to go *back* there."

*"You haven't gotten to the part of the story where you went there in the first place,"* Chk Chk pointed out.

"I'll have time to tell you most of it before we get to our destination," Tyrcell said. "Though there's a lot of undead horror to get through first. All right, dropping into conventional space... now." The view through the front windows shimmered, the shifting, colorful, fractal phantasmagoria of the Drift suddenly replaced by blackness and the hard points of distant stars. There were no moons in evidence, certainly not a thousand, but they were probably still some distance away—

The console lit up, and alarms beeped frantically, and Tyrcell began manipulating the console. "Crap, something's scanning us! It must be some kind of perimeter warning system the elebrians set up in case anyone came sniffing around the moons. Let's get some distance and then go back into the Drift and come at this from another direction, more oblique and sneaky. Crap-crap-crap."

"Do you really think the bone sages will come after you because of something you did centuries ago?" Dae asked.

"I don't know," Tyrcell said. "I sure hope I'm ancient history. But either way, I'd rather not have to explain what we're doing here to an Eoxian patrol vessel. They aren't very friendly even if you have a *good* reason to be in their vicinity, and they get touchy with people messing around in the Thousand Moons, for good reasons. Reasons that I, ah, maybe... helped give them."

*"It is wise to be cautious,"* Chk Chk said. *"I do not think the eternal rulers of Eox are likely to adhere to any statutes of limitations. Even if you committed these unspecified crimes long ago, the memories of the bone sages are doubtless even longer."*

Ty chewed on their lip. "I mean, I'm probably being paranoid. We might be OK. I only ever specifically, personally, pissed off one bone sage, so there's only one who knows my face and name and ship, and the odds are she's dead by now."

"The bone sages don't usually *die*, right?" Dae said. "They're necrovites, and they have that thing, right? That backup device?"

*"It is called an electroencephalon,"* Chk Chk said. *"A blend of technology and magic that allows them to regenerate, even if their bodies are utterly destroyed."*

Tyrcell frowned. "Right, sure, but we never heard from her again, so I always figured the other necrovites killed her for failing in her mission. She's definitely not on the council of ruling elders now."

*"Being fired from your job does not mean you automatically cease to exist,"* Chk Chk pointed out. *"Not even on Eox. And necrovites have mighty resources, whether or not they have the backing of a Pact World."*

"Why don't we just find out if she's still around or not?" Dae said. "That way, we'll know whether we should worry or not."

"How would we even find out?" Tyrcell said. "Necrovites don't show up much in the gossip rags or official records. Their whole gig is hiding their essential selves away in secret bunkers and lurking in the shadows, pulling their puppets' string while being as spooky and dramatic as possible. And they absolutely *bury* their failures."

"We can call Zo!" Dae said. "Zo! must know! He's a necrovite. And that's not me being speciesist and assuming that, like, all elves know each other or something. There aren't *that* many necrovites, and they really *must* all know each other, right?"

*"It is certainly worth a try,"* Chk Chk sent in agreement.

"Huh." Tyrcell stroked their circuit-etched chin thoughtfully. "I haven't talked to old Zo! in centuries. You think you can really get him on the line?"

Dae nodded, bouncing in their chair. "His first assistant's second assistant just messaged me yesterday to ask if I want to star in a reboot of something called *Naked and Stricken with Unimaginable Terror*, which is probably a no-go for me—*naked* is negotiable if it's for artistic reasons, but *terror* doesn't sound so great. But he'll totally take my call—he seemed really curious about you last time we talked, anyway."

"What the Hell," Ty said. "It's worth a try. Maybe Zo! can assuage all my fears."

*"There is a first time for everything, I suppose,"* Chk Chk said.

"Dae!" Zo! cried, burning eye sockets gazing out of his skull face, broadcast in high definition on the old ship's tiny vidscreen. "I am simply delighted to hear from you! This reboot is perfect for someone with your talents—"

"Um, actually, I was calling about something else," Dae chimed in. "Do you remember we were asking you about that android Tyrcell, who disappeared after the Gap—"

"Aha! Did you discover their fate? I have always wondered."

Tyrcell moved into the camera's line of sight and gave a little wave. "Hey, Zo! It's good to see you again."

Zo! dramatically clutched at his chest where his heart presumably used to be. "I am *staggered*, I am *stunned*, I have witnessed a *resurrection*! Where have you *been* all these centuries, my dear android?"

"Here and there," Tyrcell said. "Hither and yon. You know how it is. The kids here are helping me out with a little research project, and I was wondering if I could ask you a question."

Considering his undead physiognomy and eternal rictus grin, the only way to tell if Zo! was bored or angry or delighted was his tone of voice, which suddenly took a turn for the cautious. "If it's a *brief* question, of course, ask away. I have about a hundred acrobats standing on their tiptoes on a wire above a pool full of highly electric cloud rays, and I shouldn't pause their rehearsal too long."

"Right, OK, I'll spare you the backstory, then," Tyrcell said. "You're elebrian, right? I mean, originally?"

"Zo! is a citizen of the galaxy! He owes allegiance only to the audience!" He paused. "But, yes, if we're speaking strictly literally, I do hail from Eox originally."

"Do you happen to, ah, keep in touch with the other necrovites?"

Zo! chuckled. "Oh, yes, of course! I'm invited to their weekly potluck suppers, Tyrcell. We have a lively group chat where we share all the latest memetic contagions." He shook his head. "I would be rolling my eyes now if I still had organs capable of such action. No, we don't keep in touch. The other necrovites aren't terribly fond of me. As a rule, we tend to hate each other, just on principle—the kind of person who becomes a necrovite isn't usually someone you'd care to spend time with, even if you're a necrovite yourself. But you aren't really curious about my intraspecies socializing, so what's your *actual* question?"

"OK, well, during the Magefire Assault, the attack was led by a bone sage named Mnephalon, supposedly sent to Absalom Station on a diplomatic mission, who sprang a sneak attack. A rumor went around afterward saying she'd been executed for her failure, but, ah... is she still around, on Eox?"

"Ha!" Zo! said. "Having perished *once*, my dear android, my kind are quite resistant to ever perishing again, even at the hands of one another. No, Mnephalon is still undead and kicking—or, at least she was the last I heard, a few decades ago. Though she's no longer dwelling in the halls of power in Orphys. Maybe she fled execution, or maybe she just wanted to move on to rottener pastures. It's hard to blame her either way; she's young, by our standards, and when you're a junior among necrovites, there aren't many opportunities for promotions—nobody above you ever retires or dies, you see? She probably led the assault in hopes of reaping glory and rewards from her peers, so when that failed, she sought other opportunities. She eventually joined up with the separatists in the Corpse Fleet when they splintered away from the Pact Worlds. There's a lot more room for advancement among the terrorists, and I gather she's risen to a prominent role in that company."

"Oh," Tyrcell said. "That's even more unfortunate."

*"You're an enemy of the Corpse Fleet?"* Chk Chk said. *"You, personally?"* The Corpse Fleet was a renegade faction led by bone sages of Eox unhappy with their society's choice to join the Pact Worlds alliance. The armada of vengeful undead supremacists haunted the edges of inhabited systems and sought to destroy the Pact Worlds and transform the living into undead thralls or livestock.

"I am an enemy of Mnephalon, so by the transitive property..." the android said miserably.

"Admiral Mnephalon is one of the most vociferous voices for the extermination of all living beings and their conversion into the undead, actually," Zo! went on cheerfully. "She probably holds a grudge against the living for making her Magefire Assault such a horrible failure. Tell me, Tyrcell... Did you have anything to do with orchestrating that failure? You did once have a habit of getting on the wrong side of violent, heavily armed zealots, as I recall."

"Let's just say I got on her bad side. But she's not on Eox, right? So there's no reason for me to, say, avoid going within a thousand light years of the planet?"

"Hmm, well, there are certainly Corpse Fleet sympathizers in the government of Eox," Zo! said. "Perhaps try not to go within *ten* light years, just to be safe. If you do get into a conflict with the bone sages or the Corpse Fleet, I have just one request: *Film everything*, and make sure the footage makes it to me in the event of your death! I still think you're the ideal star for an epic historical docudrama." Zo! turned his head, eyes flaring, and said, "Drat, one of the acrobats just fell in, and now the rays are agitated. This is going to be messy, and we're not even livestreaming—" The screen went black.

"I wish I'd found any of that more reassuring," Tyrcell said.

"The Corpse Fleet is scattered all over the system, lurking on the outskirts," Dae said. "The odds of this one necrovite realizing you're still alive are really small, aren't they? I know we were scanned, but like you said, it was probably a monitoring station set up by Eox, or even one of the sarcesian settlements in the Thousand Moons. Plus, we're going to sneak in from another direction. What do we have to be worried about?"

*"A dedicated mind can always find something,"* Chk Chk said.

Mnephalon was the leader of a Corpse Fleet task force, a group of a dozen vessels liberated centuries before from the navy of Eox. She technically took her orders from the Undying Admiral Shathrava, commander of all the Corpse Fleet units, but in practice, the task forces were semiautonomous and given broad latitude to fulfill their strategic and tactical goals.

Alcyone and Groth were cocaptains of their own ship, a situation neither of them much liked, which was probably why Mnephalon had arranged things that way; she was opposed to comfort in her troops, as such things bred complacency.

The ghoul and the ghost took a shuttle from their sleek little fighter to Mnephalon's flagship, an immense Omenbringer called the *Necrosis*, big enough to swallow all the other ships in the fleet in one gulp. It resembled the corpse of an oceanic behemoth, with a hull shaped like a bulging rib cage. Large portions of the ship were exposed to vacuum, since many of the crew had no need for atmosphere anyway, and Groth could see the ranks of Necrogliders hanging inside through openings in the hull. The notorious, nimble fighters could spew forth like a swarm of stinging insects at Mnephalon's command, and that swarm was the last thing many an unwary mortal captain had ever seen. Crab-like drones and skeletal minions crawled all over the *Necrosis* like ants on a piece of discarded fruit, eternally repairing the hull and maintaining its weaponry.

Alcyone sighed, gazing out the view port. "Isn't it beautiful?"

"It's terrifying, so, in that sense, yes," the ghoul agreed.

Their shuttle glided into a waiting hangar bay in one of the pressurized sections of the ship, and they swiftly disembarked. A skeletal minion with cybernetic eyes was waiting, its ocular lenses flashing red as it scanned them and confirmed their identities.

"Come," it grated through a mechanical voice box embedded in its chest. "Our lady is waiting."

The skeleton lurched along unsteadily, leading them down dim and twisting corridors decorated with trophies from Mnephalon's many triumphs; the newest were still wet and dripped down the walls. At last they reached the admiral's quarters, and the minion yanked down a lever that either looked like or actually was a petrified femur. A door slid into the wall. "She awaits," the minion said.

Groth sidled into the dim cave-like space beyond, head swiveling, waiting for an inevitable blow. Alcyone glided in, as ghosts tended to do; her shape was nearly coherent at the moment, though a little ragged at the edges. Groth was a cybernetically augmented ghoul and adjusted his vision to the low light—just in time to wince and be blinded when artificial illumination clicked on in the form of a spotlight shining down on their lady. Mnephalon was always doing things like that.

She lounged in a chair that might be more properly called a throne, surrounded by draperies of purple velvet, wearing a dress of flowing black lace with bone-white buttons. Her bone scepter, a long bone staff with a double prong at the head, was propped against the throne. Groth shuddered at the very sight of it; it was the signature weapon of the bone sages, who'd used them on their undead minions in much the way a shepherd used a crook... or a coachman used a whip.

"My dear captains," Mnephalon said. "So good of you to join us."

*Us?* Groth wondered, and then a clanking sound drew his attention to the shadows behind the throne. A figure in fire-blackened armor lurched out to stand beside the throne, and Alcyone made a little sound of jealous disgust.

"You remember my misery knight?" Mnephalon said lightly.

How could they forget? The knight had replaced Alcyone as Mnephalon's bodyguard and personal attendant years earlier, a demotion the ghost had never been able to accept. Groth and Alcyone knew nothing at all about the knight's origins, or even what sort of undead being he was—their lady would only say she'd picked him up in a lovely little ruin. The knight was never seen without his armor, complete from helmet to greaves, all of it soot-stained and flame-scarred; Groth imagined a blackened husk of burnt, pulsing meat inside, but there was no telling what was in there—maybe it was just a set of animated armor. Groth wasn't even sure if the knight was intelligent, like himself, or a mindless minion that acted purely as an extension of Mnephalon's will.

Groth had once watched the knight methodically turn an arrogant diplomat from Castrovel into a sort of red paste, swinging a hammer with the regularity of a metronome, and he always treated the terrifying figure with respect as a result.

"We only wish to serve, Admiral," the ghoul said. "We assume you want us to go after this android?"

"A good servant always anticipates its owner's wishes," the necrovite said, practically purring. "I want Tyrcell brought back here, alive, so I can play with them for a while. But I also want to know what they're doing sniffing around the Thousand Moons. The last time they were there it went badly, and it could have ended much worse. I could never *prove* it was Tyrcell, but... never mind. The android might be resistant to questioning, and their kind are trickier to torture than most creatures, but the scan showed other life-forms onboard the ship, yes? That means Tyrcell has companions, possibly even friends or lovers. Threaten to hurt them badly enough, and Tyrcell will probably break. The android is a social animal. Oh. And because this is actually important... my misery knight will accompany you."

"Ah, my lady..." Alcyone began to protest. "I can assure you—"

"I was not requesting feedback." The fact that she said it sweetly was more chilling than a sharp rebuke. "The knight is going to help keep the two of you focused and on task."

Given that Mnephalon could reach directly into their minds and compel them to do whatever she wished, Groth didn't believe oversight was the real purpose. The knight must have some mission of his own to fulfill. That was fine. Groth was used to their lady's complex machinations, and it wasn't his place to ask any questions. "We welcome the assistance, great sage."

She waved the agreement away, which was fair enough; it didn't matter if they agreed or not. "Tyrcell is still traveling in the same ship they were using when we met—it must be nearly as old as *I* am. There's no telling what upgrades the wily android has made, though. I'm loaning you three my personal runabout, the *Scaphism*, which should be swift enough to catch anyone. Now go and *find* them."

Groth bowed, Alcyone shimmered, and the misery knight clanked over, blank and impassive. The knight led the way to the bone sage's private hangar and to the *Scaphism*, a modified explorer vessel that sacrificed some crew space for extra weaponry. It resembled the skull of some sleek, long-snouted predator, but with gun turrets sprouting from its base like spinal growths or tusks.

"How are we supposed to find this android?" Groth complained to Alcyone as they boarded after the knight, who was apparently planning to pilot the ship too, since he went straight for the cockpit. The interior of the ship was austere and elegant, as befit its owner. "They popped out of the Drift and then popped back in again! Unless they happen to pass by another monitoring station or spy satellite we've compromised, we'll never track them down. They could be anywhere."

"The misery knight seems to have some idea," Alcyone pointed out, and indeed, the knight *was* laying in a course.

Groth leaned over the knight's shoulder, looking at the console. "For a destination in the Thousand Moons. Our lady thinks that's where the android is going? Why?"

The knight did not answer.

"Maybe because they've been there before?" Alcyone suggested. "She thinks they're returning to the scene of some crime?"

The knight did not confirm, deny, or even appear to notice the question.

The ghoul flung himself down into the copilot's chair, and the misery knight immediately locked him out of all the copilot controls. "I didn't want to drive *anyway*," Groth said, sulking. "To confirm that you're a mindless set of haunted armor, ignore me and say nothing."

The misery knight's armored head turned with an audible creak. There was a slit in the mask the width of a finger, and Groth peered through it, looking for something—glowing red eyes, the pulse of negative energy, a grimacing skull, anything—but there was just blankness. The ghoul's guts chilled anyway. That blankness was *cold*.

The knight held the stare, if it was a stare, for a long moment, then returned to guiding their ship out of the hangar bay.

"Cheer up, Groth," the ghost said. "Maybe you'll get to eat someone's fingers soon."

"That helps," Groth confessed. He gazed inward and began to review the encrypted dossier he'd recorded, meticulously unpicking the cipher. Just because nobody wanted to tell him what the android had done didn't mean he couldn't find out.

# 8

## MNEPHALON ATTACKS

### (Tyrcell / 7 AG)

Saphenath and I were just standing up to head for the Lorespire when she pressed a fingertip to her ear and widened her eyes. "The delegation from Eox arrived early! They just came out of the Drift!"

She turned and began sprinting back toward the Eye, and for want of anything better to do, I followed her. "Where are you going?" I called. "Are you going to rocket into orbit and ambush the bone sage for an interview?"

"There's a transmission!" she called. "In the Eye!"

We'd only walked a short distance from the park for lunch, and it was a shorter run back, so we soon emerged into the great, open, tree-filled space. The immense dome above us was usually either ablaze with artificial sunlight (during the day cycles) or glittering with a thousand false stars (at night), but this was... it was different.

The dome had been transformed into an immense vidscreen, and the vast face of an elebrian necrovite smiled down upon us like a divine vision, filling the whole sky.

She could have passed for a young living humanoid if she'd worn dark glasses over her blazing eyes and put some makeup on her cheeks where the bones pushed through the skin; she even had hair, long and black and flowing. However, the hints of decay on her pretty white face and the blue flames glowing in her eyes made her undead nature unmistakable. Her smile was warm, though, and as the camera view pulled back a little to show her upper body, we could see her waving and blowing kisses.

"People of Absalom Station!" she called, voice trilling and melodious. "My name is Mnephalon, and I am a bone sage of Eox." She made hooked claws of her fingers and mock-growled. "Oooh, scary, I know, but fear not, I am here to make friends, not minions!"

The view kept pulling back until we could see her whole body, dressed in black lace that alternately clung and draped. She was, presumably, on the bridge of a ship, but her surroundings were so dark it was hard to make out details. When your eyes glow, you probably don't need a lot of artificial light, I guess.

"I didn't even know the dome could be used as a screen," I said.

"I don't think it can," Saphenath answered. "This isn't technology—it's necrovite magic."

"They're pretty powerful, huh?" I asked.

"They say the strongest ones are about a half step down from being gods," Saphenath said.

Gawkers began to fill the space around us, emerging from the Arcanamirium, the cathedral, the theater, and the various high-end residences that surrounded the park. We gathered together, our heads tilted back, gaping at this larger-than-life (or larger-than-undeath) figure in the sky. We were all silent as we listened... except for Ketavan, whom I spotted nearby, shaking his fist at the sky and shouting until enough people shushed him into mere muttering.

"There have been some serious misunderstandings between our two great worlds." Mnephalon's smile would have been sweet if her teeth hadn't looked so sharp. "I hope to clear those up. You must understand, my people never wanted to take over your home—we simply recognize the value and importance of Absalom Station to our entire system and wanted to extend our protection to you. Your station is very *small*, after all, in the grand scheme of things, and it's a cold and dangerous universe for small things. But even though you've declined to become a protectorate of Eox, we can still do much to help one another, and in the coming days, I look forward to meeting with your Prime Executive and Syndicsguild, the leaders of your communities, and ordinary citizens too. This visit will open a new and golden age of peace and cooperation between our worlds, and, I hope, will go a long way toward ending the prejudice against the undead that I fear runs rife on your station." She shook her head, her expression becoming serious and sad. "There have been *shocking* acts of violence perpetrated against innocent undead, on Absalom Station and elsewhere in the system, and there are figures who profit from spreading hatred and inciting violence." Was she talking about Ketavan? She seemed to be. Could she *see* us?

Mnephalon purred on. "Like all such interspecies conflicts, I believe these problems are rooted in a failure to *understand* each other." She held out her long, pale, black-nailed hands before her, then interlaced her fingers. "I am here to be a bridge between our peoples. The undead and the living can thrive together. We are, after all, bright lights of consciousness in a dark and merciless universe—"

An actual bright light suddenly blossomed on the screen, accompanied by a boom so loud it made the leaves on the trees tremble around us. We all gasped and averted our eyes, those of us with sensitive photoreceptors temporarily blinded. The light faded slowly, and then Mnephalon reappeared on the screen—but she was on her hands and knees on the floor, with black smoke eddying around her. Her robes were torn, her long hair mussed, and when she lifted her face to the camera (or magical focal point, or whatever), her face was streaked with soot.

"An attack," she said hoarsely, struggling up to her knees. "An attack on an invited *diplomatic mission*?" Her voice was furious and outraged, her face a snarling skull with skin stretched tight over the bones. "You try to destroy *me*?" She rose, wobbling unsteadily. "This will not stand. I will see—"

Her image flickered, and was replaced by—Ketavan? The ranting priest grinned down at us, face as big as the dome of the Eye itself. He cackled and launched into a sermon before somebody could stop him. "That's the welcome we give the undead on Absalom Station!" the talking head shouted. "You walked right into our trap, necrovite scum! Eat vacuum, bloodsuckers! We will cut off your heads, burn your bodies, scatter your limbs, toss you into the hearts of stars! We'll track down and smash the electroencephalons of every necrovite on Eox, and you'll finally taste *true* death, you vile abominations! This is only the beginning! May the empire of the living live eternally! Prepare to—"

The screen glitched, and Mnephalon reappeared on the screen, still disheveled, but with her face more composed. "It would seem the known terrorist, Ketavan the Vaticinator, apostate of Pharasma, suspected in the bombing of the Eleventh Necropolis and wanted in connection with the assassination of the necrovite Nerdegast the Wise last year, has claimed credit for this cowardly assault on our mission of peace."

I stared across the park at Ketavan, who was looking at the sky, mouth hanging open, no longer shouting or shaking his fist. The people near him were pointing fingers and backing away. *That poor idiot,* I thought. *He's being framed.* The fool had a well-known vidcast—there were countless hours of footage of him ranting about the undead, more than enough for any halfway decent programmer to create a convincing deepfake of him saying anything they liked.

"We have no choice but to apprehend Ketavan and root out his coconspirators. Did this terrorist act with the knowledge and cooperation of the Prime Executive and station authorities? Until we find out for sure, we will be forced to seize control of the station." Mnephalon shook her head, radiating disappointment. "Once we have asserted our authority, we will be questioning the citizenry... *sharply*. People of Absalom Station: Prepare to be boarded. Do not resist, or we will have no choice but to use force. *You* did this. This is your fault." The dome went dark, plunging us into night for a long moment before the lights flickered back on.

I caught sight of Ketavan running away, robes flapping behind him. No one was even chasing him. Everyone was too stunned.

"That's it, then," Saphenath said, still staring up at the empty dome. "Eox wanted a pretext to seize the station, and they got one. They *created* one."

"Did Mnephalon just set off a smoke bomb on the bridge of her ship, do you think?" I said. "Maybe we can prove there was no actual attack—"

She held up a finger, cocking her head, listening to something in her earpiece, then shook her head. "No, I'm getting word from one of my reporters that there was a real attack—a small ship in the Armada that fired on the Eoxian diplomatic vessel, though it didn't do any meaningful damage. A tiny ship like that against her immense ship? It would be like a child throwing pebbles at a mountain. Hold on... a quick record search shows the offending ship is registered to... Ketavan. Of course. Let me trace the chain of ownership." Her eyes flickered back and forth, scanning some holographic interface I couldn't see. "Oh, dear," she said. "The ship used to belong to the Prime Executive's nephew, and it appears Ketavan purchased it a few months ago for a single credit."

I winced. "It's not even a *subtle* frame-up."

Saphenath nodded. "But the pretext doesn't have to stand up to scrutiny for long, does it? Eox just needs a plausible reason to invade and take control of the station. This story will sow enough doubt to keep other powers from immediately rushing to our defense. After that, the bone sages can control the narrative, force false confessions, hold show trials... and once they're in possession of the station, they'll *never* let it go." She turned thoughtful. "If I can get to Ketavan, sit him down for an interview, and broadcast the *truth*, maybe... well. I doubt it will make any material difference. But the truth has its own inherent value, don't you think?"

Before I could answer, we were interrupted—which was good, because *how* would I have answered, anyway? A loudspeaker crackled, and the Prime Executive's voice filled the air, a rare station-wide public address.

"Citizens of Abs—" She began her announcement, and then her voice abruptly cut off.

Saphenath tapped at her ear, frowning. "My comms are down."

I nodded. "The necrovite must be jamming our systems. They planned this. *All* of this. The attack on the cathedral this morning was meant to hit the clergy of Iomedae, who were probably the people here most qualified to fight the undead. Which means we should be expecting—"

"Actual, on-the-ground fighting with forces from Eox," Saphenath said. "But how? That Omenbringer may be crammed with zombies and skeletons, but it won't be easy to get them onto the station."

"I suspect they've already got troops in place," I said. "The bone sages aren't impulsive—they must have been planning this for a while, which means there could be sleeper cells all over Absalom, placed where they can do maximum damage." I thought about Val's idea that every undead person we saw was potentially part of a sinister cabal. That was unkind, and unlikely, but... some of them probably *were*.

"There are only a few hundred undead on this station," Saphenath objected. "They're a minority among minorities."

I shrugged. "Sure, but put a few in the right places, where they can disrupt or co-opt critical infrastructure? They could do a lot of damage. There could be living mercenaries on the bone sages' payroll too. Even if there aren't, the thing about the undead is they have all the time in the world, and they're good at increasing their ranks. Every one of us who falls is a potential convert to their cause."

"I need to get back to my offices," Saphenath said. "My journalists will need to cover... whatever happens next." She touched my elbow. "Our field trip will have to wait until a later date."

I nodded. "I'll look forward to it. I'm going back to the Lorespire, to make sure my people are OK." We'd held off assaults from Hellknights in the bad old days—surely we could handle a skirmish with a handful of undead? Saphenath was right, after all. There couldn't be *that* many of them on the station. "My friend Carn knows a lot about station infrastructure. Maybe he'll have an idea about getting the comms turned back on."

She reached out, grabbed my hand, and squeezed it. "Take care of yourself, Tyrcell."

"You too."

She rushed away, and she wasn't the only one. Everyone in the park was racing off in different directions, going to seek shelter or find their loved ones or maybe even take up arms.

The citizens of Absalom Station—the long-time ones, anyway—were no strangers to fighting. If Mnephalon thought she was going to stroll in and take control just by declaring herself in charge, she had a rude awakening on the way. She was fighting for control; we were fighting for our lives.

It's an odd time when you know that horrible violence is going to happen soon, but it hasn't started happening *yet*. Apart from the failing communication systems and the panicked crowds running around, nothing was really that different on my long walk to the Lorespire. (I wasn't about to take a tram, because I did not want to be in a metal tube in a dark tunnel if zombie hordes did somehow materialize.) The lights were still on, and nobody was shooting at anybody. Then I saw armed and armored corporate shock troops pouring out of the base of Bluerise Tower and surrounding the building—those thugs could be counted on to protect their assets at all costs, but they weren't likely to lend anyone else much assistance. I passed shops in the Freemarkets where those proprietors who had security systems in place started pulling down barred gates and turning on force fields. Security bots began flooding out of hidden panels in the walls, though they didn't seem terribly organized, and some champions of Iomedae ran past me, shouting holy mottoes.

"What is going *on*?" a stately maraquoi wrapped in embroidered robes cried out querulously, shaking the gate of a closed boutique in frustration. "I had an appointment! Why is everyone rushing about like we're being invaded?"

I paused. I realized that if you weren't in the Eye for Mnephalon's broadcast, you wouldn't have any idea what was going on, since the comms had been shut down moments after her address began. That meant most people on the station only knew there was some sort of infrastructure breakdown, and not that we were under imminent attack. "Um. Actually, undead forces from Eox are about to invade. You should seek shelter."

They blinked at me, sniffed haughtily, and said, "Nonsense. If there was some sort of invasion, there would have been an announcement."

"The comms—" I began to explain, but they turned away and stormed off, muttering about respect for elders clearly not being a universal value. Oh, well. You do what you can.

I thought about Val and Carn, wondering if they knew the situation. Oh, gods, Melezheun was out in the Armada doing work for the Syndicsguild, and she was *way* more vulnerable on a ship than she would be on the station. Maybe I could take the *Venture* and get to her?

No, it was too dangerous. There would be shooting soon, and while the *Venture* was tougher than it looked, it was no gunship. I had to get back to the Lorespire, find Val, and figure out how we were going to protect our people. Val would want to take the fight straight to Mnephalon, probably, and I'd need to try to talk her out of that, since fighting a necrovite directly is like pushing your face into a fangblade.

If the forces of Eox wanted to take over Absalom Station, I wasn't honestly sure we could do much about it. The station's gun batteries were very impressive, but they were meant to drive off pirates and terrorists, not a hostile planetary armada with an effectively infinite supply of troops they could drop on our heads. Most of the station's strength came from our position as a nexus of trade and our cultural importance to the system—but that's all *soft* power, and hordes of gibbering zombies don't care about soft power at all.

The only way to really protect the Society, and the station as a whole, was to defeat the bone sages themselves, most of whom were on faraway Eox. Which seemed a bit beyond even my impressive capabilities.

The corridors were getting more crowded, and people were getting more panicked. I had a lot of experience with chaos in the halls and streets of the station, and they weren't good memories, so as soon as I got close to Drifter's End and my own neighborhood, I headed for one of the oversized maintenance panels tucked away in a little cul-de-sac. Now, I'm not *supposed* to have access to those crawl spaces, since I'm officially just an average, ordinary private citizen who steadfastly refuses all official positions of power and prestige, but... you know, I also founded the Society, so I have all the codes for our parts of the station. I convinced the panel's locks that I had authority, the hatch slid open, and I crawled inside.

These behind-the-scenes parts of the station aren't very pretty, since they're covered in exposed conduits and wires and dusted pretty infrequently, but they do make for a nice, peaceful shortcut in times of trouble.

Of course, having quiet around me gave me time alone with my thoughts, which is a horrible place to be when undead hordes are attacking. I was so wrapped up in my own dark imaginings that I almost tripped over someone doing his best to hide in a tiny crevice in the wall. His boot was sticking out, though, so it was a bit like encountering a little kid playing hide-and-seek: He couldn't see *me*, so I must not be able to see *him*.

We were very close to the Lorespire, and I take a professional interest in people being surreptitious in the walls of the place where my friends live, so I cleared my throat and said, "May I help you?"

He slowly eased out of the crevice, and I recognized him right away. Ketavan, park preacher, undead hater, and pretext for the current violent invasion of the station. "Please don't tell anyone I'm here!" he said, voice pitched like a whisper but as loud as a shout. Maybe he'd forgotten how to talk in any register other than "witnessing for the masses." He clutched at my arm. "Please, I'm innocent, I mean, I'm innocent of *this*, I didn't attack that bone sage's ship, I wouldn't do that, why would I want to give the abominations warning, I would plan to strike them by *surprise*, strike them in their *homes*—"

"I have to take you in, Ketavan." I put a hand on the nonlethal sidearm at my hip. (The other hip carried the lethal one.) "You are a problem way above my pay grade, but we'll hand you over to the Prime Executive, and she can decide what to do with you."

"She'll give me to the necrovite!" he cried. "They'll shatter my body and eat my soul and raise me up again, trap my mind inside my corpse, and force my decaying body to do... to do *horrible* things!" I thought he might attack me, and I was calculating my odds of prevailing. He didn't appear to be armed, and he looked old and weak, so those were points in my favor, but he was also a religious zealot in fear of losing his very soul, which was maybe a bigger point in his. Then, to my extreme surprise and alarm, he dropped to his knees and raised his clenched fists together, beseeching me. "Please, friend, it's a trick, it's a lie, the bone sage has framed me—"

"Ketavan, I *know*. Anybody who thinks about it for more than a minute probably knows! The Primex isn't stupid. She'll figure it out and put you somewhere safe, she'll debrief you, and she'll figure out where to go from there." Secretly, I thought there was a decent chance she'd offer to trade Ketavan to the necrovite in exchange for an end to the hostilities because, hey, it was worth a try, but I decided not to mention that. Then I tried to be reassuring and accidentally landed on insulting. "Don't worry. An attack like this requires careful planning, and a whole organization, and nobody really thinks you're capable of accomplishing anything like that—"

He lowered his beseeching hands and narrowed his eyes. When he spoke next... well, I've never heard such an imperious and condescending tone from someone on their knees before. "Do not underestimate me, apostate. I have been planning a decisive strike against these undead perversions. In fact, I will soon be poised to wipe out their entire cursed planet."

"Right," I said. "You're the chosen one, leading a holy army in a sacred crusade sort of thing."

He struggled to his feet, shaking his head, shaggy eyebrows beetling down. "No, no, *no*! This devastation can be wrought by only a few hands, in the proper time and place! For we are not the first to loathe and despise the monsters on Eox—no, long ago they were hated, and plotted against, and their enemies made plans to destroy the wretched grave world the bone sages call home! Those enemies never had the chance to use their weapon, perhaps because they forgot themselves during the Gap, perhaps for some other reason. But even now, there are devices hidden in the darkness, secrets known only to a few, the slumbering weapons of a forgotten war, quiescent but puissant!"

"Quiescent *and* puissant," I said. "Wow. That's quite a combo." Stories about treasure troves of amazing forgotten technology were common. They were also sometimes *true*. There really are remarkable artifacts out there in the black, forgotten because their owners or creators forgot *everything* during the Gap. Or disappeared. But the idea that Ketavan had just happened to stumble upon a weapon that could destroy the people he just happened to have a psychotic vendetta against seemed unlikely. He was delusional at worst, being scammed at best—

"Doubt me if you will; I am no stranger to naysayers, but I first heard the rumor five years ago, and I have been chasing it down ever since!" He was ramping up the declaiming. "Only days ago I met with a sarcesian from the Thousand Moons who sold me the location of one of these great weapons for a very reasonable price. I was only waiting for certain expected donations to arrive before I put together my expedition, as the machinery requires—"

"Wait, a sarcesian?" I recalled what Saphenath had said, about an angel of the void who offered to sell her the location of some ancient treasure in the moons. I thought the odds were pretty good we were talking about the same person—we don't get many sarcesians on the station, really. They're fifteen-foot-tall aliens with wings made of light, so they tend to stand out. "What did they tell you, exactly?"

"I'll tell you everything if you promise not to turn me in," he said. "You must swear an oath, on whatever you hold most dear!"

I considered. Harboring a fugitive seemed like a bad idea, but that had never stopped me before. If I got into trouble, I could always say I was protecting Ketavan so he wouldn't get murdered by an angry mob who blamed him for our troubles. If that didn't mollify the authorities, well, I could just run away; it wouldn't be the first time I'd evaded the law. "Fine," I said. "I swear on the Society."

"The irreligious are ever a bane to me," he muttered. "But fine. I was given a location, a set of coordinates, and certain landmarks to look for. I was promised that, within this place—the Falling Stars Complex, my informant called it—I would find ancient machinery with the power to turn Eox into space dust."

A weapon, hidden in the debris field above Eox, capable of *annihilating* Eox? I was not eager to commit a genocide, but if this information had even a tiny chance of being true, I needed to get word to the Primex, so maybe she could work out some kind of deal with the necrovite. Total destruction is a pretty good bargaining chip. "All right," I said. "I'll tell you what. I know a person who can keep you safe—she runs a news site, and she's very good about protecting her sources. You might have to give her an exclusive interview when this is all over, but she'll make sure you don't die before you get the chance. All right?"

He frowned, then slowly nodded. "I need to find refuge somewhere. Very well."

"Great." I could have knocked him out and dragged him with me, but I preferred not to have to. "After you're safe, I'll contact the Primex, and we can trade your information for protection or immunity or whatever." I'd taken to wearing this green hooded cloak with a ton of concealed pockets on the inside, plus some extra technological bells and whistles I'd had the Society's engineers work up. I fished a small respirator mask out of one pocket, then reluctantly removed my beloved travel garb and said, "Wear this. I'm going to want it back, but for now, it will keep people from recognizing you while we make our way to Saphenath's office."

Ketavan obediently swaddled himself in the cloak, doubtless remembering how his face looked projected over the entire dome, and when I handed him the respirator, he put that on too. He looked like any of the dozens of explorers who propped up various bars in Drifter's End, telling lies about all the amazing wonders they'd discovered. "We'll go as far as we can via the tunnels, but we'll have to come out at some point, and... I don't know what we'll encounter when we do."

Just at that moment—because reality has a sense of drama sometimes—there was a thunderous boom, and the tunnel shook, more dust sifting down from the ceiling.

"If the undead set upon us, I will send their souls to rest," Ketavan said, with a little of his old fire.

"I'm more worried about the necrovite bombing the station and collapsing the roof on us or blasting us out into the vacuum," I said. (It turns out, Ketavan was more right about the likely dangers than I was. Don't you hate that? I hate that.) "Come on."

I turned back the way I had come, because checking on the Lorespire had, sadly, become a lower priority for me. I needed to stash Ketavan and then take his intel to the Primex. Easy, right?

We had to exit the tunnels near Bluerise Tower, because I didn't have access codes for *their* subterranean maintenance zones. But I figured that would be a fairly safe place to emerge, because those wealthy anarcho-capitalists hire their own private security with top-of-the-line equipment, and even if there were a few undead wandering around, the mercenaries could surely handle them—

I was a little surprised then when we ran into a trio of pointy-eared, bulbous-headed ghouls playing a three-way tug-of-war with the corpse of a guy in branded corporate armor.

Then they stopped, because they noticed me and Ketavan, and I guess they had a hankering for fresher meat.

# 9

# THE RECLAIMED WASTE

## (Valentine / 7 AG)

"I've tasked my drone to keep an eye on you, Blightwind," Val said. "If you try to run, it will fire an energy beam straight through the top of your head. I'd advise you to cooperate."

The borai was rubbing feeling back into his recently untied wrists, and he nodded, face blank. "I know you're going to kill me. But I don't want it to happen right now. So I'll go along."

"Nobody's going to kill you, so long as you do as we say," Azzi rumbled.

Caspien looked up into the dragonkin's scaly face and shook his head. "Don't be absurd. You can't let me go free. I *know* you aren't acting in any official capacity—official interrogations don't happen in random back rooms, with no paperwork and no due process. You're vigilantes. You kidnapped me, tied me up, and threatened me. Even if I weren't innocent, that would be a crime. No, this ends with me suffering true death, fed into a recycling vat."

"Don't be stupid," Val said. Her initial white-hot fury had faded considerably. She'd really believed Blightwind was involved in the attack, and maybe she still did, but if he wasn't... if he really was just a luckless accountant who happened to be undead... she was, in fact, pretty screwed if word got out about what she'd done. But maybe the situation was still salvageable. She was supposed to be a politician, wasn't she? "If you're innocent, on the side of the living, then you're going to help us take down a group of undead terrorists, right? You'll be a hero, or you can keep your involvement private and we'll call you a confidential informant, whatever you prefer. I didn't kidnap you—you saw the bombing this morning, and you were moved to help us, so you sought me out as a member of the Syndicsguild."

A fleeting, hopeful expression passed over Blightwind's face. "You'd never trust me to stick to that story."

Val shrugged. "Azzi will back me up. The word of both the leader of a respected faction and the head of the dockworker's union versus the word of a borai, a people who are despised even among the undead, as you pointed out yourself? Who will people be more likely to believe?"

"You're reassuring me by pointing out how universally loathed my kind are?" Caspien sighed and slumped. "I wish I didn't find that convincing, but I actually do."

"That whole plan depends on you actually helping us, though," Val said. "Otherwise, that recycling vat... well. Accidents happen."

"All the time," Azzi rumbled, putting one immense taloned hand on the undead elf's shoulder. Val liked Azzi. They were a supportive abettor of felonies.

"Lead the way, Caspien." Val gestured.

"We have to go way down below," the borai said. "The bar I'm thinking of, the Reclaimed Waste, is deep in the Spike, on one of the lowest inhabited levels."

Val nodded. The Spike was an enormous protrusion on the underside of the station, essentially an inverted tower extending down into the void, and it was home to the poorest denizens of the habitat. She'd never spent much time in Downside, as the region was sometimes called. There were hundreds of levels of decks there, some crammed with slums, some sparsely populated because of structural instability or other dangers. There were also the Ghost Levels—no one knew how many—at the very bottom: whole decks of the station that hadn't been mapped or even explored because the drones and people who went down there rarely came back. The few who returned reported a nightmare realm of darkness, radiation, hard vacuum, and even hostile denizens of unknown species. People kept trying to go down there, though, because there were persistent rumors of hidden treasures and lost technology that could make them rich, but as far as Val knew, no one had ever emerged with anything of real value.

Some members of the Syndicsguild had agitated for sending in a heavily armed force to clear out the Ghost Levels so they could be made suitable for habitation, to ease the housing shortage caused by the station's population boom, but there simply weren't enough resources for such an undertaking. Others had suggested sending criminals down there in lieu of imprisonment, exile, or execution, since such a fate would basically combine all three, but the more progressive members had prevented such measures from passing.

Nobody who could live anywhere else chose to live even close to the Ghost Levels. People way down there had a tendency to vanish in the night; the stories said there were hungry creatures in the Ghost Levels that sometimes emerged to go hunting. Val considered it, and she thought it was an ideal place for ghouls and vampires to satisfy their grotesque urges—preying on the poor and powerless was always a smart approach, and way down in the Spike, even if people noticed disappearances, they'd blame the mysterious monsters under their feet before they thought of bloodsuckers or flesh eaters.

"I'd better call work and let them know I'm going to be even later," Azzi grumbled, fiddling with their wrist gauntlet. They cocked their head. "Huh. Val, I can't get on the network, can you?"

Valentine checked her own connections and found them fruitlessly reaching out for a network that wasn't there anymore. Her cameras were still streaming their footage to her personal hard drive, but the station's communication systems were down. "No, me neither, that's weird. There are supposed to be all sorts of fail-safes and redundancies in place to prevent total outages. Unless... this could be another step in a coordinated attack. First the assault on the cathedral, then the follow-up bomb... What if they were just the opening steps of a larger plan?"

Azzi growled. "Could be. We'd better track down Caspien's friends and see what they know."

"They aren't my *friends*," the borai protested, but Val shoved him toward the door.

There were plenty of people complaining about the network outage in the corridors, but nobody was visibly panicking around the Lorespire Complex or in Drifter's End—as the surrounding area had come to be called, catering as it did to so many explorers, traders, and interstellar vagabonds. Mass transit was still online, fortunately, so they caught an express elevator down to one of the more frequently visited levels of the Spike, Pipetown. There was a measure of organization and order down there because that level was home to the main infrastructure that supplied the station's water and electricity and disposed of their considerable sewage. Val's understanding was vague on the ultimate source of the station's water, actually. Was it elemental magic, or a portal to some plane of water, or just disturbingly efficient recycling? At any rate, Pipetown was a damp and dripping place, and it was still basically run by a gang, but it was civilized enough that you weren't likely to get murdered as soon as the elevator doors creaked open.

They stepped out into a low corridor, dripping pipes crisscrossing the ceiling overhead and lining the walls. A bored-looking orc wearing a lot of spiky black armor leaned against a nexus of conduits, patted a truncheon on his palm, and gave them a tusky grin. There was a tattoo of kinked pipes on the side of his thick neck. One of the local water protectors, there to make sure nobody messed with the essential services, Val would guess.

"I recognize you, dead man," the orc growled. "Who are your friends?"

"We're from the Syndicsguild," Val said, betting that the connection to power would make her intimidating... though it might also make her a valuable hostage. "Caspien here is helping us with an investigation."

"We don't really like investigations down here," the orc said, as if musing over the idea.

"We're just passing through," Caspien said miserably. "Heading, ah, way down."

The orc snorted. "Going down to the Morgue again, eh? The first time I saw your boy here, he was wearing a suit like any old corporate drone, but after a couple of visits to the Morgue, he started dressing all in black like his dead buddies."

Val glanced at Caspien, who hunched his shoulders.

"Morgue?" Azzi said. "They keep bodies down here?"

"Nah, nah, that's just what we call that level," the orc said. "Ever since the undead started hanging out there, trying to make their own little enclave, I guess. Nobody cares—it's a crap level, way too cold, and the environmental scrubbers don't work right, so there's toxic mold, but the dead folks don't care about all that. And so long as they're down there, they aren't up *here*, creeping us out." He waved the baton. "Enjoy speaking with the dead."

They walked down the corridor. "I think you look good in black," Azzi offered, but the borai just moaned, and the dragonkin fell silent. Caspien led the way down a branching path with a lower ceiling, which forced them to duck under pipes that hissed and leaked steam; Azzi practically had to crawl under them. From there, they took a rickety cargo elevator down, whipping past more levels than Val could count. The door was a grate, not solid, so as they descended, Val caught flashing glimpses of dim chambers, neon lights, heaving bodies on a dance floor, sprawled bodies in a dreamsnuff den, heaps of scrap metal, and the flash of welding torches before they began falling so fast that picking out details became impossible.

The car finally ground to a halt, and Azzi wrestled the recalcitrant door open. They entered a long corridor lined with bare rooms, no doors closing them off, the interiors stripped. The whole area looked like it was being renovated, but Val soon realized it had actually been gutted, the walls and ceiling torn open and the wires and fixtures inside looted and carried away to be used elsewhere. "Not much farther now," Caspien said, stepping over a gap where a floor panel had been pried up.

"If you're leading us into a trap, you'll regret it," Val said. "Don't forget about the drone above you."

"When would I have had time to set a trap?" Caspien's tone was aggrieved. "The people in the Morgue won't be happy to see you, but not because of anything I did. They don't like living people barging in down there. They might try to hurt you, but that's nothing to do with me."

"You'll just have to vouch for us," Val said. "Let them know we're friends to the undead."

Caspien didn't answer, just slump-slouched down the hall to a room that looked just like any other, until he stomped on a spot on the floor and a trapdoor popped open on spring-loaded hinges. The borai hauled the hatch up and gestured. "The ladder leads straight down to the Morgue, and the bar we're looking for, the Reclaimed Waste, isn't far."

"I'll go first," Azzi said. "People aren't as likely to jump a dragonkin." Val didn't argue that very true point as Azzi squeezed into the opening and descended.

"You next." She prodded Caspien, who climbed down, the drone tasked to watch him hovering close above his head. Val descended last and looked around the Morgue. This level was *dim*, as she'd expected, since the undead were made for life in the dark, but otherwise it was... surprisingly normal. No shrines made of skulls, no heaps of dismembered body parts, no blood fountains. Just corridors studded with doors, some of them blank, some with holographic signs proclaiming various wares and amenities. The air did smell a bit sour, but to be honest, any part of the station with inefficient air scrubbers tended to get a bit foul sometimes, even if there weren't ghouls around, and it certainly wasn't the open-pit grave stench she'd expected.

"You were expecting pools of blood and skeletons everywhere, weren't you?" Caspien sounded equal parts disappointed and disgusted. "The people down here aren't mindless monsters. They're just *people*. Don't you get that? The bone sages of Eox aren't terrible people because they're undead, they're terrible because they're vile fascists! Not all of us—"

"Just show us to this separatist bar, Caspien." Val was trying to keep her anger stoked, but Caspien's instant comprehension of her assumptions had struck a nerve. She hated being predictable.

The borai walked on, Azzi and Val just behind him, and people suddenly began to appear in the corridor, seemingly from nowhere, standing against walls or leaning in doorways like they'd always been there. Val assumed they were all undead, and one was definitely a ghoul, another some kind of immaterial spirit; but some of them just looked like people of various species... until they bared their pointy little teeth or she noticed the patches of rot and decay.

"Are you lost, blood bags?" a lashunta vampire called from a doorway, causing his compatriots to snicker. Caspien ignored them, so Val did too. They turned down increasingly narrow and sparsely populated passageways until they dead-ended at a pair of wide sliding doors, firmly closed. Holographic words canted at a slight angle over the bar read Waste Reclamation Center, letters flickering like the projector was dying.

"I thought this bar was called the Reclaimed Waste?" Val said.

"It is," Caspien said. "Somebody just stole that sign from a treatment plant up in Pipetown and hung it up here as a joke."

"Ha ha," Val said flatly. "Go on, then. Take us in and show us the Eox lovers."

Caspien didn't move. "This... this isn't a bar where living people go. You aren't welcome in the Morgue at all, really, but in *here*? It's just... not your place."

"So tell them we're candidates," Azzi said. "Tell them we want to be converts. That we're interested in becoming vampires, and we paid you to introduce us around."

Val looked at Azzi in surprise. She'd been thinking of the dragonkin as muscle, but obviously they were smart too; you didn't get to be the representative of a union as powerful as the dockworkers if you didn't have brains aplenty. "That's a good idea. Will it work, Caspien?"

The borai considered, then nodded. "It's a scam people run sometimes, sure. They bring wannabes down here and then rob them."

"And drain them and kill them?" Val said. "You left that part out. But these bloodsuckers, they're just people, right?"

"Show me a species on this station that's never murdered anybody," Caspien shot back. Apparently, being on his home turf was helping him regain some of his courage. "I'll wait."

"Let's get on with this," Val said. "Something bad is happening on this station, and we need to find out what, then stop it."

Caspien stepped up to the door and waved, presumably for the benefit of a watching camera, and after a moment, a voice hissed from a hidden loudspeaker: "We're closed for a private gathering. Go away."

"I, uh, need to talk to Malvus," he said. "I've got a candidate for the dark gift—"

"Private. Function," the voice hissed.

"She's a member of the Syndicsguild!" Caspien said. "Malvus was talking about how we need representation at the highest levels of government, and she could give us—"

"Hold on," the voice said. After a long moment, it spoke again: "Come on in."

The door slid open, and Caspien entered, followed by Val and Azzi. The main room was surprisingly large, dotted with tables and chairs and couches, with a circular bar in the center and some kind of cybernetic zombie behind it, washing glasses methodically. Various doors, open and closed, hinted at a warren of back rooms beyond.

A vampire—originally an elebrian, the indigenous people of Eox—strolled in from one of the back rooms, arms outstretched, grinning and showing off a mouth full of pointed teeth. "Welcome!" he said. "I am Malvus, owner of the Reclaimed Waste. And *you* are Valentine, leader of the Society, in the company of Azzi, head of the dockworker's union. What august personages to have in my humble establishment!"

*That explains the delay,* Val thought. Whoever was watching them on camera had run their faces through a database.

"And the two of you want to be *vampires*? Humans, well, those are easy, but I can't recall ever meeting a dragonkin vampire." Malvus circled around them, rubbing his chin thoughtfully. "In truth, you might be better candidates for other forms of eternal unlife." He snapped his fingers, and suddenly people stepped out of various doorways—and, in some cases, emerged from shadows. Some were holding weapons, and others *were* weapons. In addition to more vampires, there were a matched pair of cybernetic ysoki zombies, flesh rotting away from their metallic implants; grinning ghouls with grafted steel jaws; and a dark shape with flickering lights where its eyes should have been—a wraith? Mere proximity to this many undead made Val's bowels clench.

"How does a position as a member of a mindless shambling horde appeal to you? There's not much room for advancement, but you can't beat it for job security." Malvus gestured lazily at Caspien. "Come on over to our side, darling, you've earned it. I took you for a milk-hearted wannabe. I shouldn't have been so judgmental—it's not your fault you're a botched little freak."

Caspien cast a worried eye at Val, then shuffled away, not really joining Malvus, but standing a bit off to the side.

A couple of the vampires pointed energy weapons their way. "Oh my gods," Malvus said. "You're *captured*, blood sacks. Act like it."

Val held up her hands, and Azzi did the same. "Whoa, whoa, whoa," Val said. "Listen. We're part of a faction in the Syndicsguild that's open to the idea of joining Eox as a protectorate. We were hoping to meet local organizers with ties to Eox, so we could open up a back channel—"

Malvus tittered. There was no other word for the sound. "It's too late for all that, my Valentine. The sages back home were terribly offended to be refused when they asked nicely, and they've decided to take the station by force instead. In fact, the invasion is already happening, though word hasn't filtered down quite this far yet."

Val did her best to remain stoic, even though he'd just articulated her deepest fear.

The vampire went on, clearly in love with the sound of his own voice. "Up above, though, in your precious Eye, people must be positively soiling themselves by now. My little group has been working for months, gathering intelligence, and we've already seized control of the critical infrastructure on the station—life support, comms, and even the station defenses. Getting direct control of the Starstone Reactor, so we can control the flow of energy, has proven... tricky... but in time, I'm sure we'll crack the problem. In the meantime, we can screw around with the gravity, we can cut off the air, we can—"

"Fascinating," Val interjected. "We're all very impressed by the competence of your acts of terrorism. So what happens now?"

"Oh, I proposed just venting the atmosphere in most of the station and letting you all die, but some of my people need to breathe, and some of yours don't, and reviving all of your corpses would take forever. The bone sages don't want an empty habitat." Malvus shrugged. "They want the whole population intact, to serve as hardworking, productive citizens of the empire. So we plan to do things the slow-and-boring way. My elite squad here was just heading upstairs to take advantage of the chaos, and do you know what *our* mission is?" He threw his arms wide and grinned. Were his teeth growing longer? "We're going to round up and imprison, execute, or turn as many members of the Syndicsguild as we can! We have to get our hands on the Primex especially, of course, but anyone else is a bonus. And my man Caspien here delivered two of you straight here, no fuss, no waiting! So we'll just get you chained up in a dirty hole down here somewhere—"

Valentine had heard enough. Her drone was still hovering above her, apparently unnoticed or underestimated by her captors. She'd activated the cloaking tech that made the floating orb into little more than a shimmer in the air, preferring not to tempt thieves with a tasty bit of obvious technology.

Val was the leader of a small-but-respected faction, but she didn't walk around with bodyguards, and, strangely, no one ever seemed to wonder why. They must think she was foolhardy, or overconfident. But she *did* have a guard—her drone, always watching, and armed with more than just a camera. The priests at the cathedral of Iomedae had offered her a blessing, so her drone's reservoir was full of holy water.

She had a small exocortex, mostly to store her continuous livestream data, but it also included remote controls for her drone, and she activated it. The floating bot had subtly moved into position... and it extended its nozzle and sprayed a shower of holy water down on Malvus and his vampire pals. The spray wouldn't bother the zombies much, unfortunately, and she wasn't sure the water would work on the wraith at all, but the vampires would *definitely* feel the pain.

Malvus screamed and clawed at his face as his flesh was drenched with the blessed water, skin peeling away under his dragging claws. His fellow bloodsuckers (or energy drainers, or emotion eaters) were also shrieking and writhing, but the cybernetic zombies began lurching toward them, and the wraith flickered, moving fast—

"Light!" Caspien shouted. "They hate light, especially sunlight—"

Val's drone was, of course, equipped with emergency lighting with full-spectrum brightness, and she cranked the light as high as it would go, a searing beam shining right on the wraith. The floating shadow emitted a high-pitched squeal, more like audio feedback than any sound a living creature would make, and fled, dissolving into a cloud of mist that floated under one of the doors into the safe darkness of the back rooms.

The zombie ysoki were still coming, arms outstretched, but Azzi roared, opened their mouth wide, and spewed forth a cone of flame that engulfed them—and Malvus and one of the other writhing vampires too, which did nothing to improve the writhing *and* made the air stink of burning, rotten meat. Caspien managed to dance out of the way of the flame in time, and since he'd helped them with the wraith, Val was actually glad.

Azzi stopped breathing fire... but the zombies didn't stop coming. They were burning, but they didn't seem to notice, and the result was that Azzi was seized by burning hands. The dragonkin roared and swiped at them, but the zombies were indomitable. Val's drone was all out of water, and though an automatic fire-suppression system should have kicked in the moment the station sensed flames, the infrastructure down there was severely diminished.

Caspien strode forward with a fire extinguisher in one hand and a long baton in the other. "Here!" he shouted, tossing the weapon to Val, then hefting the extinguisher and spraying foam all over the zombies. They didn't notice that, either, but at least they stopped burning. Val whacked at one with the pole until it turned toward her, then jabbed it in the face—and accidentally triggered something in the baton, making it extend to greater length, punching a hole straight through the zombie's head and on out the back. She grunted and yanked the baton free.

With just one zombie to contend with, Azzi did better, smacking it hard enough to send it bouncing off the wall.

The vampires were starting to stir, though, and Val wasn't convinced they could dispatch them all safely—and there might be reinforcements coming. "Run!" she shouted, and Azzi heeded her advice, rushing for the door alongside her.

Caspien joined them. Val didn't complain. Either he really was on the side of the station, or he was really committed to tricking her... and from what little Val knew of undead culture, there was no scenario where a lowly borai could turn on a vampire that way and come out of the interaction intact. They got through the door and Caspien took the lead—which was good, because Val had no idea where they were going—and he swiftly led them down an alleyway to a ladder that led up, off the Morgue level. They reached the top, emerging in a storage closet, and Caspien slammed down a hatch and closed it with a sliding bolt. That wouldn't stop a determined attacker, especially one with the enhanced strength of the undead, but even the illusion of security was welcome in their predicament.

"Are you OK?" Val asked Azzi, fussing over her new friend. "Did you get burned?"

"Singed," they rumbled. "Fire doesn't hurt me much. Nice thick scales. Which also helped with the biting—I got dented by those zombie teeth but didn't bleed."

"I'm fine too, apart from a few droplets of holy water that caught my arm," Caspien said sharply.

Val turned toward him, prepared to say something cutting, then stopped. "Thank you," she said instead, "for helping us down there."

He nodded glumly. "We were too late, though, if an attack on the station is already under way. I'm sorry. I honestly thought their big talk was all just bluster. They never trusted me enough to tell me their real plans."

"I don't know about being too late," Val said. "We did some damage to the abduction squad that was going after the Primex. And we got some valuable information—we know they took control of the station infrastructure down here, at the root."

"We should tell someone," Caspien said.

"Comms are down," Azzi growled.

"We don't need to tell someone," Val said. "We *are* someone. We're going to take back control of the station. But first"—she looked at the baton in her hand—"we really need to get better weapons."

"I know a guy," Azzi said, "if we can get up to Botscrap."

"Works for me. Somebody up there might be able to tell us where the undead scum took control of the station systems, anyway." She paused. "Sorry, Caspien. No offense. I guess not all undead are scum. You did great down there."

"I'm just an accountant," Caspien moaned.

"You *used* to be just an accountant," Val said. "Now you're also a member of the Society's Citizen Defense League."

"Is that... an actual thing?" the borai asked.

"It is now," Val replied.

# 10

## HIGH STAKES

(Melezheun / 7 AG)

Master Fabricant was a dedicated murder machine, unfolding heretofore hidden limbs to slap aside the human vampire grinning at Phaera. The vampire looked comically shocked as he flew across the anteroom and bounced off one of the elegantly papered walls, landing on the floor—but only for a moment. Then he sprang upright and drew two knives, one crackling with some sort of black energy, the other giving off the blue sparks of captured lightning. "I can't eat you, robot, but I can *disassemble* you."

Melezheun didn't have any weapons, because this wasn't supposed to be *that* kind of mission, but she was a mystic, and though she didn't know a wide range of offensive magic, she was capable of seizing control of the mindless undead, albeit briefly. The skeleton minions in the entourage were rattling their way toward Master Fabricant, so she concentrated, reaching out with her mind to the nearest one, and directed it to attack its fellow minion instead. They went down in a pile of clattering, lashing bones.

A corpsefolk with glittering implants up and down their arms came at her, implanted talons ripping out of their fingertips, ready to shred her. She couldn't control an intelligent undead being as easily as a mindless creature, but she could confuse them and make them hesitate. However, her attempt to reach into their mind failed, either because the corpse's will was too strong, or because their various implants included protections against psychic meddling. The undead slashed out at her, and as she lifted her arm to block the blow, metal claws raked against it, harmlessly scraping down the links of her mindmail. She felt the impact, though, and staggered back. The corpsefolk was surprised they hadn't torn her arm off—or at least open—and goggled at her in confusion, giving her a moment to strike back.

Seven years earlier, Melezheun had been attacked by a pair of hulking thugs in a hallway and hadn't been able to defend herself against them at all; since then, she'd devoted a portion of each day to studying unarmed combat. She had another advantage too: Her mindmail did more than just defend her. The nanotechnology in the enveloping armor could augment her natural movements, greatly increasing her dexterity. She'd learned a few spells to help her in battle, including a transformation that would stretch her mouth wide and fill it with sharp teeth, letting her deliver vicious bites... but the thought of corpse flesh in her mouth was too grotesque to contemplate.

Instead, she danced away a few steps, then raised her hand to summon four orbs of hard light. They were most useful for illuminating dark places, but in a pinch, they could also be used as projectiles. She flung the spheres directly at the corpse, and though they batted the first two aside, the last ones struck them in the face and the chest, and they stumbled away, dazzled by the bursts of brightness. Melezheun took the opportunity to sprint forward, drop to her feet, and sweep the creature's legs out from under them. They went down, thumping their head hard on the floor, and Melezheun leaped on top of it, grabbed them by the wrist, and plunged their handful of extended knives deep into their own belly. The corpse howled, rolled over, and scrambled away, trailing vile fluids. She didn't dare waste time finishing them, because the elf vampire was getting up—but instead of attacking her, they vanished deeper into the ship, followed by a ghoul, the immaterial spirits, and the minions. Melezheun's compelled skeleton was in pieces, just bones scattered across the floor, along with the one it had been fighting.

That meant the only enemy left standing in the immediate vicinity was the human vampire, who had been heavily injured. Master Fabricant had severed one of his arms, and the vampire was snarling and swinging his remaining blade back and forth in wild arcs. Master Fabricant had taken some damage too, some of his extended limbs broken off and one of his legs dragging uselessly, but the robot was resilient. Phaera was stalking toward the vampire too, her body wreathed in shadows—she was a user of magic as well, it seemed. Melezheun joined Master Fabricant and Phaera to go at the vampire from three directions, forcing him to pivot and snarl. Melezheun's head was aching, but she reached out with her will once again and tried to subjugate the vampire.

His mind resisted, but he was frightened, in pain from partial dismemberment, and distracted, so she was able to find a sliver of a crack to reach into. *Friend, I'm your friend,* she whispered into his mind.

The vampire's wild swings slowed, and the point of his knife dipped. He peered at Melezheun, brow furrowed, head cocked at a quizzical angle. "I... wait, do I know you? Did we meet... was it at the flensing party, in the Inverted Palace last year?"

"That's right," Melezheun said, just as Master Fabricant extended a hinged, articulated limb that tapered to a long blade from his torso and sliced the vampire's head from his body. Melezheun stepped back in disgust when the body fell toward her, unsure if its oozing fluids were toxic or not.

The head rolled away across the deck. Phaera gestured and muttered, then knelt down and brushed her fingertips against the vampire's forehead. It burst into flame, and she stepped back, watching as the flames melted the flesh from the skull.

The casino owner turned to Melezheun and smiled brightly, her cloak of shadows receding. "Well. That was all rather unexpected."

"That was a nice trick, messing with their minds," Master Fabricant said to her with grudging admiration. "Can you do it again?"

Melezheun shook her head. "It takes a lot out of me. I'd need to rest, and I don't have the feeling I'll get much of that anytime soon."

"That's all right," Master Fabricant said. "My security forces have been mobilized. The other vampire won't be able to hide from us. Every inch of the place, apart from Phaera's private rooms, is under video and audio surveillance, and we have psychics constantly scanning for cheats and thieves. They think they can take *us*?"

"I believe the idea was to take me hostage, and then I'd do the taking," Phaera said. "Fortunately, you prevented that, Master Fabricant... and you." The void elf gazed at Melezheun for a long moment, then inclined her head in a gracious nod. "Your help was both timely and appreciated. Come join me in my office. We can monitor activity on the ship from there, and *nothing* will breach my defenses."

Melezheun nodded but said, "Not even a ghost, or whatever that wispy thing was? They can pass through walls."

"My walls are inscribed with runes of power that will, at the very least, make such creatures hesitate to enter," Phaera said. "Come on."

They hurried to another concealed door, then into a set of narrow tunnels that clearly wound under and around the public areas of the casino, to judge by all the ramps and sharp turns. Phaera took the lead, with Melezheun close behind and Master Fabricant in the rear, muttering to himself constantly—or so Melezheun thought at first, before realizing he was coordinating the security response.

Soon they were back in Phaera's office, emerging from a door behind an elaborate tapestry of a figure with butterfly wings sparkling with starlight. *A god of chance,* Melezheun thought, though she couldn't remember the deity's name.

Master Fabricant went to a wall, popped open a panel, and revealed a computer interface. He pulled a wrist-thick cable out of his torso and plugged it directly into the system. "Let's see what's happening out there."

The curved walls, and even the ceiling, all shifted, every available inch transforming into vidscreens. Melezheun turned slowly, dazzled by the array of inputs. There were screens depicting every part of the casino floor, views from the cameras of security drones and personnel, and exterior images too, showing ships of all sizes and configurations drifting or flashing past.

One large screen was mostly taken up by the glittering shape of Absalom Station. Melezheun sat down on a plush couch and gazed at the screen. She never grew tired of the opportunity to see her home world from the outside: an immense disk with irregular protrusions reaching out from the central dome of the Eye, the rings dotted by towers (Bluerise, of course, but her own Lorespire was prominent too), and the monumental Spike depending from the bottom of the station like the largest stalactite in the vast cavern of space.

Something flashed against the side of the station, and the end of one of the Arms tore away, drifting loose, dangling gantries—it was one of the shipbuilding districts, she thought, not a heavily populated area, but even so!

"Someone is firing on the station?" she said, shocked. Sure, there'd been talk of sabers rattling and tensions rising, but Absalom Station was the safe place at the center of the galaxy, and anyone who sought to destroy it would draw the ire of countless worlds.

Phaera sat down beside her, flicking at a tablet. "This visiting bone sage diplomat, named Mnephalon, claims she was the victim of a terrorist attack, and that some firebrand of a priest named Ketavan attacked her ship. She says she's taking control of the station until the perpetrator is brought to justice and his conspiracy rooted out. But it's obviously a pretext for the bone sages to seize permanent control of the station—and that includes the so-called Armada too, if our little boarding party is any indication. This is a planned, coordinated action, and I'd bet there are breaching parties all over the station as well—not to mention sleeper cells inserted months or even years ago, probably. The people of Eox are good at long-term planning." She gestured at the screen, where more fireballs were blooming at the base of the Spike and on the Arms. "I doubt those attacks are meant to do serious damage; they're just a little taste of what *could* happen if the Primex doesn't hand over control."

"Why isn't the station shooting back?" Melezheun said. "I've seen the gun batteries, they're supposed to be able to hold off an invasion fleet!"

"Don't know," Master Fabricant said. "Can't ask, either—I tried hailing your station, but the comms are disabled there. Yet more evidence in favor of sleeper cells. It's also possible that bad actors have seized control of the station's guns. Or maybe they just don't dare open fire because there are too many friendly ships in between their cannons and the Eoxian flagship. It's a monster of a ship called the *Marbhan*. And its escorts—look, they're gunships, which makes sense for an honor guard, but now they're firing on civilians. Permission to hail the other ships and implement an evacuation plan, boss? If we can clear the field a bit, open up a clear line of fire, the station might have a better chance."

Phaera frowned. "What? Why? This is none of our business."

"That bone sage sent a boarding party of vampires and ghouls and more to try to take *your* vessel," the robot pointed out. "You're prepared to let an insult like that stand?"

The void elf gazed into space for a moment, tapping a long, pointed fingernail against the tablet screen. "The enemy does seem to think I'm part of this Armada, and therefore part of Absalom Station, so I suppose I could lend a hand to the cause. In exchange for certain considerations later, of course. Such as permanent tax-exempt status?" She smiled at Melezheun.

"Can you provide real, material assistance in defense of the station?" Melezheun asked. "If so, we might be able to make a deal."

"Absalom Station isn't the only object in this system capable of holding off a fleet," Master Fabricant said. "We've been attacked by pirates seven times. Do you know how many times they made off with any loot?"

"None?" Melezheun hazarded to guess.

"That's right. And do you know how many pirates lived to tell the tale?"

"Also none?" she repeated.

"No." Phaera spoke up. "One. After the seventh time, we decided we should leave one alive to tell everyone to stop trying. The *Offshoot of Design* isn't anybody's easy pickings, including a bunch of grasping, avaricious necrovites."

"I've been wondering," Mel asked. "What does the name of this ship mean?"

"It's from an old quote I read once," Phaera said. "'Good fortune is an offshoot of design.' The idea, as I understand it, is that the harder you work and the better you plan, the more good luck you have." She waved a many-ringed hand at Master Fabricant. "Go ahead and hail the other ships, coordinate a response... and let's show that bone sage we don't appreciate being meddled with."

The large screen showing the bombardment of Absalom Station shifted to a view of the Eoxian flagship, the *Marbhan*. A similar model to the *Necrosis*, it was an immense, bloated, grotesque vessel, like the corpse of a sea monster, its hull shaped like a giant rib cage. It couldn't *actually* be made from the bones of a dead leviathan, could it? The ship loomed on the edge of the Armada, and Melezheun realized it would indeed be impossible to shoot at it without risking all the other ships in the way.

The bone sage had no such compunctions. The missiles the small Eoxian fleet launched at the station mostly hit their target, but a few clipped or outright smashed into smaller vessels, which burst into silent fireballs or lurched away smoking and trailing debris.

Many of the smaller crafts were scattering like birds who'd seen a predator, and some vanished into the Drift, but a few brave souls were firing back at the enemy. None of them were doing enough damage to crack the warship's shields, but their courage heartened Melezheun.

"Should we fire on their vessel too?" Phaera asked.

"That's up to you," the robot said. "We can damage their shields badly enough that they'll probably shoot back to stop us."

"Can we prevail in a firefight?" she asked.

"We can certainly bloody their nose," Master Fabricant said. "If necrovites have blood. It's not supposed to be a warship, just a diplomatic vessel, so it might not be stuffed full of their nasty little Necroglider fighters, but they obviously brought bigger guns than you'd expect. If I were calculating the odds on who'd win, based on my current knowledge... I'd say fifty-fifty."

"I prefer a better bet," Phaera said. "Let's hold off on shooting for the moment. Focus on getting those smaller ships out of the way so the good people of Absalom Station can do their own shooting. And capture those freeloading invaders still at large in my casino."

"About that. The ghost is still at large, but the ghouls are in custody, and... we've just secured the elf vampire," Master Fabricant said. "We're having him dragged into a cell now, so you can question him if you'd like."

"Is that safe?" Melezheun said.

Master Fabricant chuckled. "We have several priests on board because people like to get married when their luck is good, and we also have an array of blessed objects and holy water. You'd be surprised what gamblers try to use as collateral. The creature has been suitably restrained."

"Make contact with the necrovite diplomat," Phaera said. "Maybe she'll want to trade for the rest of her people. Otherwise we can just send all their bits and pieces back."

"I'll do what I can. Sending a request for—oh." The robot swiveled around, unfolding numerous arms tipped in an alarming variety of spikes, spines, claws, nozzles, and other implements of destruction. "We have a visitor."

"I wanted to see the inside of this place anyway," the bone sage Mnephalon said, sitting in the large chair behind Phaera's desk. She was white-skinned and sharp-faced, her eyes bright and glowing faintly blue, her hair long and dark and lank, her garments composed of shredded black lace and bits of gleaming obsidian. She propped high-heeled black boots on the desktop.

"She's not really here," Master Fabricant said. "It's some kind of projection, but I can't tell if it's magical or technological."

"Could be both," the necrovite said brightly. "Often, it's both! Magitech's come a long way." She wiggled her ringed fingers. "So... What did you want to talk to me about... Phaera, is it? Did you want to swap girlboss tips?"

"You sent a team of boarders to invade my vessel," Phaera said.

"Officially, I did no such thing. They were junior diplomats who acted impulsively and without orders, and I'm very cross with them." She mock-scowled ferociously and bared her small, sharp teeth, then relaxed into a mask of placidity. "Off the record, yes, of course. Your vessel is actually capable of causing me some mild inconvenience, and I wanted to take control of it, obviously, but the people I sent were fools, and as I said, I *am* very cross with them. I'm sad to say I don't have the best people on my team—there was some debate, back on Eox, about the wisdom of seizing Absalom Station this way, and my resources are more limited than I'd like. Still, once I'm in charge here, they'll all come around and claim they supported my idea from the beginning. You know how it is; you run a casino. Everybody loves a winner."

"You can't get away with this," Melezheun said. "Absalom Station is the crossroads of the system; we're crucial to the economy of countless worlds. You can't just take us over!"

The necrovite shrugged. "The people we pay to worry about things like that assure me we'll be fine. Nobody really cares who's in charge, as long as commerce keeps flowing, and Absalom Station has remained steadfastly neutral, which means we aren't triggering any nasty treaty provisions. The cowardly attack by your terrorist Ketavan is sufficient pretext for my little maneuver. There might be grumbling from some of the other planets, but we're undead—we're used to everyone hating us and thinking we're terrible. That doesn't really *bother* us, darling."

"So then you won't mind if we send your vampire back to you in pieces?" Phaera asked.

"You'd be saving me a bit of trouble, truthfully. Do you think I let people who fail me live?" The necrovite glanced over at one of the screens and chuckled. "Do you see that?" She pointed a long, bony finger.

Melezheun looked and frowned. The screen showed a scene from the casino floor, people waving their arms as, on a big screen before them, numbers shifted alongside diagrams of Absalom Station—

"They're betting on the outcome of the assault." Phaera sighed. "Of *course* they are. Our systems allow betting on any situation where the outcome is in significant doubt."

Mnephalon took her feet off the desk and rose. "I suppose casino employees are banned from betting. But if I were you, Miss—Melezheun, is it? I'd put all my money down on the success of Operation Magefire. A grandiose name, I know. One of the other sages came up with it. But the outcome isn't *really* in doubt. My troops are swarming all over the station, in far greater numbers than you can imagine. We've seized your weapons batteries, we have control of your life-support systems, we'll have access to the Starstone Reactor soon, we've crippled your comms—"

Melezheun's gauntlet suddenly beeped, and a holographic projection emerged from the nest of lenses without her even accepting the call—which meant it was an emergency override contact from one of her most trusted contacts. That could only be Valentine, Starla, Carn, or—

"Tyrcell!" she shouted as the android's face appeared before her.

"Excuse me," the bone sage said in a voice as cold as cryostasis. "I am not finished speaking."

"Mel!" Tyrcell said, face flickering as the audio broke up: "—my ship, we need to—found a way—pick you—" The signal died. Mel moaned and tried to call them back, to no avail. Then she noticed that the screens in the office, which had just shown so many angles of Operation Magefire, were all suddenly blank.

"Our ship-to-ship comms are being jammed," Master Fabricant said. "That's your doing, necrovite?"

The bone sage's image swiveled back and forth in the chair. "A little trick we picked up from the Order of the Eclipse, yes. I don't like being interrupted. Nothing anyone has to say is as important as anything *I* have to say. I also don't like all the coordinating you're doing with the other ships in the Armada, trying to get them to evacuate. I consider those little ships under my protection too—"

"We weren't trying to get them to evacuate," Phaera said. "We were trying to get them clear so the station could fire on you without endangering them."

"I *told* you, my agents on Absalom Station seized control of their gun batteries, so they can't shoot back even if they want to. The living are so bad at listening."

"You said you'd seized control of the station comms too," Melezheun said.

The necrovite cocked her angular head. "And? So?"

Mel shook her head. "Nothing. Never mind." But she was thinking, *I just got a call from someone on the station. So maybe...*

The bone sage snorted, opened her mouth—and then froze, mouth hanging open. "What? Those foolish, incompetent—"

Mnephalon's projection vanished from the chair, and Master Fabricant said, "Our comms aren't being blocked anymore. Ha. Look at this." The screens came back on at his gesture, and this time, all of them showed the necrovite's flagship, rocked by explosion after explosion as the formidable artillery batteries on Absalom Station bombarded their attacker.

Melezheun tried calling Tyrcell again, and this time, the connection was sharp and clear.

# 11

# A HIDEOUS CONCATENATION OF ALIEN FLESH

**(Carn / 7 AG)**

I'm going to explain that whole calling-up-Melezheun thing when I can, I promise, but first, let's get back to Carn and the horrible infestation at the docks.

Zombies were breaching the walls all over. The kill box made of stacked crates held, at least, and that part of the plan went off without a hitch. There were always tanks of various grades of industrial nastiness tucked away in docks like this, and Carn and the workers had gathered some of the worst of the toxic materials and arrayed them around the interior of the box. Thirty or forty zombies flowed down the chute and into the square pen at the end, and a watchful worker triggered the tanks before the zombies could start climbing out of the box canyon they found themselves trapped in.

Cryogenic gases burst out of two dozen cylinders, spouts arrayed to cover pretty much the whole interior of the holding area, and dozens of the zombies were immediately flash frozen, transformed into silently snarling statues of themselves. Those closer to the center of the horde, blocked from the spray by the bodies of their unluckier comrades in decaying arms, only had the odd limb turned to blue ice, but even that served to slow them down and allow some of the remaining sharpshooters at the top of the wall to pick the survivors off.

Of course, that still left some uncountable number of zombies climbing over the walls farther back and flowing through the breach the behemoth had made.

Carn stood in a loose line with a dozen workers, most of them big bruisers, all armed with makeshift clubs—pry bars, enormous wrenches, and the like. Carn's hammer swung back and forth like a horizontal pendulum, smashing heads and caving in chests and breaking arms. Unfortunately, only the first one did any reliable good—if you smashed a sizable dent into a living person's torso, or made their elbows bend the wrong way, they'd at least slow down a bit, but these zombies didn't feel pain or fear, and they didn't fear being maimed or disfigured. They just kept fighting until their bodies fell apart.

Still, the defenders were holding their own. The fallen undead piled up on the ground, making it harder for the ones behind them to find solid footing. The sharpshooters had fallen back to climb on top of crates close to the hangar bay doors so they could pick off zombies without too much risk of accidentally hitting their allies.

The real problem was the behemoth. Carn was splitting his concentration, half his mind on keeping the undead behemoth pinned to the floor with gravity, the other half on firing concentrated graviton particles at any zombie unlucky enough to stumble within fifteen feet of his mote.

He couldn't immobilize the beast fully. The monster was just too big and too strong, and he'd only succeeded in slowing it down. His head began to throb with the effort. So far, the other workers hadn't broken and run, despite the broken skulls, the gore, the stink, and the chattering, moaning, gibbering chorus of the horde, but if that behemoth got much closer, they would probably flee in terror. Carn wouldn't even blame them.

"I am here, praise Iomedae!" a voice boomed, and Carn risked a glance behind him to see one of the runners they'd sent earlier, hurrying in alongside a fully armored human knight in the white and gold of the Lady of Valor. She held a sword aloft like a flag as she dashed to the front line, where Carn and the other defenders were slowly losing ground. "Let's scatter this rabble!" she shouted, raising her other hand and calling out a prayer.

There was a burst of holy fire, a flash that reduced many of the zombies to charred lumps and caused the rest to flee, scattering in every direction that could plausibly be called *away*, scrambling over one another in a blind panic. Many of them crashed into the behemoth, which, sadly, *wasn't* trying to flee—but it did snarl, snap, claw, and gore the zombies that got in its way, mowing down many of its own allies in the process.

The holy knight began to shine with a golden light and stepped into the gap next to Carn. The ysoki felt a flood of strength and calm fill him, and his simmering fear of these horrible undead creatures ebbed away. *The gods are good for something, after all,* he thought.

"Shall we send the dead back to their graves, my friends?" the lady of Iomedae boomed, and the invigorated workers shook their weapons in the air and surged forward, Carn among them. "Form a wedge!" the champion shouted. "Don't let yourselves get surrounded!"

The defenders weren't exactly trained in small-unit tactics, but many people on the station had taken part in one pitched battle or another in the years after the Gap, and the old-timers demonstrated for the rest. They straggled out into two lines to form a spearhead shape, with Carn and the champion at the front. The fleeing zombies were much easier to cut down from behind—the only hard part was *catching* them while keeping their whole group in some kind of formation. As the champion got closer to the remaining scores of zombies, they became more panicked, some trying to claw their way through the metal bulkheads of the docking bay to get away.

Carn noticed that his fellow defenders slowed down as they got closer to the still-plodding undead behemoth, taking their time smashing zombies to bits. Nobody was eager to clash with that thing directly, apart from the knight. Carn wasn't too keen on the idea himself, but when she looked at him with a wild grin, his spirits were buoyed. It was some kind of holy morale boost, and while Carn wasn't a big fan of being manipulated, even for a good cause, he had to admit, her boon made doing the next thing easier.

"You take out its arms and legs, and I'll go for the head?" the champion said.

"Whatever you say!" Carn called.

She grinned and flicked the hand holding her sword. It rippled, revealing itself to be made of thousands of tiny interlocking plates, which shifted configuration until it ceased to be a sword and became a double-headed axe. Some kind of transformative weapon? Neat.

The behemoth was suddenly directly before them, reaching out with those long, claw-tipped arms, and Carn grunted as he tried to pin them down with gravity, to give the champion a chance. The long arms lowered, slowly, until the claws touched the floor, the beast roaring its outrage all the while.

Then the knight raced up one arm as if she were running up a ramp, her whole body glowing with golden light, axe held aloft. She swung the blade into the monster's skull, right between its metal-coated horns, making it roar and try to rear back. The champion grabbed onto a horn with one hand while she tried to wrest the axe free with the other, but the blade seemed stuck fast.

Carn took advantage of the beast's distraction to duck around its long arms and come at its flank. Up close, he understood why he'd been unable to determine the species of the beast—he could see the places where its various body parts were grafted together, elements of different creatures melded by some horrible mixture of necromancy and biotechnology to create a monstrous undead necrografted chimera. There were chitinous elements of a monstrous insect, the thick fur of some tundra hunter... and were those the scales of an aquatic predator? The bone sages sure were sick weirdos.

Well, whatever the thing was made of, it had knees, and those were always a weak point, so Carn reared back with his hammer and smashed the nearest one as hard as he could. The behemoth listed to one side, howling—that howl would have sent Carn fleeing in mindless terror if he hadn't been still suffused with extra courage from the champion.

He smashed down on one long arm's elbows next (it had three of the joints in each arm, which seemed excessive), making the limb flail and flop about uselessly. The champion, meanwhile, had gotten her axe loose, and she turned it into a long lance, which she shoved deep into one of the thing's empty, glowing eye sockets.

Carn worked his way around the back, smashing the thing's hideous, patchy-furred body with the hammer, until he got to the other side. There he disabled its other leg, leaving it stranded on the floor, roaring, and swinging its one good arm wildly. The other defenders moved in. It seemed they'd put down the rest of the zombies without losing too many people in the process, though everyone looked like they'd rolled around in a pile of guts, and they stank as bad as the zombies did, with the added aroma of animal sweat. With the collective might of the workers raining blows upon it, and the more focused attention of the champion, the behemoth crashed over onto its side.

Cronch and another nuar came over carrying a long loop of heavy wire between them, and Carn got the idea immediately. He helped them get the wire wrapped around the still-snarling skull-faced monster's neck, and then everyone grabbed onto one end of the wire or the other, and they heaved, like a game of tug-of-war, every pull tightening the loop.

It took some work, but the wire finally cut through the thing's flesh and muscle, nearly decapitating it, though they couldn't quite sever the spine. The champion helped with that, though, raising her polymorphous weapon—back to an axe, single-bladed this time—to hack through the bony column until the head rolled free, landing on its side, black fluids oozing slowly from its neck.

She gazed at the mess thoughtfully. "It's got the body of a caypin, I think. Definitely the horns of a crest-eater. These are... the spines of a ksarik? What a hideous concatenation of alien flesh."

While she was doing her anatomy lesson, the dock defenders whooped and danced around and congratulated one another.

All of them except for Carn, who was, instead, counting.

His extra strength and devotion suddenly ebbed away, and in the sudden absence of holy zeal, he felt even more tired than he might have otherwise. He sidled over to the champion. "Hey, thanks for the help. I'm Carn."

"I'm Dania. I haven't fought off a horde of the undead in *years*. That was *bracing*!" She kicked the behemoth in the side. "And how about this monstrosity? The blighters on Eox are inventive, you have to give them that—"

"There aren't enough zombies here," Carn interrupted. "Sorry. We did great, for sure, but... there are a couple hundred zombies here, tops. There were more like a thousand crates in the warehouse, though, and even if there was only one zombie to a crate, which there wasn't, this is just like... a fraction."

Dania didn't seem bothered by this revelation. She just hefted her sword (it was a sword again) and said, "Then let's go kick their crates open and slay what we find inside! Port defenders! To me!"

She rushed for the torn-open hangar door, and Carn followed with the others. None of them seemed as thrilled about more fighting as Dania was, but then, none of them had signed up to be champions.

Cronch fell into step beside Carn. "I want a bath and a drink," the nuar lowed. "Now we have to fight *more* of them?"

"Looks that way, pal," Carn said. "I don't know why so many of them are hanging around in their crates, though. Maybe whatever spell was supposed to wake them up misfired?"

The champion strode through the warehouse, kicking at piles of broken-open crates, prodding wreckage with her lance (When had it become a lance?), and shaking her head, pinned-back golden hair flicking peevishly back and forth. "There's nothing here!" she shouted, at what seemed her one singular volume. "All empty! Where did the filthy things go?"

"Uh-oh." Carn looked around, stuck his finger in his ear, twiddled it around thoughtfully, and then walked toward the back of the warehouse. He had a pretty good sense of direction and a solid mental map of the station. They were in one of the Arms, the radiating protrusions that extended away from the central station, with all the docks and hangars, plus businesses that provided the kind of, ah, *basic* entertainment that long-haul spacers most enjoyed. They were over on the Fardock side of the station—though not *that* far out on the edge of things, sorta halfway down—in a prime location for docking cargo ships.

But it wasn't like the Arms were isolated from the rest of the station. The Arms connected to the Ring, a network of passageways and corridors that ran all the way around Absalom Station and connected the docks to the central bulk of the habitat. The Ring was one of the most heavily populated areas on the whole station. It wasn't the poverty and slums of the Spike way down below, and it wasn't the hoity-toity luxury apartments in the Eye: The Ring was where most of your everyday, average denizens of Absalom Station lived in comfortable, low-key neighborhoods.

Carn headed for the bulkhead wall in the back of the warehouse, Cronch following him. "Oh, gods," Cronch said, and Carn nodded. They could use some gods, that was for sure.

There was a hole cut in the bulkhead, with multiple welding rigs discarded off to one side. It was a *big* hole, as wide and tall as the cargo door they'd come through... big enough to admit things the size of that stitched-together behemoth, say. "How can zombies use a *welding torch*?" Cronch demanded.

"Must have been some smarter undead tucked away in a few of those crates," Carn said. "Lieutenants, you know, to boss the rest around."

Dania joined them, raising a hand aloft and shining a holy light into the darkness beyond the hole in the wall. "Where does this lead?"

Carn shook his head. "Where *doesn't* it lead? It looks like they cut their way into a service corridor. From there, they can get into the Ring, and after that... they can go anywhere they like. Or everywhere, most likely. They probably split up their forces. They sent us just enough zombies to keep us busy and distracted while they escaped into the station. Now..."

"Now we have rats in the walls," Dania said, then glanced at Carn and winced. "Ah. Sorry. I didn't mean... you know."

Carn shrugged. Some ysoki got upset when people compared them to rats, but he, personally, had a lot of respect for rats. They were clever, and they could survive just about anywhere. "Can you call your champion and priest pals and warn them, send them to help people?"

She shook her head. "The comms are down everywhere, I'm afraid. Your runner just happened to stumble across me in a corridor."

"I meant more of, I dunno, some kind of mystical message? Send them a divine vision or whatever?"

"Alas, my skills are more martial in nature," Dania said.

"Oh, well. It was worth asking." He turned to the assembled dockworkers, who were standing around, filthy and tired, apparently waiting for someone to tell them what to do next. "I'm going to follow this trail here and try to kill anything already dead that I find. Anybody want to come with me?"

"*Want* to?" Cronch said. "Nope. But if there are zombies running around in the Ring? Then *want* doesn't have much to do with it. I'm with you."

Some of the others agreed, though a few said they had to go check on their families, and Carn could respect that. They ended up with about ten people in their party, counting Dania, who couldn't help herself from taking the lead—that was champions for you, though. Carn was happy to follow along just behind her. She was the one with the proper undead-fighting skillset, after all. He just knew how to hit stuff with a hammer. Fortunately, that worked on zombies about as well as it had on everything else so far.

"So what do you think the point of all this is?" Carn said. "Releasing a bunch of zombies in the station? It doesn't seem very organized. Or strategic. You know?"

"If it's an attack from Eox, then everything is meant to confuse and demoralize the population, sow chaos, and keep the station's defenders occupied with skirmishes in the corridors," Dania said. "The bone sages will also be attacking on other fronts—trying to seize control of infrastructure and our defenses and likely mounting an assault from ships in orbit too."

"So the zombies are just a distraction?" Carn said.

"Strategically, yes, but... saving the lives of innocent people is never a distraction, is it?"

"It's not," Carn agreed.

They reached a branching corridor in the service tunnels, and Dania paused.

"Can you tell which way they went?" Carn asked.

"I can sense undead if I'm close enough, and... they went in *both* directions," she said. "I'm afraid you were right: They split up. With so few of us, I don't want to split the party, so we'll have to pick one."

"That one," Carn said, pointing left. "It leads to a more populated sector."

"Good enough," Dania said, and led on.

In truth, either direction led to equally populous areas. But heading left would take them toward the Lorespire Complex. The Society was there. All Carn's nearest and dearest friends lived there. If he couldn't save everybody, he could at least try to save *them*. Maybe that wasn't the most perfectly and ethically pure way to decide, but ethics were better suited to situations where undead monsters weren't trying to eat your friends.

Pretty soon they heard screaming, and the defenders broke into a run. It didn't take long before they reached one of the residential sectors of the station, where people raised their families in cozy homes and went about the mundane business of their private lives. This was a neighborhood with apartments made of stacked shipping containers welded together into jaunty piles like children's blocks—a clever way to convert old warehouse space into habitations for the ever-expanding population of the station. The long, rectangular houses were painted cheerful colors, with windows cut in the sides and flowers in pots outside, and there was even a little park in a courtyard surrounded by the angled containers, with a patch of scraggly grass and a play structure for the little ones, including swings and a chain ladder up to a plastic slide. Cheerful chalk drawings covered a concrete slab marked for harkolo, a sort of psychic ball game lashunta children often played.

The neighborhood was under siege by zombies. As Carn and his people arrived, terrified parents were pulling their children into the containers and slamming the doors as zombies stumbled and lurched toward their dwellings, a few dozen undead already pounding on the walls and tearing at window shutters. The champion held up a hand to bring their group to a halt and considered the scene before the ravening undead noted their presence.

"This place has no strategic value," a dragonkin dock defender muttered. "Crippling the ports, I get that, but why are they *here*?"

"To demoralize the populace," the champion said. "This is the work of bone sages, all right. They use this tactic when they want to subjugate a habitat. It doesn't take long before the locals agree that it would be better to have the zombies working with them, instead of trying to eat them." She flicked her wrist, and her sword reoriented itself into a warhammer. Dania winked at Carn, who still held his own hammer, and he blinked at her. Was this champion flirting with him? She couldn't be. She just liked his style of devastation, probably.

"There are about thirty of them—that's only three zombies apiece. Shall we save these nice people?"

Without waiting for an answer, Dania rushed toward a zombie trying to tear a bright yellow door out of a wall. This one was an ikeshti—lizardfolk, some called them, though Carn figured that was like the people who called ysoki ratfolk, so, maybe not so nice. Its tail and neck frill were mostly rotted away, and there were strange bulges all over its back, like there were mechanical implants under there.

Carn went down a mechanical turn of mind, because he'd seen a whole lot of booby traps in the bad old days on the station, and he had a sudden, terrible intuition. "Dania, no!" he shouted, just as the champion raised her hammer to smash the ikeshti across its knobby back.

Carn lifted his hands and exerted his personal gravity to shove Dania roughly away from the zombie before she could land a blow. His gravity slammed into her hard, though, making her hammer fly out of her hand and collide with the zombie—

There was a blinding white flash as the explosives embedded in the zombie's body went off, and a pressure wave rocked Carn back on his heels but didn't topple him. As he stumbled forward, ears twitching and ringing, he thought, *It wasn't a big payload, it wasn't meant to do structural damage, just to tear off the arms and legs of anyone who happened to be close by—*

In this case, that was mostly other zombies, and there were rotting limbs scattered across the courtyard. The houses were mostly unharmed—they were made from sturdy containers that got loaded on and off freighters all over the system, piled up in stacks that rose hundreds of feet high, and thus made to withstand a lot of punishment. The dwelling the ikeshti had been closest to was streaked with soot and sported a huge dent that would take some time to hammer out again, but Carn thought the inhabitants were probably OK. The zombies who hadn't been blown to bits were disoriented, bumping into each other and into walls and crawling on the ground.

"*—bombs in them?*" Cronch was shouting into Carn's ear. "How are we supposed to hit them if there are *bombs* in them?"

"Real carefully," Carn said, hurrying toward Dania, who was getting to her feet by the playground and scowling. "The explosives were sewn into that zombie pretty crudely, so I could see the bulges and the stitches. Keep an eye out for that sort of thing, I guess?"

Carn offered a hand to Dania, who shook her head, and he thought she was furious with him—but then she grabbed him in her powerful arms and lifted him off his feet. "You saved my life, Carn," she shouted into his ear—maybe because she was deafened by the blast, but probably because she was just a shouty person. "I would have lost my *head* if I'd whacked that bomb." She set him down, then went to fetch her weapon, cast off on the floor. The explosion had reverted it to factory settings, apparently, and it looked like a thick broom handle more than anything else. "These monsters are *crafty*!" she boomed to the defenders. "Keep your eyes open for nasty surprises and proceed with care and protect each other! Be like Carn!" She spun the staff around in her hands, and it shifted smoothly into an elegant spear. Dania planted her feet, twisted her hips, and hurled the weapon at the nearest zombies, who were beginning to regroup.

Her javelin went through one's eye, out the back of its head, and right through the ear of another zombie, and they both collapsed in a heap. Dania ran forward, roaring, arms outstretched and glowing with golden light, then seized a human zombie by the face, hideous smoke streaming out from beneath her burning hands.

"You gotta appreciate someone who loves her work that much," Carn observed, and Cronch nodded.

"I have never been too excited about checking shipping manifests, myself," the nuar said. "But I can see what she likes about her job. I wouldn't want to do it, but I get it."

"Should we help her out?" Carn asked.

"If we hurry, there might be a couple of zombies left for us," Cronch allowed, and hefted his pry bar.

*Oh, there's plenty of zombies left,* Carn thought, pausing to listen to distant explosions and screams that were growing closer.

# 12

## A HURTFUL REUNION
### (326 AG)

The *Venture* dropped out of the Drift and plotted an oblique course to the Thousand Moons. It's never a smooth ride through that dense field of clustered shrapnel, which comprises over a thousand objects ranging in size from boulder to moon. These remnants, left by some ancient destruction, formed a ring around the planet Eox that was visible from the surface, an array of detritus big enough to seem sort of like the Diaspora in miniature.

"Do sarcesians live here?" Dae asked. "I know they're all over the Diaspora."

"A few do," Tyrcell said. "More of them certainly would if the bone sages didn't chase them off. The necrovites really don't like people messing around in here."

*"There was an assault launched against Eox from here, wasn't there?"* Chk Chk said. *"Three hundred or so years ago."*

Ty nodded. "That's what the histories say."

"All these rocks used to be part of planet Eox?" Dae peered at the viewscreen, watching as immense asteroids drifted by and Tyrcell threaded a passage through them.

"That's the theory," Tyrcell said. "There was some horrible cataclysmic war, long before the Gap. That's why there's a crater the size of a continent on Eox, and why the whole planet is incapable of supporting actual life—the surface was scoured, irradiated, and the atmosphere burned. Bits and pieces of the planet got flung into space during the conflict. Every necrovite who looks at the sky and sees the glittering arc of the Thousand Moons is reminded of the violence in their distant past." The android went silent, obviously contemplating their own violent past.

*"And the attack on Eox?"* Chk Chk said. *"It was revenge for the Magefire Assault, correct?"*

"It happened *during* the Magefire Assault," Tyrcell retorted. "And it wasn't about retribution. The attack wasn't supposed to happen at all..." They trailed off.

*"You were there, weren't you?"* Chk Chk said. *"That story you were telling us about the assault on Absalom Station, it ends with you coming here, doesn't it? That's why you've seemed so troubled and distracted about returning."*

"Me, troubled and distracted? Androids are famously impassive. I'm sure I didn't seem troubled or distracted at all." Tyrcell pressed the heels of their hands to their eyes and made a sound best transliterated as *gragh*. Then they looked back at the others. "OK, yes. There's a trap out here in this asteroid field—a planet-killing trap. As far as I know, that trap is still active because there's probably no way to disable it without triggering it, so the bone sages don't dare try. They have taken steps to seal up the control center they know about, though, and there are obviously sensors in place to detect intruders and disturbances—which is why we got scanned. I just didn't expect sensors scanning that far into the outskirts. You don't get to be an immortal mage without being pretty paranoid, though."

*"When you say 'trap,'"* Chk Chk said. *"What does that mean, exactly?"*

Tyrcell waved at the viewscreen. "All these rocks floating up here in space? On a magical level, they still remember that they're part of Eox. They can be 'encouraged,' with the right combination of technology and magic, to *return* to Eox. At tremendous velocity. All at once."

*"A planetary bombardment on a massive scale."* Chk Chk made an appreciative click-whistle.

"Oh, wow, it would turn that whole planet into chunks!" Dae said. "Flying... chunks!"

"Yeah." The normally chatty Tyrcell lapsed yet again into silence.

*"Who created this dreadful weapon?"* Chk Chk asked.

The android shrugged. "Sarcesians are the best bet—they aren't the greatest fans of the bone sages. Eox is a cruddy home world by most accounts, but at least it's home, and sarcesians don't even have that much anymore. A lot of them believe they're descended from the ancestral enemies of the elebrians, who are the original people that lived on Eox before they all turned undead, and that the war that devastated Eox was the one that completely destroyed their home planets of Damiar and Iovo, creating the Diaspora asteroid belt."

"I thought Damiar and Iovo smashed into each other a long time ago," Dae said, banging their fists together and making noises that were probably supposed to approximate the sound of colliding planetary bodies, though they mostly just sounded like *boosh*.

Ty shrugged. "Nobody knows for sure what happened, since the disaster took place before the Gap, and so many records were lost. But one theory goes that the elebrians are the ones who *made* those planets smash together. Anyway, yeah, most likely sometime before the Gap, sarcesian rebels slipped into the Thousand Moons and built this weapon so they could strike back against Eox, but it was never set off. Nobody knows why—maybe they made a peace treaty, maybe somebody got cold feet about committing genocide, maybe they were planning to fill the rocks with murderous killbots before flinging them down at Eox. Who can say? But the trap just sat out here, for who knows how long, waiting."

*"Until it was triggered during the Magefire Assault,"* Chk Chk said. *"And yet Eox is still here. Did the trap fail?"*

"It's not that the trap failed—" Tyrcell began, and then the console started beeping. The android swiveled their chair around to consult the controls. "Huh. We're getting a distress signal from a ship, and it's right on our route. *Exactly* on our route."

*"You think it is a trap?"* Chk Chk said.

"This is the place for traps," Tyrcell observed. "Hold on, there's an incoming signal—"

The viewscreen briefly blanked, then returned to show a ghoul wearing a shiny blue uniform with a high collar. Chk Chk could find beauty even in horrible things, but this ghoul was simply... *lopsided*, with an embedded exocortex bulging out the back of his head, all gleaming metal and blinking lights. "Thank all the gods and their blessed saints," the ghoul said, clutching his clawed hands together in front of his chest. "It's the brave and noble android Tyrcell, hero of the Magefire Assault! We're saved from certain death!"

"I'm afraid you've mistaken me for someone else," Tyrcell said. "Totally understandable. But my name is Bentley—"

"And yet you are on Tyrcell's ship, the *Venture*," the ghoul said. "We compared your specs to a scan taken by one of our vessels only three hundred years ago, so it's nice and fresh by our standards. And your face certainly matches the images in our dossier." A dozen still images of Tyrcell flashed up on the screen, most of them grainy and off center, as if they were ancient screen grabs from surveillance systems—which they probably were.

"Yeah, I get it," Tyrcell said. "This happens to me all the time. But I'm an android. You know how mortality works with us, right? When an android body is created, it attracts a soul, and that consciousness inhabits the body for a time. When an android dies, the *body* doesn't die—the soul just moves on, and then a new soul moves in." They spread their hands. "This body used to belong to Tyrcell, but they moved on, oh, a century ago, and my soul moved in. I'm Bentley, like I said. Pleased to meet you. Tyrcell was nice enough to leave their starship and a few other things for me to inherit, which is customary among androids, but I can assure you, we're not the same person." They chuckled. "Believe me, it's a situation I've had to explain to more debt collectors than I'd care to remember. How did you know Tyrcell?"

The ghoul frowned, and something—a humanoid figure, but shifting and luminous—briefly entered the frame. The ghoul spoke, but he had muted the signal so there was no sound—the body language and expression made it clear some kind of argument was happening, though. The ghoul turned back to the screen and unmuted. "My name is Groth. And if you're telling the truth, Bentley, I am *very* sorry, but the sins of your parent have caught up with you."

"Hmm, the term *parent* isn't exactly right, it's more like... there's a kind of crustacean in the aquarium on Absalom Station that doesn't have a shell of its own, so it crawls into the shells of dead creatures it finds, or sometimes it will even use a discarded food container for a shell... But anyway, that's not important. I thought you were in distress? You sent a distress signal?"

The ghoul glared at something offscreen. "My associate thought we could lure you onto our ship, since Tyrcell is a notorious do-gooder, but I told her it would be an obvious trap that you'd never fall for, which didn't stop her from setting off the distress beacon anyway."

"If you need to take a step back and workshop your plan, that's fine," Tyrcell said. "We're just passing through on our way to explore a ruin on Triaxus—"

"You are the fugitive criminal, Tyrcell!" the ghoul roared. "Or perhaps merely the body of Tyrcell, but our lady will want to investigate that personally, and once she reaches her fingers right into your mind, she'll find the truth in an instant."

"Your lady," Tyrcell said flatly. "Who might that be?"

The insubstantial figure floated into the frame again, roughly humanoid, translucent, and luminous: a ghost. "Alcyone, you're passing through my arm; you know I hate it when you occupy the same space as me," the ghoul complained, but the ghost paid no attention.

"Our lady is the great bone sage Mnephalon, a deputy admiral of the Corpse Fleet, and she has tasked us to bring you to her alive, so that she may minutely examine your every entrail and flay your mind while you lie screaming—"

"Got it, so that means you're not allowed to kill me," Tyrcell said. "That's all I needed to know. Goodbye." They snapped off the comms, shut off the interior and exterior lights, and then shoved a lever that caused the whole ship to hum at a frequency that made Chk Chk's mandibles vibrate.

"Bentley?" Dae said.

"It's an alias I use sometimes. That stuff about soul migration really is how androids work, so it's totally plausible, and it's gotten me out of some unpleasant reunions over the years more or less unscathed. Crap-crap-crap." Tyrcell banged a fist down on the console. "And crap again. This was going to be tricky enough without the attention of a necrovite who once told me she was going to turn me into a charcuterie board for ghouls."

"*We are already defying the gods in our pursuit of knowledge,*" Chk Chk said. "*We knew the way would not be easy.*"

"I was hoping it would be!" Tyrcell said. "Why can't *anything* be easy? OK. I've engaged *Venture*'s cloaking system, which is very good—tippy-top-of-the-line. We're not far from the coordinates for Yaraesa's next happy-fun dungeon. If we can get there, get in, and get out before Alcyone and Groth detect us, then maybe I can avoid a reunion with their lady—"

"You didn't miss me?" Mnephalon said, stepping through the dark viewscreen to perch on the edge of the console.

Tyrcell leaped out of the pilot's chair and fell backward onto the deck, and Chk Chk and Dae scrambled away too.

The bone sage snapped her fingers, and the lights on the bridge came back on. She was dressed in a sleek midnight-blue uniform like Groth's, though with a lot more silver accents, accompanied by a flat cap with a short brim that wouldn't have fit over the ghoul's exocortex. Her lips—or the part of her face where her lips should have been—were painted a vivid purple, bright against her white skin and the glimpses of bone that showed through beneath her burning blue eyes.

*She is beautiful and terrible,* Chk Chk thought, and almost against his will, he began to imagine an installation that could convey the same effect as being in the presence of a necrovite—or even her psychic projection. There would have to be fire, of course, but also an area of extreme frigid cold, and that new black metamaterial that actually bent light in its vicinity, and—

"It's been three hundred years since I saw this ship," Mnephalon said, "and it's *still* a piece of garbage." She cocked her head and giggled. "You're Tyrcell, all right. I can smell the shape of your mind."

"Why are you here?" Tyrcell said. "On that ship? This close to Eox? You're Corpse Fleet, you're a renegade—"

She chuckled. "The rulers of Eox aren't as opposed to the Corpse Fleet as they'd like everyone to believe. Not all of them, anyway. But, no, I'm not on the *Scaphism*. I'm quite far away, actually. I've just gotten much, much stronger in the centuries since your friend saw me last. I told you I was like a god then, Ty, but I had no *idea* how strong I could become. Projecting myself across this distance is trivial for me now. I have duties to attend to and a whole fleet of ships under my personal command, but I sent a few of my most trusted puppets—I mean, lieutenants—to bring you back to me."

"Alcyone," Tyrcell said. "I remember that name. That's the commander you axed because the Magefire Assault didn't go your way, the one you said was obsessed with you!"

"She still is. It's tiresome. But she's loyal to me, and personal loyalty is a rare and precious thing. They're coming for you, Tyrcell. But"—she tapped her chin with one black fingernail—"your little bug friend there said you were 'defying the gods'? I'm intrigued. What exactly are you doing out here? I assumed you'd come to finish the job of destroying Eox, but it's something else, isn't it?"

"Nothing I'm going to tell you about," Tyrcell said.

"Hmm. Androids are a *tiny bit* harder than most people to pry secrets out of. But I bet your little friends know your secrets too."

Chk Chk had been watching her with fascination and horror—Dae just with horror—but the pahtra suddenly arched their back and stood on their tiptoes, as if being lifted off the ground by wires. They threw their head back and gasped, and their eyes rolled, showing the whites. Chk Chk rushed to his friend's side, but Dae seemed entirely unaware of his existence.

"Leave Dae alone!" Tyrcell shouted.

"Oh, it looks very dramatic, I know, and I don't *have* to paralyze the pahtra and rack them with spasms," Mnephalon said. "It's just more entertaining that way. Hmm, oh, interesting, the secret of lost Golarion, hidden away by Yaraesa—that's a tedious deity if I've ever heard of one, so focused on individual excellence when the best use of any individual is to become an extension of *my* will. Ah, Tyrcell, you navigated a dungeon full of puzzles that any half-bright student could have overcome with ease, only to find, ha, a bread crumb that might, if you're lucky, lead you to *another* bread crumb, and it took you centuries to even get *that* far?" Mnephalon flicked her fingers, and Dae collapsed, moaning, to the deck.

The bone sage slid off the console and stood almost nose to nose with the android. "Ty! This is almost interesting. Do you know what? I'm going to let you and your little crew skip along to this mysterious asteroid to see if you can find Yaraesa's next no-doubt-baffling missive. I saw in your friend's memories that the last time you went into one of these temples, you were pursued by Hellknights, and I can't help but think that added stress spurred you to even greater feats of mental and physical accomplishment. Since I care *deeply* about your betterment, I'm going to send my friends—the ghoul, the ghost, and a special someone you'll be *so* excited to meet—to chase after you this time, so you won't find the experience too dull and unchallenging. Then, when you're done, I'll take whatever you've found for myself." She clapped her hands. "This will be so fun!"

The necrovite vanished, and Tyrcell immediately went to Dae, who was sitting upright and sipping from a bulb of water held out by Chk Chk. "Are you OK?"

"That felt like fingers in my *brain*," Dae said. "Just rifling through..." The pahtra winced. "I'm sorry, Tyrcell. I didn't mean to give up secrets. She just *took* them."

"It's all right," Tyrcell said. "Honestly, if Mnephalon hadn't found out what we were doing, we'd have a ghost and a ghoul dragging us all off to the meet the Corpse Fleet immediately. At least this has bought us a little time."

*"She might have dragged* you *away,"* Chk Chk said. *"Why would she have any interest in me or Dae?"*

Tyrcell shook their head. "If she thinks snatching up the two of you would hurt me, she'd do it."

"Why does she hate you so much, anyway?" Dae asked.

The android looked down at the scuffed deck of the *Venture*. "Because three hundred years ago, she dismissed me as irrelevant, and let me go... and as a result, I ruined all her plans." Ty looked up, and though android eyes didn't flicker with arcane fire like a necrovite's, theirs nevertheless seemed ablaze. "Let's ruin her plans this time too."

# 13

## COMMON ENEMIES

(Tyrcell / 7 AG)

OK, so, about me calling Mel on the *Offshoot of Design*. Here's how that happened.

Ketavan and I had crept out of the maintenance hatch into the corridor. The plan was to make our way through the Eye to Saphenath's office, where Ketavan could hide, and then I could go on to the executive offices of the Primex to share what I'd learned. Like all my plans, it almost immediately exploded into shrapnel.

The very first corner we turned, we ran into three ghouls playing tug-of-war with the corpse of a Bluerise corporate-security goon. One ghoul gripped him by the head, and the other two clutched one leg each. As far I could tell, they were trying to tear his head and limbs from his body like kids pulling apart a wishbone after Reunion dinner.

The ghouls looked at us and dropped the corpse, the head bouncing off the ground. One of the ghouls was wearing some random bits of body armor that had probably been stolen from its victims, including a chestplate that barely fit around its huge barrel chest. I drew my lethal sidearm—the one that spits blobs of metal, superheated until it's practically plasma—and aimed for the big ghoul's head. But the moving target, combined with a stench that was so strong it was basically giving me mental damage, messed up my aim, and I just grazed a hulking shoulder instead, which had the result of making the thing *angry*. The ghoul held up long-clawed hands and bared its teeth in a mouth big enough to snap off the top of my head, then charged at me.

I did the obvious thing, which is to say, I ran away. We were in a corridor not far from an entrance to Jatembe Park, and I wanted to get to a place where I had more room to maneuver—and where that stink wouldn't be quite so concentrated by confined quarters.

I confess I completely forgot about Ketavan, and I have no excuse, except that, really, that *smell*—you can't imagine, it was like sewage backing up into an overstuffed morgue where the air conditioning was broken, and I had to get away from it. Fortunately, Ketavan was similarly affected, and he ran in the same direction I did, and he soon caught up with me—for an old guy, he was fairly spry, but being pursued by two ghouls and a superghoul tends to light a fire under you.

"We—must—fight—" Ketavan gasped, clutching at my arm.

"No, we must run!"

We rounded a corner and burst into the park, and I realized we were running from mere danger and into total doom.

The park was a war zone. Hazy palls of smoke drifted across the ravaged landscape. Trees and bushes burned. Groups of staff-wielding priests and gun-toting champions faced off against hordes of skeletons and zombies. Among the fighting dead were people who'd been priests and champions not long before—there must have been a necromancer around somewhere, turning our fallen troops into their undead ones.

Worst of all, from a psychological standpoint, was the dome—it held that bone sage's leering face, and she was laughing and telling the defenders they were doomed. "There is no hope. Lay down your arms and welcome the embrace of undeath. Join your new siblings in eternal fellowship!" Her smooth, melodious voice spoke in a chant-like cadence, and I could feel my own will to flee ebbing away. What was the point? We were fighting death itself, and *nothing* can stand against death—even androids die eventually.

"Don't listen!" Ketavan shook me hard and maybe used some of his own holy power on me, because my mind suddenly cleared, and I was able to shake off the clinging ennui her voice wove around my senses. "She's trying to get inside your head! All of our heads!"

"It looks like ra-a-in," Mnephalon singsonged, putting her face close to whatever camera or magic crystal she was using to project her image onto the dome so her ghastly, gorgeous features filled the sky like the face of a cruel and mirthful god. Black droplets began to spatter down on the troops, but the dark rain only fell on the champions and priests, making their armor smoke and eating right through their robes, and the priests screamed and tore at their clothes.

"What *is* that?" I asked, gaping.

"Negative energy," Ketavan said. "Void rain."

The priests managed to erect magical shields over their heads, but the tide had turned, and the zombies, skeletons, and smarter undead were pressing their advantage.

"Got you," a guttural voice roared behind me, and I spun around, reminded quite unpleasantly that we'd been running away from something. The superghoul was there, flanked by two more ghouls, and there was nowhere to retreat except into the melee of champions and zombies—

*"Forward!"* a voice boomed, unnaturally loud. Everyone, living and undead alike, swiveled to see who'd called such a thunderous command.

A phalanx of armed and armored Hellknights marched into the park in a clamor of chains: rank upon rank, spiked armor gleaming, cruel weapons thrust high, all proceeding in perfect order, approaching the back of the zombie horde. My old unfriendly acquaintance Mikiel was at the head, holding a shock lance even longer than he was tall. He lowered the tip, pointing toward the zombie horde. *"Charge!"* he shouted, and the Hellknights did as they were told, breaking into a trot that moved very fast, considering the heavy plate armor burdening them.

Mikiel caught a zombie in the back with his lance and flung it into the air, where it flew in an arc and got snagged in the branches of a burning tree. Then it was tactical butchery as the Hellknights battered the zombies into charnel leavings.

I almost wanted to cheer for them. I gladly took advantage of the distraction they provided to draw my pistol and fire again, this time sending a plasma bolt right through the superghoul's left eye and out the back of its head. It smelled even worse when it crumpled into final death. I should've turned off my olfactory input.

The ghouls were not, unfortunately, demoralized, and they came at me, claws and jaws scrabbling for any part of me they could grab. I did *not* enjoy the sensation of being someone's idea of an appetizer. I tried to dance nimbly away. Unfortunately, Ketavan had the same idea— he retreated clumsily into me, and we fell into a messy tangled heap.

The ghouls stood over us, drool dripping from their mouths as they doubtless imagined the taste of our entrails. I lifted my sidearm and one of them kicked my hand, sending my weapon spinning away. That was not good.

Then both the ghouls' heads exploded, showering me and Ketavan with foulness, and their headless bodies fell over. An imposing figure in gleaming armor stepped forward and grinned down at us, an arc rifle resting casually against his shoulder.

"You've got bits of ghoul in your mustache, Mikiel," I croaked at him, and then I got to my feet, helping Ketavan up once I'd accomplished it myself.

The Hellknight leader flicked the filth off his face with an absent-minded gesture. "One of the perils of war. I was just fighting a skeletal battalion over there and couldn't help but notice you were in a spot of trouble. I hope you don't mind that I intervened."

"I can forgive you this once."

"What brings you to an active battlefield, Tyrcell?" Mikiel raised one bushy eyebrow. "And in the company of Absalom Station's most wanted?"

"Listen, it's a frame-up," I said, before Ketavan could start ranting about something or other.

"Obviously," Mikiel said. "I've heard of Ketavan. A rabble-rouser, and thus not one of my favorite people, but I know he's not capable of orchestrating coordinated terrorist attacks."

"I could if I wanted to," Ketavan muttered, though quietly, by his standards.

"I'm trying to get him to my friend Saphenath, she runs a news site—"

"I know *her* too," Mikiel said, frowning. "Our friend Astrachios wanted to bomb her offices because she spreads disruptive propaganda."

"That sounds like him," I observed.

"I do quite like their amusing cartoons, though," Mikiel mused. "And the theater reviews are top notch. Do you enjoy musical theater, Tyrcell?"

"Is this, ah, really the place for this conversation? Or the time?" I gestured at the battle—which had seemingly turned a bit in our favor, with the help of the Hellknights—and the leering necrovite face on the ceiling. "Mnephalon hasn't noticed our friend here yet, but..."

"Indeed." He turned, cupped his hands over his mouth, and shouted, "Calcedony! Take command! I have an urgent mission I must attend to." Mikiel turned back to us. "All right, come on, I'll escort you to the offices of Saphenath's libelous media empire."

"What? Why?"

"Because I am sworn to protect safety and order on this station," Mikiel said. "And you, running around with the putative cause of this invasion, are the very definition of *disorder*. I need to see you both squared away, and I'm not letting you out of my sight in the meantime. There's no telling what damage you'd cause. Besides, protecting *you* demonstrates how impartial and honest the Hellknights are these days, under my capable leadership."

"I disagree with your assessment but gratefully accept your protection," I said as an explosion flung zombie parts in all directions not fifty feet away from us.

"Very wise." Mikiel clamped one gauntleted hand over Ketavan's shoulder, making him wince. "Let's take the long way around rather than strolling straight through the battlefield like you'd planned, eh?"

We looped around the edge of the park, approaching Saphenath's offices more indirectly, scurrying down side halls and cutting through back alleys. It wasn't like we encountered zero resistance, but it was mostly skeletal minions armed with melee weapons, no really intelligent enemies. I'd retrieved my sidearm, Mikiel had weapons aplenty, and Ketavan, it turned out, could still smite the undead with flashes of holy light and healing spells if necessary, so we got through without more than scratches.

"I admit, I wondered if maybe the Hellknights would side with Eox," I said as we walked down a deserted corridor past shops locked up with bars and force fields.

"Why would we do that?" Mikiel asked.

"Well, you all like order, and Eox is *very* orderly—like, their leaders don't even ever die, so their society is totally static and unchanging."

"Mmm. There are significant doctrinal differences between our respective worldviews that I would not expect you to comprehend," Mikiel said. "But quite apart from all that, they've attacked my home, filled the corridors with dirty ravenous undead, and done a great deal of property damage."

"Plus, they killed a bunch of people," I quipped.

"Death is inevitable, but there's no reason for anyone to go around breaking innocent windows," Mikiel said. "The point is, these elebrians brought chaos into my domain, and that cannot be permitted. For the moment, you and I are very much on the same side. I'd recommend you enjoy it before you argue yourself out of a heavily armed escort."

"That's a fair point," I allowed.

"We are all of us on the side of life, standing together against the onslaught of foul abominations—" Ketavan proclaimed, and Mikiel and I said "shut up" simultaneously.

"Why exactly are you harboring the most wanted fugitive on the station?" Mikiel asked.

"Why aren't you taking him into custody?" I shot back.

"I didn't say *I* wanted him," Mikiel said. "Frankly, he seems like a great deal of trouble."

"I am a sword of tribulation unto the undead horrors," Ketavan said, but without much conviction.

"He knows something that could be useful in stopping this assault."

Mikiel kicked down a flimsy barricade of overturned benches and scrap metal someone had erected in the middle of an abandoned arcade, peeked through to make sure no one had set an ambush, then waved us ahead. "Stop being coy, Tyrcell. We're no longer enemies. Just tell me."

He had a point; everyone on Absalom Station had a common enemy, for once. It was a strange change from our old state of civil war and gangland conflict, and even the more recent political bickering and backbiting. "Ketavan has made destroying Eox his entire personality, and he found out about an ancient installation in the Thousand Moons, a dormant weapon system that can destroy their entire planet."

"Once we annihilate the grave world, the galaxy will be cleansed of their foul—"

"War crimes, Tyrcell?" Mikiel said. "That doesn't sound like you. Anyway, if you actually succeeded in destroying Eox, the remnant of their society laying siege to the station would hardly be motivated to spare us."

"Yes, Mikiel, I know, give me a little credit. But if we can get control of the weapon system and threaten the bone sages, we can tell them to back off or we'll unleash Hell. The bad kind of Hell. Not the good kind that you like."

"That could work," Mikiel mused. "Mutually assured destruction is as good as a strategic alliance, assuming rational actors on both sides, and say what you will about necrovites, they tend to be rational. They are entirely without morals, of course, but they don't often act impulsively."

"No!" Ketavan said. "I've spent years tracking down this information! We must use it to destroy all the necrovites and their foul empire, not merely threaten them!"

"We have to save Absalom Station," I countered. "That's our first priority. Your crusade comes second. Or third." Or never, by my count.

Ketavan scowled, fury radiating from beneath beetled eyebrows, and I could see how he'd attracted a following of malcontents and bigots; he did have a certain intensity about him. "Fine," he grated out. "But my crusade will not be forgotten."

"The whole plan is ridiculous, of course," Mikiel said. "You'd have to get off the station in a ship, escape the Eoxian blockade, fly to the Thousand Moons, and find this mysterious weapons installation, which may not even exist..." He shook his head. "But it's not as if we have a lot of other options, with the enemy in control of our communications and our station defenses disabled. Did you know the gravity has been turned off in portions of the station? Then ghosts and wraiths float in to seize control. And there are sectors where the life support has been shut down, and skeletal minions—who don't mind a lack of breathable air—have been sent in to take the territory."

I groaned. "No, I hadn't heard."

Mikiel nodded. "I sent a squad of Hellknights down to the Spike to try to retake control of our essential systems, but I have no idea what became of them—I imagine they got distracted fighting zombies on the way. There are undead and phantasmal horrors roaming all over, seemingly on every sector and level, based on the scattered reports I've received. The bone sages must have been planning this assault for a long time, getting resources in place before they sprang the trap. I don't know where they were hiding all these zombies, though. In the Ghost Levels, perhaps? What a frightful lapse of operational security. If we don't all die, I'll have strong words for the Syndicsguild about it."

We turned a corner, and Mikiel pointed to a heavily fortified structure emblazoned with flickering holographic projections that probably once read "The Absalom Advertiser: All the News You Need to Get Ahead," but I could only read "Absalom the New head," and barely that.

"As pledged. Your friend's establishment."

"It looks like they're expecting to hold off a siege!" The windows were barred, the doors were blocked with metal barriers, and there were gun emplacements set up. "Which they are, but why were they ready for that?"

"I told you, Astrachios hated them, and he threatened to send his Order of the Eclipse to silence them all." Mikiel puffed out a breath that made his mustaches fluff. "He was posturing, but they took it seriously—"

The front doors opened, and Saphenath appeared, looking left and right nervously, then gesturing for us to come in. "The head of the Hellknights, the founder of the Society, and Ketavan the Vaticinator, all together on my doorstep?" She shook her head. "War does make for strange relationships."

She took us through the dark and empty lobby, up to a control room filled with consoles and vidscreens that had all gone dark. "What's happening out there?" she asked.

We filled her in as best we could, and I concluded with: "So I need you to take care of Ketavan while I make contact with the Primex so she can negotiate with the necrovite," but Saphenath was shaking her head.

"I just heard from one of my reporters that an undead snatch squad tried to abduct the Primex, led by some horribly scarred vampire. They failed, but the Primex got spooked, and she's retreated with most of the syndics to a heavily fortified bunker in the heart of the station. There's no way to get in there, at least not in a timely fashion."

I swore. "So what do we do? Ketavan has information that could shift the course of this conflict, but..." I trailed off.

Mikiel smiled nastily. "They say if you want something done right..."

I groaned. I looked at Saphenath, who was staring at me with a calculating expression. "Aren't you going to say, 'Tyrcell, you can't go look for this weapon on your own; it's too dangerous?'"

She shrugged. "It is dangerous. So is staying here, waiting to be torn apart by ghouls."

"Yes!" Ketavan said. "We need not appeal to secular authority when we have the inherent authority of righteousness—"

"Just give me the coordinates," I said wearily. "And tell me everything you know about this weapon."

"I know it's a complicated system," Ketavan said. "My source told me it looked like at least three people would be needed to activate the weapon, and even with your plan to frighten the bone sages, you will need to turn on the system to prove you're a real threat." He pressed a hand to his chest. "I will, of course, join you on this sacred mission."

I groaned even harder and looked at Saphenath even more pleadingly. "You heard rumors about this weapon too—that corroboration is the only reason I trusted this old coot at all. Is what he's saying true?"

"It... matches what my source told me," she said. "They said I would have to assemble a team if I hoped to get my hands on the mysterious treasure. Even if Ketavan has the coordinates and the authorization codes... it might require more than one set of hands, yes."

"I don't suppose you want to go with me?"

Saphenath considered the idea, to her credit, but then shook her head. "My people need me here. And the events on this station need to be documented." She paused. "Also, if I'm being honest, you'll probably die, and I don't want to die with you."

"Death in the service of glory is no—" Ketavan lectured, and I shushed him.

"That's fair," I said, and took a deep breath. "So, Mikiel, I know we've had our differences, but I could use—"

"The fighting is here," the Hellknight said. "Here is where I'll stay. Your little gambit is a long shot at best, and frankly, my talents can be put to better use than"—he flapped his hand—"pulling a lever or pushing a button on some remote ancient installation. I'm sure you can find someone eager to flee the station to act as your third set of hands. Take one of them."

"I can't just take some random—" I protested, and then the console behind Saphenath lit up and a babble of voices poured in. Saph spun around and began punching buttons, then whooped.

"The comms are back up! All my reporters are trying to call in at once."

"My knights must have made it to the Spike and vanquished the agents who seized control of the station's systems," Mikiel said.

I thought he was quick to take credit with very little evidence, but this wasn't the time to point out Hellknight arrogance. If the comms were back... "Can you reach the Primex?" I asked Saphenath, feeling a glimmer of hope about off-loading this responsibility onto someone else.

She snorted. "No, Ty, I don't have a direct line into our leader's secret bunker. There are channels I can use to get a message to her, but I doubt those channels are operational right now anyway."

Hell. I always end up having to do things I don't want to do.

But this *did* give me an idea about our third crew member, so I activated the communications device on my wrist. I considered Val, of course, but I assumed she was taking care of things back at the Society, and I figured Carn would be there too, running point on security; between the two of them, I was confident my home and friends were well protected, and I didn't want to distract them from their cause. Mel, though—she was on that casino ship in the Armada trying to shake down the owner for tax money (not Mel's words, but that was the gist). That meant she was already off the station, so I wouldn't have to find her and get her to my ship, just arrange to pick her up. She was completely trustworthy (she went behind my back once and the shame nearly killed her), cool in a crisis, and most importantly, my co–best friend. I called her direct line, and she picked up right away.

"Mel!" I said, delighted to see her face, pinched with worry as it was. "Listen, I'm going to get my ship, and we need to go to the Thousand Moons. You won't believe this, but I think we've found a way to force the bone sages to call off this invasion. I'm going to pick you up—"

The connection broke, even though Saphenath was still receiving messages, and I groaned. "What happened?"

"Overloaded circuits?" Saphenath guessed. "Everyone on the station trying to call everyone else all at once?"

"Speaking of." Mikiel rose. "There's no telling how long our comms will last, so I need to coordinate the Hellknight forces while I can. There's a lot of disorder out there to set right."

I cleared my throat. "Thank you for... you know. Everything. Saving us."

"You'll face judgment eventually," the Hellknight said placidly. "In the meantime, you may yet be of some use to the forces of order."

"It's the first time anyone has ever told me *that*," I said, but he was already leaving. Me and Mikiel were going to be great friends someday, I could just tell. Under that thick layer of fascism, I was sure there was a gooey heart of, well, probably bigotry, but under *that*—

My bracelet pinged with an incoming call, and I hurriedly accepted. "Mel!" I said. "Will you go with me and a somewhat unhinged priest on a field trip to try to save Absalom Station from certain destruction?"

The holographic projection of Melezheun looked at me and blinked, and then she smiled and said, "How could I possibly turn down an invitation like that?"

# 14

## BOTSCRAPPING

### (Valentine / 7 AG)

"I hate that we're going to waste time searching for these sleeper agents," Val said. "It's not like there's one central control room for all the station's infrastructure. We should probably focus on restoring the comms first."

Valentine stopped at a T, looking left down one corridor lined with conduit, then right down a basically identical corridor. Azzi scratched their chin, also looking both ways. They had said they knew the way to a friend in Botscrap, but it turned out, they only knew part of the way.

"We should have interrogated one of Malvus's crew," Val grumbled. "To find out exactly—"

"Please don't mention interrogation," Caspien said.

She winced and looked at Azzi, who didn't meet her eye, then cleared her throat and faced the borai. "Look, about that... the whole... thing we did. I'm sorry, I just... I jumped to a conclusion when I saw you in the park, rushing away after the attack on the cathedral."

"I am a junior accountant in the Bluerise district," Caspien said. "I live in a windowless room, and I work in a windowless room. So on my break, I like to go out into the park, see the trees and the flowers, and feel like my life is more than a series of windowless rooms." His voice crept up in pitch and volume, and he squeezed his hands together. "And I ran away after the attack because there was an *attack* and I was *afraid* of being *attacked*! Then you took me to another windowless room and threatened me—"

"You could have told the authorities about the separatists you met," Val said, but without much conviction.

"Undead are a despised minority on this station!" he shouted. "*Of course* some of us are mad about that! I'm mad about that! You hate us and want us all to go to Eox, where things are just as bad, or worse—if you're not high up in that hierarchy, your existence is basically worth nothing; any necrovite can have you torn apart for their own amusement! They can stream the video of you being torn apart for the amusement of *others*! I didn't know Malvus was working for the bone sages—how could I? I thought he was just complaining! I never heard any plans." He shook his head. "I saved your life when I could have turned on you, my *kidnappers*, because I think we're basically on the same side, and after all that, the best I get from you is, 'Oh, I guess not *all* undead are scum.' How many awful things have humans done, Valentine?"

She closed her eyes, biting back the furious responses that built up inside her, and then said, "You're right. I'm... I'm sorry."

"You *are* right, Caspien," Azzi offered. "I've got no excuse. There are people who hate dragonkin too, think we're all mindless brutes or that we want to steal their stuff and sit on it like a hoard or force them to bond with us so we can control their feelings, just really stupid things like that. We were scared, and we made stupid decisions, and you suffered for them."

"You're all right, Caspien. It was wrong of me to judge you." Val held out her hand.

"Why would I want the approval of a bigot?" the borai said, looking at her hand with undisguised loathing. "Let's just do this. Get to Botscrap, get the weapons, and stop these terrorists from cutting off the life support or whatever they're planning to do. All right?" He turned and marched off down the left-hand side of the corridor.

"That sucks, but it's fair," Val said. "Is he going the right way?"

"I'm going to say yes," Azzi said. "But the next chance we get to go up a level, we should take it."

"Who exactly are we going to visit in Botscrap, anyway?"

"I know this ysoki, high up in the salvage union—the ones who deal with all the broken machinery on the station, the stuff that can't be handled by the usual recycling programs? They're basically the government down here."

"They have a representative on the guild, yeah? An ysoki who doesn't talk much?"

"They prefer not to get too involved in politics, honestly," Azzi said. "It's a different world down here, just decks and decks of private junkyards and recycling and repair operations. A lot of gray-market, and some black-market, stuff involving scavenged military tech. Mostly their rep is there to provide an early warning if the Primex ever decides to try to exert more control over the Spike. Which, so far, she hasn't tried to do."

"Never piss off the people who control your water, energy, air, and sewage, is my feeling," Val said.

"Right? Anyway, me and Scunge met through organizing; my union and his have coordinated on some actions in the past, and he's got his own little junkyard and repair shop. I know he has a sideline in self-defense items. He's outfitted half the crews who've gone down to explore the Ghost Levels."

"None of them have ever come back! Not exactly a ringing endorsement."

"Yeah, but it wasn't because of the equipment they had. That was top-notch," Azzi said.

They caught up to Caspien, who was standing indecisively at another intersection, and he stayed with them after that, though he didn't talk much. He also didn't just leave, though he could easily have escaped to Downlow or one of the other enclaves in the Spike. He was actually trying to help, despite how much he (understandably) despised his current companions. Val kept revising her opinion of Caspien upward, and the only problem was that it meant revising her opinion of *herself* downward.

They found an escalator—surprisingly *operational*—that led up to the next level, and a few turns later, they were in Botscrap.

"Oh my gods," Val said, gazing at the seemingly infinite, cavernous expanse before her. "Is it all just... one big junkyard?"

"It is many small junkyards," Azzi said. "And a certain amount of... junk held in common." They were surrounded on all sides by heaps of scrap. Some of that scrap was identifiable—old appliances, broken drones, busted transports—but much of it was a jumble of metal components, plastic, wire, and broken glass in a rainbow of colors. There were pathways, of a sort, winding among the heaps, some of which would have qualified as hills or maybe even small mountains if they'd been on a planet. The lighting was irregular, with blazingly bright beams shining down here and there, serving to highlight the pools of dimness in between. Cranes moved in the distance, and there were the sounds of clanging hammers, welding torches, and miscellaneous shouts. The smells of burning metal and plastic were acrid in her nose.

Robots of various configurations scuttled or trundled past them, and scavengers clambered over the piles or crept down paths, mostly ysoki with battered cybernetic enhancements (and some fanciful prosthetic limbs—it must be dangerous working down there, but at least there were plenty of replacements handy). Azzi led them through the winding paths, and when they passed one pile of especially disreputable-looking trash, Val spun around when some of the rubbish cascaded down behind them.

A creature emerged from the base of a pile, looking like nothing she'd ever seen before—it was the size of a human child, with tentacles extending from beneath a bulbous shell made of mismatched metal plates and plastic scraps glued together with some kind of goo. Was it a botched bot or some kind of biological mishap with trash stuck to it? It waved its pseudopods in her direction.

Val reached for her knife, but Azzi touched her arm. "Hey, whoa, you're not in danger." The creature waved its tentacles a moment longer, then turned with surprising alacrity and burrowed back into the junk heap.

"It's a gnarefuroid," Azzi said. "They're a little strange, but they're basically just scavengers. Smart, though—smarter than you'd think, for a space snail. Pretty much harmless, unless you're a piece of old tech they get interested in disassembling and repurposing."

"Not *every* unfamiliar thing is a threat, Valentine," Caspien said, prompting a surge of shame inside her, which was becoming a depressingly familiar sensation. Then he turned to Azzi. "Are we almost there?"

"Just around the bend," the dragonkin said. They reached a post with a sign on it that read "TRESPASSERS WILL BE DISASSEMBLED AND SOLD FOR PARTS" in bright red paint. "This is the place."

They went to a gate decorated with spikes and the skulls of small animals with a guard shack next to it. A bulbous black robot inside consisted mostly of guns and camera lenses, all trained on them.

"It's Azzi, here to see your boss!" he called.

The guns didn't move, but the robot beeped, which Val chose to take as acknowledgment rather than a threat.

A few long, stressful minutes later, the gate trundled open, and an ysoki with a mechanical left leg sporting extra joints strode out toward them, wearing a welding mask and some kind of fireproof apron.

"Scunge!" Azzi cried, and the ysoki threw open his arms and embraced the dragonkin—which, given the height disparity between their species, mostly meant hugging Azzi's leg. When they parted, Azzi gestured at their companions. "Scunge, this is my pal Val from the Society, you know, over in the Lorespire?"

"They send down a lot of broken data crystals," the ysoki said from behind the welding mask. His accent was odd, vowels flattened strangely. Some kind of Botscrap dialect, Val supposed. She'd never been down there before.

Azzi gestured. "And this is Caspien Blightwind; he's an accountant."

"He is also a borai," Scunge said.

Caspien winced and hunched his shoulders, waiting for whatever unpleasant remarks would follow.

"We have borai down here," Scunge said. "In the union even. One of them, she says to me she likes being in the salvage union because being a borai is like *being* salvage; you were something people thought was broken, but it turns out, no, there is use for you. There can be a purpose still. There can be a life. I welcome you, Caspien Blightwind."

"I... thank you?" Caspien said.

"What is it I can do for my friend Azzi, my sibling from another union?"

The dragonkin looked over. "I don't know if you know this, Scunge, but the station is under attack."

Scunge lifted his mask, revealing a face crisscrossed with scars and a muzzle with a lot of white in it—an old ysoki who'd been through a lot. "That is why the comms are down, then. Who is attacking?"

"Eox," Azzi said.

"Ah." Scunge looked at Caspien. "A worse time than usual to be undead on Absalom Station, eh? Come to my workshop; we will speak more there in private." He led them through the gate, which rolled closed after them. The world inside the fence of his junkyard wasn't so different from the outside, except that the scrap heaps were better organized. "This attack, it perhaps explains why a ghoul tried to break into my special storehouse just an hour ago."

"Wait, what?" Val said.

"Yes, yes, I have a... special private reserve... for friends and very special clients. There are scrap piles here that contain great wonders. Alien technology. Unknown marvels. Relics from long before the Gap, from worlds with names we do not know. I look for these. I collect them. Especially the useful ones. The ones that will help adventurers, explorers, delvers. I specialize in this. Do you know why?"

"Why?" Val asked. From the way Azzi was grinning, it was clear the dragonkin already knew, and they thought it was hilarious.

"Because these people who wish to explore the Ghost Levels, they have little sense, and so they pay very well, and because they usually die on their adventures, they never come back to complain or ask for refunds." He made a wheezing noise that took Val a moment to realize was laughter. "I could cheat them, but I do not, because I have pride in my work, and because it is more interesting to rebuild or repair or reconfigure something so that it works than it is to make a piece of useless junk into a different, more complicated piece of useless junk. This is what I believe. But, yes, I have a secure area behind my workshop, and a ghoul was caught in one of my traps. Would you like to see this ghoul?"

"I'm sure she'd like to interrogate this ghoul," Caspien said. After a moment, he said, "Which... would be fine. We should find out what they know."

"Yes, good, then." Scunge escorted them to a low building with a roof made of scrap metal and a surprisingly imposing door that opened with the aid of several keys and a palm print. The door clicked its electronic approval and swung open, and the ysoki led them into a cluttered workshop full of long worktables, neatly arranged shelves, and tools hanging on the walls. There was most of a disassembled autocannon on one table, next to a large glass container of what Val suspected was acid.

They passed right on through the workshop to an open area in the back, surrounded by a solid wall studded with cameras and guns. There was a metal hatch set in the ground, promising secrets hidden below.

There was also a ghoul—humanoid, with an angular face, elven ears, purplish skin, and taloned fingers—wrapped up tightly in what looked like strings of decorative lights, blinking red and green. The ghoul hung vertically, held upright by wires extending in various directions to fixed points on the surrounding wall. "He triggered my automatic net," Scunge said.

"I almost got past all your stupid defenses, rat," the ghoul spat, struggling fruitlessly, arms pinned to his sides. "Slipped right past your cannons, your robots, I had my claw on the hatch to your vault—"

"This is not hatch to my vault," Scunge said. "Is decoy, to fool people like you. Big obvious shiny hatch in ground! Yes, that is where I will put my treasures. Pah. Is stupid one." The ysoki gestured at the ghoul. "Question, do what you will; I will make us tea, yes?" He puttered off.

Val and Azzi looked at the ghoul. Val opened her mouth—

And then Caspien strode forward, drawing a long collapsible stun baton from his belt, and jabbed the electric ends into the ghoul's neck, making the creature hiss and writhe as electricity sparked.

"Where did he get *that*?" Val whispered.

"Must've picked it up in the confusion at the bar," Azzi said. "Girl, you're lucky he didn't jab *you* with that thing."

"You kidnapped him too," Val said. "I don't know why I get all the grief."

"You were *way* more racist about it all than I was."

She groaned. "I know. I know. I have a lot of things to unpack. I'm going to work on it. I hate myself."

"Just hate that *part* of yourself, maybe," Azzi said. "Other parts aren't so bad."

Meanwhile, Caspien was speaking in a low voice. A few hours earlier, Val would have thought he was conspiring with the ghoul against them. Instead, she was thinking he was probably just trying to be intimidating, like the operatives he'd probably read about or seen on his vidcasts in that windowless room of his.

The ghoul was not so quiet. "Traitor! You should be working with us, for the glory of Eox—"

Caspien jammed the stun baton into the ghoul's neck again, making him gag and sputter.

*It's probably distressingly satisfying to interrogate someone after you've been interrogated,* Val thought.

"Stop!" the ghoul squawked. "I'm just a freelancer. I work down here in Botscrap—one of the elebrian agents hired me to help out with the assault! Everybody knows Scunge has the nastiest weapons, so I was going to liberate a few and give them to this squad I know, to help them fulfill their mission!"

"And what's their mission?" Caspien said, more audibly.

"They want to seize control of the *Starstone*!" the ghoul said.

"Not possible," Scunge said, returning with a tray that held several teacups. Val and Azzi took theirs, and the ysoki set the tray down on the fake hatch before squinting at the ghoul. "Been tried. Automated defenses. Technological and magical. Beyond anything anyone else has seen anywhere. Nobody gets in. Nobody needs to. Power source never malfunctions, always produces reliable energy. People messing with it could only make it worse. Builders of the station, in the long-ago, they built that system right. No one can even get close to the *Starstone*. Nothing in my vault could help with that."

"That's what I always heard," the ghoul said. "But they're from Eox, and they think they can do anything, and they pay well. What do I care if they waste their time? Listen, will you let me loose? I learned my lesson."

"What else do you know?" Caspien said. "We heard there were agents from Eox trying to take control of life support and gravity and temperature control and comms and everything. Where are they, exactly?"

"How would I know?" the ghoul cried. "I told you, they just hired me for local knowledge, and that's not local knowledge I have!"

"It is knowledge I have," Scunge said. "I know where I would go if I wished to seize control of all those things at one time."

"You do?" Azzi said. "We were honestly just going to look for clusters of conduits and hope for the best."

"No, no need for that," Scunge said. "All the systems down there, they are separate, yes? To take them all over, you would have to go here and there, from air supply to gravity control, back and forth, up and down, all over. Too much trouble. If it was me..." He looked at the ghoul, sniffed, and then prodded at the chunky metal bracelet on his wrist. The ghoul stiffened as electricity coursed through the wires wrapping him up, and then he slumped, shocked into unconsciousness. "I do not like to say secrets in front of people who sell them," Scunge explained. "You vouch for these two, Azzi?"

"I do, pal," the dragonkin said.

"OK, then." Scunge rubbed his hands together. "Long time ago, before the Gap probably, somebody decided the people of Botscrap might someday need... leverage. In case the people from upstairs decided they could come down here, interfere, tell us how to live or what to do, yes? And so those people, they reached down and ran around and wired things up and hid those wires away, and now—in the headquarters of the salvage union—there is a special room. In this room, there are controls for everything, consolidated in one place. The lights, the gravity, the air, communications. All of it. *That* is where I would go, if I wished to control or hurt the station all at once."

As a member of the Syndicsguild, Val found this revelation alarming, but as a freedom fighter, it was promising. "Do you think the agents from Eox could have found out about this control center?" Val asked.

"Only top people in salvage union know," Scunge said. "But some... some are not in this business for the love of making new things from old things, you know? Some... they mostly love money." The ysoki shrugged. "So I say yes. Probably. If the agents of Eox asked around, offered money, pretended to be part of the union even, yes, they could find out." He paused. "We should go see about it, maybe. Either the undead are there, in control... or we can use the controls to take *back* control."

"Let's go," Azzi said.

"Yes. But first, we should go to my real vault."

No thief would ever have found Scunge's genuine secret stash. The ysoki led them into his workshop, pressed a hidden release somewhere, and made a hinged section of the floor rise up on hydraulics, the tables and loose junk on top somehow *not* sliding off into a messy clanging pile but remaining in place, as if epoxied down. "Gravity trick," Scunge explained when he noticed them gawking. "Useful is gravity. Some places, they have it naturally, but here on station, we make our own." He led them down a set of stairs to a reinforced door bristling with security measures and whistled to himself as he punched in the codes and offered the biometric proofs necessary to unlock it.

The door opened, and Scunge ushered them inside.

Val had seen a vid once about a legendary thief who found a map that led to a secret treasure chamber under a mountain, and she always remembered the shot when he finally entered the hidden room: a close-up of the actor's awestruck face, gazing in wonder, lit up by the light reflecting off all the gold and jewels inside. Scunge's vault was like that, except it was Val's awestruck face, and it was light reflecting off polished chrome and steel and mirror-bright precious materials in prismatic swirls of color.

"I can put together one good suit of power armor to fit any of you," Scunge said. "A little bit of this and that, but all together, it will be good. And for the others, we have heavy and light arms, lots of those."

Val looked at Azzi. "You want the armor?"

"I come with my own armor, really." They thumped their chest.

"You, Caspien?" she asked.

The borai considered, then shook his head. "I like the idea of being wrapped up in armor, it's true, but I would probably do more damage to myself than anyone else. I've never really been in a fight, besides at the bar; when things were bad after the Gap, I got killed almost immediately. You can wear it."

"Oh, well," Val said. "If you insist." She grinned. She'd never worn powered armor before.

"It will be easiest to work with you, anyway." Scunge tapped the side of his head. "You have neural hardware already, for your little drone, yes? We can connect the armor to that, make it easier for you to control."

Val spent a lot of time standing still with her arms outstretched while Scunge fitted her with various bits of modular armor, clearly salvaged from half a dozen different models, all with his own modifications. It reminded her of the time Starla got her a bespoke-suit fitting for one of their anniversaries.

Gods, she missed her wife. She was probably OK—they lived right in the heart of the Society's territory, and the Lorespire Complex was as secure as any place on the station, other than the Starstone Reactor and maybe the Primex's residence—but it sure would be nice to hear her voice.

Azzi, meanwhile, was oohing and aahing over other bits of vicious ordnance, strapping on gauntlets and hanging grenades and guns all over their body. (Ty here: I considered slowing down the footage and trying to identify all the specific weapons, but, eh, I've never been much for gun porn, and Scunge made so many changes to the base specs that I probably couldn't do it justice anyway. I'll just describe the consequences of using the weapons later.)

Caspien found a cape of some oily black material that Scunge waved at and said, "Take, wear, it deflects incoming." So the borai wrapped it around himself. Then he picked up a long white staff tipped with a golden spearpoint. "What's this?"

"Ah, this *was* Eoxian bone staff," Scunge said. "Used mostly to hurt people, to make them do what you want, yes? But end of staff was broken, no horrible pain came out anymore, so I upgraded, put a holy relic I found in a trash heap on the end. Now if you stick that into someone, they don't like it so much, and if they are undead, they *really* don't like it."

Caspien gave the staff an experimental twirl and didn't hit himself in the face or knock anything over. "I'll take this." With his staff and cape, he looked like a hero in a historical epic—apart from the wormy veins of negative energy crawling across his face, but even that gave him a sort of tragic antihero vibe, Val had to admit.

"Looking good," Val said, just as Scunge lowered a helmet over her head.

"You too," Caspien said. "Especially now that I can't see your face."

Azzi chuckled. "Burn," they said, and puffed out a tiny gout of flame.

"I deserve that." Val waited in darkness as Scunge fiddled with the armor's sensors. "I really am sorry, Caspien."

"Words are wind," Caspien said. "Show me you're sorry, and then I might believe you."

"I'll do my best," Val said as her view lit up with scrolling infomatics and targeting overlays.

"OK, then." Scunge picked up some sort of chunky gun with multiple barrels and lowered his welding mask. "Now we are off to be saving the station."

# 15

## A HEARTFELT REUNION
(Melezheun / 7 AG)

Thanks to the Hellknights (and *that* is a phrase I really don't like writing) pushing back the assault on the Eye, the corridors were clear enough that I was able to get Ketavan down to the hangar where my ship, the *Venture*, was waiting, without having to slaughter a thousand zombies on the way, and we set out to pick up Mel on the *Offshoot*.

"There is a ghost in the slot machines," Master Fabricant complained, still plugged into the ship's systems. "They're spraying jackpots all over the floor, sending the customers into a frenzy!"

"We'll clean it all up," Phaera said, standing alongside Melezheun, watching the orbital battle on the screens. "Concentrate on the space battle for now, please. Internal security won't matter much if we get destroyed."

The necrovite's flagship was being bombarded both by Absalom Station's ferocious autocannons and the impressive weaponry on the *Offshoot of Design*. (Phaera was willing to shoot as long as her vessel wasn't the biggest thing doing the shooting, thus becoming the most obvious target for retribution.) Some of the smaller vessels in the invasion fleet had already been destroyed. Since the big guns were finally fighting back, many of the remaining ships in the Armada had decided to join in the action, zipping around and taking potshots at the *Marbhan* and its allies.

"Ah, I think your friend is on the way," Phaera said. "The *Venture*, isn't it?" She pointed to a screen showing a view of Absalom Station, and a small dot lit up in green, moving away from the habitat. "We just picked up their transponder. I'll hail them."

Tyrcell's face appeared on the screen. The android wasn't always the easiest to read, but their face lit up when they saw Melezheun.

"Mel! We're on our way. Thanks for agreeing to come along."

"There's no one I'd rather go on an impossible mission with," Melezheun said.

"Shush," Master Fabricant said. "No talking about operational details on an open channel."

"I think we can be sufficiently vague," Phaera said. "I make my living calculating the odds, Tyrcell, and I must say, I wouldn't bet on you. There are too many variables."

"Always tell me the odds," Tyrcell said. "Then it's so much more satisfying when I beat them. Wow, are you seeing this? It's a full-on space battle out here! There are undead mages on the bridges of those Eoxian ships, flinging destructive spells that shouldn't have anything *like* this kind of range! You don't throw lightning at a spaceship with your *hands*!"

"The joys of magitech," Master Fabricant said. "Science melded with the arcane, machines animated by occult powers. The bone sages specialize in that sort of thing. But brute-force physics still has plenty to offer. Our railgun is charging. That's going to give the necrovite flagship a headache."

"We can hold these ships off," Melezheun said. "But what if Eox sends reinforcements? It's not such a long trip from there to here through the Drift."

"If that happens, we're doomed," Phaera said. "I'm sure the bone sages would rather seize my ship than destroy it, but they *will* destroy it if they feel they have no other choice. Which is why I wish I could give your plan better odds. I doubt Absalom Station will be vaporized—the bone sages want to control it, not reduce it to dust—but they'll have no such compunctions about annihilating me and mine."

A human with bulging eyes and a long white mustache shoved his face into the video screen's frame. "This is Ketavan the Vaticinator! Fear not, for if you are slain, I will avenge you—"

Tyrcell gently pushed the man off the screen. "So where should I dock?"

"I am sending you instructions," Master Fabricant said.

"See you soon, Mel." The screen flickered off.

Phaera looked down at Melezheun with great hauteur, then

softened her expression into a smile and took the lashunta's hands in her own. "It has been *so* interesting meeting you, and your help has been most welcome. Don't forget to tell your Primex how very helpful I've been, hmm? I daresay the station would have fallen by now without my intervention."

"You might be right," Melezheun offered. "I like you a lot more than I expected to when I first got here."

"When you arrived, we were at odds," Phaera said. "Now we have a common cause. I find that makes all the difference. Now, go, join your friend, and save us from certain death, hmm? I run a casino, and there's nothing I find more boring than certainty." She patted Melezheun on the cheek and then turned back to watching the fray.

A small hovering drone appeared to lead Melezheun through a series of service corridors and cargo elevators, giving her a few moments to collect herself and her thoughts. Even on the secure Society communications channel, Tyrcell had been carefully vague about the details of the plan. She knew only that they had to go to the Thousand Moons to secure a weapon that could threaten Eox. She was curious to find out more... and to find out why this boisterous Ketavan fellow was a necessary element of the plan.

The drone left her waiting at an airlock, and a moment later, Master Fabricant's voice grated over a loudspeaker. "The ship has docked. Proceed through the airlock."

"Thank you!" Melezheun called. The doors hissed open, and once she passed through, those doors closed behind her, and then the ones before her opened, linked with the hull of the *Venture*—and there was Tyrcell, standing in the tiny cargo bay of the explorer ship, arms outstretched. Melezheun rushed into their arms and grabbed them tight, rocking back and forth. "I was afraid I'd never see you again or Val or Carn or Bindi or Starla or the Society or *anything*!"

Tyrcell kissed her forehead and then released her. "I've been trying to reach Val, but she's not answering. No luck reaching Carn or the Lorespire either. I think everyone is trying to call everyone else, and the station's systems are getting overloaded. But I'm sure they're fine, right? *I'm* fine, and you're fine; Val and Carn are at least as good at this stuff as we are."

Melezheun took Tyrcell's hand as they returned to the tiny bridge of the *Venture*, which contained a pilot's chair, a copilot's chair, and not much else. "Where is your new friend?" Mel said. "Or is he your spiritual adviser?"

"His advice is kind of all the same," Ty said. "'Kill all undead.' Which, though they aren't my favorite kind of people at the moment either, seems a bit extreme as an overarching worldview. I sent him to the galley to get something to eat, even though he seems to run entirely on spite and fanaticism."

"Why does he hate undead so much, anyway?" Mel asked.

Tyrcell dropped into the pilot's chair and Melezheun lowered herself into the copilot's seat. "He's a priest of Pharasma, or used to be, and undead are an interruption to her spiral of rebirth. Ketavan does seem to go far beyond typical religious doctrine, but I haven't asked him for his reasons. I'm afraid he'd tell me—in great and graphic detail. What do you say we get a little farther away from all this mayhem and then pop into the Drift?"

The android tapped at the console, and the viewscreen shifted from a view of the side of the *Offshoot of Design* to one of the cameras at the rear of the *Venture*. There were ships streaming away from Absalom Station in all directions. "Getting off the station was impossible earlier, because the *Marbhan* and the other vessels were shooting at anyone who tried to flee," Tyrcell said. "Once the station cannons started firing on the necrovite fleet and providing some cover, though, the exodus began. Tons of people with ships docked in the Arms are jumping off station and fleeing the area, and it's hard to blame them... but it works well for us, because we can sort of blend in with the general outward flow, and this Mnephalon won't pay any particular attention to us."

"I met her, sort of," Melezheun said. "Mnephalon projected herself onboard the *Offshoot of Design* to make threats. It was horrible, like she was really *right there*."

"Ugh, really? She projected herself across the dome of the Eye, a thousand times bigger than life, leering down at all of us, but it was like seeing Zo! on a screen, not so up close and personal."

"That sounds horrible in different ways," Melezheun said. "The worst part of it all is, she seems to be having so much fun. I thought the bone sages were supposed to be cold and deliberate?"

"I get the sense she's young and fiery by necrovite standards." Tyrcell guided the *Venture* away, following the curve of the larger ship's hull for a while, since it was between them and the *Marbhan*. But inevitably, they had to proceed into open space, and that was chaos. Even the smaller ships from Eox were constructed with an eye toward intimidation, with cadaverous hulls dotted with crawling skeletal minions. Some of those minions were leaping from the ships to sail through the void and land on the hulls of ships in the Armada, where they used breaching charges and welding tools to break through the ships' exterior. One Eoxian ship, like the corpse of a sea monster with one giant glassy eye, had a battlemage standing in the front view port, gesturing with a bone scepter, sending lances of purple lightning through space to strike at any ship that dared to fire on them.

"I wish the *Venture* had more guns," Tyrcell said.

"Opening fire would only draw attention," Melezheun said. "We have a more vital mission. Which is... what, exactly?"

"There's a hidden weapon in the Thousand Moons," Tyrcell said. "Probably, anyway—that's what the sarcesians say, and they live there, so they'd know. Probably a remnant of some ancient war, maybe even the one that created the Thousand Moons, when Eox destroyed two neighboring planets—the survivors concocted an elaborate revenge plot. According to Ketavan, the weapon will turn the Thousand Moons *themselves* into weapons. The asteroids can be launched at the surface of Eox in a devastating orbital bombardment."

"Throwing rocks down gravity wells," Mel said. "It's definitely effective."

"Try this one simple trick for extinction-level events," Tyrcell quipped. "There are planetary defenses to prevent that kind of thing from happening by accident, but there's some kind of stealth technology or something that makes this weapon more effective, in theory. Several thousand giant chunks of rock impacting Eox would make the place uninhabitable even for undead. So we'll find this weapon, turn it on, call up the bone sages, and tell them—"

"Hello there," a voice purred—not emerging from the comm system, but from the air around them. "This is Mnephalon. You're Melezheun, isn't that right? I can't believe you're already leaving."

"So much for slipping away unnoticed," Ty muttered.

Mel didn't know if the bone sage could see inside their ship, but she hoped not. She'd rather Mnephalon not know that Ketavan, the pretext for the whole invasion, was on board too. "Can you hear me?" she asked tentatively.

"Of course I can hear you! I'm a *necrovite*. Compared to you people, I'm basically a god. I shouldn't even be calling you *people*. You're more like insects, really, or those tiny, microscopic shrimp that fish eat on Kalo-Mahoi."

"I've never bothered to have a conversation with a tiny, microscopic shrimp," Tyrcell said. "Also, saying 'tiny, microscopic' is redundant."

"It was a deliberate intensifier, to further highlight your insignificance. Hold on, I don't like being a disembodied voice—ah, there we are." A figure appeared on the bridge, standing between the two of them, and Tyrcell and Mel both got up from their chairs and retreated several steps—Mel did so automatically, without even intending to, the appearance of even the necrovite's psychic projection acting directly on the parts of her mind that experienced fear and revulsion.

The necrovite took no notice of their hasty retreat, and just kicked at the control console, or appeared to; Melezheun wasn't sure how these psychic projections worked. Mnephalon certainly *seemed* to be right there. "This ship is like a scrap heap furnished with trash from the dump. I don't even like being on board this thing mentally."

"Don't bad-mouth the *Venture*," Tyrcell said. "It doesn't look like much, it's true, but it's got a lot going on in the engine room and under the console panels. I won it in a bet from a smuggler. Who I guess probably had to find another line of work, since I took his smuggling ship. I've—"

"I don't care," Mnephalon said. "I just came to mock Melezheun for running away. Cowardly, but prudent."

"That's our motto," I said cheerfully. "I keep meaning to get it engraved on some kind of family crest, but first I need to get my hands on one of those."

"I can't believe that casino ship is *firing* on me," the necrovite said. "After I sent such a polite boarding party to take control of the vessel, instead of just annihilating it! My elders always tell me that my kind heart is a liability."

"Shouldn't you be attending to the battle?" Melezheun said. "Instead of wasting time with us cowards?"

"Please. I can talk to you with a fraction of my attention while I attend to more important things. Besides, I thought it was important for you to know that I know what you're up to."

Melezheun's heart sped up. The necrovite knew! She knew about the Thousand Moons! She knew about the plan!

"I can't believe you're taking up with the terrorist Ketavan," Mnephalon said. "Why risk your lives to protect that fool?" Mel could feel the necrovite trying to invade her mind. It was like greasy, oily fingers pawing at her brain. Up close, a necrovite could scoop out her thoughts like someone eating a melon with a spoon, but being so far away—and getting farther all the time, as the *Venture* sped into the black—apparently limited her capabilities, and Melezheun managed to hold her thoughts fast. The bone sage knew about the priest, then, but there was no evidence she knew about the weapon in the Thousand Moons, or she'd be a lot more hostile. "Where is that bony sack of bad ideas, anyway?" the bone sage asked.

"Ketavan, you say?" Tyrcell shook their head. "Never heard of them."

The necrovite sighed. "I still have eyes and ears on the station, android. I know you've been harboring the terrorist and that you recently spirited him away in your flying garbage wagon."

Tyrcell shrugged. "If you say so. Who am I to contradict a sage of bone?"

Mnephalon leaned back in the pilot's chair and drummed long fingers on the arm. "You two could scurry away, and I wouldn't care. But Ketavan is a problem. We didn't choose him as our scapegoat at random, you know. He's been traveling all over the inhabited worlds of our system for years now, trying to stir up resentment against Eox. We don't really approve of that sort of activity. I promised my fellow sages that Ketavan would be captured so we could have a show trial and a messy public execution. We think it would be a valuable object lesson for everyone watching."

"Ah, well," Tyrcell said. "No plan survives contact with... well, me, really. Losing Ketavan hardly seems like your biggest problem, anyway. Your failed invasion of Absalom Station seems like a bigger problem. You might end up being the one messily executed instead."

Melezheun wondered whether Tyrcell was immune to the constant low-level fear that being in the presence of a necrovite caused in her, or if the android was just better at hiding it. Or maybe Tyrcell just talked shit automatically, whether they were afraid or not; they certainly had a gift for that sort of thing.

Mnephalon shook her head. "Nonsense. I haven't failed."

"The comms are back online," Melezheun pointed out. "The station's defensive batteries are up and running, and they're hammering away at you. You've lost numerous smaller ships already."

"I didn't say *no one* failed. Clearly, some of my agents on the station did." Mnephalon kicked her booted feet up and rested them on the console. The boots were very black and shiny, with heels that could have easily doubled as implements of torture. "One sleeper cell managed to seize control of comms, life support, and the security systems, as planned... and then somehow lost control of everything. A group of sympathizers was supposed to abduct the Primex and as many syndics as possible, to hold them hostage, and *that* doesn't appear to have worked out either—shouldn't have used Absalom Station castoffs instead of reliable people from Eox." She clucked her tongue. "That same group was meant to grab Ketavan and deliver him to me on my ship, and you know how that went. So, yes, there were failures, and there will be consequences for all of these failures. I already personally tore the head from the body of Commander Alcyone, who oversaw all our preinvasion planning. The poor dear was quite obsessed with me." Mnephalon sighed. "Rather more obsessed with me than I'd realized, actually, since she seems to be hanging around in the form of a ghost, with precious little left in her head *but* that obsession. Still, she could be useful. But I digress." She leaned back, lacing her long fingers together and resting them across her sunken belly. "My point is the invasion is ongoing. We've had a temporary setback, yes, but I have the full backing of Eox behind me. Reinforcements are coming out of the Drift soon, and then the choice for the people of Absalom Station will be: Submit to our rule or be reduced to vapor and fragments. We'd rather *own* the station—that was the whole point—but if we can't have it, no one will."

"If you destroy Absalom Station, the other inhabited worlds will turn on you," Melezheun said.

"Possibly. I think it's more likely they'll fear us. And we'll still have our cover story, after all—Absalom Station hid a terrorist who attacked a diplomatic mission, and we simply responded to that outrage with necessary force." She leaned forward with a leering grin. "Actually, you fools running away with Ketavan helps that narrative. I've looked up both of you now—cofounders of the Society, one of the station's little fiefdoms, clearly acting in an official capacity to protect the terrorist! After we mop things up on the station, we'll send a hunting party after you too. You two can go on trial alongside Ketavan. Maybe we'll drop you on one of the irradiated plains of Eox, where the ghouls driven mad by starvation congregate, and vidcast you getting devoured. I'd watch that." Her projection began to flicker.

"Sorry, sage, you're breaking up," Tyrcell said. Absalom Station was receding in the viewscreen, like a spinning top floating in space, surrounded by flickers and flashes of light as the ships continued to make war on one another. "It was really lovely talking to you, though. I hope we never meet again."

"Oh, we'll meet," the bone sage said, her form fading in and out of focus. "We'll meet, and then you'll *be* meat. For the ghouls. Is what I mean."

"I did get that," Tyrcell said. "But thanks for clarifying."

"I never forget people who annoy me, Tyrcell and Melezheun, and you have both *annoyed* me."

"That's a shame," Tyrcell said. "I thought we really hit it off."

The necrovite opened her mouth, doubtless to deliver a devastating rejoinder, and then she vanished from the chair.

"I think we're beyond the range of her psychic projection now." Melezheun shuddered. "She was trying to get into my head the whole time, but I don't think she managed. She didn't seem to discover our true mission."

"Huh, really? I didn't notice anything like that."

"You're an android," Mel said. "Also, you have an exceedingly thick skull."

"I'm famous for it," Tyrcell said. "One of my many fine qualities, right up there with the ageless beauty and nanofilmament-sharp wit. It's a good thing Ketavan wasn't here. He would have blurted out the whole plan. 'Soon your world will be a cinder, abomination,' and so forth."

"Do you think the plan will actually work?" Mnephalon said.

Ty sat back down in the pilot's chair, leaned back, and closed their eyes. "I couldn't venture a guess. But I'll tell you one thing. Any plan that starts with you and me running away from a pitched battle between Absalom Station and the technomagical might of a bone sage is a good enough plan for me."

# 16

## A BLOODY HOMECOMING

### (Carn / 7 AG)

Meanwhile (or actually a bit earlier, because keeping this in strict chronological order is beyond my capabilities), back on Absalom Station...

As the dock defenders ripped through the Rings, their forces grew in number. After what Dania called "the Battle of the Playground," they picked up a couple of furious orc women from the neighborhood, armed with family heirloom waraxes (probably; with the Gap erasing everyone's histories, you couldn't be sure, but the weapons were old and well cared for). The duo—Krella and Axe-Marie were their names—left the human father in their polycule to watch over their kids, dromaars who stared around at the carnage from their adorable faces, doubtless soaking up all kinds of trauma. They'd need some counseling after all this was done, for sure. Carn tried not to worry about that part. The most important thing was to survive; you could deal with all the damage and pain that happened because of surviving later.

Still, Carn made a point of dragging the elongated body of one of the insect-like trox zombies off the children's slide. That had been the last of the creatures to go down, he and Dania both pounding on it with their hammers until its armored exoskeleton finally cracked, spilling out all manner of foulness. Carn only wished he had a rag to wipe all the fluids off the playground equipment, but again, that was a problem for another time.

They gathered more fighters as they went on, ordinary citizens of Absalom Station who wanted to defend their homes or get revenge for the indignities inflicted upon them. It seemed like Dania would have been the obvious choice to lead their merry band, having combat training and occasionally a literal holy aura around her, wearing all the armor, and having a big loud shouty voice. But in practice, Dania really just liked killing zombies and yelling encouragement, not so much strategizing or organizing or trying to make sure their burgeoning army of killers of the undead didn't get too many of themselves killed by putting enthusiasm ahead of caution. As a consequence, those responsibilities ended up falling to Carn, sort of by mysterious default, with Cronch as his lieutenant, while Dania acted as kind of a free-range war machine and morale booster. Carn had never entirely understood how he came to be one of the leading members of the Society, honestly, and the same thing was happening again. Was it just that he was willing to step in and do stuff? Maybe sometimes, that was all it took. He didn't feel qualified, but who *was* qualified to lead a group of civilians on a mission of street-level house-to-house fighting with undead hordes?

Many of the volunteers from the neighborhoods they cleared out came armed; a lot of them were veterans of the bad old days of the gang wars. Carn urged the ones with rifles and pistols to pick more close-range melee options, sometimes with significant pushback from the prospective zombie killers. One dwarf was positively bristling with guns—sidearms on each hip, another in an ankle holster, and a nasty-looking energy rifle slung across his back—and he went red in the face when Carn asked if maybe he had a crowbar or something he could use instead.

Carn tried to explain: "It's just, well, zombies respond better to blunt-force trauma or a comprehensive beheading than they do to projectiles hitting them. They don't really do pain, you know, so you gotta really upset the machinery of their actual biology. You can't just shoot them in the gut or the heart and call it done. Plus, well, friendly fire is an issue—"

"I am an excellent shot," the dwarf insisted.

"I don't doubt it," Carn said, extremely doubting it. In his experience, people with that many guns were more into aesthetics than regular practice. "But when there's an actual horde of zombies tearing around in every direction, and a bunch of our people are wading in there swinging heavy things at the heads of said zombies, *nobody* is that good of a shot, unless we're talking some kind of trained assassin operative. Are you a trained assassin operative?"

"No," the dwarf muttered. "I do supply-chain logistics."

"That's gonna come in handy later, probably," Carn said. "In the meantime, even something like a real heavy frying pan can be a good weapon."

Then Dania screamed a war cry and Carn ran off to join her.

They soon fell into a pattern. The dock defenders (the Ring defenders now, really) would clear out an apartment block or a cul-de-sac or a street lined with homes, assign a few defenders to keep watch in case more zombies came by, and then press on to clear the next knot of zombies, moving inexorably toward the Lorespire district, Carn's secret actual destination.

Battle was one thing. Your mind focused on that, and it all sort of blurred together after a while. The worst part was the little details you noticed in the quiet moments. A discarded stuffed dragon toy in a courtyard. A body floating in a fountain. A grill knocked over on its side, still smoking, sausages scattered on the ground beside it. Potted plants that had been inexplicably charred. Brightly painted front doors scarred by shrapnel. Those were the images that would linger in Carn's mind, long after all the fighting was done.

One tricky part of the whole situation was keeping an eye open for the occasional improvised explosive zombie and trying to detonate those well away from everyone else. One osharu zombie had seemed laughably harmless, slow-moving and portly... but it turned out to be stuffed not just with explosives but also wicked shards of shrapnel, and a couple of the dock defenders went down with terrible wounds. Fortunately, they'd picked up some medics along the way, off-duty doctors and priests and emergency medical techs (including a couple who worked for Dr. Bindi's street-care initiative), and they got the patients stabilized.

Not all the defenders were so lucky. They didn't suffer a ton of casualties on their side, all things considered, but most people weren't professional fighters, and Carn and Dania (and the surprisingly competent Cronch) couldn't watch out for everyone at once. A few of their people went down with nasty bites and shredded flesh and couldn't be saved. They lost an orc named Hardian when he strayed from the group and got piled on by zombies; a halfling, Cantino, was caught in an explosion and had an artery nicked by shrapnel; a lashunta called Vandela was dragged off down a side corridor, and there wasn't much left when they reached his remains. Carn made careful mental notes of all their names because there would be a memorial later. He'd see to that.

When it came to saving residents, well, that didn't always work out, either. Sometimes they were too late. One time they rushed into a broad and vaulted complex of airy apartments arranged in complex stacks and overhangs, with ornamental metalwork railings on the balconies and the flags of a dozen worlds and factions hanging in riotous display, only to find the zombies had come and gone already, leaving only bloody smears and the occasional corpse. Dania poked her head past the broken door of one building, looked around, and came out, frowning. "There aren't enough corpses here. I think the enemy is swelling its ranks."

"They're turning our people into zombies?" Cronch said. "I thought that whole thing where a zombie bites you and you turn into one of them was made up!"

"There are lots of different kinds of mindless undead minions." Dania twirled her staff idly, looking around at the devastation, as their nearly fifty-person-strong army gathered around to listen to her. "Some are created by magic, some by technology, some by fusions of the two—I could tell you stories about bioengineered parasitic worms that gradually erase the mind of their victims, making them into weapons who exist only to spread more parasites. There are plenty of zombies that *do* convert their victims, but it's usually a slow process, and it takes at least a couple of hours, often much longer, before the victims rise again as undead. Even for those bitten by a vampire, they don't generally come back to unlife for three nights. For this to happen so fast... we're dealing with necromancy. Not all our enemies are mindless. As Carn suspected, there are officers among the horde, intelligent undead from Eox, directing this terrorism. If we can find and destroy the leaders, the zombies and other undead minions will lack direction, and become much easier to dispatch."

"These officers are probably leading from the front," Carn said. "Right? Heading for some destination and dispatching their forces to attack the citizens as they go."

Dania nodded. "Any idea what that destination might be?"

Carn put a finger in his ear. "In this direction, the major landmark is the Lorespire Complex. I don't think it has a ton of strategic value, honestly, because it's mostly a hall of records, and most of *those* turned into nonsense during the Gap, but..." He winced. "Actually, there are an awful lot of weapons in there. The tower is the center of one of the old factions, the Society. That's actually my faction. We're real serious about our security. After everybody made peace and started to play nice on the station, we took out the autocannons and the smart mines and the perimeter defense drones and all, but we've still got that stuff in storage. It's not a real big secret. If I was in charge of an army of undead troopers, I'd much rather control that stuff than risk having it turned against me."

Dania nodded. "Then I propose a small group of us hurry to the Lorespire in search of the leaders, to remove the thinking members of the horde and stop the invasion. The rest of you should continue your methodical sweep, taking out the zombies and protecting our citizens. Carn, would you care to accompany me? Since you know this area? And perhaps we could also bring the terribly competent and very angry orc wives?"

Carn nodded. "Cronch, do you think you can keep everybody here on point?"

"You got it, boss," the nuar said. "It's not really all that complicated. See zombie, make sure zombie isn't full of bombs, kill zombie."

"That about covers it." Carn agreed. He clapped Cronch on the—well, not on the shoulder, since that was far above Carn's head, but on the elbow, anyway. "Keep pushing toward the Lorespire. We'll see you there."

"Can't wait." Cronch turned to the crowd of defenders. "You heard the man! Let's go kick dead ass!"

"Is there a faster way to the Lorespire?" Dania asked. "One that won't require us to fight our way through zombie hordes every few hundred feet?"

Carn nodded. "Oh, yeah. We've got tunnels."

As the four of them made their way through the dark, narrow maintenance corridors that wound through the walls and under the halls of the Lorespire district, Carn pointed out landmarks that none of them could see, since they were on the other side of bare bulkheads. "We've moved out of the residential district now, and we're moving into Drifter's End, which is where a lot of the spacers and traders and explorers hang out. There are bars upstairs, cheap hotels, pawn shops, junk shops, military surplus stores, music and comedy and immersive sims and betting parlors, and anything anybody could want after coming back from months and months all alone in the inky black. The zombies are gonna have a harder time in there than they did in the residential areas—a lot of these people are the kind who start bar fights for fun, you know? But I think most people are likely to hole up. There must be rumors spreading about the zombie horde at this point. We get the occasional drunken riot around here, you know, so the shops and clubs all have sturdy security doors and gates and all that. They might be safe."

The champion nodded. "Good. How long until we reach the Lorespire?"

They turned a corner, and Carn grinned. There was a cargo mover down there—basically an anti-grav platform with a steering wheel, two seats in front, and a storage area in the back. "Much faster now. Climb on." The orc wives clambered into the truck bed while Carn jammed himself behind the wheel and Dania hopped onto the seat next to him. Carn entered the emergency override codes that all the founders of the Society had, and the mover hummed to life.

They covered ground a lot faster after that, zipping through the curved corridors, past access hatches and bundles of conduit and ladders leading up to populated areas and down to regions of less hospitable infrastructure. "These tunnels are how we stayed alive during the bad old days," Carn told Dania. "They let us move around undetected, outflank our enemies, hide on those occasions when we got invaded until we could regroup for a counterattack..."

"Good memories?" Dania asked.

"Unforgettable ones, anyhow," Carn said.

"We're lucky the zombies didn't get into these tunnels," Dania said.

"We are," Carn agreed. "The hatches are reinforced pretty well, and they're monitored, with the access codes closely guarded, but if you have enough time and equipment you can get through just about anything."

Carn's impeccable mental map told him they were getting close to the Lorespire Complex, and he slowed their transport as they approached a familiar elevator platform. Once upon a time, he'd gone up in that elevator with Mel and Ty, hunting for the secrets of the universe, and found a bunch of murderous Hellknights instead. Here he was again, once more hoping for one thing and likely to find another.

"We're here," he said.

"I haven't been to this part of the station before," Dania said. "What should I expect up there?"

"There's a lot of open space," Carn said. "It's not as big as Jatembe Park, but there's a similar feel, lots of grass and trees and all that, with artificial sunlight beaming down from above. There are plenty of small buildings scattered around, used for everything from storage to libraries to community gatherings to worship, but the main attraction is the Lorespire Complex, one of the biggest towers on the station—it extends up and up, actually on up through the roof, and if you go to the very tippy-top upper floors, you can look out the windows at the stars and down at the shape of the station below."

The Society hadn't explored those upper floors for years because the stairs had been hidden with illusions and hologram projections, making the structure appear to end much sooner than it did. Once Melezheun and Tyrcell realized there were secret higher floors, they'd been all excited, but what they'd mostly found up there were dusty empty rooms and vermin droppings. At the *very* top they'd found a vault, which rekindled some excitement, and after days of effort (mostly on Carn's part) to crack it open, they finally succeeded, finding it crammed with racks of data crystals, all of them erased, corrupted, or hopelessly garbled by the history-destroying magic that caused the Gap.

"And where are these weapons you mentioned?" Dania asked.

"They're in the basement of the tower, in a vault inaccessible except by going through the tower itself. Even if you had a *bunch* of welding torches. Apparently really important information used to get kept in the Lorespire Complex, and the secure storage areas down below are majorly secure."

"Then let's make sure the forces of hideous necromancy don't get their hands on them," Dania said. "To the heights!"

It was a dramatic way to say "get on the elevator," but the four of them crowded onto the platform, and Carn entered the appropriate codes to make said platform ascend. The ceiling slid open to allow them through. In the old days, this elevator was a hidden access point that led up to a little storage shed, but since then, they'd moved the shed and made the arrival a little more hospitable.

They emerged to find themselves surrounded by guns and armored drones the size of Carn himself and people holding lances that crackled with black lightning. The orc wives growled and raised their axes and Dania opened her mouth to probably start yelling, as Carn said, "Wait-wait-wait!"

"*Carn?*" a familiar voice cried. A small human woman with spiky dark hair shoved her way in between a menacing drone and a dwarf wearing bright white ballistic armor. "You came back!"

"Starla!" Carn embraced her, a little awkwardly since he was still holding his hammer and trying not to bash her with it. "I am so glad you're here and not a zombie. How's—"

"Have you heard from Valentine?" she pleaded, her expression strained.

Carn shook his head slowly. "No. I saw her in the park earlier, and then she was going to the Syndicsguild meeting, and she called me to ask me to go check up on a problem at the docks, but since then, it's been... well, you probably know, right? About the undead?"

"They're pounding on the gates," Starla said. "We've pulled everyone in from the outlying areas into the Lorespire Complex itself." She glared at the dwarf. "This is Carn, Strewth, if you go up enough levels, he's your boss! Let them through."

The dwarf security guard nodded, and the drones moved back to open a pathway out but kept their vigilant watch on the elevator.

Starla led them past the soaring bulk of the Lorespire, toward the main blast doors that led out to the rest of their neighborhood. Those were usually left standing wide open, but they were all sealed, for the first time since the bad old days. "We didn't want to seal off the elevator access," Starla reasoned. "In case some of us tried to come home through the tunnels."

"That's good," Carn said. "If the elevator hadn't worked, my new friends here woulda started to doubt my qualifications." He introduced the orc wives and the shouty champion, and said, "And this is Starla, one of the founders of the Society—"

"Not really," she said. "I was just around back then is all, and I'm married to our leader. I'm mostly a chef. Though I had to leave the restaurant behind when we heard about the *hordes of undead* coming for us. Now that Carn is here, *he* can take over telling everybody what to do."

"Oh, good," Carn said. "I didn't want a nap or anything." He looked around at the clumps of people huddled together here and there on the grass or in the shadows of outbuildings and thought they could *all* use a nap.

Starla patted his arm. "Don't worry. Dr. Bindi is here, and she's mostly running the show. I'm just dealing with the stuff she doesn't have time for." Starla led them to a makeshift command center—basically a whole bunch of piled-up crates and computers and screens, with some folding chairs scattered around—where Bindi, their android head of medical services, was furiously smacking a touch screen.

"Hey, Doc," Carn said. "What's the situation here?"

There was a sudden, booming thud, and the blast doors shuddered. Which was a bit like a mountain shuddering; those things were supposed to be impregnable.

"The situation is bad," Bindi said, voice mild. "We closed all the security doors in the sector—the starship-grade airlocks that are supposed to be able to withstand direct artillery fire? And the dead things have cut or smashed their way through every one, to reach our final barrier." She nodded at the shuddering wall of reinforced metal.

Carn winced. "That's worse than I thought. Have we lost many people?"

She shook her head. "Surprisingly, no. A while ago people started running in here screaming about the undead, and we all knew something was wrong when the comms died, so we were already preparing our fallback plan. By the time the horde arrived in Drifter's End, people were either sheltering in place or sealed up in here. If that main door looks like it's going to fall, we can retreat into the Lorespire and barricade in there, which will buy us some time, but it's not like Bluerise Tower—we're rather less heavily fortified. I don't see many other options, though. We can always descend into the tunnels, but if they follow us down there, it will get very ugly very fast. There's just not enough room down there to maneuver."

Carn imagined trying to fight zombies while jammed into the narrow tunnels and suppressed a shudder. "You're right about that. Now, we've been fighting groups of zombies all the way here, but when you say 'horde'..."

Bindi turned a large vidscreens to face them. "Here's a compilation of the security footage."

At first, it looked like a parade: ranks of people of a wide variety of species moving in tandem together down the broad avenues of the Lorespire district. There were lots of humans and orcs and elves and dwarfs and ysoki and lashuntas, but also some antlike formians and immense four-armed shobhad giants from Akiton.

There were bigger things in the marching mass too, towering over the people, moving along steadily with the flow. Those weren't parade floats, though: They were chimeric beasts like the one Carn and Dania had killed at the docks. There were four of them, all different, all alarmingly horrible, cobbled together from bits of dragons and jungle beasts and sea monsters and giant bugs. The beast at the very front of the procession was the largest, and far more biomechanical than the rest, with legs of gleaming metal. *Those* knees would be a lot harder to break. The crowd swarming around that creature moved with less robotic precision, instead loping and gamboling and apparently leaping with the pure joy of anticipated slaughter.

"Most of the ones up front are ghouls, some with lots of cybernetic enhancements, it looks like," Bindi said. "There are a couple of wraiths or ghosts"—pointing to shimmers on the recording—"who haven't tried to come through the walls yet, fortunately. We've got high-powered lights, which should drive wraiths away, and we have some mystics who say they can dispel the ghosts, though only temporarily—they reform, apparently, in a day or two, no matter what."

"Oh, this will all be over, one way or another, in *much* less than a day or two," Dania said. "Who's the one riding the lead monster?"

Carn squinted, and realized someone *was* riding on the largest of the undead beasts, a figure swaddled in black robes. "Does she have a chair up there?"

"Looks like it," Starla said. "A little throne, perched between the horns."

"I thought that was some kinda hat," Carn said. "I was wondering why they would put a hat on that thing, and the answer is, they didn't. They put a necromancer on it instead."

Bindi nodded. "The cameras have trouble focusing on her, but we think she's an undead elebrian, based on eyewitness reports. She has some kind of long weapon, and we thought it was a bone scepter, like the necrovites use? But hers has a skull on top, and those witnesses say she was gesturing with it and making our dead rise to join her army... which is now at the gates. They destroyed the video cameras on the other side, but it's pretty clear that their undead giants are trying to smash through."

"Their leader isn't a necrovite, I don't think," Dania said. "I doubt one of them would consent to be locked in a crate for months."

"A crate?" Bindi frowned.

"Long story," Carn said. "So, not a necrovite. That's good news, right?"

The champion smiled. "Oh, yes, indeed. If we had to directly face a necrovite, I wouldn't think much of our chances. Fortunately, those creatures don't like to venture into battle themselves—the strongest are nearly demigods in terms of their power, but they consider actually getting into fights rather beneath them. That's why they have lieutenants and minions. I suspect the leader of this band is some variety of vampire—they're fairly high up in the unofficial hierarchy of the undead, and being elebrian would give them greater status on Eox too. Yes. *That's* the head we need to cut off. After we take her out, we should focus on the ghouls and ghasts next; as long as they get enough to eat, they're as capable of tactical planning and complex thought as anyone else." She narrowed her eyes. "And I'm sure they've eaten entirely too well today."

"We're making a stand, then?" Dr. Bindi said. She sounded neutral about the idea, but androids were notoriously hard to read.

"I am, anyway," Dania said forcefully. "I won't insist anyone else stand with me. But I'd welcome volunteers."

The blast doors shuddered again, and... Was that a little gap down at the lower right corner, where the barrier was shearing away from the floor?

"There's no point in trying to hole up and wait this out, really," Carn said. "That sort of thing depends on somebody coming to the rescue, and I get the feeling stuff like this is happening all over the station."

"I hope Valentine is OK," Starla said. "Everyone else too, but... especially Valentine."

"She's pretty tough," Carn said. "And everywhere she goes, she's got that drone full of nasty surprises to back her up. I should know; I programmed some of those nasty surprises in myself. She's probably holed up in some kind of safe room for VIPs with the Primex and the other syndics."

"Maybe," Starla said. "She'd really hate that, though. She always wants to be in the fight." Starla squared her shoulders. "So I'll be in the fight too. I remember a few moves from the old days. Count me in, Dania."

"Glad to have you!" she bellowed. "I don't know how long those doors will hold, so we should see who else wants to go out in furious glory—"

"Well," Carn said. "I was thinking, we've been doing a lot of one-on-one fighting, because we didn't want to go around hurling grenades and firing plasma rifles at innocent civilians. But there's no civilians coming through that door, you know? So... before we have a noble, heroic doomed last stand to the death, maybe we could go down and get some of the really *nasty* guns from out of the basement. I've got the codes, you know." He shrugged. "Being as I'm the head of security."

"I do not fear death," Dania said, "but I confess I would welcome the opportunity to delay it a bit!"

# 17

## YARAESA'S JEWEL
(326 AG)

After Tyrcell blocked their transmission, Groth howled in frustration. "That was embarrassing." He took a swipe at Alcyone, though that was about as effective as slapping mist. "You embarrassed me in front of the misery knight." Groth pointed to the impassive, unmoving, char-covered figure sitting off to one side, where he'd been sitting ever since they came out of the Drift to look for the android.

"We should have done my plan." Alcyone's voice had been wheedling even in life, and the atonal howling that backed every utterance since she'd become a ghost made it even worse. "They would have tried to render assistance, and we could have scooped them up easily! Now we have to track them down again, and they're all cloaked. We won't be able to find them with active measures. Try the passive scanners—"

"We're in an asteroid field!" Groth shouted. "We're surrounded by solid objects approximately the size of a spacecraft! With their energy signature and their lights hidden, we'll *never* track them down—"

The misery knight lifted a gauntleted hand and pointed at the screen Groth had turned away from. He shifted back, and there was a bogey on the screen again, a ship putting out light and energy, uncloaked. "They dropped their stealth?" the ghoul murmured. "Why? Is it a trap?"

"It doesn't matter," Alcyone said. "Go, move in, let's get them! Pilot us close enough to launch the skeleton boarding party." There were skeletons clinging to the outer hull, plus a launch bay in the belly of the *Scaphism* tightly packed with folded-up skeletal minions, all armed with explosives and cutting tools, waiting to be fired through the vacuum of space, to slice and blast their way inside another ship. It was a favorite tactic of the Corpse Fleet. Sure, the explosive decompression of such a forceful boarding action often killed the crew of the ships they were attacking, but what did that matter?

Mnephalon or her necromancers could simply raise their corpses as new members of the fleet anyway. People were so much less trouble when they were dead. (*Except for Alcyone, of course,* Groth mentally amended.)

These skeletons would be more careful, though, because their lady wanted the android intact, and they'd take Tyrcell's companions alive too, just in case—

"Hello, you unlovable incompetents," Mnephalon said, appearing and draping herself across the console like a cabaret performer sprawling atop a grand piano. She flung her hand dramatically over her head. "I'm having the most *interesting* conversation with Tyrcell."

"So it is Tyrcell," Groth grunted, sliding his chair away from Mnephalon. It wasn't smart to crowd her, even if she *was* just a magical projection. "I knew that Bentley stuff was nonsense."

"Don't worry, my lady!" Alcyone said. "We are closing in and we'll soon have them in our clutches, ready to spirit back to the Corpse Fleet—"

"No, no, *no*, you stupid phantasm." Mnephalon turned on her side and propped her head up, supported by an arm bent at the elbow. "That is the old plan. I am here to tell you the *new* plan, which I wouldn't need to do if we were still following the old plan, now, would I?"

"Of course not, my lady." The ghost sounded, as always, incredibly gratified to be corrected.

*I guess abuse is at least a form of attention,* Groth thought.

Mnephalon slithered down off the console and sauntered across to her misery knight, sitting on his lap as if he were a particularly uncomfortable and unlovely chair, then wrapping her hands around his neck and planting a kiss on the side of his helmet. "It turns out Tyrcell is in pursuit of a secret hidden away by a god, and in fact, it's an ongoing quest, one that the android has been pursuing for centuries." She ran her fingertip over the knight's helmet. "I do wish I'd known about all this business with gods hiding secrets away earlier. That would have been interesting to me. People should really tell me interesting things. Don't. You. Think?" She punctuated the last three words with hard slaps against the knight's helmet.

He remained immobile, prompting Groth to wonder once again if there was any mind at work in there at all, or if the creature was just a puppet for Mnephalon. The ghoul knew that *he* was just a puppet for Mnephalon too, ultimately, but at least he was allowed to have opinions about the situation—some opinions, some of the time, anyway.

"Oh well. I'm sure we'll all strive to do better in the future." She patted the misery knight's helmet with her palm more gently before rising to her feet, then stood to face Groth and Alcyone, clapping her hands together briskly. "So! The *new plan*! Follow the *Venture* to whatever unlovely rock they're aiming for. Watch them as they seek entry to the secret god temple hidden therein. Give them, oh, a few minutes for a head start—we want this to be sporting, after all. And then..." She smiled her terrible smile. "Go in after them. Chase them. Scare them. Maim them. Have fun with it! Enjoy yourselves! Feel free to kill the pahtra and the shirren, but not too quickly, of course. Let Tyrcell make it all the way to the end, though. It will hurt them so much more to get close to the goal, don't you think? If there *is* a secret hidden away in the dungeon temple place, take it, and take Tyrcell too, and bring them both to me. Perhaps I can have my fun, and get my overdue revenge, and even learn a little something about the nature of the universe in the process. Knowledge is power, Groth. Never forget that. Of course, it's not as much power as you get from being a necrovite for several centuries, but a little more power never hurts. Does everyone understand the assignment?"

"Yes, my lady," Groth and Alcyone obediently chorused.

Mnephalon slowly turned and looked at the still form of the misery knight. "Do *you* understand, my treasure?"

The knight slowly inclined his head down, and then back up, in a scraping, rusty nod.

"Dee-lightful," Mnephalon singsonged. "I'll try to look in on you from time to time in the temple if I can, but if it really was created by a god, it might prove inhospitable to my psyche. Some of those divinities get terribly bent out of shape with those of us who have the good sense to cheat death forever." The necrovite gave a twirl—less dramatic in her dress uniform than it was in her usual scraps of torn lace—and disappeared.

"I detected subtext." Alcyone pointed an accusing, insubstantial finger at the misery knight. "There were *words unspoken*! I demand you tell me the exact nature of your relationship with our lady and why her voice just *dripped* with implications when she spoke to you!"

The misery knight didn't respond at all, and Alcyone gave a shriek of frustration before floating over to the armored figure, clearly intending to pass through him and *into* him.

A lot of things could happen to you when a ghost inhabited the same space you did, ranging from a cold chill to bodily possession. Groth looked on with curiosity to see which it would be.

But before Alcyone quite reached the misery knight, he reached out with one gauntleted hand—and seized the ghost around the throat. Alcyone thrashed wildly, clawing pointlessly at the burned and rusted armor that somehow grasped her spectral flesh.

Groth laughed aloud—there must be enchantments in the armor that enabled him to interact with ghosts as if they were made of flesh! The knight shook Alcyone and flung her aside, and the ghost lost coherence, turning into a dripping blob of yellowish light for a moment before gradually pulling herself back together into a roughly humanoid form.

"Fine," Alcyone huffed. "Be that way. But this is no way to improve unit cohesion!"

"Shut up, ghost," Groth said. "And cheer up too. Didn't you hear our lady? We get to go on a hunt." He wiped a string of drool from his mouth. He hadn't eaten in hours.

Dae was not feeling their usual super fantastic self after having a necrovite frolicking through the deepest recesses of their mind, and it took a while to shake that off, but the very shiny rock that suddenly appeared in the viewscreen made them gasp. "It's like a giant jewel!"

"It's a single enormous diamond," Tyrcell confirmed, looking at the sensor readouts. "Not even a raw diamond—one that's been cut and shaped. It didn't show up on the sensors at all until we reached the exact coordinates specified in Yaraesa's message. The only explanation for how a diamond the size of a warship went unnoticed in the Thousand Moons this long and why it hasn't drifted into space at all for centuries is divine intervention. So this must be the place." They groaned. "I can't believe Yaraesa's next horrible space dungeon is *here*. I was just here, hundreds of years ago! Like, basically exactly here, within a few hundred kilometers! I could have detoured over this way easily. Although Melezheun was with me at the time, and she was always good at keeping me on task."

Dae was usually interested in lore drops about Tyrcell's past, but they couldn't stop looking at that immense jewel. "Imagine how much it's worth!" Dae said.

*"It is a little big to set into a ring,"* Chk Chk said. *"I would have gone for something more dramatic—onyx, ideally, or at least chalcedony. But the purity of a clear white gem does seem in keeping with Yaraesa's guiding virtues of clarity and perfection."*

"There's a spot on the surface that isn't quite so shiny," Tyrcell said. "See that pentagon of darker material? That must be our way in. Let's get suited up."

They went down to the airlock and got into their environment suits. Dae had brought their own—it was tailored in their current signature colors of coral and plum—while Tyrcell put on a suit that really belonged in a museum of obsolete technology, and Chk Chk wore the same old boring black one he'd been using forever.

They tucked the *Venture* away on the far side of the largest nearby asteroid and set out from the airlock with propellant packs, sailing through empty space toward the glittering temple. Dae thought enviously about the sarcesians and their gorgeous golden wings that let them propel themselves through the void under their own power. Maybe Dae could get a set of fake wings made, and wear an antigravity rig, and do an aerial dance routine at the next PactVision competition—

"We have company!" Tyrcell shouted over their comms, jolting Dae out of their reverie. They looked around, glad they had the 360-degree-crystal helmet on, so they didn't suffer a total lack of peripheral vision like Tyrcell did. That meant Dae got a perfectly good look at the sleek, long shape of the Corpse Fleet craft as it slipped through the tumbling asteroids toward them; it looked like the tapering leg bone of a leviathan, and were those *skeletons* clinging to the outside of the vessel?

Dae pushed their propellant to maximum, and their friends did the same, zipping through space toward the great diamond. They couldn't go anywhere near as fast as a ship, of course, but the ship was unlikely to set a collision course for the temple, so being small and nimble was an advantage in this particular situation.

The trio reached the huge diamond, slowing themselves down and sailing toward the hatch. It had looked so tiny, but it was easily ten feet to a side up close. Magnetic boots were no good on diamond, but the hatch was metal, and they managed to attach themselves and then clamber to the center of the pentagon. There was a sliding puzzle there, a square with eight movable tiles and nine spaces, so you could arrange the tiles to form a picture. The markings just looked like jumbled lines to Dae. "What do we do?"

*"Allow me,"* Chk Chk said, as he began to deftly slide the tiles around.

"We've got skeletons incoming," Ty said.

*"I am adept at these sorts of puzzles,"* the shirren said calmly. *"This is obviously meant to be one of Yaraesa's holy symbols, a stylized brain with—"*

"Less talky-talk, more slidy-slide!" Tyrcell said. Dae deliberately didn't look away from the puzzle. How would it help to know how close the skeletons were?

*"There,"* Chk Chk said, putting the last tile in place. The panels of the hatch slid open just enough to let the three of them tumble through, the interior gravity seizing them and dropping them on the floor of a corridor, the hatch set in the ceiling a dozen feet above them. Dae looked up, tilting their head back to see three skeletal minions sailing straight at them, arms outstretched—

The hatch sealed itself shut, blocking entrance to their pursuers, and the trio got to their respective feet. "Let's hope those mindless undead minions aren't quick visual thinkers like you," Tyrcell said.

There was a muffled boom from above, though the corridor didn't even shake.

Tyrcell clucked their tongue. "They tried to use a breaching charge? Yaraesa doesn't really reward brute force. There are consequences for trying that sort of thing in her territory."

Dae took in the corridor, which stretched ahead of them for a few yards before curving around and out of sight. The walls and ceiling were smooth and glowed with a steady white light. "The diamond was kind of shaped like a brain, wasn't it?" Dae said, just realizing.

"Huh," Tyrcell said. "I think you're right. I thought it was sort of a funny shape for a gemstone." They started walking down the corridor. "I really hope this is easier than the last temple we had to navigate. It's got to be, right? We made it this far. There has to be some reward for making progress."

*"Is it traditional, at a university, say, for the tests to get easier as you progress?"* Chk Chk asked.

"I wish you hadn't said that," Tyrcell groaned.

# 18

## THE THOUSAND MOONS

(Tyrcell / 7 AG)

I dropped the *Venture* out of the Drift as close as I could to the Thousand Moons. You don't want to pop out of another level of reality right in the middle of a dense, ever-shifting asteroid field, because that's a good way to get a bunch of holes blown through your ship and then, by extension, through yourself.

"I have never been this close to Eox, the rotting grave world, source of all necrotic foulness in the galaxy." Ketavan was sitting in the copilot's chair (despite my many hints that he should wait elsewhere), staring at the screen, filled as it was with the floating pieces of old Eox, asteroids the size of people, the size of houses, and almost the size of moons, floating silently in the dark like a landslide caught in a slow tornado.

"I've been to the Diaspora," Melezheun said from the jump seat behind us. "This is much the same."

"Ah, but the Diaspora is the remnants of two great planets destroyed by the necrovites long ago, a monument to their terrible cruelty," Ketavan said. "The Thousand Moons are pieces of Eox itself, blasted from the planet by a counterstrike, and so this is a monument to the terrible weakness of the bone sages."

I sighed. "Nobody knows any of that for sure. It's all just speculation." The Gap had wiped memories and garbled records all over the galaxy, including the truth about Eox and its blown-up planetary neighbors. Melezheun and I happened to know that the main thing the Gap seemed aimed at suppressing was the existence and fate of a planet called Golarion, so there were more hints to be found about the true history of other places, but still: How Eox ended up a horrible dead rock full of horrible dead people was a matter of some debate.

"I know the truth in my heart," the priest said, with the confidence of the truly faithful.

"How did you come to be expelled from the church of Pharasma, anyway?" Melezheun asked, in that surprisingly sweet and curious voice she used sometimes when she was deeply, deeply annoyed at someone.

The priest hunched a little. "I wasn't expelled. I was invited to leave my ministry and instead take the good word to the people of the galaxy. There are... elements in the church hierarchy... that I clashed with, I admit. But Pharasma's commandments are very clear! She is the goddess of birth, death, fate, prophecy, and time. Undead in all their forms are perversions of her tenets. We her followers are commanded to destroy them on sight. And yet some people in the church argue that not all undead are abominations, that some are victims of circumstance, like those loathsome borai. Others say that ghosts just need *counseling*"—he spat the word—"to help them move on to their proper reward or punishment. Some have even argued that necrovites might be forgiven because the Gap has erased their memories and their reasons for choosing such an unrighteous path to immortality, and therefore their sin is wiped clean. Pah!" He shook his head. "The leaders of my church see an entire planet of the undead, with scarcely a living soul at all on the surface, and yet they don't whip up a holy crusade to remove this blot on all that is right and good? I cannot understand them."

"Where does the church stand on ghouls and zombies?" I asked, genuinely curious.

"Oh, dispatching zombies or any mindless minion is a mercy; everyone agrees on that." Ketavan waved a dismissive hand. "As for ghouls, they are sometimes seen as victims, but no one really objects overmuch to killing them on sight too." He paused. "It's the smell, you see, and the... infectious possibilities. They are a public health hazard."

"And since your church wouldn't go militant enough, you began researching ways to destroy Eox yourself?" Melezheun asked.

"At first, I sought to muster my own army—that is why I created my vidcast, to warn people, to inspire them, to gather our forces! And some of the faithful did come to me, yes, but they were not always the most experienced fighters or tacticians. Some understood instinctively that all undead must be eradicated, like I do, but when confronted with an actual undead creature to dispatch, many tended to scream and run away. Others killed our foes adroitly enough, but they did so through an unseemly love for violence, or else they merely wanted to be part of something—anything. I could not trust either sort to carry out the mission, and *only* the mission, without collateral damage. Alas, I never gathered near enough competent faithful to do more than launch the occasional attack on small undead communities." He raised a bony finger. "But then things began to turn. I met sarcesians, here and there. Many of them loathe all undead, and almost *all* of them loathe Eox, and they have been trying to piece together their history from even fewer fragments than the rest of us have. The angels of the void have as many questions about the past as anyone, but few of them doubt that their home world was destroyed by the bone sages, and they want revenge. Many of them began to explore the Thousand Moons, following rumors of anomalous objects, and eventually I met a sarcesian with *real* information."

"Or a con artist who sold you a fake treasure map," I said. "I don't see anything out here but rocks."

"If sarcesians hate Eox, and they found a weapon to strike at the bone sages, why didn't they just use it themselves?" Melezheun asked.

"Ah, well, the treasure hunters who discovered the planet-killing trap and tracked down the access codes were more interested in getting rich than getting revenge. But that is all right. I had some trouble building an army, but I have never had difficulty getting donations, and my coffers were full... at least until I purchased this information. I was waiting for more funds to launch my expedition."

"It must have been a scam." I scanned the area for anything that *didn't* look like just another rock. We were near the inner edge of the debris field, and I caught occasional glimpses of Eox below: a blackened cinder of a world, bereft of oceans or greenery, laced across its surface with artificial lights. No wonder the bone sages had launched the assault on Absalom Station. My home was beautiful and wonderful, and theirs was ugly and dreadful.

"It was no scam!" Ketavan asserted. "They provided ample video evidence."

"But not an exact location," I pointed out. The word *roughly* had been appended to the coordinates Ketavan had given me.

The priest nodded. "Ah, well, that's tricky. The Thousand Moons shift around a bit. Everyone knows that, those who know anything about them. And it's a chaotic system, so you can't predict *exactly* where any of the asteroids will be at any given time. But we should be close enough. I told you, they put a daub of transponder paint on the right asteroid, and once we get within a thousand yards or so, we'll detect it."

"Getting within a thousand yards of an asteroid in a moving starship is begging for a collision, Ketavan. Sarcesians can fly around on wings of light out there, but we are not that nimble—"

"Ty." Melezheun pointed at the console, where a telltale light was blinking.

"Oh," I said. "We're picking up a transponder signal."

I still had nagging doubts about the reliability of the priest's purchased intel, but at least we had a place to investigate. The asteroid in question was immense, equal parts black stone and milky ice, almost the size of a dwarf planet. When we got close, Ketavan told me to transmit a complex alphanumeric code on a particular frequency... and when we did, the rocky side of the asteroid irised open, revealing a dark interior tunnel, like an immense throat.

"I just... fly in there?" I asked.

"Unless you want to take a shuttle and leave your vessel behind," Ketavan said.

I preferred the armor and armaments of the *Venture* to the flimsy protection of my third-hand shuttle; my vessel wasn't a warship by any means, but it did have *some* exploding bells and dangerous whistles. I floated in through the opening, which was big enough to admit a ship twice our size, and once we were fully inside, the asteroid closed up again, camouflage restored.

Lights came on inside the tunnel, bars of illumination spaced at intervals, though about a third of them just flickered once and then died. An ancient guidance system attempted to interface with my navigational controls, but the computers were speaking different languages, and the automated system soon gave up. "It's fine," Ketavan said. "Just go straight ahead, and there should be a docking platform."

The tunnel eventually widened out into a vast hangar, the deck below us scattered with the remains of small ships that looked like they'd been messily stripped for parts. I'd completely misunderstood the scale of the place we were going. I'd been expecting a small control room tucked away into a floating rock, but this was a full-fledged military installation—abandoned, yes, but once clearly a very serious undertaking.

"Just set down anywhere!" Ketavan was practically bouncing in his chair, he was so excited to find his treasure at last. I suspected he was going to be a problem. We needed to figure out a way to disable this place when we left, or Ketavan would come back later and destroy Eox for real.

I found a relatively clear portion of the hangar floor and settled down. We got into our environment suits—Ketavan had to wear the spare and grumbled as it adjusted itself to fit his scrawny contours—and then we descended the *Venture*'s ramp. The artificial gravity in the hangar still worked, better than the lights had, so maybe other systems had remained intact too.

"Here we are in a weird space dungeon again, Mel." We walked slowly into the graveyard of cannibalized ships. "Did you miss it?"

"As long as we don't have to do math puzzles to proceed this time," she said.

Ketavan wasn't interested in our banter or our little trip down memory lane. He set off briskly toward a set of stairs that were all out of proportion for our bodies—even before sarcesians adapted to life in the void, they must have been a statuesque people, assuming their ancestors were indeed the architects of this place.

We clambered up the switchback steps until we reached a platform that faced an imposing door in a blank wall emblazoned with red-and-yellow warning signs in language I didn't recognize. There were about three hundred knife-switch levers on the wall on either side of the door, all their handles pointing upward. "Look for the levers with blue paint," Ketavan said.

Melezheun and I each drifted in a different direction and found levers with marks on their handles—mine was high enough off the ground that I'd have to jump to reach it. Ketavan found one too. The handles were scattered far apart, enough that even long-armed sarcesians couldn't have pulled two of them at once. "You don't actually need three people, though," I said. "Drones and bots can flip a switch."

"They cannot flip these," Ketavan said. "All the controls in this place are enchanted to detect life, and only the living may activate them! We seek a weapon built to kill the undead, Tyrcell, and the undead are incapable of accessing it."

"Huh. OK. That's pretty smart." We all yanked our levers when Ketavan said "Go," and the door went *thunk* and swung open.

"Now, apparently, it gets a bit dangerous after this," Ketavan said. "My contacts told me to beware of 'guardians and traps.' They said they disabled all the threats they found, but there could be more."

"Guardians and traps. Great." I had my pistols, and Melezheun had grabbed a spare staff she kept on my ship, one with some nasty elemental magic wrapped around the shaft.

"Let me lead the way," I said. "I've got a good eye for traps." No one argued with me—when someone volunteers to be a goblin mine detector, people usually don't—so I led the way down the tall, narrow corridor, the walls of which were emblazoned with more warnings I couldn't read.

I hit the first trap only a hundred yards in, and it wasn't very subtle. The holographic projector was old and busted, and the fake floor flickered in and out of sight.

"There's a pit trap here." I took aim with one of my pistols and sniped the tiny projector, and the illusion vanished entirely, revealing a hole in the middle of the floor. It was a messy hole, like it had been brutally carved out with hand tools, making me think it was an addition that came *after* this place was mothballed, not part of the original specs.

I shined a light into the hole and whistled. There were spikes down there, of course, but they were an assortment of jagged pieces of scavenged metal in all different shapes and sizes, gleaming wetly with whatever toxins they'd been doused in. "Let's just sidle around this."

There was clearance on both sides of the hole, though not a *lot*, and we put our backs against the wall and began to shuffle sideways.

There was a click as I stepped on a pressure plate on the floor, and I realized I was *meant* to see the pit trap, and *expected* to shuffle along the side, where I'd inevitably step on the trigger for the actual trap. There was a giggle from up above as the ceiling collapsed on us—

A glowing golden barrier appeared over our heads, rubble showering down on both sides. Ketavan had some divine magic after all. Melezheun muttered and made mystic passes with her staff, and a shimmering crystal bridge appeared across the pit trap.

Huh. Maybe I should try to learn some magic.

We stepped onto the bridge and hurried across, and once we were clear of the collapsed area, Ketavan let the magical shield drop. Rubble fell, but it wasn't the *whole* ceiling, just enough tonnage to crush a few unwary dungeon delvers. The cave-in had the nice bonus of filling in the pit, so we'd be able to come back this way more easily once we finished threatening a genocide.

I looked up at the dim ceiling. "Did anyone else hear laughter right before the roof caved in?"

"I did," Melezheun said. "We are not alone in here."

"Guardians and traps," Ketavan said smugly. "Shall we go on?"

I led the way again, but *much* more slowly and cautiously, because the whole goblin-mine-detector thing is kind of funny but also pretty dark. (The idea is, goblins send the most useless member of their band into a dungeon first, and they detect any traps... by triggering them and getting turned into paste. It's very effective. A necromancer could have sent a whole bunch of skeletons into the dark to trigger all the traps on the same principle. Maybe I should learn some necromancy.)

Over the next thousand yards of hallway, I managed to avoid a laser trap, disable a trash-compactor trap, deactivate some nozzles that would have sprayed acid or spores or poisonous gas or something on us, and turn off a disintegrator beam. There were no more giggles, but there were some wails of frustration coming from the ceiling and wall vents as we consistently failed to die.

The traps got, for want of a better word, *jankier* as we moved deeper into the complex, taking turns according to Ketavan's instructions.

There were improvised explosives, deadfalls, spring-loaded spikes, and even greased floors and homemade caltrops. "A lot of these traps were just built from random junk," I said.

"Those ships in the hangar were taken apart and stripped," Melezheun said. "Someone must have used those parts to build more traps. But why? Did goblins find this place and move in at some point?"

"It's hard to imagine how they would have made it all the way out here," I said. "Also, this is a *lot* of traps. Goblins would have gotten bored and tried to stab us by now. We—Ketavan, no!"

The priest had gotten ahead of me, eager to lay waste to his enemies, and he stepped on an honestly not-very-well-hidden plate on the floor. Darts shot from the wall beside him, but he managed to conjure a shield when I shouted, and the projectiles bounced off without hitting him.

"That was a close—" he began to say in relief, and then a shriek of outrage burst from the ceiling, and a *thing* came down—it was like a pile of scrap metal and hoses, but it had arms made of hinged lengths of metal, with improvised claws dangling from the underside. It hovered before us, and there was the faint outline of a spectral skull floating above the metal jumble, gnashing its teeth. The thing screamed at us and then flashed past, flying just over our heads and disappearing around a turn in the corridor.

"What in the layers of Hell was *that* thing?" I shouted.

"As I suspected," Ketavan said. "A gearghost. It is a most insidious form of the undead."

"I thought undead couldn't get in here?"

"That gearghost was *made* here," Ketavan said. "When an operative dies in a trap in a place like this, their outrage at being bested and their shame at their failure can combine to make their soul persist after death. When that happens, they become a spirit, often building a new body out of the very machinery that killed them. They roam the ruins and forgotten places where they died, and they are compelled to build more traps, to kill others. They also repair and reset traps that have been sprung, which explains why we've encountered so many, even after the sarcesians came through here."

"How do we kill the thing?" Melezheun asked. "Or, ah, release it from its torment?"

Ketavan counted on his fingers. "Sanctify the ground, douse the gearghost in holy water, and destroy all the traps in its territory. That should prevent it from reforming." He shrugged. "It is sad, and I will try to dispatch it later, but we have other priorities now. The fact that the ghost is so furious with us most likely means we have defeated all its traps, which also means our destination is at hand."

Ketavan boldly walked ahead of us, right into a trip wire, and got a spike of metal as long as my arm driven right through one side of his calf and out the other.

Somewhere behind us, the gearghost tittered, pleased with itself.

We pulled the metal out, Melezheun did some light healing to stop Ketavan's howling, and then we limped together up a short set of steps that led to the control room of the planet-killing device.

You have to believe me. Melezheun and I really didn't intend what happened next.

# 19

## THE SALVATION OF CASPIEN BLIGHTWIND

### (Valentine / 7 AG)

The Battle of the Lorespire—more about that later—is generally seen as the most significant clash that took place on the station itself during the Magefire Assault. It was certainly the biggest, in terms of people fighting on both sides, and in terms of casualties taken.

But I don't think it was the most consequential battle. For me, that distinction goes to a much smaller fight, one that happened way down in the Spike, between a handful of station defenders and a handful of invaders. *That's* the clash that really shifted the balance on the station and ultimately enabled us to stop the Magefire Assault.

And it was all thanks to Valentine and her new friends.

"We take special salvage union transport," Scunge said, leading Azzi, Caspien, and Valentine (feeling invincible in her power armor) past the unconscious ghoul and through a gate in the formidable fence. The space beyond was one of the usual narrow paths through infinite scrap heaps that seemed to typify Botscrap's landscape.

"What kind of transport?" Val asked. "A junk wagon with rockets strapped on top?"

"You think we move tons of material in *wagon*?" Scunge said. "Well, OK, some do. But senior guild members, we have better ways." They followed him to a particularly large and unsteady-looking junk pile, one that had an entire wrecked shuttle embedded within the mess about ten feet off the ground. Scunge hummed tunelessly to himself as he fiddled with his wrist gauntlet.

A seamlessly welded-together section of the pile swung open at the base, revealing a freight elevator gate and a large platform on the other side. "We go down." He opened the gate, they all piled onto the platform, he closed the gate, and they began to descend with a sudden jerk. "We have whole transport system down in space between levels," Scunge said. "You might need to be ducking your head sometimes down here, though, Azzi."

"Story of my life," the dragonkin muttered.

Val wasn't sure if they were going very slowly or very far down, but it was a long trip, and she passed the time playing with the controls in her heads-up display. She flagged her current companions so the weaponry wouldn't hit them with friendly fire (assuming they didn't leap in front of a projectile or something) and set up various shortcuts so she could deploy her weaponry with the flick of an eyeball. The arms and legs of the suit were hooked into her exocortex, so she could walk and punch and grab as easily as thinking it.

Val had, admittedly, moderated her stance on thinking all undead were irredeemable monsters, but *some* of them were, and soon she'd get to beat the crap out of *those* ones. This was going to be fun.

And she was going to make sure Caspien came through this fight in one piece, since it was her fault he was there at all. In fact... "Caspien, I dragged you into all this, very much against your will. If you want to hang back and wait for us here, or even go back to the workshop, that's absolutely fine—"

"I am a citizen of Absalom Station," the borai said stiffly, staring straight ahead, wrapped in his void-black cloak. "It is my duty to defend this place just as much as it is yours."

Val wanted to reach out and touch him but was afraid that would be unwelcome—and also, she was wearing power armor, and it was hard to give someone a friendly shoulder pat when you were strong enough to rip an airlock door off its hinges. "When we're done here, Cass, there's a place for you in the Society if you want it. We may not pay as well as your bosses in Bluerise Tower, but we can offer you something better than a windowless room. We can offer you a home. A community."

Caspien turned to look at her, eyes narrowed, but was there something like a glimmer of hope? "I'm borai. We aren't welcome anywhere."

"The Society has a reputation for welcoming everybody," Azzi rumbled. "They got their start as something like a microcosm of the population of the station—founded by an android, a lashunta, an ysoki, and a couple humans—and before long, they were welcoming all kinds of people into the ranks."

"And you're part of the station now too," Val said. "It's past time we opened our doors to you and yours. If you want."

"I'll think about it." You could have used Caspien's voice to hammer dents out of sheet metal, it was so firm and unyielding, but it wasn't a no. Val had a lot to make up for, but maybe she'd made a good start.

The elevator shuddered to a stop, and Scunge—who'd seemingly paid no attention at all to the fraught exchange happening around him—hauled up the gate to let them out. The elevator opened onto one side of a long, dim corridor that resembled a tram tunnel, wide and rounded, stretching off in both directions. Trash was piled up against the bottom of the walls on both sides, but there was a clear space in the center of the floor wide enough for vehicular transport, the decking worn smooth by long use. The place reeked of engine oil and burned metal and something unidentifiable but sour.

The piled trash across from the elevator moved with a crackle and a crunch, and Val wondered if there were squoxes or some other critters down there, nesting.

Then Scunge muttered, "I know that smell." He stepped forward, holding up his hand, a bright light shining from his wrist gauntlet and illuminating a heap of rags and plastic. "Globkin! Come on out."

A goblin popped out of the trash heaped against the base of the tunnel, his huge oblong head bristling with teeth. He was dressed in rags that fit right in with the garbage strewn around him. Goblins weren't huge, but they weren't tiny either, and Val was amazed he'd been able to conceal himself in the mess. Her heads-up display lit him up in a purple glow, which seemed to mean, "Is this a target or not?" Val withheld judgment. She'd heard Botscrap was full of goblins, scavenging among the remnants, and she suspected they were a lot more dangerous than gnarefuroids.

"Why are you hiding in here?" Scunge said. "You usually stay over by the Blasted Boltbox or whatever it's called."

"Bad ones came," the goblin said. "Fangsters and stinkers and bone folk. Tried to eat Globkin and Globkin's kin!"

"Does he mean... vampires and ghouls and skeletal minions?" Caspien hazarded, and Val shrugged, though the movement didn't really translate well to power armor.

"Probably," Azzi said. "You gonna introduce us, Scunge?"

"Eh?" The ysoki tilted back his head to look at Azzi, then looked back at the goblin. "This is Globkin, leader of the Busted Bolt band. You escaped attack from undead?"

The goblin nodded his oversized head. "All of us, almost, except one or two who are stinkers now." Globkin gestured, and suddenly all the trash in the tunnel, on both sides as far as they could see, moved, revealing hidden goblins dressed in garbage-strewn camouflage. There were at least scores of them, possibly more; counting them was beyond the limits even of Val's armor-enhanced vision. The goblins were armed with everything from metal poles to kludged-together ray guns. Globkin went on, "We came down here because nobody knows about these underneath places so much... so we can sneak up on them."

"You're going to attack the undead invaders?" Val asked. She had the idea that goblins were cowardly creatures, but was that just more bigotry? Maybe one goblin could be cowardly. They were, infamously, a lot more courageous when they were in a horde, and this was looking like a horde.

"They ate my friends," Globkin said. "They can't eat my friends." He put a hand to his chest. "Only *we* get to eat our friends!"

"Do you know where the stinkers and such are now?" Scunge said.

"In the secret salvage union headquarters that no one is supposed to know about, but we do," Globkin said.

"That sounds right." Scunge gestured at the goblins. "They hide in scrap heaps and vents and pipes and listen and look and learn. There's no keeping secrets from a goblin. We were going to fight the undead too. May we join your band?"

Val wanted to object—surely these lowly goblins armed with junk would be joining *them*, not the other way around! Except the goblins had been there first... and there were a lot more of them. Ugh. She had a lot of work to do on her own brain, didn't she?

"Yes, join," Globkin said. "We were going to go, when the elevator rumbled us to hide. We thought maybe more of the dead ones were coming. But only one dead one. Is friend?" Globkin pointed at Caspien, and there was suddenly an overcomplicated chrome-and-glass pistol in his hand.

"Is friend!" Caspien and Val and Azzi all shouted at once, and Scunge nodded too.

The goblin moved the end of the gun fractionally away and grinned—or maybe his teeth just looked like that. "Yes, then, all friends. Let's go burn the dead things."

"Or something like that," Val said.

"I was going to call transport," Scunge said. "But there is not room for all these goblins. It is not so far to go, though. Come, come."

They all let Val take the lead, since she was a walking war machine. Caspien and Azzi followed at her back, with Scunge and the goblins behind them, though the goblins were also ranging up and down on both sides, vanishing into cracks in the wall that seemed too small for them to fit through, and generally acting as scouts. She'd always imagined goblins as noisy, squabblesome creatures, but they were eerily silent. They could also be pack hunters or ambush predators, it seemed.

The group didn't encounter anyone else for hundreds and hundreds of trudging yards, until Scunge said, "Here, wait, is secret door."

"Globkin knew about it," Globkin said with a trace of pride.

"Globkin knows more than is good for him." Scunge walked to a perfectly unremarkable stretch of wall and pressed it in several perfectly unremarkable places, and then a section of wall slid aside, revealing a set of metal stairs beyond. The doorway was low—Azzi would definitely have to duck—but the passageway opened up wider on the far side.

Scunge said, "Undead will be guarding approaches to salvage union headquarters, surely. But this leads up to storage area in back. Is hidden entrance to mostly empty room, so double hidden, maybe they don't know about it? But maybe they do." Scunge shrugged.

"I'll go first." Val clomped forward as quietly as she could in a large metal suit, reached the base of the stairs, and looked up at the hatch on the ceiling, about ten feet above. She tested the steps with one foot, worried the metal would bend under her armor's weight, but it didn't even creak. The salvage union knew what they were doing.

"Hatch should open when you press up on it," Scunge said.

Val went up a couple of stairs and pressed. The hatch yielded briefly and then stopped. She grunted, then braced her feet, put both palms against the hatch, and *shoved.*

Something above her squawked when the hatch door ripped loose from its hinges and flew upward, slamming against the ceiling. Val leaped up through the opening as the trapdoor tumbled down, and she batted the square of metal aside. Then she looked down at the ghoul, dazed and bleeding from the face, who'd been on *top* of the hatch when she shoved it and had subsequently been thrown across the room.

The ghoul was pretty banged up, but Val banged him up more, grabbing him in one mechanical claw, lifting him by the neck, and giving him a shake. From inside the power armor, she couldn't really smell him, though there was a warning about contaminated air in her HUD. "How many of you are there?" she demanded.

"More of us all the time," the ghoul wheezed, scrabbling pointlessly at her mechanical grip. "We aren't like you, growing babies in our bellies. We can grow our families with our *teeth*." The ghoul gnashed at her helmet's faceplate.

Val had honestly never been great at *calculated* violence. She had a bad temper, and when she had been defending her home or her wife or her friends during the bad days of chaos on the station, she'd fought and even killed people, but always in a rage-induced righteous haze. As she held this ghoul's life in her hands, knowing she could pop off his head with but a thought, even knowing he was working for the downfall of her home, it was hard to actually—

The ghoul screamed as a golden spearhead burst out of its chest and then ripped back out again. The hole smoked and sizzled, edges charred. Val dropped the body and looked at Caspien, cloaked in black, holding his holy spear. "Thanks," she said.

"I've been bullied by a lot of ghouls," Caspien said. "This could actually be cathartic for me."

Azzi clambered out of the hole, followed by Scunge and then Globkin, though his horde mostly hung out on the stairs, since the storage room was only so big. "We should have plan, maybe," Scunge said.

Val nodded. "Me and Caspien and Scunge and Azzi can go to the control room and stop the undead from messing with the station security systems and comms. Globkin and his people can... sow chaos and confusion?"

"These are Globkin's middle names," the goblin chief said. "Globkin Chaos Confusion Busted Bolt." He rubbed his hands together.

"Works for me," Azzi said, and the others all nodded.

"Scunge, where are we going?" Val asked.

"Out of here, turn right, turn left, go through double doors into grand ballroom—"

"The salvage union has a grand ballroom?" Val interrupted.

Scunge cocked his head curiously. "Yes. Where else would we hold annual grand union ball?"

"Of course. Silly of me. Do we have to go through this ballroom? That just doesn't sound like a stealthy route."

"Is only way," Scunge said. "Secret control room is on other side of ballroom, no other paths."

"Right, left, through the doors," Val said. "OK, that should be easy enough."

The first two parts were. Caspien eased open the door, looked into the corridor, and declared the all clear. The lights in the hall had been shattered—undead weren't, as a whole, big fans of illumination—which gave the place a haunted, derelict air.

They crept along, though Val couldn't help but clank a bit, and took the next turn—and there were the large double doors, guarded by a pair of skeletal minions holding large battle axes they'd probably been buried with centuries earlier on some planet where technology hadn't advanced beyond hitting people with sharp bits of metal.

The minions sensed them and immediately ran toward them, axes upraised, and, even worse, they emitted high-pitched keening screams that sounded more mechanical than voiced. *They're alarms,* Val realized with dismay, and lifted her hands, blasting both skeletons with concentrated bursts of projectile fire from the launchers on her arms and scattering their bones into shrapnel, though the keening went on.

"Let's go!" she shouted, rushing for the doors, and she smashed through them, her power armor tearing through the metal like it was paper. The doors slamming off their hinges did an admirable job of scattering the first wave of undead who'd come in response to the alarms, their bodies flying back and off to the sides... only to lurch upright again with zombie resilience.

The ballroom was a wreck even before Val started doing damage, with the ruins of an elaborate chandelier smashed in the middle of the floor and most of the wall sconces shattered too, leaving only faint illumination. The doors at the other end of the ballroom opened, less explosively, and a crew of a dozen non-mindless undead—mindful undead?—entered, bearing arms. There were vampires, more ghouls, corpsefolk, a couple of borai, and the shimmering, inconstant form of a ghost among them.

*"Get them!"* Val shouted, voice amplified by the power armor, and rushed toward the vampire.

What followed next could be described generously as a ballet of violence. Less poetically put, it was an ugly, violent melee. Val's camera drone floated up toward the ballroom ceiling and took positions to record the fight from every useful angle. What the footage showed was Val grabbing a vampire by the neck with one armored hand, grabbing it by the head with the other hand, and twisting the head clean off, her earlier hesitation with the ghoul nowhere in evidence now that a true battle had been joined.

Caspien whirled around with surprising agility, the golden tip of his spear making the zombies it touched flee in terror, some of them actually trying to run *through* walls.

Azzi swiped with their powerful claws and aimed short, controlled bursts with their fiery breath before remembering that their body was literally covered with weaponry, and they started firing at the undead with pistols in each hand.

Scunge stood in a corner of the ballroom with his complicated cannon and took careful aim at the undead leadership, his firing solutions so perfect that he must have had targeting software running inside that welder's mask. The cannon's functions were myriad. One ghoul was struck with a glob of expanding foam that glued it, shrieking, to a wall. One of the borai was neatly bisected by a spinning blade that embedded itself in the wall, shearing off most of a zombie on the way. The ghoul was wrapped up by an electric net that first stunned it… and then it began to *contract*, squeezing and squeezing until the creature's unlife was compressed out of it.

Then there were the goblins. They swarmed the zombies, blasting and hacking and, yes, biting; the appetites of goblins are legendary and prodigious, and their stomachs are famously capable of digesting just about anything organic, including corpses. Globkin sought bigger game, befitting his status as chief, and he shot the kneecaps off one of the corpsefolk before gleefully jumping up and down on its face.

There were injuries and casualties on the side of the station defenders—a couple of the ghouls had ranged weapons, and they managed to take out numerous goblins before they went down under a flood of small but furious bodies. Azzi's left arm was grazed by an energy blast, searing a charred line across their bicep that made them scream, charge, and dispatch their attacker. Caspien lost most of his right ear, though he didn't notice until much later, and even careful review of the footage doesn't show exactly how or when it happened—he was spinning that spear and stabbing every zombie he could reach the whole time, and, even in slow motion, was a bit of a blur.

The most significant casualty on the side of the defenders, though, was… Well. Here's what happened.

It was all because of the ghost.

The apparition floated toward Val in her power armor while she was blasting a ghoul in the face with a plasma torch embedded in the palm of one armored claw. The ghost floated into her armor… and then the interior lights flickered, and the power armor powered down. Val was suddenly stuck inside a metal coffin, unable to move her limbs, and a horrible static-and-feedback noise filled her helmet as the ghost moaned in her ear. She panicked, the intangible undead acting directly on her amygdala to flood her with fear, and thrashed as best she could, trapped inside the armor. But she managed to control her flailing enough to grab the emergency-release lever, yanking it upright and opening the front panel of the armor.

Val slithered out of the cockpit, gasping, breathing hard, and trying to shake off her terror. She made it to her feet, finding herself suddenly unarmed and unprotected. The armor's lights flickered back on as the ghost—one of the technologically adroit sorts, apparently—took control of the suit and lifted its lethal arms.

The embedded grenade launcher on its left arm hissed open, the wide aperture pointed at Val like a sightless eye.

Then the armor pivoted, taking aim not at Val, but at Caspien, who was jabbing the point of his spear-staff into the body of a zombie.

Why did the ghost aim for Caspien? Maybe because he was undead, and the ghost thought he was a traitor. Maybe because the weapon he wielded was actually capable of harming the ghost. Who can say? The point is, the ghost focused on the borai elf and launched a projectile.

And Val leaped into that projectile's path. The grenade struck her in the chest, hard enough to crack her ribs and send her tumbling to the floor. But the grenade wasn't a projectile weapon meant to tear through flesh and bone, so it didn't kill her. Not then.

It didn't bounce off her chest, either. The ghost had fired—probably at random—one of the sticky grenades, the sort that strike their target and then adhere, so there's no throwing it back or running away.

You can see on the drone footage as Valentine tugs at the grenade, trying to tear it away from her chest, but she only succeeds in getting her hands stuck to it instead. You can see the moment on her face when she realizes that this explosive is *on her* and isn't going anywhere.

She turns her head and looks at Azzi—who doesn't even notice her plight, busy fighting a zombie of their own—and then she looks at Caspien. You can't hear her on the video, because the whole situation is too noisy, with the gunfire and the gibbering of the goblins, but it's easy enough to read her lips.

Val says, "I'm so sorry." Then she looks up, right into the hovering camera, and says, "I love you, babe."

After that, Val runs for the power armor and climbs back *inside it*, headfirst, even as the ghost within tries to pull her out with the armor's claws, clumsily manipulated.

The grenade goes off, a burst of light and fire and sparks showering out of the armor, and then the whole power suit falls over, catastrophically damaged, pouring smoke. The ghost emerges, shimmering, from the wreckage, just in time for a sobbing Caspien to stab it over and over and over again with the holy spearhead, jabbing wildly at the air even after the ghost is dispelled, before finally collapsing to his knees next to the wreckage, where Scunge and Azzi and Globkin all join him, their foes vanquished... along with their friend.

Another important thing happened at the salvage union headquarters, of course, though the drone didn't record it, programmed as it was to stay with Val's body instead. But I heard the firsthand accounts: how Scunge took them all to the secret control room, where they dispatched a few more undead and then restored the station's weapons systems, life support, gravity controls, and, maybe most importantly, the comms. (The Primex, naturally, had the salvage union's backdoor control nexus deactivated once everything calmed down, and the union didn't even squawk about that, since it *had* been revealed as a pretty major weak spot in the station's defenses. Next time somebody wants to take over Absalom Station's essential functions, they'll need a much bigger team in a whole lot more places.)

Once Scunge and company returned control of the station to rightful hands, our defensive batteries were finally able to shoot back at Mnephalon's flagship, and I was able to contact Melezheun, as you saw earlier in this manuscript, and *that* eventually led to... well, you'll see.

So it's true that Val sacrificed herself to save Caspien, yes... but she also sacrificed herself to save the station—to save all of us. That's why her name is at the very top of the memorial in the Lorespire that Carn put up to honor the fallen after everything finished. You could make a plausible argument that Val would have gladly given her life to save us all—that it's exactly what she would have wanted.

Maybe. It wasn't what *any* of the rest of us wanted.

# 20

## BLACKMOON RISING

### (Melezheun / 7 AG)

Obviously the timeline in this manuscript hasn't been entirely linear. You just read the bit where Val's team defeated the undead to restore the comms and the defense systems to station control, which happened way before me and Mel and Ketavan lit out for the territories. Well, what can I say? I originally tried to organize this document in a strictly chronological fashion, and honestly, that was *more* confusing. Just assume that everything was happening everywhere all at once, in all the worst ways possible.

The end is coming up, folks. It just wasn't the end that we meant it to be.

The three of them entered the control room, and it was more or less what Mel had expected from the priest's descriptions: a square about twenty feet to a side, with a console against each wall except the one with the door. The control panels were covered in unlit lights, with dead screens above them. Each console had a single large black button right in the center. There were no chairs, but that was fine—everything was built to a larger scale than any of their bodies, and they would have needed to stand to reach the controls, anyway.

There were holographic words, all different, hovering above the consoles. "I wish I could read those," Ty said.

"I can," Ketavan said. "It's an ancient Sarcesian dialect. One console says 'Initiate,' one says 'Accelerate,' and one says 'Execute.' When all three of those systems are triggered, the bombardment of Eox will begin, and with it, a new era of peace and prosperity in all the civilized worlds." He walked over to the first console—"Initiate," Mel assumed—and it lit up brightly. The screens began to display what looked like telemetry data and impact simulations. "See?"

Ketavan said. "The machinery still works. It detected my life force and turned itself on." He cracked his bony knuckles.

"Careful, there," Tyrcell said. "Don't go poking anything."

"It takes all three of us acting in tandem to launch the planet-killing attack," Ketavan said. "Calm down. I am just looking things over... Ahhh. What a beautiful damage projection." Ketavan was practically drooling as he leaned toward a screen that showed a sphere being peppered with thousands of asteroid impacts. "The necrovites won't even be able to hide in their tombs and their caves and their pits. We're going to shatter this planet down to its rotten core!"

"No, we're not," Melezheun protested. "We're going to threaten the bone sages with destruction. That's all."

"Of course. But it needs to be an *effective* threat. We have to switch on the weapon, so their sensors can detect the danger."

"Won't they launch a strike against us immediately?" Mel said.

Ketavan shook his head, face lit up by the screens. "The Thousand Moons arc across the entire sky of that planet. They won't be able to detect our precise location so quickly. Besides, just tell them that any attack will trigger the weapon to activate automatically—I think that might even be true." He gestured. "Go on. Approach your consoles."

Tyrcell stepped toward the "Accelerate" wall, and the systems woke up, screens displaying models of dozens of different asteroids surrounded by equations. They looked over at the priest. "So your console, what, turns on the system, and mine accelerates the asteroids toward Eox?"

Melezheun went toward her console, "Execute," and it came to life too. "And mine... executes the command?" Her screens showed asteroids exploding into shrapnel, over and over again.

"I don't have a user manual," Ketavan said, "but that seems plausible. Although I think your console also primes warheads hidden inside some of the asteroids, Melezheun."

"Gods," Mel breathed. "The people who built this place were *thorough*."

"You may as well call up the bone sages and make your threats," Ketavan said.

Tyrcell nodded and pulled their hood over their head, then covered the lower half of their face with a scarf. Whoever delivered this threat to the bone sages wouldn't be very popular on Eox, and if you were going to anger the leaders of a whole planet, it was best to do so anonymously. Mnephalon might recognize their shape and their voice, but with luck, she wouldn't get looped in.

They'd released a series of drones along their journey so they could relay a message from Ty's gauntlet through the *Venture*'s communications system without the sages instantly being able to pinpoint the source of the call.

Contacting a bone sage wasn't easy—you couldn't just contact the Primex on a whim either—but Ty worked their way through various levels of secretaries by claiming to be a representative of Absalom Station with the power to destroy Eox. They did have Syndicsguild authentication codes—Val had shared hers—and eventually someone took them seriously enough to check their planetary defense sensors and notice what was apparently an immense energy signature spreading right across the whole of the Thousand Moons.

Finally, an actual necrovite appeared in the display over Ty's gauntlet. Ketavan and Melezheun stayed off to one side and out of sight, but Tyrcell positioned themself so a console would appear in the background behind them, with its animations of asteroids tumbling in clear view.

"To whom am I speaking?" the bone sage snapped. He had a face like a metal skull with fires burning inside it and wore a crown decorated with silver-plated canine teeth and black jewels.

Ty pitched their voice lower than usual. "I represent the interests of Absalom Station. We've come to demand an immediate end to hostilities there, the withdrawal of all your forces, and a binding oath to forswear any future unprovoked violence against us."

"Some anonymous humanoid makes demands of *us*?" the necrovite sneered. "We could wipe your pitiful space station out with the snap of our fingers!"

"I could destroy your entire planet with the push of a button," Ty countered. "You've heard the rumors, I'm sure, about the planet-killing trap in the Thousand Moons?"

"A baseless sarcesian fantasy—" The bone sage began his rebuttal, but then a cringingly servile vampire entered the frame and whispered in the sage's ear before scuttling away.

The necrovite was silent for a long time. "Well. It does seem like *something* is happening in the debris field. Enough to make... opening negotiations... seem reasonable. Your demands are obviously absurd, and we won't agree to anything of the sort, but—"

"No negotiation with the dead!" Ketavan shouted as he launched himself at the "Initiate" console, slamming his palm down on the large black button. The screens all flared with light, and a series of shifting glyphs that looked disturbingly like a countdown replaced the holographic display of words floating above.

The priest flipped one toggle on the console and reached for another, but Melezheun swept his legs out from under him with her staff, sending him to fall onto his back. She walked to the console, looking for any kind of abort button, but what few markings there were appeared in a language she couldn't fully understand. The screens showed a single stylized asteroid, one almost perfectly spherical, outlined in red, and then, slowly, the orb began to drift across the display. How could she stop it? How could you unthrow a rock?

"What is happening there?" the necrovite demanded.

Tyrcell slammed the mute button on their gauntlet so the sage couldn't overhear and spun toward the fallen priest. "Ketavan!" they shouted. "What did you do?"

"I cast the first stone!" the old man cackled from the ground, not even trying to rise, apparently content with the damage he'd wrought.

Tyrcell shook their head, unwilling to accept the reality that Melezheun had already absorbed. "But... it's supposed to take all three of us to launch the attack. We have to initiate, and then accelerate, and then execute—"

"Ha!" Ketavan sneered. "I can't do *everything* without your help, I can't launch *all* the stones, or accelerate them to deadlier speeds, or arm the bombs inside them, but I can get things *started*, by the gods, and I did!" He kicked his feet in supine glee. "Death! I am become Death! Death to the undead!"

Melezheun stared down at him, numb with horror. Even just a single asteroid… what would it *do*? Maybe… if it struck an uninhabited area—

"What have you *done*?" the bone sage demanded. "Our sensors are picking up—a single asteroid? Estimated area of impact is—by the blood and bone, you launched one at *Murthal*?" The sage's face twisted into a vicious snarl, then smoothed out. "Oh. I see. A show of force, then? To prove that you're serious? An act of mere mass murder to show us that you aren't bluffing? Fine. Yes. Message received. I must… consult with my colleagues." The holographic projection wavered and vanished.

Ketavan rose and moved toward his console again, and Tyrcell drew a pistol and shot the control panel, sending up a shower of sparks and making the priest stumble away. He turned on Tyrcell, snarling, eyes popping, spit flecking the corners of his mouth. "Ha! The damage is done, android! And it's only the beginning of the cleansing fire I will rain down!"

Melezheun had been quietly circling around the priest, and she suddenly jabbed him in the small of the back with her staff, jolting him with a shock strong enough to drop him to his knees, muttering and whimpering and curling up into a ball.

Tyrcell and Melezheun looked at the screens above the remaining consoles, which showed that lone asteroid falling, falling, falling toward the stylized sphere of Eox.

Tyrcell here. Let me take a step back from the chaos of that moment and tell you what happened on the planet below us.

Ketavan managed to activate the first stage of the Thousand Moons trap, and as a result, one of the largest asteroids in the debris field was magically drawn toward the surface of Eox. The rock was supposed to be further accelerated with a combination of inertial technology and magic, but since Melezheun and I didn't trigger those controls, the asteroid wasn't fired like a bullet from a gun. It was just dropped, like… many thousands of tons of rock and metal falling from a great height. Which is better! It really is better. It's just not all that *much* better.

There was a city down there on Eox called Murthal, one of the greatest necropolises on the surface, home to hundreds of thousands of undead citizens. The place was famous for these ancient towers that looked like finger bones pointing accusingly at the sky, which is a strange thing to be proud of, but it's not like they had beautiful gardens or tranquil lakes to tell tourists about.

That asteroid tumbled, and it tumbled fast, and it utterly crushed Murthal—and sent out a shock wave of dirt and stone and energy that scoured everything within a thousand miles. Where Murthal had been, there was just a devastated area, and looming in its place a chunk of rock the size of a mountain, almost a perfect hemisphere.

Now, if the trap had gone off as the builders intended, that rock would have been moving a lot faster and would have transferred a lot more energy to the planet and would have destroyed everything within *ten* thousand miles—and it would have been just the opening salvo in an escalating bombardment that would have flung every asteroid of significant size onto the surface of the planet, one after another, faster and faster, turning Eox into an overlapping mess of blast craters, until the planet itself was cracked apart and became an asteroid field itself. So. Things could have been worse. They could have been *so* much worse.

Later, the locals looked at that new mountain, that headstone for the grave of a whole city, and named it Blackmoon. It became the tallest summit on Eox. It's one of the tallest mountains in the whole system.

There are rumors that people are still conscious down there under Blackmoon, or even living within the mountain itself, since many of the asteroids are riddled with tunnels and chambers that date back to the old days, when they were part of Eox itself. Some subterranean portions of Murthal might have survived, driven deeper into the ground, and the undead are very hardy creatures, capable of surviving—in their own way—devastation that would annihilate the living. So there could very well still be undead down there, in the dark, cut off from the rest of the world... forever.

That's my fault. I let that happen. I will carry that burden for as long as my soul clings to this body. Melezheun isn't the only one who feels the guilt.

"We surrender." The necrovite flickering over Tyrcell's gauntlet was impassive, apart from those burning eyes. "You have proven your point with the destruction of Murthal. No further demonstrations of force are necessary."

Tyrcell matched the bone sage's impassivity, but Melezheun knew her friend well enough to realize the android was suppressing strong emotion. "Good. We don't want the violence to escalate any further."

"You have destroyed many, many, *many* more citizens of Eox than have been harmed on your space station," the necrovite pointed out. "This was in no way a proportionate response."

"A proportionate response might not have persuaded you to end your hostilities." Tyrcell sounded like an actor mouthing lines they didn't believe or understand.

"That is true," the necrovite concurred. "We do respect strength. We have recalled Mnephalon and her fleet, and we will bring back the ships we dispatched to act as her reinforcements. I speak for the rulers of Eox when I say that we disavow all claims to Absalom Station and will cease all hostility in aggression. In return, Absalom Station will cease all hostility against us, and its agents will vacate the Thousand Moons immediately."

"As soon as I get word from the station that your forces are gone, we'll leave," Tyrcell said. "And you won't try to stop us."

"Agreed," the necrovite said. "I believe our business is concluded. But... I don't suppose you'll tell me your name? For our records?"

Tyrcell laughed. "I'd prefer to be able to sleep at night without worrying about being abducted and turned into a zombie, so, no. Consider me an anonymous patriot of Absalom Station."

"Mmm. We wouldn't turn you into a zombie. Zombies are unaware. Zombies don't suffer. For you... we would do other things. Farewell, then, patriot. Just remember: Necrovites have long memories."

*Don't we all,* Mel thought as Tyrcell shut off the comms. "Now what?" she said.

"Now we monitor Absalom Station's comms until we hear that the dead people all went home, and then *we* go home."

"No!" Ketavan uncurled, sat up, and punched his fist into his open palm. "The fools think we made a deal! Now is the time to finish the job!"

"We *did* make a deal, Ketavan, and we will hold to that deal." Tyrcell unholstered their pistol.

"These monsters attacked your home," the priest sputtered. "They may have killed your friends, and raised them as abominations to do their bidding! And you're going to just let them walk away?"

"We destroyed a whole city!" Melezheun shouted, her outrage bubbling up. "We're not going to follow that up with a genocide! There are innocent people down there on that planet just trying to survive!"

"There are no innocent undead!" Ketavan bellowed, and then he stalked away, fists clenched. He paced back and forth in front of the door, talking to himself. Tyrcell didn't put their pistol away but stared, watchful. Ketavan couldn't launch the full bombardment alone, but he'd proven he could do significant damage.

It didn't take that long for the comms traffic whispering in their ears to take on a jubilant and triumphant tone. There was an announcement from the Primex, broadcasting from a secure bunker: "The bone sage Mnephalon has reached out to apologize. She explained that the assault on her ship was revealed to be the work of a jealous underling named Commander Alcyone, who conspired to frame Ketavan and implicate the authorities on Absalom Station in the crime. This Alcyone has been summarily executed, and the forces of Eox are in the process of retreating." She paused. "Discussions of restitution for property damage and... lost personnel... are in the early stages, and there may be... rogue elements and Eoxian sympathizers still at large on the station... but the worst is over, and our security forces will soon restore order. I will provide more information as we have it. In the meantime: Stay Absalom strong."

Tyrcell rose. "That's our cue to get out of here before the necrovites send forces to secure this place. They may not be able get inside easily, but they can certainly cordon the whole asteroid off. I'm afraid this is the end of your mission, Ketavan. You'll have to content yourself with the destruction of a whole city."

"Fools," he muttered. "This is just one of the facilities the sarcesians or their ancestors set up in the Thousand Moons. There are rumors of other complexes just as capable of bombarding Eox, and I will find them and finish this job. Ha! Once word spreads of the damage I've already done, of the crushing blow dealt Eox by the hand of Ketavan the Vaticinator, new followers will flock to my banner! I will lead an army ten million strong, and the living will finally vanquish the dead!" He stormed out the door and went clattering down the steps.

Ty stood next to Melezheun. "He means that, doesn't he?"

"He has tasted the doom of his enemy, and he will not rest until he eats his fill," she said.

"So what do we *do*? Turn him over to the station authorities? Let them lock him up?"

"Why would they arrest him?" Melezheun said. "He is the savior of Absalom Station. Without him, we would have been overrun and forced to become a protectorate of the bone sages."

"He doesn't even feel guilty, Mel. Thousands gone, tens of thousands, maybe more, and to him, it's just an appetizer."

"They're not people to him," Melezheun said. "They're the enemy. And now he knows a way to destroy them all forever."

"So what do we do?"

She bowed her head. "I think we both know."

They went down the steps after the priest. Ty had their hand on the hilt of a pistol, the one with the lethal settings. Ketavan was storming away ahead of them. Mel could sense Tyrcell's struggle: They didn't want to shoot an old man in the back. Not that shooting him in the front would be much better.

Melezheun glanced at Tyrcell, then began to twist sections of her staff, preparing to deliver a lethal attack. Ty had done so much for her. She could spare them this grim duty.

They were fifteen feet behind Ketavan. Then ten. Then five. Then—

Ty opened their mouth to say something and then closed it and put a hand on Melezheun's arm to stop her from walking forward. The android inclined their head toward the floor, and Melezheun saw.

While they were busy committing war crimes, the gearghost had been busy with its own work, resetting and rebuilding and refining its traps.

Ketavan didn't notice the nearly invisible beam that crossed the corridor at ankle height, a motion-sensing trip wire of light.

This time it wasn't darts or lasers. It was spears, about a dozen of them, made from old spaceship parts, irregular and of different lengths and diameters, but all wickedly sharp and barbed. They sprang across the corridor, emerging from artfully hidden holes in the wall, and because Ketavan cast no spells to protect himself, the spears pierced him in a dozen places, turning his white-and-blue robes red with blood. One spike went right through one cheek and out the other side and ripped his tongue out along the way.

Melezheun turned away, retching. Androids don't suffer much from nausea, so Tyrcell kept staring. Bearing witness. "I could have warned him," Tyrcell breathed. "I could have said 'No, Ketavan!' again. I didn't." Ty shook their head. "But he saved people, didn't he? Ketavan did. Everyone on Absalom Station."

The spears withdrew, and Ketavan's corpse dropped onto the floor.

Melezheun took Ty's arm. "We had no choice. No good choices, anyway."

They walked past the dead priest and made their slow, careful way through the complex, disarming or skirting around the traps as they went. They didn't try to banish the gearghost when they left. Ketavan was full of fury and unfinished business and might become a ghost himself, after all.

Maybe the two of them could keep each other company.

Tyrcell here. So. Now you understand why the official accounts of what happened at the end of the Magefire Assault tend to be a little vague. Melezheun and I didn't want to share the details, and we certainly didn't want to take credit, and Ketavan wasn't around to film a ten-part vidcast series about the whole thing.

So. That's how Mel and I returned home, the saviors of Absalom Station.

# 21

## THE BATTLE OF THE LORESPIRE

(Carn / 7 AG)

The bone sages stood down and sent word to Mnephalon and her forces to withdraw. She may not have *liked* the order, but she packed up her skeletons and her battleships, and they all vanished into the Drift, as far as I know, never to be heard from again. I figured the bone sages probably executed Mnephalon for her failures—if they were feeling merciful, I guess they might have just buried her in a cell beneath the surface of Eox.

Our attack on Eox stopped all the warfare outside the station, and I understand a lot of expensive bottles got popped by the people on board the *Offshoot of Design*, and a few of those bottles might even have been on the house.

The fighting on the station didn't end right away, though, because ground-level battles always outlast diplomatic decisions. The final mopping-up by Absalom Station security forces took days, and there are still rumors of fugitive undead hiding down on the Ghost Levels, but the last truly consequential battle of the Magefire Assault happened while Mel and I were navigating the Thousand Moons, and it happened right in my neighborhood.

I have to say, it's a good thing Carn and Starla and everyone else at the Battle of the Lorespire didn't know about what happened to Val; finding out your leader has died, even for a good reason, is a brutal blow to morale, and the fight might have turned out differently then.

I guess I should admit that nobody else really called it the Battle of the Lorespire. For one thing, there have been a *lot* of battles at the Lorespire over the years; the Hellknights spent a few years trying to obliterate the place, after all. Carn mostly called that final clash the

Day of the Undead. But I can't help it; *I* have a sense of occasion, and "the Battle of the Lorespire" has a certain gravitas.

This next part of the manuscript is going to be a little different than what you've read so far. I've been writing up these chapters based on interviews with the survivors, surveillance footage, firsthand accounts written by other people, and my own suppositions, while trying to present all that in a coherent and unified way.

But when it came to the Day of the Undead, when I started interviewing Carn about the experience, he said, "How about you just let me write this part myself? You seem to find this whole writing thing pretty good for putting your mind at ease, and I could use some ease. What do you say?"

If someone wants to give me the opportunity to do less work, who am I to argue? And so, I now yield these pages to Carn: one of my best friends, the Society's head of security, and a good man to stand behind in a battle, as long as you're far enough behind that he doesn't clip you with his hammer on the backswing.

This is Carn, which probably you can tell, on account of how I bet I write pretty different from how Tyrcell does. I don't know all the fancy writing tricks they use that Ty learned from writing up whole books of history and all that, so I'm just gonna put this down basically like the way I talk, and hope that's good enough.

So, the Day of the Undead, we had this elebrian vampire and a horde of hundreds of undead minions, plus a bunch of ghouls and skeletons and all like that, hammering on the gates of the Lorespire Complex. We can't have that. So before they busted down the doors, I led some people down to the basement and used my biometrics and some one-time keys and passcodes to open up the gates to the secure vaults.

See, over the years, I bought and bartered and collected by right of conquest a whole lot of wonderful, beautiful, nasty toys, and that's how we held out against all those Hellknight incursions and other sorts of ugliness. But then when we all started playing nice together on the station, we didn't need that stuff so much anymore, so we stripped things back to pretty basic defenses and put the technology that falls more into the potential-war-crime category downstairs, where it would be safe, but also, I made sure the mechanics kept the weapons all maintained, just in case. Once you've seen society break down and a whole space station turn into a lawless gangland-chaos type of thing, you lose your faith in the inevitable stability of civilization a little bit.

I didn't wanna let Tyrcell write this part down for me because they would have listened to everything I said and then been all, "We brought a bunch of cannons upstairs and shot at the undead with them," and that's just showing all my wonderful stuff no respect. Let me tell you what we had down there.

I gave Axe-Marie and her wife a matched set of disintegration machine guns, which the Primex has tried to outlaw a few times, not that I'd give them up even if she *did*. These are nasty little submachine guns that draw about as much power as an apartment building, and what they do is they fire a beam, and anything that beam hits gets disintegrated. You're thinking vaporized, but that's not what I said. Dis-in-te-grat-ed. Molecular bonds broken down. Turned into what in the security trade we call sludge.

I gave Starla a starfall pistol, a nasty little zap gun that spews superheated plasma, mostly because it matched her name, and it didn't require much experience to use.

For my new friend Dania the champion, I brought out my precious rocket pauldrons, which integrated pretty well with her armor, I gotta say. The way it works is the big old shoulder pads are full of micro-rockets, and there's an integrated holographic heads-up display, so you can deploy those flying missiles with voice commands or even the movement of your eyes. (I didn't have time to really train Dania, so I disabled the eye-movement part. I didn't want her accidentally giving me the side-eye and exploding my head off my body.) Those came with a matched set of rocket bracers too, though she grumbled about taking off her armguards to wear them. She basically had enough ordnance on her body to take out a whole armored division, and I warned her to be careful not to shoot at the walls—we're not too far from the outer hull in some places around here.

They were my favorite people, so they got my favorite toys, but I handed out some of the best goodies to other members of the Society too. We had a skyfire sword, which is basically a thing that spews fire all over, contained by a magnetic field into a kind of blade shape. Good for cutting through people and things. One of our quickest runners got a set of modified battle gloves that let you punch somebody's face off but can also let you do these wild leaps in the air by aiming the concussive blasts downward—so you can blast off, fly in an arc, and land on your enemy fists first. Our resident acoustic genius Chordelia got the conveniently named chordpocalypse, which looks like a concert-ready musical instrument but is actually a brutal sonic weapon.

That was the fun stuff, the rarest of the rare. I also doled out grenade launchers, projectile weapons, energy weapons, cryo-weapons, thermal weapons, and a couple of sets of power armor. Then we got some burly folks and drones to bring the *really* big guns upstairs. We had some autocannons, sure, but also a mounted apocalypse beam, a portable artillery laser that you have to brace real good before you start firing it, because if you lose control of the thing, it'll cut your house in half. Along with all your friends. We put up some strategically placed barrier cannons too, to generate layered force fields for our shooters to fall back to once the undead broke through.

Tyrcell calls this kind of stuff "gun porn," but that's because they don't appreciate the inherent poetry of violence and stuff. That's OK, nobody's perfect.

While we were getting our gun emplacements established, the blast doors were gradually getting overwhelmed by a combination of brute force and cutting torches. I was calibrating an autocannon so smart you could practically play board games with it when there was this extra big sound of squealing metal, and a triangle of open space appeared at the bottom corner of the blast doors, big enough for a humanoid to come through, but not the big stitched-together necrograft monstrosities. At least, not yet.

I raised my arm to signal our snipers in the tower to get ready. The zombies would have to squeeze through that gap one or two at a time, and with well-placed headshots we could maybe even clog the opening with their bodies—

But then a tiny drone zipped through the hole instead, no bigger than my head, a white hovering sphere, and I thought, *We're screwed, it's a bomb*, because a sufficiently nasty flash-bang would disorient my people, and an EMP could disable most of our beautiful weapons.

But instead, the drone projected a life-sized hologram of that elebrian in the dark blue robes, creating an almost-realistic image of the necromancer hovering a few inches above the grass. Her image spoke in a screeching voice. "Greetings, future citizens of glorious Eox! You are truly blessed to come under our protection! Those who are *not* under our protection get torn apart and eaten by monsters, who *are* under our protection! Some of you have seen what we can do! I will now graciously accept your unconditional surrender!"

There was a long moment of silence, and Dr. Bindi and Starla were looking at me, so I sighed and called out, "No, thanks, we're good here."

The hologram swiveled, like it was staring right at me. Maybe the vampire *was* looking at me, with mind powers or through the drone's cameras or something, who knows? "You are the leader here? You are... Valentine of the Society?" she called.

"Val's busy doing more important stuff," I called back. "She sent me to deal with you. I told her we shoulda just hung up a sign that says 'No Solicitors,' but she thought that was too rude."

"You *joke*?" The vampire seemed genuinely shocked. What can I say? Sometimes I joke. Even when things are terrible. It's not like jokes make things any worse, and at least that way maybe somebody gets a chuckle out of it. "My name is Helicarnassus, blood bag. I have been sent by the great bone sage Mnephalon, long may she shatter the skulls of her enemies, to seize control of the Ring and the Arms, and your pathetic Lorespire Complex shall serve as my command center!"

"If it's pathetic, why do they want it?" I asked Starla, who giggled, a little bit in an unhinged way, understandably. We were pretty close to the tower, behind a whole bunch of overlapping layers of force fields, but still, it was a scary situation, knowing what was on the other side of those big doors.

I went back to yelling, thinking again that this would have been a better job for Dania than me—she had the pipes for this kind of stuff. "Listen, Helical... whatever... sorry, I can't be remembering all that. Vampire lady! I'm gonna give you a chance to surrender, but if

I'm being honest, that's mostly because I know you won't do it. But will you?"

"I stand at the head of an army of the dead!" she shouted back. "My troops know nothing of fear or pain! Your rabble know nothing *but* fear and pain, and soon they will know death, and glorious resurrection under my control! If you do not lay down your arms and surrender now, you will find yourselves killed by the walking corpses of those you once loved!"

"I think we're at what you might call an impasse," I shouted back. "So, you know. You do what you have to do."

"Fools," the vampire said. "But I am *glad* you're putting up resistance. Your gruesome deaths will serve as an object lesson for others on this station who might foolishly think to do the same!"

"OK, then!" I called back, which seemed to annoy the vampire, who flickered off, the drone zipping back underneath the crack in the door.

"What do you think the odds are they were bluffing?" I asked. "That they realized they're totally outgunned, and were just hoping we'd fold on a winning hand—"

A giant armored horn ripped through the center of the blast door, tearing the whole right half of the door away, leaving an opening that was about ten feet high and ten feet wide, plenty big even for the real big monsters to get through if they didn't mind ducking their heads.

The mindless minions came first, which we expected: They're the definition of cannon fodder, after all, reborn for the purpose of dying all over again in service to glorious Eox and whatnot. Rank after rank of them came rushing in, three abreast, and it was less like watching an enemy charge, because when that happens, even the most well-trained and disciplined group is still kinda made up of *individuals*. These minions were operating under the control of a single authority, though, more like extensions of their necromancer boss than troops under her command, so the impression they gave was more like a kind of force-of-nature-type thing—an avalanche coming at you or a lava flow or a tidal wave. The snipers took some shots, but there were way too many of the zombies for that to make any real difference, and even with targeting technology and a lot of practice, landing a disabling shot on an animated corpse is pretty tough.

But that was OK, because we had a different first line of defense, even before the zombies reached the force fields generated by the barrier cannons. That first line wasn't very high-tech at all, and I'm saying "line" so much because it's a pun, and like I said, I make jokes sometimes. We had whole big spools of nanofilament wire in our supply storage, and that stuff is incredibly strong and incredibly thin and incredibly useful and incredibly dangerous. You gotta wear special gloves when you deal with it so you don't slice yourself to ribbons, and special glasses so you can even *see* the stuff, since it's so thin it's next to invisible to the unassisted eye.

Zombies don't have very good eyes (some of them don't have eyes at all, just the holes where the eyes used to be, with or without gross goo in there). The minions ran right into the layers of nanofilament wire we'd strung horizontally in front of the blast doors, each line a few inches above the next, starting at ankle height and going up about ten feet.

I dunno if you've ever seen one of those automatic meat slicers, or maybe the wire you can use to turn a block of cheese into tissue-thin slices? This was a lot like that, only a billion times more disgusting. The first zombies were running so fast they just pushed right through the wire and came out on the other side, and the filaments were so thin the minions even stayed upright and intact... at first. Then, inevitably, different parts of their sliced-up bodies started to shift and slide, and they just collapsed into heaps of neatly dissected (because they're dead, right, even if they were moving) zombie. Three of them fell, six fell, nine fell, twelve fell, and my people behind the barriers were cheering... except some of them were gagging and some of them were throwing up. It was so gross. Alive people would have been worse, I think, because their insides are more fluid and splashy, not as dried up as zombie insides, but even so. And the smell? I won't even try to describe the smell. Whatever you're imagining, it's like that but way worse.

After about fifteen or twenty zombies got turned into cold cuts, the necromancer running the show must have realized something was happening, because the horde stopped and slowed down and stood there, swaying a little, which was good for the snipers, because they got a bunch of them picked off.

Then the zombie horde parted and some skeletal minions came through. It's funny, skeletons all look pretty similar, like, it's hard to tell a skeletal elf from a skeletal human, like death is the great anonymizer. These were *definitely* mindless minions, definitely magical undead, and they were all armed with these shock batons that were about three feet long each, but a lot of the minions looked like they had metal bones, or at least like their bones had been *coated* in metal. They started chopping wildly with their batons, and whatever their weapons were made of was strong enough that the wires couldn't cut right through them, so the filaments started to snap instead, with a sound like the strings on a musical instrument breaking. Some of the metal-boned skeletons hurled their own bodies at the wires and jumped up to reach the highest lines, seeming to hover in the air while dangling from the invisible filaments.

My people were shooting, of course, but those skeletal undead, they can take a lot of punishment, and you basically have to break them into pieces to disable them, and even then, the skulls snap their teeth at you. We hadn't run into any of that kind of minion at the docks or during our house-to-house fighting, I guess because Helicolossus or whatever was keeping them for the main assault.

Then came the main assault. Once the skeletons had cleared the wires, the zombies took the vanguard again. They'd pile up against our force fields, and our snipers would snipe, and then the pressure of the zombies would overwhelm the force field, and we'd all fall back behind the next barrier, and so on. Meanwhile, the *big* beasts were coming through the door, and the idea was clearly to overwhelm us with zombies and then mop up the rest of us with the behemoths.

But we had autocannons. Not the *best* ones on the station—those we gave *to* the station, for security against pirates or invasion, and I surely hoped they were blasting away at whatever ships the Eoxians had floating around out there around us. But these were our *second*-best autocannons, the ones that had severely bloodied the noses of the Hellknights on no fewer than three occasions, and they were plenty good at dealing with a bunch of bitey flesh monsters. Our carefully placed barriers led the horde right into our predesignated kill zones, and the cannons laid down fields of overlapping fire in the form of projectiles, including grapeshot designed to disable ships. When you shoot what's basically a spinning chain of kinetic energy at a *guy*, what happens is there's no more guy anymore, and at most you've got a pair of boots standing up at the bottom with the feet still in. Even the skeletal minions couldn't stand up to *that* kind of pressure, and bones went flying everywhere and bouncing off our force fields, and then *everybody* was cheering.

The autocannons probably took out about half of Heliopatra's forces, but that still left... a whole other half, and we only had so much ammo. Some of those remaining troops were ghosts too, and they started passing *through* the cannons? And I did not know this about ghosts, but they can disrupt electrical systems and even take control of computer systems. At least, *these* ghosts could, because they made some of the cannons stop firing, and some of the others turned and started bombarding our force fields, which we were not prepared for, and that was my biggest failure of that part of the battle, because some of our people got shredded up real good too. The only good thing was that a lot of their bodies were so badly damaged they couldn't be reanimated to attack us, but that's a real thin silver lining, I gotta say.

The rest of us managed to fall back, and the limited ammo was an advantage for us at that point because the possessed cannons all sputtered to a stop in pretty quick succession. There were easily a hundred zombies left, coming right at us, plus the ghosts and wraiths, the ghouls and more skeletons, and that damn vampire necromancer. She was through the door, still riding her giant stitched-together monster, with the other monsters padding along in a wedge formation after her, a living wall of scales and spines and teeth and tongues and tentacles. We still had a few force fields, and the snipers were still sniping, but it was gonna come down to fighting up close real soon.

Now, there weren't that many of us defending the tower, not really. Oh, there were hundreds of us in the complex, but that included old people and kids and their caregivers and people who weren't up for the fight for various reasons and Dr. Bindi and her medical support people, who we wanted to keep alive so they could keep *other* people alive. All those noncombatants were back in the tower, some going up to the highest levels, some down to the security of the vault, where there was a lot of room because all our weapons were outside now.

In terms of actual *defenders*, there were maybe a hundred of us, and if it had just been the zombies, we would have been OK, but... it wasn't just the zombies. And then Heliogabble went and raised her staff and got this black aura of negative energy crackling all around her, and some of our people who'd fallen lurched upright, missing arms and half their faces sometimes, and they picked up weapons and came toward us.

"Dania, now!" I shouted, but great minds think alike, because she was already walking out of the Lorespire where she'd been waiting, because she'd had the idea that if a champion showed her face on the front lines, the vampire would throw everything she had at killing her right away.

Dania raised her hands and smiled, and she was radiant.

Scores of micro-rockets burst from her shoulders and from her outstretched hands. A bunch of them went for the skeletal minions, exploding on impact and spraying metal-coated bone shrapnel in all directions, doing a great job of cutting up the zombie horde in the process. The remainder were aimed straight for the vampire, though, since Dania's whole thing was "cut off the head of the undead snake." Heliocrapulous *dived* off that beast and flickered out of existence as far as I could tell, some kind of hiding-in-the-shadows magic, most likely. The giant chimera didn't fare too well, though, with rockets blowing great big holes in its face and sending its mechanical legs flying, one of them spinning so fast it scythed the legs out from under *another* necrografted monstrosity.

I signaled for our people to drop one of the last barriers, and my buddy Raisfeld was manning the apocalypse beam, which we'd set up off to one side, to provide him with a lot of target options. A beam of light lanced out, so bright we had to turn our faces away, and it seared holes through the other three beasts. They turned and started to charge the weapon, and that's when the orc wives popped out of a concealed maintenance hatch near the beam and aimed their disintegrators, and the roaring monsters practically melted in the force of the beams, their limbs turning to sludge.

Order kinda broke down after that, as it does. The last barrier flickered out, and we still had zombies all up in our faces. I was swinging my hammer like I was trying to beat the high score at a carnival strength-testing game, and my mote was blasting little bursts of suppressing fire. Sonic blasts erupted behind me. Starla sprinted by, blood smeared on her face, blasting away with her starfall pistol, trying to take down a ghoul—those could think, and they *could* feel pain, and they didn't like getting a bunch of plasma in the face. Dania was out of rockets but never out of her ever-morphing melee weapon.

Honestly, we did pretty good. But it wasn't enough. We were losing, especially because that damn vampire was popping up all over, stepping out of shadows, waving a stupid staff, and making our fallen allies get back up and try to kill the rest of us. Every one of ours that fell became one of *hers*, and that's just not real promising math.

We were all focused on our own desperate fights, with no more order or coordination to be found. I'm not a general, and even if I was, I couldn't tell what was going on to give orders anyhow. I just hoped we could buy some time for our people to hide, and maybe thin out the horde, for whatever that was worth. Eventually I got mobbed by zombies, and they pressed in so close that I couldn't even swing my hammer anymore, and my solarian powers were getting pretty worn out. It's exhausting, changing your density and blasting people with solar light, it takes a lot out of you, and I'd had a long, long, long day.

I didn't wanna be a zombie, but probably nobody who becomes a zombie does.

They didn't kill me, though. Just forced me down to my knees. Like I'm not short enough already, compared to most humanoids.

Then the elebrian vampire was standing in front of me: wide, fanged smile, bloody and smoke-smeared robes, stupid staff with a skull on top. "I got you," she said.

"You gonna drink my blood now?" I asked. "I hope you choke on it."

Heliopopulous stepped even closer, nostrils flaring. "I am already drinking you. I feed on emotions, rat, not blood. All this pain and fear is flowing into me and giving me strength. I think I'll allow you to keep a fraction of your mind when I slay and resurrect you—enough of your consciousness and memory so that you can suffer and provide me with a steady trickle of energy from your despair. Doesn't that sound—"

"Carn, duck!" someone shouted, and I will say, one of my good qualities is when somebody says something like that, I don't question it, I just do it, so I dropped. Kinda lucky I was on my knees at that point, you know? Closer to the ground.

The zombies around me all dropped too, but that was because their heads were popping like melons dropped off the back of a transport truck. The vampire spun, outraged, raising her staff, and then *that* got blown out of her hand, along with most of her hand.

I peeked past her and saw Cronch—I thought I'd recognized his voice—leading a *huge* army: the dock defenders and what looked like half the citizens of the Ring, all armed, all shooting and smashing and taking the zombies and the ghouls from the rear, totally surprising them and damn near wiping them out in one go. Even the ghosts were in trouble, because there were some priests and whatnot in the bunch. It was like one of those amazing cavalry rescue battle stories you hear about, but it was just *some guys*. My guys!

Cronch and them shot the vampire a bunch of times, and they must have hurt her enough that she couldn't get away through the shadows, because she didn't flee, just sorta wobbled.

I'm not gonna make a real big thing about telling this part. The vampire tried to say some haughty threatening stuff, so I summoned up the energy I had left and did something I don't do too often, which is I reached in and squeezed her organs with my mind. The undead don't use their organs much, but vampires have this thing about their hearts, so I squeezed that as hard as I could. That wasn't gonna kill her, but it didn't do her any good, and she fell to her knees and struggled to get up again and ended up on all fours, her head hanging low. "You're all... so joyful," she gasped. "It's so... it's so bitter..."

Then Dania stepped in and cut her head off, and everybody cheered, and that's how we won the thing nobody other than Tyrcell ever called the Battle of the Lorespire.

We were all real happy, though. And that was nice. The sad bits, with Val and all, came a little later.

But if there's one thing I've learned about life, it's that any kind of life worth living is gonna include a good helping of the good and the bad, the happy and the sad. That's just how it goes.

I'm done writing now. I'll figure out later whether or not writing this helped me. But maybe it helped you.

# 22

## THE MYSTERY OF THE MISERY KNIGHT

(326 AG)

"This feels just like how you described making your way through the other temple of Yaraesa!" Dae looked at the closed door at the end of the corridor, made of cloudy white crystal inscribed all over with mysterious sigils.

"My group was being chased by Hellknights, not the undead, last time," Tyrcell said. "So it's a little different. But... entirely too much the same." They put a hand against the door. "Does this stuff make sense to anyone? Chk Chk?"

The shirren had come prepared with a hard drive full of esoteric knowledge. *"Let me consult my notes... Hmm, these symbols appear to be elements of an equation involving heat exchange, rendered in a rather obscure script. I think we just have to balance both sides."*

The android and the pahtra stepped back and let him manipulate the symbols.

"What do you think we'll find inside?" Dae asked. "A map to the location of lost Golarion?"

"That's the hope," Tyrcell replied. "Though the planet has to be in another plane of reality, right? Otherwise, someone would have found it by now, you'd think. Maybe it's in the Drift someplace? We know the Drift pulls bits of other planes into itself, so maybe it pulled something *really large* in once?"

"Space is awfully big," Dae mused. "It's possible that Golarion is still out there, hidden away somewhere in the vast—"

*"Done!"* Chk Chk proclaimed, and the door opened.

From there, it really was like the last temple, room after room and puzzle after puzzle. They manipulated a series of mirrors and lasers to illuminate a light-activated switch that let them exit the next chamber. They wore tiaras that read their brain waves as they practiced relaxation techniques to slowly roll three balls across a track; the balls only moved if you were perfectly calm, which was difficult when they could hear distant shouting and thuds as the undead made their own blundering way through the passages and test chambers. They folded up thin sheets of paper to replicate a fiendishly complex origami model of a wading bird. They competed in a trivia contest against a grinning, animated mosaic of a lizard that mocked them whenever they answered incorrectly. They opened a crate full of wheels, cogs, levers, gears, and pins, and used them to build a mechanical system that could transfer a single cup of water from one pool to another across the room. They manipulated sound waves to create tones of perfect mathematical harmony, which resonated with a crystal box, shattering the container and allowing them to reach the golden key hidden inside.

"Actually, this *is* a nicer temple than the last one," Tyrcell said after fitting that key into the door. "Last time, we had rooms that flooded and traps that threatened to kill us while we solved puzzles. This temple seems more playful—practically friendly. I guess there *are* some rewards for making it this far."

"You two are useless," Groth complained, solving the latest puzzle to open the latest door, without any help from either of the others, *again*.

They'd given up on forcing their way through the doors after they lost most of their minions and all their explosives at the hatch and in the first hallway, trying and failing, with nasty consequences. The magic that governed the temple really didn't like that sort of thing. The misery knight had shaken his head the whole time they were setting charges, like he was trying to warn them against trying brute force, but what did he know about it?

"You can only solve these puzzles because you have an exocortex," Alcyone said. "It's not like any of this understanding is really *yours*. There's just a computer stuck in your head."

"It's still my mind operating the computer, you translucent loser," the ghoul said.

The misery knight had nothing to contribute.

Ty opened the next door, and instead of another small room with a puzzle to solve, they entered a long crystal cavern, lined on either side with round pedestals topped with cylinders of blue light. Each pedestal held a statue or a smaller artifact that floated at eye level within the light.

Chk Chk approached one of the cylinders and reached out, tentatively, toward the light. *"It feels smooth, like glass,"* the shirren said. *"Some kind of force field."*

"There's a plaque set here in the ground, just inside the door," Dae said. "I can't read it, though."

Tyrcell looked down at the polished rectangle embedded in the stone floor. "I know that language. It says 'A remnant of a remnant. Behold the treasures of lost Golarion.'"

*"These aren't statues?"* Chk Chk looked at what he'd taken to be a sculpture of a goblin riding a hairy four-legged quadruped and brandishing a nasty-looking sword.

"I think they're actual specimens preserved in some kind of stasis." Tyrcell peered at a longsword that seemed to be made of magical ice, floating vertically point-down above a small pile of gold coins heaped atop the pedestal. Another cylinder held something that *looked* like a pistol, but impossibly primitive and encrusted with clockwork gears. The next display case over held a figure that looked a bit like a robot, its face blank and shining metal.

"There are crowns and jewels and things!" Dae said from the other side of the room.

*"This looks a bit like a nuar."* Chk Chk gazed at a figure with the head of a bull, holding aloft a scarred battle axe. *"But... not quite. Are these really from lost Golarion?"*

"I see no reason to doubt the word of a goddess," Tyrcell said. "Yaraesa loves knowledge, and she must have taken the opportunity to preserve a few things."

"These must be worth a *fortune*," Dae said. "Artifacts from a vanished planet? There are collectors out there who would give us our own private moon for just one of these things."

"Unless you know how to turn off a force field that a god turned on, I don't think we're going to be able to loot anything in here," Ty said. "We should move on to the next puzzle. There are two doors at the other end of the chamber." One looked like it was carved from a single giant emerald, the other from a single giant sapphire. "We've got green and we've got blue. Maybe there's a clue somewhere about which one we should open—"

The blue fields around the cylinders on either side of the chamber closest to the doors at the end of the corridor flickered and went out. The huge creature with the horned head and the axe stepped off its pedestal and took up a position blocking the green door. The silver-faced robot thing stepped off its own and joined it, standing in front of the blue door.

"One door leads to certain death," the creature with horns lowed. "The other, to the treasure you seek."

"Ah," Tyrcell said. "I don't suppose there's a way to tell which is which? Is this just a fifty-fifty chance sort of thing? That doesn't seem like Yaraesa's way."

"You can ask either one of us a single question," the robot said, voice surprisingly melodious. It had the quality of a prepared spiel rather than an answer to Tyrcell's question.

Dae snapped their fingers and grinned at their friends. "I know this one! One of the guards always tells the truth, and the other one always lies!"

"He always lies," the not-quite-a-nuar said, pointing at the robot.

"Nonsense. She's the liar," the robot said.

"Uh," Tyrcell grunted, but Dae patted them on the shoulder.

"Don't worry. I've got this!" Dae cracked their knuckles and pointed to the hulking horned figure. "Would the *other* guard tell me the blue door is safe?"

"No," the not-quite-a-nuar said.

"Great!" Dae grabbed Ty's hand in one of theirs and Chk Chk's in the other. "Then that's the door we want!"

The guardians stepped smoothly aside, allowing access to the doors, and didn't interfere with their progress when Dae dragged them toward the sapphire.

*"Are you sure this is right, Dae?"* Chk Chk asked. *"I do not mean to doubt you, but—"*

"Yes!" Dae said. "When we read about that other dungeon Tyrcell went through, and all the puzzles they had to figure out, I reviewed those puzzle resources you sent me on classic brainteasers, and this puzzle with the doors was one of them! If you ask about the right door, they'll both say no when you ask what the other guard will say! The truthful guard will *truthfully* tell you that the liar would say the right door isn't safe, and the lying one will *lie* and say the truthful one would also tell you it isn't safe! If I'd picked the bad door, the answer would be yes, whichever one I asked, and then we'd go green instead!"

*"I could have figured that out on my own,"* Chk Chk said. *"Had I only been given a moment."*

"I still don't understand it," Tyrcell said. "But I'm happy to let someone else do the thinking for me."

Dae nudged open the sapphire door with one foot and led them through.

Groth stood over the dead horned humanoid with the axe and the twitching disabled not-quite-a-robot beside it. The nuar-like thing had been easy to kill, one plasma shot through the forehead, but the robot had taken several vicious blows from the misery knight's electrified mace.

A skeleton pushed open the emerald door, revealing a frame lined with teeth as long as Groth's arms. Black tentacles—or were those *tongues?*—whipped out to pull the skeleton into the dark maw before the door slammed shut again.

"There must be some trick to picking the right door," Groth said. "We just used up our last minion!"

"At least it died for a good cause," Alcyone said as the misery knight kicked open the blue door and disappeared inside.

"Does he seem angry to you?" Groth said. "He usually seems like nothing much at all, but here lately..."

"Maybe he hates puzzles," Alcyone suggested.

After the sapphire door, there was a short corridor, and then a blank stone wall with a head-sized purple crystal embedded in the center. "Looks like a dead end," Tyrcell said. "Is this crystal the… the thing? Do we stick it in a really big projector?"

The crystal glowed, and a spectral figure appeared before them: a lashunta woman wearing flowing gray robes and a complicated tiara that looked like a molecular model of some unknown compound. "Greetings, pilgrims," she said in a melodious voice.

"Oh my gods, is that Yaraesa?" Dae squealed.

"I am not Yaraesa," the projection said. "I am an automated semiautonomous spectral interlocutor, here to administer the final test before you will be permitted to enter the sanctum."

"Of course you are," Ty said. "So what's the test?"

"It is very simple," the lashunta said. "Come close to me, each of you, one by one, and tell me something you've learned."

They all exchanged glances. "Just… anything we've learned?" Dae said cautiously.

The lashunta smiled placidly. "Come close to me, each of you, one by one, and tell me something you've learned." Her intonation was utterly unchanged.

"I've learned plenty of things over the years," Ty muttered as they stepped closer. A shimmering bubble of purple light enveloped the android's head, like a fishbowl helmet made of moving clouds, but Ty didn't start flailing around or acting alarmed, so it must have been all right… or else they were paralyzed. Dae looked at Chk Chk, who shrugged helplessly, and after a moment, the purple light vanished and Tyrcell stepped back, blinking. The projection nodded, smiling. "Very good."

"It's fine," Ty said. "Not dangerous. Go ahead."

Chk Chk went next, head vanishing in the same opaquely swirling sphere, and it remained for a bit longer than Ty's had. *"Apologies for the delay,"* the shirren said upon emerging. *"First I recited a poem of my own composition, but she said it had to be something I'd learned, not created, so I recited Antonin the Bleak's ode to slow asphyxiation—"*

"And you?" the virtual lashunta said brightly to Dae.

The pahtra stepped forward and then gasped as the sphere enveloped their head. Dae had expected something claustrophobic, but it was more like being immersed in a sim: They seemed to be standing on a vast plain outside one of Yaraesa's distinctive library temples, and the lashunta interlocutor stood before them, hands clasped at her waist. "What have you learned?"

"I've learned that the android Tyrcell is the true founder of the Starfinder Society, which is a pretty big secret thing," Dae said.

"Indeed it is." The lashunta agreed. "A secret that is known to the goddess already, of course, but we cannot expect every pilgrim to add to our body of knowledge; we merely ask... and hope. You did well."

The light vanished, and Dae was back in the antechamber. "Go ahead." The lashunta projection turned and gestured, and the wall opened up like the blossom of a flower. They entered the inner temple.

Groth didn't know what Alcyone had told the lashunta hologram, of course, but judging by the puzzled expression on the projection's face, it was probably something like the exact way that Mnephalon liked to have her toes licked. But the hologram, or whatever she was, nodded, so the ghost's answer must have been good enough.

For his part, Groth stepped forward confidently, and when he entered the projected landscape, he said, "The great ghoul mathematician Klinchpin proved that for all but a negligible fraction of real numbers *x*, the coefficients *ai* of the continued fraction expansion of *x* have a finite—finite!—geometric mean that is *independent* of the value of *x*!"

"That is true," the lashunta said. "You have passed the test, but may I ask, What prompted you to tell me about that rather obscure constant?"

"Oh, family lore says Klinchpin was the progenitor of my line, passing ghoul fever to the ghoul who passed it to the ghoul who passed it on, and so on and so forth, until it got to *me*."

"How interesting." The lashunta considered. "But that is *not* true. Your direct progenitor from Klinchpin's contemporaneous era was a ghoul with no given name, generally referred to by the sobriquet Feces Eater." She beamed. "And now we have added to *your* knowledge!"

"Much appreciated," Groth growled.

Next the misery knight stomped forward and stayed wrapped in the bubble for as long as Groth and Alcyone had combined. When the bubble vanished, the lashunta projection seemed paler, and murmured, "We... did not know that. Thank you. And... oh, how horrible." Then her face flickered into a smile. "Thank you all for sharing your knowledge. You may proceed. Your friends are already inside."

The wall opened, and—

"Get them!" Groth screamed.

And so the three agents of the Starfinder Society entered the final sanctum of the goddess.

Tyrcell had seen a chamber like it once before, hidden away on that unlovely moon so many centuries earlier, when it was pristine and unmarred by smoke and fire. A crystal cavern, like the inside of an immense geode. This time there were pillars of shining jewels dotted about the interior, glowing with soft light to illuminate the domed space.

Last time there'd a been a tunnel that led to a cozy nook and a set of data crystals, but this time, the layout was less complicated. In the center of the chamber there stood a simple stone altar, waist high, inscribed with Yaraesa's holy symbols. Resting on top, on a neatly carved stand of pure diamond, was a jeweled bone scepter, two feet long, inscribed with tiny glyphs that probably translated to something ambiguous and maddening, knowing the god's mysterious ways.

Tyrcell stepped forward, toward the altar—and then the wall opened on the other side of the chamber, and Groth the ghoul, Alcyone the ghost, and some horrible rusty, charred ambulatory suit of armor burst in, the first one doing a lot of shouting. The undead invaders must have been following their own route through the temple, not exactly following right behind them; Yaraesa's last temple had done funny things with spatial reality too.

The ghoul flung himself at Tyrcell, and the ghost floated toward Chk Chk and Dae, forcing them all to retreat and raise their weapons.

The thing in the armor paid no attention to any of them, just walked up to the altar and tilted its helmet down to regard the scepter before picking it up. Then it bellowed, "Stop!" in a voice like rocks crushing a robot to death.

They were all so startled that they *did* stop, the living and the undead alike, there facing one another across the chamber.

"The misery knight *talks*?" Alcyone wailed.

"Hello, Tyrcell," the dead knight grated out.

"Uh, hello. Do I know you?"

The misery knight laughed—or at least, it must have been a laugh, though there was precious little mirth in the sound. The knight scraped a gauntleted hand across his chest, clearing away soot and ash to reveal the dull gleam of battered armor underneath. His filthy, rusted hand couldn't really clean off a filthy, rusted cuirass, but it succeeded in moving the filth and rust around enough to reveal a previously hidden sigil on the breastplate: a solid black disk, surrounded by an aurora of spiky red lines.

*"That is the symbol of the Order of the Eclipse, is it not?"* Chk Chk said, and Tyrcell drew their sidearm and immediately began firing at the knight. Groth dived behind a crystal pillar, and Alcyone just floated there, unbothered by projectile fire but obviously bewildered.

The hulking figure didn't react to the gunfire much at all, even though one of the shots pierced a smoking hole in his armor. He reached up and wrenched his helmet away, revealing a face that had once been human, but was now gaunt, with skin like torn old leather stretched over a frame of sharp bones. "Tyrcell," the undead knight said, his voice a rasp on old metal. "It's been such a long time."

Another shot from Tyrcell tore off one of the creature's leathery ears, and the knight scowled. "Stop shooting at me, Tyrcell. I've been dead for centuries. You can't really hurt me. Mnephalon wove these protections around me herself. You'll only ruin my looks."

"Not possible," Tyrcell said, but the rejoinder had a sort of automatic tone, like the android was just going through the motions. "You were already at maximum ugliness when we first met."

The knight turned his head toward Chk Chk and Dae and bared his teeth. "My name... is Astrachios."

"Nooooo," Dae said, eyes wide, and Chk Chk had seen his friend say the same thing with the exact same expression on their face when a long-lost twin came back from the dead on a vidcast show they watched: This was a twist. This was *lore*.

"In life, I founded the Order of the Eclipse,"Astrachios went on, "and led it, for a long time."

"Until Rakhiel ousted you, and you crawled off in disgrace," Tyrcell said. "I heard you went into exile."

"I went into... all sorts of places... and finally found one... I didn't come out of." He gave something that was probably meant to be a smile, but since you could always see his remaining teeth through the holes in his cheeks anyway, it didn't have quite the same effect it might have in life. "But Mnephalon found me there, and brought me back, to delve through my mind for knowledge, and she relit the spark of consciousness in me. I'll always be grateful for that, despite the anathemas she forced me to perpetrate in her name. She knew about our history, and she sent me along, knowing I'd enjoy the opportunity to face you again. I'm grateful for that too." He sighed, though it didn't look like he really needed to breathe anymore. "I'm afraid I have to leave her service now, though." Astrachios held the scepter up to the light. "The secrets hidden here are too dangerous for a necrovite to possess. There's no telling what she'd do with this forbidden knowledge. Even in death, I must protect *order*, and finding out the fate of Golarion would be the most disruptive event in galactic society since the Gap. I won't let that kind of chaos happen again. I'm going to make sure no one *ever* deciphers this."

"Traitor!" Alcyone shrieked. "No one disrespects my lady!" The ghost went flying toward the knight. Astrachios reached out, almost casually, and seized the ghost's flickering body in one gauntleted hand—and then used the scepter to rip her in half like an old rag, flinging the pieces aside, where they dissipated into specks of glowing spectral remnants before they could even reach the ground.

Beside Chk Chk, Dae gaped. That knight really *did* have magic wrapped all around him!

Tyrcell ignored the whole business with the ghost, attention still fixed on the knight. "Astrachios, I *know* you wanted to preserve the Gap so no one would find out what horrible crimes you'd committed in the times before. But that was all centuries ago, and you've doubtless committed much worse crimes since then! You were disgraced, and you aren't even acknowledged as the founder of your own order anymore. What does any of that matter? We can find out the truth now!"

Astrachios shook his head. "I once acted for selfish reasons. But I have come to truly embrace the values I once simply spoke. The gods hid the truth about Golarion's fate away for a reason, and whether that reason was good or bad, it defined the entire shape of our society and our worlds and all of our lives. To undo that now would simply be too disruptive. Goodbye, Tyrcell. In recognition of our long relationship, I will leave you alive." He paused. "There are so few of us still around, from the old days, after all."

The knight tucked Yaraesa's scepter down the neck of his armor into his breastplate, put his helmet back on, and walked ploddingly toward the exit. Tyrcell kept shooting at him, and Groth too, but the knight paid no attention to either of them, simply leaving the chamber through the hole he'd entered.

Then Groth and Tyrcell turned on each other, weapons aimed. Chk Chk unstrapped his painglaive, and Dae took a long, winding whip of light from their solar mote, giving it a few experimental cracks in the ghoul's general direction.

"Well, void dust," the ghoul said. "Seems we're at an impasse, then."

"Not really, because you're not allowed to kill me," Tyrcell said. "You couldn't kill me even if you wanted to. Mnephalon's commands can't be ignored, not by puppets like you."

"How can you say that, when you *just* saw the misery knight, or Astrachios, defy our lady?" The ghoul raised the pistol, bared his teeth—and then flung the weapon away, dropping to his knees and howling. After a long, gasping moment, the ghoul looked up. "The bindings still work on me, then. I thought maybe this temple was blocking them. But no. Astrachios just... overcame them, somehow."

"He never was very good at following other people's orders," Ty said. "That's why he founded an order of his own. We're leaving now, ghoul."

"Go on." Groth flapped his hand. "I'll be punished regardless, with the way *this* went. What's another hundred years in a pit full of bone vipers, more or less?"

The three of them turned toward the door, and then Dae paused and said, "I'm sorry about your... ghost friend."

"Don't be," Groth said. "It's almost impossible to dispel a ghost permanently. She'll pull herself back together in a day or two." The ghoul brightened. "And then *she'll* be punished too. That's nice."

*"So... what do we do now?"* Chk Chk asked as they passed back through the hall of lost Golarion's salvaged treasures.

Tyrcell draped one arm over the shirren's shoulder and the other over Dae's. "Do you two want to quit? Head back to the Lorespire and see if you can still join that expedition you were angling for originally? I might have a string or two I can pull, to help you out. I wouldn't blame you. I paused this quest for literal centuries, until you two came along and got me interested again."

"I don't want to stop!" Dae said. "Except I want to stop *Astrachios*! He stole our *clue*!"

"He did," Ty said. "I'm not going to let him get away with that. It felt like I spent years being chased by that man. Now it's my turn to do the chasing."

*"We are with you,"* Chk Chk sent.

The android grinned. "Good. Astrachios is pretty big. I might need help knocking him over and kicking him a bunch of times."

"You don't seem too upset about all this," Dae said.

"Oh, I'm upset. I thought I was *done* having my life disrupted by that armored conglomeration of self-righteousness and bad ideas. But I figured we'd be chasing down clues at another shrine of Yaraesa, and in a way, we are—that clue is just tucked away inside a dead Hellknight's breastplate. All the other times I fought Astrachios, he had the full force of his order behind him. Now that he's on his own, and on the run himself, it's a whole different situation. A much more even match. And I'd be lying if I claimed I didn't like the idea of settling my absolute oldest score."

"I only met Astrachios this one time," Dae said. "And I don't like to judge people too much, I mean everyone is just doing their best, but I have to say... you're right. Astrachios sucks."

*"Indeed,"* Chk Chk chimed in. *"Let us venture forth, and, as Dae might say, kick his desiccated butt."*

"I would *not* say that," Dae replied.

"Tyrcell *escaped*?" Mnephalon demanded, on comms this time, instead of in the form of a psychic projection, which was some condolence, at least. "And my misery knight *betrayed me*? I sent him after Tyrcell as a *treat* because the two of them have history together! He was going to help me cut the android into very small pieces, each piece still capable of experiencing pain!"

"I only know what I stated in my report, my lady." Groth pressed a cryopack against the side of his head that didn't bulge with implanted computer. He'd bashed his head at some point while flinging himself away from android gunfire. "Alcyone will corroborate my account once she reconstitutes herself."

"This is unacceptable," Mnephalon said. "Something must be done! I will not be disrespected this way!"

"Yes, my lady," Groth said. "Of course, my lady." When Mnephalon said something must be done, something got done. It just wasn't very often anything that Groth wanted any part in doing. Not that it mattered.

"Come back to the *Necrosis* as soon as Alcyone has reformed. I will not allow this insult to go unanswered!"

Groth opened his mouth to offer the proper servile agreement, but the bone sage cut off the transmission. The ghoul hunched forward, head throbbing, miserable—

And then exhaled. For once, Mnephalon wasn't plunging her bony fingers into his mind, and the misery knight—Astrachios, was it, once upon a time some important Hellknight?—wasn't creaking and rasping and clanking, and no one was shooting at him or screaming. Best of all, for the first time in centuries, Alcyone wasn't yammering at him, a bundle of neuroses and regrets and yearnings in spectral form. There was only this little ship in the void, and blessed, rare, precious solitude, and the promise of the same for another whole day—maybe two, if Alcyone took longer to pull herself together.

When your life was eternal toil, you had to learn to appreciate the moments of rare peace and rest.

The ghoul leaned back in the pilot's chair, turned up the sound system, blasted his favorite industrial shattercore music until the hull vibrated, and screamed along with every word where nobody else could hear.

# EPILOGUE: THE ASCENSION OF CASPIEN BLIGHTWIND

(Tyrcell / 7 AG)

Val didn't leave much in the way of remains, but Azzi and Caspien brought her drone back to Starla and told her how Val had led their group and fought for them and given her life for them—for us.

Starla did *not* think it was a good trade. She was a wreck, and it took a lot of drugs from Dr. Bindi and a lot of therapy with some of the station's better priests before she began to actually heal, and you never really heal from something like that. Maybe you know that already.

Caspien went to Valentine's memorial service—the Primex went too, among other dignitaries, but I was more interested in Caspien. The borai didn't stand up to speak when we shared stories about Val, and he slipped away afterward, before any of us could try to talk to him, even Scunge and Azzi.

While she was packing up Val's things, Starla found an encryption key tucked away in their safe with a note for Starla, saying that in the event of Val's untimely demise, she wanted Starla to be able to access her video life log. Starla's biometrics opened the key, which opened the camera… and Starla asked me to watch the footage from the assault and tell her about it because she couldn't bear to watch it herself. I watched it all, more than once, and then I gave the widow a carefully edited account. Neither Azzi nor Caspien mentioned the whole abduction and interrogation thing to anybody, so neither did I. Officially, Caspien was a patriot who'd helped them save the station.

I did show Starla the clip of Val's last words professing her love. I am not great with crying or strong shows of emotion generally, but I got a lot of practice with both that day.

The Society carried on in the aftermath. We repaired the damage from the Battle of the Lorespire. We selected Dr. Bindi as our new president. (Carn already had about five jobs, and Melezheun wanted to accompany me on my expeditions, since it turned out we'd both been lonely; and spending time together, even in such terrible circumstances, with such terrible consequences, was good for both of us.) A bunch of us collected some secret commendations from the Primex. My first, but not my last.

And, of course, we kept Val's promise to Caspien Blightwind. I was the only one, apart from Azzi, who knew how the two of them had really met, so I went to see him in his extremely depressing and windowless quarters and interviewed him for this document, and then I said, "So, what do you think? Want to move into our neighborhood and help us balance our books?"

Caspien had been through a lot, and he'd clearly been changed by his experience. He looked less like a dead bookkeeper playing a part and more like a warrior, even while he was sitting unarmed in a chair. He still had his holy spear and his defensive cloak, though the former was leaning against the wall, and the latter was hanging on a coat hook. "Do you really need an accountant there?" he asked me.

"I am assured that we *always* need more accountants," I told him. "Our head of security and logistics has never entirely grasped the concept of receipts."

"I'll... give it a try," Caspien allowed.

I helped him pack up a few things, suitable for a probationary stay in the Society, and we caught a tram to the Lorespire district. There were faint bloodstains on the floor of the tram car, a reminder that the Magefire Assault had raged everywhere and that all the stories I'd heard and footage I'd watched displayed just a fraction of a fraction of the whole battle.

I took Caspien in through the impressive main doors of the Lorespire itself, then up an elevator to one of the higher floors, where we kept the good views. Our Society was growing, so we were expanding our housing. Word had gotten around about Carn's heroism, and there was a version of Val's story spread by the salvage union where she was unambiguously heroic too. That kind of acclaim drew new people to the neighborhood, even if Mel and I remained blessedly anonymous to the public regarding our parts.

I opened the door to a generous corner suite. "You can have these rooms if you like." Caspien walked inside tentatively. Then he walked over to the windows.

There were a lot of windows, basically covering two of the walls. That's why I'd chosen this apartment for him. There was a sprawling view of the stars on one side, and you could look down on the dome of the Eye, with its replanted park and elegant spires, on the other. Stand in one space, and look upon the world here and the world beyond.

Caspien Blightwind let out a long breath. "This is really all for me?"

"Welcome home," I said.

THE END

# ACKNOWLEDGMENTS

Thanks to the Starfinder team: Thurston Hillman, Mark Moreland, and all the game designers and artists who brought this world and these characters to life. Special thanks to Starfinder Creative Manager Jenny Jarzabski, who was a real delight to work with. My gratitude also goes to my agent, Ginger Clark, who's the best advocate an author could hope for.

I couldn't do this job without my closest loved ones, especially Heather and River and Sarah and Katrina and Emily and Aislinn, who support me in so many ways.

I'm also thankful to the Starfinder setting creators for being so inclusive. I am genderfluid, and strive to include trans, nonbinary, and otherwise gender-nonconforming people in my work, but there was no striving needed here; that kind of thing comes built in to the setting. Especially in this current moment, with the rights of my brothers and sisters and siblings under renewed assault, that kind of representation feels especially vital.

*—Tim Melody Pratt*
*Berkeley CA*
*June 2025*

# ABOUT STARFINDER

*Assault on Absalom Station* takes place in the universe of the popular Starfinder Roleplaying Game, a science-fantasy tabletop roleplaying game that puts players in the roles of intrepid intergalactic explorers, weird aliens, and more. Launched in 2017 as an offshoot of the tabletop fantasy RPG staple, Pathfinder, Starfinder has sold more than 2.5 million copies of rulebooks, adventures, setting guides, and gaming accessories. In August 2025, Starfinder Second Edition debuted, bringing the game into full compatibility with the bestselling Pathfinder Second Edition rules set. Starfinder has been adapted into board games, comics, and the Starfinder on Alexa interactive skill, starring Nathan Fillion and Laura Bailey. *Assault on Absalom Station* is the second novel set in the Starfinder setting.

For more information about Starfinder or to subscribe to get future releases sent to you automatically, visit **http://paizo.com/starfinder**.